THE GRAVEBORN SERIES
BOOK TWO

THE BOOK OF SHADOWS

R.G. WESLEY

For those who struggle with the voices in their head. Healing isn't linear, but there's light at the end of the tunnel—even if you can't see it.

CONTENTS

AUTHOR'S NOTE

Welcome, readers. I'm so glad you're here. Before you embark on this journey with Seph, I'd like to share some content warnings. *The Book of Shadows* is intended for an adult audience, and depicts the following:

- Graphic violence
- Death
- Explicit sexual content
- Addiction
- References to off-page sexual assault
- Mental health issues such as depression, anxiety, grief, self harm, and suicidal ideation
- References to forced birth
- Animal death (In context of hunting for meat. The dog doesn't die, don't worry.)
- References to miscarriage/fertility issues

For a list of specific chapters, please visit my website: https://www. rgwesleywrites.com/content-warnings

PART I

"Would you tell me, please, which way I ought to go from here?"

"That depends a good deal on where you want to get to," said the Cat.

"I don't much care where—," said Alice

"Then it doesn't matter which way you go," said the Cat.

"—so long as I get somewhere," Alice added as an explanation.

"Oh, you're sure to do that," said the Cat, "if only you walk long enough."

— LEWIS CARROLL, *ALICE IN WONDERLAND*

1

It turned out that being broken wasn't easy.

When Alex had been dragged into a bubbling hell-pit by a demon prince, part of me had cracked wide open like a fissure splitting the ground after an earthquake. That line separated the old-me from the broken-me.

The old-me, the Seph who was on her way to wholeness, who'd found family and love and magic.

The broken-me, the woman who was empty, powerless, so entrenched in her own misery she could barely keep moving.

The simplest of tasks became a monumental effort, complex and coated with a salt-crust of hopelessness. Eating, talking, putting one foot in front of the other as Simon and I trudged through this wretched forest that I hated with every fiber of my being—I almost wanted to lay down and let the moss grow over me, becoming indistinguishable from any of the other lichen-covered boulders in this place.

Yet, I kept going in spite of the agony. Or maybe because of it. Each step, each morsel of dirty roots I consumed, each croaked whisper to Simon, put me closer to saving Alex. He was out there somewhere, alive. Hoping for me like I was hoping for him. And I wouldn't let anyone or anything stop me from getting to him. Even if I had to go to hell itself.

The actual task of rescue seemed farther away than it had been four days ago when Simon and I landed in the sun-dappled clearing of this wildwood world. We had no resources, apart from a few daggers and Simon's superior talent at plant identification that kept starvation at bay. There'd been no signs of civilization, unless we counted the primordial trees draped with thick, woody vines, or butterflies as large as my hand that winged around delicate flowers in patches of marshy ground. And, worst of all? There was no magic.

Correction: *I* didn't have any magic. My power seemed to have flamed out after facing Magoth in the prison world, deader than a flower after a killing frost. Whenever I tried to pluck the black and gold threads, all I found was a dry, dusty riverbed where there had once been a torrent. Simon's theory was that it was the emotional shock of it all, and that the magic would come back in time.

I wasn't so sure. Something essential inside of broken-me wasn't simply out of alignment, but missing altogether. If I were to unzip the skin between my ribs and draw back the aching muscles, I'd find a hollow space devoid of everything that made me human.

It wasn't only due to the agony of Alex's disappearance, although that was most of it. My actions had led to Simon leaving the comfort of the only home he'd ever known. My Guardian friends who had become family—Davina, Casey, Hollis, Sage, and Sylvan—were god knows where, and thought Alex was still safe with me. Fern betrayed us. I didn't defeat Magoth.

I was a snow globe in perpetual motion, except instead of those little white plastic flakes I contained rage and fear and hopelessness. After the first night in this moss-laden world when I made the decision to go after Alex, I'd put all of those damnable feelings in a box and secured the lid. The only problem was that the hinges rattled constantly. If I acknowledged them, they'd consume me. I would drown in my own sorrow, and Alex would be stuck in hell forever. So I just kept going.

And then, it happened—again. An overwhelming sensation of emptiness engulfed my chest, stopping my breath. I paused mid-step, leaning against a damp tree for support. Dizziness was a given these days, but this was different. This was the feeling of air freezing in my lungs, of a knife carving out my insides and leaving me gasping over the vacancy. It was a bloodless wound, but no less lethal.

You're going to fail. Alex is dead. Your friends came to their senses and went back to the Diurne. You're going to fail. Fail, fail, fa—

"Hey." Simon's gray eyes peered into mine, worry written into their tight corners. He grasped my forearms to steady me. I clung to him, counting the beat of his pulse beneath my fingertips. "You're all right. Just breathe."

I nodded, trying to convince my body to work again. He knew exactly what to say, because he'd coached me through this a dozen times already. It happened whenever I thought about Alex and the Guardians, or the battle in the prison world—so, all the time.

It was impossible to keep them all out of my head. Not that I really wanted to. At night I lay awake analyzing every aspect of the battle, replaying my mistakes and where it had all gone so terribly wrong. I saw Magoth's horrible yellow eyes, heard my screams, watched Alex's mask of calm shatter into fear, then smooth into lines of acceptance, as he was dragged into the pit. Felt Simon's arms, animated by some borrowed power, lock around and drag me through the swirling black gateway.

The images played in a loop, their only competition the unanswered question that clawed brutally at my mind—where was Alex?

"That's it," Simon encouraged quietly, smoothing his worry into steadiness. "In and out. That's the way." I took another deep, shuddering breath, and the emptiness eased. "Let's stop here, eh? Rest for a bit."

"Sorry," I wheezed. The phantom pain in my shoulder where Fern had shot me pulsed, and I pressed the spot with my thumb. It was always doing that, too, although the wound had healed over instantly when I'd sucked power from Simon in the prison world. "We should keep going. It'll be dark in a couple hours."

Simon rubbed the reddish stubble covering his jaw. I'd never seen him unshaven, or anything less than put together, despite his worn and patched clothes from Canhaben. But now his formerly white shirt was soiled and riddled with tears, his vest missing buttons. Dirt streaked his face, and he smelled of stale sweat and mud. I knew I wasn't much better—probably worse, actually. I tucked a stringy wave behind my ear and tugged on my own stained shirt.

"You need something to eat," he insisted. "You'll feel better for it."

His answer to everything was food, so I didn't stop him from crashing around in the undergrowth as he foraged for something edible. I rested against the base of the tree, glad dark spots no longer crowded my vision. And for the thousandth time, I brooded about how we wouldn't be in this situation if I had power.

My throat dried, just like the bare riverbeds of my power source. I missed my magic, and not just its usefulness. I missed the confidence it gave me, how strong I felt when I called flames to my fingertips with barely a thought. It had become an indivisible part of me in such a short time, and just when I thought I'd figured out who I was...well, that was old-me.

"Simon," I called in my rusty voice, thighs groaning as I stood. "I promise, I'm fine. Let's just go."

But instead of his accented baritone, a strange sound reached me. It wasn't like any of the usual forest noises—the trill of a bird, or the rustling of a furry creature in the canopy. No, this was a deep groaning, like tree roots being wrenched from the forest floor.

My heartbeat skipped even as I tried to convince myself it was nothing. He might have wandered farther in his search than I realized. "Simon?" I called again, looking for his telltale chestnut head amidst the perpetual wall of green. "Is that you?"

Twigs snapped under my feet, and I fought with mossy vines and damp branches to push my way through the forest. "Simon!" The clammy air seemed to swallow my words. I broke into a jog, head spinning with the effort. Right as I passed a rocky outcropping that resembled a sleeping giant, my eyes caught a flash of white shirt. I slowed as relief flooded through me so violently that my knees buckled.

Simon was crouched, facing away from me with his head bent as if studying something beneath his feet. I let out a choked laugh. "God, don't scare me like that."

I expected him to frown at me, maybe say something about how I should worry about myself instead of him. But when he answered, his voice was strained and thin. "Don't come any closer."

My stomach dropped, and for a moment I felt like I was suspended weightless amidst the treetops. The forest's usual giant ferns and pale, vanilla-scented blossoms attached to the climbing vines surrounded us. Nothing was out of place. "What is it?" I whispered.

He looked over his shoulder at me, frozen from the chest down. His eyes were wide, his forehead dewy with sweat. "Run."

"Wha—"

A thick vine whipped out from a nearby tree, snaring my ankle. I hardly had time to flinch before a second appeared and threaded around my waist, wringing the air from my lungs. Simon lurched toward me, revealing the vine that held him in place. It coiled up his body and was soon at chest height, heading for his neck.

Icy panic sluiced through my veins while I tore at the vines, writhing to escape their grip. "Simon!" I screamed, as he struggled with the one going for his throat. He managed to slip a hand beneath it, tugging it away from his neck.

"Use—knife," he gurgled, then was dragged to the ground.

Knife. My thoughts were frozen, but my body reacted, drawing the dagger from my weapon harness and hacking at woody tendrils. I sliced and sawed, not caring if I cut myself in the process. They loosened enough for me to wriggle away, and I lunged for Simon. He grappled with the vine, rolling on the forest floor as his face purpled.

"Hold still!" I cried. Between my shaking hands and his frantic movements, the blade could just as easily pierce his jugular as free him. He took a deep, rattling breath, then stilled. I managed to sever the vine that choked him and ripped it free of his neck.

Another vine knocked my outstretched arm and my dagger went flying into the underbrush. The vine knotted around my bicep, then I was being dragged over the soggy earth toward a leviathan of a tree, its trunk easily the width of a minivan. One hand fumbled for another dagger while the other pawed the ground for purchase. Simon was crying out, but his yells died suddenly.

I slammed against the massive tree and was yanked upright. More vines bound my arms and legs, some slithering across my mouth to gag my screams. I could see Simon now, and a wave of fresh horror swamped me. A writhing mass of vines covered him from head to toe. They looked like snakes, or worms risen to the surface after a hard rain. A scream built in my throat, but I was unable to release it.

This was it. I had led Simon to his death, and I'd never save Alex. We were the only ones in all the worlds who knew what had happened to him, and that knowledge would die with us.

I was so wrapped up in the ending of our stories that I almost didn't notice the ball of flames that arced across the mossy ground. I blinked, hard, but it didn't disappear. The fireball cut across Simon's vine-wrapped grave, and the mass of them parted, retracting and fleeing the orange flames. I caught a glimpse of him looking still as death before the fireball changed direction and hurtled toward me. It passed within inches of my face as it blazed over the vines anchoring me to the tree. Hot air scorched my lungs, but that didn't matter because I was free and sliding to the ground. I landed on hands and knees, fighting for breath and trying to make sense of the fact that I wasn't dead.

My arms and legs were leaden, but I crawled for Simon. He was hunched over in the dirt, coughing and massaging his throat. Angry red lines circled it, and the rest of him wasn't much better.

"Are you okay?" I rasped. My own throat felt like I'd swallowed a hot poker.

He nodded and tried to speak, but only garbled hacking came out. I caught him in a one-armed hug. Fuck. We were alive, and nothing else mattered right now. I went boneless, collapsing into Simon's chest. We held each other for the space of another heartbeat before a snapping branch had me bolting upward and scraping for missing magic. I twisted around, heart in my throat as I threw my arms out to protect Simon from...

The best way I could describe the creature would be to compare it to a four-foot-tall vole, although that didn't really do it justice. Its head was covered with downy, fawn-colored fur, and the paw wrapped around a short knife had small pink fingers that ended in pointed claws. It was cute, honestly, but for the dark eyes that spoke of a wisdom older than time.

It took a second before I found my voice. "What—who are you?"

The creature's whiskers twitched, and it sheathed the knife. "Durl. And you?" Durl's voice was the low grinding of boulders scraping together, the words accented but recognizable.

Did I risk telling this creature who we were? I looked back at Simon, who was still massaging his throat. He offered a helpful shrug. Right.

"I'm...Steph. And this is...Sam." Simon made a throaty sound behind me. I choose to interpret it as agreement.

Durl nodded. "Come." It—he?—turned and began picking a path

through the forest. His wide, padded feet were soundless and barely disturbed the leaf litter.

"Hold on." I levered to my feet, brushing mud from my arms. Christ, I felt like I'd been run over by a truck. "You sent the fireball?"

The vole creature slowed, then faced us. His eyes were inky-black in the forest's fading light. He nodded.

"Why?"

"A Knerl helps where help is needed. Follow if you want food and warmth." He started off again.

Simon and I traded disbelieving stares. He extended a hand at the same time I lowered mine to pull him up. We scrambled after Durl as his small form disappeared into the darkening forest. I noticed for the first time that he wore a little vest and short trousers with a hole for the skinny tail poking out from his seat. He was...adorable, but I had to remember that he'd created a fireball out of nowhere.

"Do—" Simon cleared his throat, voice gravelly as Durl's. "Is this safe?"

I had no idea, but our other option was to spend more time in the forest with the knowledge that deadly vine-monsters were on the loose. "We'll just have to take the chance," I whispered back, injecting lightness into my tone. "And run like hell if that thing tries to filet us and cook us for dinner. Although in the state we're in, we wouldn't make for very good eating." A grin flickered around the edges of Simon's mouth, and he swallowed a laugh in a cough.

The small bit of horizon visible through the trees had blurred with the lavender sky by the time we reached a small clearing. My supernatural vision made out a stone cottage in the clearing's center, a column of smoke drifting lazily from a chimney. Shutters framed its windows, and tidy rows of gardening beds were bordered with a picket fence. It was, again...strangely adorable.

When we arrived at the front door, Durl gestured to our feet. "Boots off." He wasn't wearing any shoes, but wiped clawed feet on a doormat made of moss and brush. We toed off our boots before crossing the threshold into a warm, welcoming room. I swallowed around a lump in my throat.

The floor was a sort of fuzzy, spreading plant that felt sublime against my aching feet. The cottage's stone walls and ceiling were covered with rushes and cattails, creating the effect that we were inside a tree. Fire blazed in a wide hearth, and a large cookpot hung on a hook above it. Whatever was inside emitted a smell so mouthwatering that I had to push down the urge to run over and scoop it out with my bare hands.

This place was a *home*, cared for and tended with dedication borne of love. Something in my gut told me that we didn't need to fear this Knerl any longer.

Durl pointed to a scrubbed wooden table that sat low to the ground. "Sit."

We did as we were told, and plopped into two heaps while the vole set the table with polished wooden cutlery and stone bowls. Gratitude welled in my chest when he filled our bowls with the contents of the pot, which turned out to be a rich and creamy soup. I couldn't identify the chewy lumps in it, but I was past the point of caring.

He leaned silently against the wall and observed us as Simon and I attacked the food. After our third helping, we finally sat back. Warm ease and heaviness flowed through my limbs, my stomach painfully full.

"Cheers, mate," Simon croaked, putting his bowl aside. "Really, we can't thank you enough. For the food, and for saving our skins."

"How did you do that, by the way?" I asked, thumbing the hilt of my dagger. The cold metal cut through my drowsiness.

Durl retrieved a large glass jar from a side cupboard. Inside were orange-scaled lizards the size of my pinky nail, laying upon clumps of moss. He said a word that sounded like rocks being crushed into gravel. Then, in English: "Fire newt."

"Handy," Simon mumbled, before scraping the non-existent remains from his empty bowl. He was going to start licking it clean in a minute.

"What were those things? The vines," I asked, fighting a shudder as I recalled the way they'd encircled my throat.

"A Knerl calls them a name you could not understand. They are forest spirits who live in the trees. Always hungry. They do not like noise."

I thought of Simon crashing through the underbrush in his desperation to find food for me. I lowered my gaze to my empty bowl. "Please tell us how we can repay your kindness."

"Kindness does not need repaying," Durl grumbled. Then he paused, the silence weighty. "I have met your kind before."

My heart thudded hard, once, twice. "What do you mean?" What if the Diurne's minions had been here, looking for us? Would Durl turn us in, and would that mean running off into the night again? My sweaty palm slipped on the dagger's handle.

"Those fleeing the broken worlds."

"Oh." My heartbeat settled again, for the moment.

Durl nodded once. "You are not the first I have offered refuge. They come from the south, always soaked to their bones and running from the spirits."

"Where do they go?"

"On through the forest. Some stay for a night. Some for longer. Less come each cycle. But all look the same."

"What, like this?" Simon said, rubbing bare skin through a hole in his sleeve.

The Knerl shook his head. "Some hairless-skins, some scale-skins, some no-skins. All different kinds, but the eyes...the eyes are all afraid."

My shoulder jerked as a shiver ran through me. Refugees coming from the south, all soaked to the bone? There was some kind of pattern there, but my exhausted and over-wrought brain couldn't put the pieces together. I needed to sleep, at least for a few hours before we moved on.

"Stay here if you wish," Durl said, like he read my mind. More likely he noted the way my eyelids drooped and my whole body sagged toward the floor. "Leave tomorrow if you must. I will not harm you."

I glanced at Simon, who was making eyes at the soup tureen. "Excuse us a moment?" I told him, taking Simon by the elbow. I led us outside, halting just past the door. A light rain had begun to fall and dripped softly from the eaves. "What do you think?"

Simon yawned wide. "I dunno. He seems all right. The bloke barely reaches my waist, anyway. I don't think we're in danger."

"Fire newts," I said, enunciating slowly.

"Yeah, but he doesn't want to use them on us. It's like you're trying to find reasons not to stay. This is what we've been looking for, isn't it? Food, shelter?"

He was right. We were in survival mode, too busy trying to stay alive instead of formulating a plan. Old-me would've acknowledged the sense

Simon made. Broken-me wanted to keep marching forward without stopping, knowing that every second we didn't have Alex was one that Magoth did. And who knew what kind of torture he might be undergoing?

"I—"

"Please, Seph. Please. I'm begging you. We can't carry on this way." Simon's brow was knit and his shoulders stooped like an old man's. He was so different from the person I'd met at Jupiter's Books and Stationery. That version of Simon was taciturn and cranky, but with such wry wit he always made me laugh. The Simon standing before me was defeated, crushed under the weight of grief and exhaustion.

I could give him one night.

"Okay," I relented, trying to fight off the itch of unease beneath my skin.

The lines around his mouth softened, and he blew out a long exhale before squeezing my hand. "Thank you."

Durl provided us with hot water and rags. Every inch of mud I scrubbed away made me a little more grateful for the decision to stay. He even had some clean—if musty—clothes from a large trunk. I stepped behind a screen woven of rushes to don the sack-like shirt and trousers. They were stitched from coarse threads, but more comfortable than my blood-stained jeans.

Once Durl had bid us goodnight and disappeared into the cottage's second room, we each bedded into little nests of some sweet-smelling grass. The fibers were soft as down, as good as any mattress I'd slept on.

Simon's soft snores filled the room within moments. I wished I could fall asleep so effortlessly, but my mind fought my weariness. There was something about the refugees that was important. But every time I tried to grasp the edge of a thought, it slipped away.

Giving in to wakefulness, I reached for the photograph I'd slipped into my pocket when I changed. It was creased, the edges worn from how often I'd held the picture my father had left behind for me. It showed him and Simon's father, Lucas, along with my former neighbor Mrs. Parham—Evangeline—and her husband Uriel, all in Canhaben. Though I could barely make out their faces in the dark, I had their cheerful expressions memorized. Lucas and Uriel were dead, my father cursed, and Evangeline...I didn't know where she'd disappeared to.

The sadness I felt upon looking at the photo was still there—it was always there—but a foreign feeling of warmth joined it as the pieces fell into place.

I knew why it was important that all of Durl's refugees came from the same direction, soaked to their bones. The warmth spread into my face, and for a moment I went lightheaded.

There was a seam in this world, somewhere to the south. The place between worlds where the boundaries had rubbed against each other and grown thin, eventually splitting open and allowing the passage of people in and out. And it had to be in a body of water.

I bolted straight up, heart pounding. "Simon," I whispered. When he didn't answer, I shook him.

"Wassit?" he mumbled, throwing my hand off and rolling over.

"There's a seam here. We can get out."

"S'nice," he answered, a snore sounding in the same breath.

I snuggled back into the nest, breathing slowly to get my heartrate under control. I couldn't fight the excitement and that warm feeling— what broken-me hadn't realized was a tiny, flickering spark of hope.

2

The seam was not eager to be revealed, and I was beginning to doubt its existence. We swam to the muddy bottoms of ponds and rivers and waded in streams, but nothing gave way like the oak tree into Canhaben. After each failed search attempt, the warm light of hope in my chest dimmed. But still, I kept on. And that was how one night with Durl turned into two, then two turned into three.

My desire to move on chafed at the rhythm of routine, never allowing me to settle. Simon had argued that staying with Durl provided us a home base from which to search for the seam. I'd agreed, reluctantly, because the purple rings beneath his eyes softened with each passing day. He was thriving in the little cottage in the woods, and part of me hated to take that from him.

The part that wanted Alex was stronger.

On our fourth morning, after Durl went out to forage, I cornered Simon in the kitchen. "I know you're having a great time learning from Durl," I began. "But we need to move on. It's time." Simon didn't answer until I tugged on his sleeve. "Are you listening?"

He scratched the back of his neck. "Hm? Oh, sorry. You know, I was thinking about that pondcress stuff we had for dinner last night. There might be a way to dry it and make flour."

"Oh my god," I muttered, tugging at my hair. "Leave the pondcress. We need to get out of here."

"Why? If we need to go farther afield, we can take longer trips—camp overnight, or something. I'm sure Durl wouldn't mind us being away."

I blew at a little spider that descended from the rafters on a silken strand of web. It swayed, then reversed course and crawled back up the thread. "Of course Durl won't mind. He's used to being alone. We are guests here. Visitors. And coming back each night wastes time. He's given us clothes, supplies, and food. I think we've done enough chores to pay Durl back for anything he's lent us. Let's thank him and get going."

"What are we even going to do when we find the seam, Seph?"

I took a deep breath and rolled my shoulders, which had crept toward my ears. "We've talked about this."

He scoffed and sidled a hip against the counter. "Yes, and your plan is predicated on running away."

I stilled, caught off guard by his flippant tone. "It's not running away. We stay on the move so that the Aureum doesn't catch us. Then we'll get my power back, find where Alex is being held, and rescue him."

The details would fall into place later. *It'll work out*, the hopeful spark whispered. *You'll find him.* Because the alternative was too awful to bear. My mind strayed to torture, to hellfire and chains and gruesome iron implements. No, it was never a good idea to let my wild imagination run loose with my fears.

"Let's give it a little more time," Simon said to his crossed arms. "Just a few more days here. You couldn't have expected us to just fall into it the way you did Canhaben."

"Why not?" That's exactly what I'd thought would happen. "Never mind. I'm not arguing about this. We're going." Simon's caution usually wasn't a bad thing, but right now it was costing us time we didn't have.

Simon's mouth twisted like he wanted to make a face, but was using all of his energy not to. "I don't think it's fair for you to dictate that," he replied slowly. "I've given up my life to be here with you. To do this...." He didn't say *suicide mission* out loud, but I could almost hear the words forming on the tip of his tongue.

"Which you agreed to," I snapped. "I didn't ask you to come with me. You volunteered."

He scooped a hand through his thick chestnut hair and blew out a sigh. "Well, it seemed like a good idea at the time."

I kneaded my forehead and tried to keep breathing through the pressure in my chest. If Alex was in our position, he'd probably have already found a way out. When I thought about his fierce desire to protect others, his kindness, his heart-stopping smile.... I blinked the image away, swallowing.

"I have to do this, Simon," I said with the flat certainty of a woman who was out of options. The knowledge crawled along my skin, rattling my bones, tearing at my hair and my ribs with a furious clarity.

"You don't," he countered. His gray eyes were hard like shards of flint. "You think this is your burden, but you could just as easily set it down and walk away without killing yourself. That's what Ezekial wanted for you. He wanted you to live a normal, *human* life, away from magic."

That was a low blow, bringing my father into it. Because that *is* what he'd wanted, but it wasn't meant to be. The father I'd needed, the community I'd searched for, the greatest love I'd ever known—none were within my reach.

My heart twisted sharply. A dull ache radiated through my chest, every beat spelling out Alex's name. I couldn't speak for a moment, couldn't catch my breath. Simon ducked his head.

"So, what, you want to bail on me? Play house with Durl forever? Or go back to Canhaben, which could be crawling with Guardians?" I tossed the questions at Simon like I would the knife strapped to my waist—unrelenting and brutal. Broken-me was harsh and cutting and downright mean. But I couldn't stop the words from spewing.

"No. I don't. I told you I'd come, and I won't leave you alone." He finally looked at me, and I saw truth in his eyes. I released my pent-up breath. No matter what I said to Simon—now that he was here, I didn't want to be alone.

"Then you need to be all in. I'm not going to half-ass this, or fantasize about what can't be. We cannot stay here, Simon. You need to accept that. The longer we're with Durl, the more attached you're going to get, and the more painful it will be to leave. I'm sorry, but it's the truth."

Simon kept his head bowed for a long moment. "True that may be, but you're not the only person who's lost someone. You put Eames on a pedestal so far above everyone else that you don't even notice the bruises you've left elbowing people out of the way to put him there. I have needs, too. This isn't all about you."

I spluttered for a moment, my face growing hot. How could he think that? It was about Alex, and him alone. "You don't think I know you're using this to run away from your own shit? Don't blame me for making you leave your precious knitting because I'm willing to face reality and you're not. I'm going to find us a way out of here. Do what you like."

He wasn't nearly as adept at hiding his feelings as I was. Pain, anger, grief, and guilt flashed across his face as each claim drew blood from unhealed wounds.

I didn't stay to watch the fallout, because such overpowering shame flooded me that I couldn't remain in his presence. I snatched my bag from beside the door and fled into the misty forest.

Who the fuck did Simon think he was, leveling those accusations at me? I'd never elbowed anyone out of the way, much less ignored his needs. *Haven't you?* asked an unwelcome voice in the back of my mind. *You're pushing him to leave, to do what* you *want, even though you know he'd like to stay. You've never once thought that your feelings for Alex blinded you to everyone else?*

I kicked the voice out of my head. Simon was a grown man, free to do as he pleased. If he wanted to stay, I wouldn't stop him. I, however, was going to find this damned seam.

I stalked through the forest, fuming. An observer might have said that I stomped my feet in self-righteous anger, but that observer might find themselves on the wrong end of a blade.

Eventually I cooled down enough to strip my pack off and dig out the rough map Durl had drawn for me. A small settlement sat about sixty miles north of us, but otherwise there were no large population hubs in the world of Orrm. According to Durl, Knerls were solitary creatures by nature and wouldn't survive without close access to the natural world. They were a race of earth-dwellers, not made for concrete and crowds.

But the forest itself seemed so vast that I wouldn't be able to plumb all of its secrets even if I lived there a hundred years. When I looked at the map, I saw failure. We needed *help*. We needed my magic.

I turned inward and reached again for what in my heart of hearts I knew wouldn't be there. Flakes of rust speckled the edges of the obsidian door in my mind. The meadow surrounding it appeared to be in a drought, with large patches of yellowed grass. When I opened the door, it released a harsh squeak.

The landscape of my power source hadn't changed—the hills were still covered in lush grass, dotted with tiny white flowers that looked like stars. The cloud cover was thick and gray, swirling with hints of a storm. But the life underneath it all, that pulse of energy that lit me up from the inside out, was dead.

I went to the edge of a riverbed, one of two that was the wellspring of my magic. Usually, the twin rivers that ran through the valley between hills, winding together like a pair of snakes, would be full of glinting black and gold threads, ready to be called and fulfill my desire. But now they were dry and barren.

Kneeling, I sank my fingers into cracked earth and reached for the barest drop of moisture. It felt as lifeless as everything else. Just like it had every time I'd tried to get in touch with my magic over the past several days. It only added to my foul temper, and I slammed my fist into the nearest tree.

"Shit," I grunted. The skin on my knuckles was torn and a salty, metallic tang already tickled my nose. Blood beaded, then trickled down the back of my hand. The scrapes throbbed dully in time with my heartbeat.

Blood was what started this. My blood spilled in the cemetery all those months ago, breaking the ties that my father had bound my power with and releasing the secrets that had been kept with them. Those secrets had landed me where I was now, bleeding and broken in the wildwood of another world.

I stilled even as my pulse thundered. My blood didn't just belong to the gods-touched Guardians. My magic wasn't just arcana. I was a

Watcher through my father's side, and Simon had taught me about my heritage back in Canhaben. Watchers were descended from the Nephilim, the first demons, and summoned spirits to work their magic.

I could summon a demon.

Why hadn't I thought of it before? Better yet, why hadn't Simon thought of it? Unless he had, and was trying to delay us further. The drowsing beast of my anger woke again, spitting fire.

Although...maybe I shouldn't, a more rational voice chimed in. I didn't have the proper kit, only some day supplies—dried fruit and a water skin, a candle stub and flint, some bits of twine, and a small pouch of salt Durl said would ward off the forest spirits. I had no idea which demon to call, what would show up if I tried, or if it would even work. Not all demons were evil, but not all of them were good, either.

But I would never know if I didn't try. This was an opportunity, as much a tool as the handheld spade in my pack. That restless, flickering flame of hope surged. *Alex needs you. And if you'd been taken, he'd do the same.*

My hands shook as I upended my bag onto the ground. I crouched, sifting through the items as I considered my options. When I'd summoned in Canhaben, I had fire, water, earth, and air, along with spirit. At least I had salt with me, which would hopefully contain anything that appeared.

"Right," I breathed. "You might be insane, but let's see." I used the spade to dig deep into the boggy ground. Water seeped into the hole, and I finished filling it to the top from my waterskin. Next came salt, which I scattered in a circle around the depression. The candle took a few tries to light, but at last the wick caught. I cupped the dried fruit in my slick palms, arranging it at the four points of the circle.

My makeshift altar was humble, but just maybe it would work. I cleared my throat, casting back in my memories to find the words that would call a demon.

"Spirits? I mean, um, spirits, of air, earth, water, and fire, heed my call. Please, uh, help me in my time of need, and accept this—er, humble offering. Your daughter calls you."

The water's surface sat almost too still, a sure sign of failure. The butterflies winging in my stomach faded with each passing moment. I folded my arms to try and contain the emptiness threatening to split me apart. My breath juddered in my chest, and the phantom pain in my shoulder pulsed once, twice, three times.

No. This whole thing was clearly a bad idea. I gathered the dried fruit and blew out the candle, then washed the sticky blood from my hands in the pool of water. The surface clouded, turning murky red.

"Well met, daughter." The voice was only a whisper, but it was smooth as satin and twice as alluring.

My stomach clenched. I glanced around, but the forest looked the same as it always did: quiet, damp, and green.

"Who are you?" I whispered.

A slight scoff. "You called me. Now, tell me what you want. What you *need*."

I leaned over the salt circle and peered into the water. My reflection stared back at me. Eyes bright with fear and ringed with dark circles, along with the lines worry had dug into the corners of my mouth.

"Help," I whispered hoarsely. "Please."

"What do you seek, young one?"

A man with a kind and fierce heart, one who would lay down his life for his friends in an instant. "His name is—"

"I do not deal in mortals," the voice said in a superior tone. "Find another demon to help with your heartache."

"Hold on," I blurted to my reflection, even as my heart sank. "I need to leave this world. Please, show me the way out."

"Hand me your offering," it ordered.

"What?"

The voice sighed loudly. "You did bring an offering, didn't you?" A face suddenly materialized in the water's surface, overlaid by my own. The effect was jarring and grotesque. I scooted backward over the damp ground, my heart thundering.

"No need to be frightened, daughter. Come back, now. Yes, that's right," the voice said, as I crawled forward to the altar.

Dusky gold skin, large, dark eyes, and ruby red lips. Round cheeks and long black, shining hair. The demon was androgynous and stunning, possessing far more beauty than a mortal ever could. They were perfect. So perfect that the effect was eerie and unsettling, like walking through an empty museum filled with exquisite works of art.

"Who are you?"

Its features turned haughty. "If you don't know who you're calling, I may as well leave."

"No, wait! Please." I picked up the dried fruit and dropped it into the water.

The demon puckered their lips, flicking their tongue out. "Ah, delicious. I am Gamori, she who holds truths, and the keeper of secrets."

"Gamori," I repeated, digging in the recesses of my brain for any facts about her. While at Aureum headquarters I'd spent hours poring over grimoires to memorize the names of demons. I couldn't place Gamori's, which worried me.

"Now speak," the demon commanded.

I cleared my throat. "I have to find a way out of this world. I'm looking for the seam."

The water's surface rippled, and the demon's jaw sharpened, then softened again. "A break between worlds?" Gamori scrutinized me. "And why do you need my help for that, daughter?"

I bowed my head, unable to meet her eyes as I told the truth. "I'm broken. Something inside of me has gone wrong, and I don't know if I'll be able to fix it."

Gamori clucked her tongue. "Pity is not becoming to anyone, human or creature. Dry your eyes, daughter. What will you give me in exchange for my help?"

I considered her exquisite beauty again. Did I want to do this? Make a deal with a demon? Simon was waiting for me back at the cottage, probably still furious. Our argument replayed in my head, but the heat around it had faded, remorse taking its place.

"What do you want?" I asked.

The demon's answering smile made my breath catch in my throat. It reminded me of Magoth's, full of danger and a terrible knowing, like she could see every awful thing I'd ever done. "Let's say...a favor, to be called in at a time of my choosing."

The inside of my mouth felt like I'd been chewing on sandpaper. "No. No way." Even I wasn't foolish enough to owe a demon an open favor. I scooted away, but she called me back.

"All right, all right. I will accept the completion of a task."

"What task?" I managed.

"Oh, nothing too complicated. I need you to fetch me the stone of Vadyron."

I blinked. "The stone of...what?"

Gamori rolled her lovely eyes and pronounced the word again, slower this time. "Va-dyr-on."

"What is that?"

"A stone of power, and that is all you need to know. I am unable to come into the mortal plane at the moment, otherwise, I would get it for myself. It will be simple, daughter."

Yeah, right. I shook my head. "I can't. I don't have time. I'm looking for—"

"Yes, yes, I know. I will give you the span of a year to fetch it for me. Does that soothe your high-strung mortal nerves?"

A year? I thought of how the days seemed to be slipping by like the grains of sand through an hourglass, too quickly for me to count. "Can I have some time to think?" I wished for Simon's steady presence and practically encyclopedic knowledge of demons.

"No. Take it or leave it, youngling." Gamori's reflection rippled, then began to fade.

We could call another demon when we were prepared. Simon would know what to do. But I had Gamori here now, a solution dangling within reach. Were we likely to get a better deal than this? Perhaps. Or perhaps not. Finding Alex was going to be difficult. No, not just difficult. It was becoming clearer by the second it would be the hardest thing I'd ever done. We wouldn't get to him without taking some chances.

This was my choice, and the risk would be mine and mine alone to handle—I'd keep Simon out of it.

We'd find the way out of Orrm, track down Alex, then worry about getting the stone of Vadyron to Gamori. Surely it wouldn't take more than a year to do all that? My stomach was a tangle of knots, my breath coming shallow and making me lightheaded.

"I'll take it." And in saying so, I signed my first deal with a demon.

"Excellent." Gamori smiled again, her white, sharpish teeth and blood-red lips her only features still visible. "You will find the stone in the world of Audirne, in the priest's temple."

What the hell was Aundirne? "Where's the seam?" I asked, the words overlapping in my hurry. The water's surface blurred, or maybe that was panic clouding my vision. "You promised—"

"Yes, yes. To find the crack between the worlds, you must follow the stars." She faded away completely, the surface of the water glassy smooth once again. I rocked back on my heels, disconcerted and dazed. Follow the stars? *What* stars?

"Fucking demons," I hissed. They could never make anything easy.

3

The forest's usual green haze deepened to dusky purple as the sun slipped behind the horizon. In my former life, I would've found a clear patch of sky and stopped to enjoy the beauty of nightfall. Now, it was just a reminder of everything I'd lost.

I didn't see any stars to follow on the way back to Durl's. Then again, I wasn't sure what I was supposed to be looking for. Maybe a constellation pointing the way, or a mark on a tree? But there seemed to be as many trees in the forest as there were stars in the sky. If only Gamori could've been kind enough to put up a billboard with *Seam Here!* flashing in neon lettering. I snorted, almost stumbling on a tree root.

The task of finding a way out of this world without my magic seemed more impossible than ever, and already I felt buyer's remorse. Simon was going to skin me when I told him about the deal, and I deserved every bit of his ire. I'd sprinted across the line from irresponsible to idiocy without looking back.

The outlines of Durl's cottage had just appeared through the closely packed trees when a sharp *snap* sounded from behind me. My heart slammed into my ribs, and I pivoted, preparing to face a forest spirit or something worse.

But there was only empty, darkening woodland, tangled vines draped over the trees to create shadow puppets of hulking beasts.

My heart sank back to its normal position in my chest. I was just jumpy after my encounter with Gamori, that was all. It was a rodent or something, or Durl returning late from foraging.

"Durl?" I called softly. "Is that you?"

No response.

That probably meant he was already back, and the snap I'd heard was utterly normal and completely, definitely explainable. Totally.

I crossed the clearing, but couldn't help glancing over my shoulder until I reached the safety of the front step.

Simon was bent over a pot on the large hearth, stirring the contents with a wooden spoon. We locked eyes as I latched the door behind me, and every harsh word from our earlier argument unfurled between us like a minefield.

"Durl not back yet?" I asked, breaking the silence.

"No," Simon grunted, then removed the spoon and sniffed it. Apparently satisfied, he used a rag to take the pot off the fire and set it on the low table. A pungent, vegetal odor wafted toward me.

I wrinkled my nose. "What is that?"

"Poison," he said, a little too casually for my liking.

"Uh—for me, or...."

A small smile crossed Simon's face, but he quickly scowled. "No. Thought I could do something useful, since apparently you don't like my knitting. This's absorbed through the skin, takes effect almost immediately. I've already made one batch and bottled them."

I glanced over at the windows, noting with relief they were open. Hopefully Durl wouldn't have a problem with us brewing dangerous substances over his fire.

"I need to tell you something, starting with an apology. I was out of line earlier."

"You were," he acknowledged, folding his arms.

Okay, I deserved that. "I'm not myself," I offered, though that was a fully inadequate explanation.

"I know," Simon answered. "I'm not myself, either. I don't know if we're ever going to be ourselves again, Seph. But if this is our new normal, we need to find a way to work through it without fighting and storming off every time there's a problem."

I wasn't used to irritable and normally borderline rude Simon being the peacekeeper. But he was right; we were both irrevocably changed. The fissure between old-me and broken-me yawned wide. Our worlds would never be the same as before, no matter what world we were in.

"Okay," I agreed. "You're right. I can't guarantee it won't happen again. I'm rude and impatient and don't have it in me to care most of the time. But I do care about you. Please believe that."

His eyes were the soft gray of an overcast sky, filled with a sadness that would've made my heart bleed had it been working. "I do. And I know I'm fucked up, too, but...we're all each other have left. For now," he added. "Until we find Eames. I don't want to lose you, even if you're acting a right arse."

I smiled, taking a deep breath for the first time since coming through the door. "Same goes."

He gestured to the pot. "This is just about cool enough for bottling. Help me?"

"Sure, but I have one other thing to tell—"

The door slammed open with a resounding crash. I spun around, shoving Simon behind me, unsheathing the knife at my waist while my pulse skittered.

Durl was being held at knifepoint.

I recognized the woman holding the blade to his throat from my time at Aureum headquarters. She would've been unremarkable, with her dishwater blonde hair and regular features, except for her towering height. Durl seemed like a stuffed toy compared to her. His usually twitching nose was still, and his ears lay flat against his head. My heart twisted.

"Fucking hells," Simon breathed.

Every muscle in my body tensed to spring, and I instinctually clutched at my nonexistent magic. "Let him go."

Three more Guardians edged into the room, dressed in all black and bristling with weapons. "Drop the knives, Hart," said the woman. What *was* her name? Nicole? Jessica? Something like that. "Or we'll kill your pet beast."

I took another step back, herding Simon away from them. Had they been watching us? For how long? More importantly, did they know I was powerless?

"Oh, and here I was thinking you showed up for a friendly chat," I retorted.

"Drop it. You're outnumbered, and we don't want to hurt you." Her eyes flicked around the room. "Where's Captain Eames?"

The cavernous hole threatened to split me open again. "He's gone." My breath came shallow. "Magoth has him."

"I don't believe you." Her grip tightened, and Durl let out a soft choking noise. The blank look of shock on his whiskered face scared me more than if he had been terrified. And suddenly, I was seeing another face, and green eyes instead of black.

No. Stay here. Durl was too kind, too good to be a casualty in our war. Nicole/Jessica was right. We were outnumbered, and without my power, there was no way in hell we would be able to win.

"Believe what you want, it's the truth."

She traded glances with the other Guardians, a silent exchange playing out.

"Simon?" I breathed, so low that I almost couldn't hear the words. I prayed he would. "Any ideas?"

He squeezed my arm in response, but didn't say anything. Nicole/Jessica drew her blade tighter to Durl's throat and nicked him. Blood welled and matted his fur with a dark stain.

"Okay!" I shouted. "Let him go. I'll come with you." I dropped to my knees and let the knife clatter to the floor, raising my arms above my head in surrender. The Guardians were on us in less time than it took to blink. Simon struggled, and they threw him to the ground and kicked him in the ribs. I yelled again, but one of the men backhanded me and my head snapped sideways. Hot blood filled my mouth from a split lip as dull pain coursed from the wound. They wrenched my hands behind me, gripping my wrists so hard bone ground against bone.

"Don't hurt him!" I cried, but it was too late for that. Simon was curled in a ball on the floor, and pain sang through my arm into my shoulder. The woman didn't let go of Durl, but he stood tall and digni-fied while the remaining Guardian that wasn't holding us ransacked his home.

We had been caught. Only days into our journey, and we were going to be kidnapped and probably murdered. Durl, one of the kindest souls I'd ever encountered, was hurt, his sweet home in the process of being torn apart. And Simon...he'd agreed to come with me, had *trusted* me, and I couldn't keep him safe.

I wasn't enough. Not strong enough, not smart enough, not powerful enough. I was going to fail everyone I loved.

My vision went red around the edges while I trembled with the need to crush someone's skull. But my rage had nowhere to go.

"Let Simon go," I begged my captor in a wavering voice. "He has nothing to do with this. I forced him into it."

"We know what he is. A Watcher." The man spat it like a foul word. Then, he leaned in close so that his spittle landed on Simon's cheek. "And he'll tell us where the rest of them are hiding."

Terror burned in my belly, so hot that I went cold. So it would be torture first, then murder.

"How did you find us?" I demanded, even as sweat pooled at the base of my spine. If I could keep them talking, maybe a miracle would appear and save us.

"You left the prison world with a little gift," said the Guardian. He rubbed his upper arm, then grinned. "Took a while for it to activate, which leads to the very interesting question of why you haven't been using magic."

I looked down at my shoulder, where my sleeve covered the circular scar from a gunshot wound. Where the phantom pain had been pulsing these past few days. There *had* been more than just pain when Fern shot me. And I'd summoned a demon this afternoon—not using Guardian arcana, but magic all the same.

"Found these," called the man who was searching. He raised our satchels aloft. Mine held the daggers Alex had gifted me. My gut twisted at the idea of this man pawing at them. They were the only part of him I had left, apart from the tattoo on my forearm.

"Bring them," Nicole/Jessica said. "And take those two outside."

The man holding me stank of sour, fear-soaked sweat. I leaned away from him even as he jerked me through the door into the night air.

Waves of power vibrated from the ropes they'd used to tie our hands. I struggled against them but quickly stopped because of the burning sensation from where the bindings rubbed my skin. Based on his muffled grunt of pain, Simon had just learned the same thing. I tried to catch his eye, but our captors shoved us back to back.

A sound carried through the night, crushing my already ruined heart; a short, sharp cry from Durl, then silence. The woman who had held him at knifepoint exited the cottage, wiping blood from her blade.

"No!" I screamed, as Simon went stock still. "You fucking bitch!"

"Shut your mouth, or we'll shut it for you," she said with a coldness that matched the ice spreading through my veins. The man holding me tugged my ropes and I fell to my knees on the soft, damp ground. The woman grasped my chin and tilted it upward, turning my head from side to side. She studied me like I was a prize steer up for auction. I tried to wrench away, but she kept a tight hold on me.

"What did Captain Eames see in you?" she mused. "It's hard to believe that such weakness could hold any interest. Pretty, though, I'll admit. That's men for you." I bared my teeth and snapped at her hand. She wagged a finger in my face. "I told you, behave or you'll have to take a little nap."

"Where are you taking us?" Simon coughed, and blood trickled out of the corner of his mouth. Oh, god, his ribs. Had they punctured a lung?

"That goes for you too," his hooked-nosed captor barked. "Shut your fucking mouth."

"No need for language," the woman reprimanded. "We're the civilized ones, remember? Now, come on. We're wasting time."

"Sorry, Tiffany," my captor grunted.

I was going to be kidnapped by a bitch named *Tiffany*? A hysterical laugh bubbled from my lips, before B.O. yanked me to my feet.

Then somehow, after a moment of mind and stomach-bending movement, we were back at the clearing with the waterfall where we'd first arrived in Orrm. What I saw next was enough to make my bile rise. Durl's body lay at our feet, along with a heap of other dead Knerls.

Of course. They would have to make a graveyard in order to open a gateway.

"Fucking monsters," Simon growled from behind me.

I couldn't agree more. I focused on breathing so that I wouldn't desecrate the bodies further with vomit. The hook-nosed man must have hit Simon again, because I heard a body thump to the ground.

B.O. threw me down next to Simon. He joined Tiffany in clearing the earth to dig a mass grave. The third man, who had searched poor Durl's house, kept half an eye on us while lining up the bodies of the Knerls in a tidy row. A heavy weight settled in my limbs, pinning me to the ground where I lay.

"I'm so sorry," I whispered, both to Simon and to Durl. It was a meager apology, of course, for causing a friend's death. But it was all I could do.

"S'okay," Simon said, though the way his mouth twisted told me he was holding back some powerful emotion. Then: "Look here." I glanced down at the pocket he gestured to with his chin.

"What?"

"Poison," he murmured, glaring at the Guardians. They began digging the mass grave, scooping out clods of dirt with magic. "I snuck two vials into my pocket before they got to you."

"*Simon.*" All thoughts of submitting to whatever Tiffany and her ilk were about to do to us vanished. "You're a goddamn genius. Here, turn a bit so I can get them." He obliged, sitting up so that he was positioned behind me. I leaned back and reached for his pocket. It took a minute until I found it, and I realized that if we lived through this experience it was going to get a bit awkward that my hands had been all over Simon's lap. But finally, my fingers closed on the rounded glass vials. I slipped one to Simon.

"There's something else I have to tell you," I whispered as we both struggled against our bonds. I swallowed a yelp of pain and gritted my teeth, even as warm blood slicked my palms. But they loosened, and I left my wrists inside the slackened ropes. "I did something earlier."

"For Asael's sake, what's so important you have to tell me now? They're almost done," he hissed.

"I summoned a demon." I continued through his muttered oath. "I made a deal to get us out of here. They said to follow the stars."

"Stars? What stars?"

"If I knew, I wouldn't have to ask you."

"Seph, if we get out of this alive, I'm going to kill you."

"You have my full permission," I assured him, renewed with the vigor of escape. "But we need to figure this out, so look for the fucking stars."

I craned my neck, searching in a last-ditch effort for anything that could be construed as a star. There were the actual stars of course, which were now out in their full glory, dotting the sky in a spray of paint from an artist's brush. But they were far out of reach unless I suddenly sprouted wings.

They were also reflected in the pool of the waterfall that was some fifty yards to our left. It was a beautiful sight, the light of the stars twinkling in the current like they were winking at us. Beckoning, almost.

The realization struck me just as the dull thud of bodies hitting the bottom of shallow graves signaled that the Guardians were finished. *They come from the south, always soaked to their bones and running from the spirits.*

The waterfall was the seam. The Guardians' voices faded away for a moment, and I was left with my heart thundering almost as loudly as the falls. We just needed time, a distraction to draw them away while we made a run for it. And what better distraction could there be than an angry forest spirit?

"Do you trust me?" I asked Simon.

"Unfortunately, yes."

"Then follow my lead, and when I scream, you do it louder."

Simon's brows drew down. "But that'll—"

B.O. jerked me upward. I would consider myself the luckiest person in all of the worlds if I lived to see the bruises he left. Hook-nose did the same with Simon, and we were half marched, half dragged to the undisturbed earth beside the bodies. I could only hope Simon had caught my meaning.

Tiffany made the familiar motions of opening a gateway, her fingers searching for the invisible latch that would open a door between worlds. I stared straight ahead, afraid that making eye contact with Simon would give us away. Then the atmosphere changed, and the midnight silk of the gateway undulated against the dark of night.

"Go on," B.O. snarled, and pushed me ahead of him. I stumbled, dropping to the ground. When he reached to pull me back up I sent a shattering headbutt straight to his nose. There was an audible crunch. He shouted and reeled back, clutching his face as blood spurted between his fingers. I pulled out the hand I'd worked free of my bindings, then uncorked the vial of poison and threw it into his gaping mouth, backhanding him with all my strength. I didn't wait around to see what happened, but if the bloodcurdling screeches were any indication, it wasn't good.

There was a muffled grunt behind me, while Tiffany, her face drawn tight with anger and surprise, rushed us. I sprang up, blessing my Guardian reflexes, and shot a foot out to trip her. She was too agile and struck out with power, knocking me back to the ground. Good—let her think I was stunned. She put a knee on my sternum and leaned forward. I wheezed as my breath fled.

"You little bitch," she hissed, inches from my face. "I might as well save the Diurne the trouble and kill you now. Everyone knows that unfortunate accidents happen during a—"

I cut her off by unleashing an ear-splitting scream that was so piercing my pulse stumbled and my throat burned with the effort. That scream was for Durl, for Simon, for me and Alex and our friends, and most importantly, for the forest spirits. If they hadn't been summoned by the noise of the Guardians burying the Knerls, this would surely bring them running.

Tiffany's mouth formed an *O* of surprise, and she jerked backward. I bucked her off, then snatched a stone off the ground and slammed it into her temple. She went limp, and in that moment, I was so full of fury I didn't care if I'd killed her.

I spun to see Simon splashing the vial of poison into hook-nose's face. He kicked the stunned man in the balls, sending him to the ground. Simon released a cry of rage, then we were both shouting at the top of our lungs.

"What are you on about?" the third man roared. We never got the chance to answer him, because a dark shape flickered in the corner of my vision. I groped for Simon's hand and yanked us back, away from the diaphanous blot that became more solid by the second. The shape groaned like a heavy bough sighing in high wind.

The forest spirit finally solidified into a creature of knotted thorns that were as long as my forearm. It was vaguely human-shaped, towering above us, glowing red eyes trained upon the third man. He yelled, then sent a jet of green flame at it. The creature caught fire, but that didn't stop it from lashing out with a thorn-studded vine.

"Come on," I urged, not bothering to keep my voice down

anymore. I'd called a bigger bully to take out the Guardians, but as soon as it lost interest—or the third man killed it—we weren't safe, either. The gateway Tiffany had opened was shut now, perhaps closing when she'd lost consciousness, or—

"The waterfall," I cried, and we ran, feet squelching along the marshy ground. Another masculine scream rent the chill air, then stopped abruptly.

A shadow slid across my peripherals, and a forest spirit materialized before us. Blood rushed in my ears. It was even larger than the last one, who, from the sound of it, had finished off the third man. A sizzle of adrenaline surged through my limbs, and I darted around the beast, pulling Simon behind me. He was panting in harsh, pained gasps, and I remembered the blood trickling out of his mouth.

Whip-like strands of thorns raked across my stomach. I cried out, releasing Simon to cradle the wounds. They felt so deep I feared my guts might spill out. A similar cry came from behind me, but when I turned the thorns lashed me again. Blood poured from the lacerations, drenching my destroyed clothing. I felt like I was the one fire, bleeding and burning and screaming.

"Seph," Simon croaked. He lay prone, face half-buried in mud. We were at the waterfall's edge. So close to freedom.

The beast bellowed, and I looked up to see it looming directly over-head. This was it, then. I curled my body over Simon's, knowing it was useless but trying all the same. I'd signed our death warrant by calling the spirits. This was my fault.

But the killing blow never came. Instead, the creature groaned, its tree bough sigh morphing into the crackle of kindling catching fire. Bright orange flames consumed the spirit. The scent of woodsmoke filled my nostrils, and my eyes stung with it. I slid my arm under Simon, who was alert now, and heaved us out of range of the falling embers.

As I did, I caught sight of Tiffany. The side of her face was drenched in blood and cast in a demonic glow by the fire.

"I am going to kill you," she snarled, skirting the smoldering pile. The murderous expression on her plain face sent a strange sense of calm through me. We'd survived death by inches tonight, and I wasn't about to let her finish the job.

Snatching another large stone off the ground, I staggered to my feet and drew her away from Simon. She prowled toward me, a hunter set on her prey. Her focus reminded me of Davina's single-mindedness once she had a target in her sights. Bad news for me.

Tiffany shot a hand out, then curled her fingers inward. Pressure clamped around my neck, and I tore at the invisible noose. My head buzzed, vision darkening at the edges as I tried and failed to draw breath.

I just hoped she'd have mercy on Simon, that the Aureum would go after Alex since I couldn't.

Except, for the second time that night, Tiffany's jaw went slack, and her eyes rolled back. She fell to her knees, revealing Simon standing behind her with his hand held aloft, clutching an empty vial of poison. The dying fire threw harsh shadows over him and turned his fox-like features into a ghoul's mask.

"Weapons," he wheezed, then folded in half at the waist with his hands on his knees. "Get our bags."

Right. I lurched toward hook-nose, who still lay on the ground unconscious, and snatched the satchels before crossing to Simon. I no longer felt the pain of my wounds. In fact, my whole body was numb, and my head seemed like it was floating on top of nothing.

"You're brilliant." I coughed, hauling his arm over my shoulder and splashing into the icy pool of the waterfall. "Can you swim?"

"Yeah. That thing didn't get me as bad as you, but my side's on fire where they kicked me. So maybe I should be asking you that question."

"No choice," I gasped. The freezing water cut through my numbness, and my wounds throbbed again.

We fought hard against the current to get to the falls. But once we were several feet away from the plunge area, the swirling flow shot us beneath the overhang. Lucky for me, because I was beginning to see stars, and not the kind that were in the sky.

"Where is it?" Simon yelled. I had to read his lips, as nothing was audible over the rush of water. I mimed hammering on the slippery rock that formed the cave behind the waterfall, and he swam to the far end of the pool, searching for the weak point of the seam where world rubbed against world.

There was real fear in Simon's eyes now, and I knew it was for me. I was fading fast, clinging to the rock with the tiny amount of strength I had left. The swim had washed away most of the blood caking me, but I knew I'd lost far too much.

Simon returned from the far end of the cave, securing my grip around the point of a rocky outcropping. "Don't let go!" he mouthed. Then, he dove beneath the churning surface.

I shook my head to prevent my eyes from closing. I was so tired. It would be easier than falling asleep to let go and slip into the water. Just when I was thinking what a good idea it might be, Simon breached the surface.

"Got it!" I read the triumph on his lips, then took a deep breath before he grabbed my hand and took us under.

The water buffeted us so that we were pulled in all directions while Simon fought the current. Luckily, he was a strong swimmer; I'd have to ask him about that sometime. I hoped I'd have the chance. My eyes burned as I opened them underwater, but I was able to make out a long, gaping split in the rock. The inside was blacker than a gateway, and more terror curdled my stomach.

I hated small spaces. Hell, I could barely walk down a staircase if someone was coming the other way. Tightness banded my chest, and I automatically tried to kick back to the surface. But Simon was stronger, so he succeeded in pulling me through the crevice and into oblivion.

4

"Morning," Alex murmured. He skimmed his knuckles down my side, over the curve of my breast to the flair of my waist.

We faced each other in bed as the gray dawn broke and sent silvery light to caress our bare skin. I shivered, then rolled into him, finding his lips with mine. The kiss was soft and sweet as the new day, and I hummed with pleasure in the back of my throat.

I drew away just to take him in, absorbing every ridge of muscle and line of ink covering his arms. I could never get enough of looking at Alex, in this lifetime or any others. His skin was pale and smooth, save for where scars puckered his flesh. So many scars. I traced a fingertip across a faded white slash that ran along his ribs, and his abdominals bunched beneath my touch. He grabbed my wrist, then closed the space between us and claimed my mouth again. This time, there was no trace of gentleness. I opened for him, and he swept his tongue against mine, tracing my lower lip and taking the kiss deeper. My blood went from a slow simmer to a boil that sent heat straight to my core.

"You're so beautiful," he whispered into my throat, nuzzling the hollow of my neck. Every touch made my nerves sing with lust.

I wove my fingers into his dark locks, reveling in their silkiness. His skin burned against mine. I drew him upward so that I could look into the dark green of his eyes. He smiled his beautiful, heartbreaking smile that made me want to fall to my knees.

And it all came back.

The demon, the hell-pit from the prison world, and the horrible acceptance on his face as he was dragged down into the dark.

Alex touched my cheek and drew away a wet fingertip. "Why are you crying?"

"Because you're not real. None of this is real."

"Isn't it?" he asked, smiling softly.

———

I woke up with *I love you* on my lips, my throat tight and hot. My hands felt heavy, and when I tried to move them, something tugged on my skin. Several thin plastic tubes were attached to my hand with tape and needles.

The four white walls surrounding me held a sterility that screamed "hospital." I turned to the side, noting the all-over ache that came with it. Low beeps sounded from a monitor with a green line undulating across the screen.

It was hard to think through the pounding in my head, but I grasped for memories of how we'd gotten here. All I remembered was the crashing waterfall, the fear of slipping into the water and drowning. Simon had gotten us out somehow.

He sat slumped in a chair in the corner of the room, chin nodding to his chest in sleep. A wave of gratitude swamped me. He looked like someone had kicked the shit out of him, bruises purpling his face and a gash on his temple. Our canvas satchels from Durl's—god, Durl—lay at his feet.

I attempted to say his name, but my throat was so dry that only a gasp escaped. I coughed and tried again. "Simon."

He startled awake immediately. "What's it? Oh, gods, Seph. You're up." He limped over to my bed and laid a gentle hand on mine, taking care not to disturb the IV lines. "You scared me for a moment there."

"Water," I croaked. He handed me a plastic cup with a bendy straw from the adjustable table beside the bed. I drank greedily, draining the cup dry. I handed it back to him and he just held onto me, staring. His eyes were dull and lackluster, and the dark circles under them almost matched the color of his bruises.

"Where are we?"

"In hospital."

"In what...world?"

"Yours."

I tried to bolt upright but was caught by wires and a tugging sensation around my midsection. "Fuck," I gritted out, the word sticking in my throat.

"Shh, lay back." He gingerly pushed me down onto the pillows. "It's all right. We're in a place called Old York. No, that's not right. New York, I believe. And, ah, the hospital is named after a mountain?"

The monitor next to me beeped loudly, the little graph shooting skyward as my heart raced out of control. "Mount Sinai?"

"Yeah, that's it. It's an odd place, this. No one batted an eye when we fell out of a public washroom, soaked to the skin and sliced to ribbons."

I groaned. What were the chances that out of all the infinite possible worlds to find, we had landed back in mine? The Aureum must have a huge presence in the city, given the sheer number of dead bodies buried here.

"What's important is you've got stitched up. None of the, ah, lacerations were too deep. Missed all your vital organs, thank Asael, and you didn't lose enough blood to need a...transduction, I think she said." He arched a brow. "I would have been supremely annoyed if you died on me."

Now that I was more alert, I recognized the tight tenderness along my abdomen. I winced when I brushed my hand over the wounds and felt stitches through my hospital gown.

"I'll do my best not to. What about you?"

Simon shook his head. "Got one cracked rib, three of those cuts, and these." He raised his bandaged wrists, which matched the bandages on mine. They ended a few inches below the swirling black lines of the protection tattoo on my forearm. "They've wrapped the ribs nice and tight and told me to take it easy. Fat chance of that happening, given your penchant for running into people who want to commit murder."

His gentle ribbing was meant to make me smile, but I felt a surge of sticky guilt instead. The thud of Durl's body, of his cry as Tiffany slit his throat, rang in my ears. "I'm so sorry. I fucked up with summoning that demon. I fucked up bad, Simon. That's how they found us."

"Well...it's over now, I s'pose." He wouldn't look at me head on, instead rising halfway out of his seat and turning toward the door. "The healer said to tell her when you woke. I should find someone."

"Hold on a second." I tugged on his sleeve to pull him down into the chair. "We need to take care of this first."

I rubbed my left shoulder. The sleeve of a polka-dotted hospital gown draped over it. Stealing power from Simon in the prison world had healed all my wounds instantly, including the hole in my arm from Fern's bullet. Which meant, if I wanted to remove the tracker.... I caught his eye.

"What?" After a beat, his chair scraped along the floor as he scooted away from the bed. He shook his head fervently. "No. No bloody way."

"Simon," I said in my calmest, most reasonable voice.

"Seph," he answered, using a warning tone.

"If we don't take it out, they're going to come for us again. It's only a matter of time."

Silence unfolded between us. He knew I was right. I would win this one.

"Bloody, bollocking fuck. You're asking too much."

"I've already been slashed once. I don't think this will hurt as badly."

That was the wrong thing to say. He shoved up, stomping around as best he could while limping.

"When you finish your tantrum, you need to steal a scalpel. It's a tiny knife on the end of a—"

"I know what it is," he interjected with a scowl.

I continued as though he hadn't spoken. "There's probably iodine, tweezers, gloves, and bandages in those." I inclined my head toward the row of white cabinets above a sink on the opposite wall. "Hurry up."

Throwing a glare over his shoulder, Simon stormed from the room. I closed my eyes, taking short, shallow breaths through gritted teeth. All this talking wasn't doing me any favors.

Simon returned a short time later, muttering something about stubborn women. After another peek down the hallway, he closed the door and locked it. Then he pulled a scalpel from his sleeve. I cringed inwardly, but nodded. "Let's get this over with."

He rolled up a wad of gauze. "Open," he instructed. When I looked askance at him, he said, "To bite. So you don't yell."

I grimaced but did as he asked, the gauze absorbing all the moisture from my mouth. He probed my upper arm. "I think I can feel something," he murmured. "Right, keep an eye on the door and tell me if anyone's coming." He swabbed a large patch of skin with the iodine, then placed the scalpel's blade against my arm. I released an involuntary shiver.

"Do it," I mumbled through the gauze, focusing on the doorknob.

To my credit, I didn't scream, only emitted a tight groan as tears of pain streamed down my cheeks. And to Simon's, he was fast and efficient, his hands surprisingly steady. When he emerged from the bloody mess of my arm with a tiny, cylindrical metal device in his hand, I sagged back against the pillow.

He placed the device in my palm, then picked up the needle and thread. "This honestly might hurt worse. Sorry."

"Why would you tell me—*fuck*." The tracker bit into my palm as I clenched my fists.

"What should we do with it?" he asked, as he secured a bandage around my arm. It was almost like Simon had done this before.

I shrugged, then flinched as the movement pulled my stitches. "Flush it down the toilet. The Diurne deserve a trip to the sewers."

Simon gathered up the many bloody bandages and shoved them in the garbage, tying off the bag then disappearing from the room. As soon as he'd returned, a nurse in pink scrubs and a halo of dark curls knocked on the door and entered. Simon jumped, throwing her a guilty glance.

"How're you feeling, honey?" The nurse checked the clipboard hanging from the end of my bed.

"Uh, fine," I answered, trying not to squirm.

"Heck of an accident you got into. How'd it happen?"

"Erm—one of those, ah, separated train cars," Simon answered, pasting a terrifying, wide smile on his face. Oh, no. I shook my head at him furiously, and his brows lifted.

The nurse's pen paused on the clipboard. "You from Australia or something?" she asked, cocking her head at Simon.

"He's joking!" I interjected, forcing a laugh. "It was a regular car accident. Yeah, we're tourists. Not used to the big city, you know. Stepped out right in front of a cab."

"Uh-huh," she said, casting a wary eye over both of us. "Well, let me go see when the doctor can come in to check your stitches."

Once she was gone, I tore out the needles taped to my hands and arms.

"What do you think you're doing?" Simon demanded, grabbing my forearm. I shook him off.

"Getting the hell out of here. She's not buying it. Where are my clothes?"

Once dressed, we snuck out of the hospital room and down the corridor into the chaos of the emergency room exit. Luckily our jackets were still in our satchels, so we were able to cover up the worst of our blood and ash-stained clothing.

We spilled out of the hospital onto the chilly, teeming streets of Manhattan. Central Park stretched along one side of us, Madison Avenue on the other. It was bizarre and unsettling to go from the world of forests and meadows to seeing Starbucks and McDonald's on every corner. Car horns blared, and stale air wafting up from subway grates mingled with the scent of roasting street meat. I cringed at every new assault, gripping Simon by the elbow to keep him close. His head was on a swivel, eyes huge as he took everything in.

I took a quick mental assessment of just how screwed we were, and it was as bad as I'd imagined. We had no money, so we couldn't get food or a place to stay, or plane or bus tickets. We had no way to know whether there was another seam in the city we could travel through, and I couldn't open a gateway, not without my power—and even then, it was touch and go. There was no way in hell I could call my mom and ask for her help. If the Aureum had any intelligence at all, which they did, they were likely staking out her house. That left one other option: Bri.

"So, we're fucked," I told Simon.

"Tell me something I don't know," he groused. "D'you think we should go back to Canhaben?"

"Are you sure there's just the one seam coming through Jupiter's?"

"Definitely. Penn—" His throat bobbed as he swallowed hard. "Penn looked, and Diana, too. There's only one way out."

I blinked as I got a sudden head rush. Black spots appeared in my vision, and I stumbled into a passerby.

"Watch it," they groused before pushing on. I felt exposed, even with the crowds. What if Guardians were walking these same streets?

Simon took my arm, steadying me as we walked. "Do you know of any other seams in your world?"

"There must be others around, somewhere. But we need money to travel."

"What, can't we trade? You surely don't need all those weapons, and some of them are quite nice."

"Oh." Although I was loath to part with anything Alex had given me, we needed money more. "I guess we need to find a pawn shop."

We hadn't gone two blocks when we came upon a storefront that had a flashing neon *We Buy Gold!* sign.

Simon gaped at it. "Your world is rich, isn't it? We haven't seen the likes of this in Canhaben in a hundred years. And imagine, just going out to the shops and buying anything your heart desires! This world has so much *stuff*. No wonder your dad came here."

"Most places aren't like this." I approached the middle-aged man who sat behind thick plexiglass, fiddling with his phone. He smoothed a hand over oily, slicked-back hair before sliding the partition open a meager inch.

"Put 'em up," the man said, still staring at his screen. I drew the daggers out of my bag, holding one back to keep. The shiny metal seemed to get his attention, because he put the phone down and squinted at me. "What's a lady like you doin' with those?"

I smiled, baring my teeth. "I'm not a lady. And I'm not here to chat." A year ago, I'd never have said that aloud. Crazy what a change in priorities could do to a person.

"Aright, aright," he said. "I don't accept stolen goods."

Like hell he didn't. "They're not stolen. I need four-fifty for all three."

He guffawed. "You're funny, kid. Slide 'em through." I pushed the blades through the gap beneath the glass, waiting until he returned one to send the next. The man scratched his chin. "I'll do two hundred for three."

"That's insulting." I swept them into my bag and made to walk away.

"Hold on now, hold on. Touchy, ain't she?" he said, looking at Simon and winking.

"No," Simon answered blithely. "She's not."

The man blew air through his lips, then fingered the gold hoop in his ear. "Two-twenty."

I snorted. "Four-twenty."

We went back and forth for several minutes until we landed on a semi-decent price. I was folding the wad of grubby bills he shoved through the window when the man spoke again.

"I'll throw in an extra hundred for the ring." He gestured to my hand. "Pure silver?"

I twisted the ring on my thumb that I hadn't taken off since we left Canhaben. My dad had left it behind along with his photograph and letters.

The ring's origins were a mystery. I didn't know what significance it held to him, but it was still a reminder of the man he'd been. The man my mother had fallen for, who'd risked his life and run so that the Aureum and demons wouldn't find me. I just wished his sacrifice hadn't been in vain.

I tied the fastenings on my bag and slung it over my shoulder. "It's not for sale."

The man was grumbling about suckers missing out on easy money when we left.

"You would've been a force in the markets back home," Simon said. "That was impressive."

"I've never haggled for anything in my life," I admitted. "I never spoke much, if I didn't have to. Before...all this."

"You wouldn't be able to tell now. You're a natural."

I shrugged off Simon's praise. "You hungry?"

The diner was classic and old-timey, with a lunch counter and red vinyl booths. It smelled of apple pie and burnt coffee, and we ordered both, along with heaping blue plate specials. I hadn't had meatloaf since elementary school, and it filled me with a yearning for simplicity. We tucked in, not saying a word until both our plates were clean.

"I think I know where we can get help," I told Simon. I'd thought about it while we stopped in a cheap, knockoff electronics store where I bought a prepaid cell phone. Simon was captivated by touch screens, and I'd had to forcibly drag him out.

"Eh?" he asked, making a face at the bitter coffee. "Does this place have tea?"

I flagged down the waitress who had an honest-to-god bouffant hairstyle and smoker's wrinkles lining her thin, hot pink lips.

Once she'd brought the tea, I started again. "Well, it's not so much a where as a who. There's a woman from Gravesville that I'm almost positive is supernatural."

"Who's that?" Simon asked, sipping from the new mug. "Ah, much better."

"Her name is Constance. I met her last year, right after...." I was going to say right after I met Penn for the first time. I didn't want to bring up Simon's twin again, to remind him of his death by my father's hand. The dull sheen of grief had just begun to lift from Simon's eyes, and I didn't want to be the one who put it back there.

"After all this started. She's a psychic, or at least was posing as one. She gave me this protection charm." I touched the brown, striped stone pendant hanging around my neck. "I think it's real. At least, it might've helped me before." The demon Ventusiel's sharp beak flashed in my mind, and I suppressed a shudder.

"Why wouldn't it be real?"

I sighed. "The supernatural isn't an accepted part of this world. Regular humans outnumber them...us, hundreds, thousands to one. We have to hide in order to survive."

"Sounds right terrible. Having to hide who you are, just because folk are too small-minded to understand."

"It happens here more than you would think, and not just in regard to magic. Did you notice how that security guard was following me when I bought the cell phone, even though I was holding a wad of cash?" I asked, stirring more cream into my bitter coffee. "And wasn't paying attention to you, even though your hands were all over the tablets?"

"Er—no. I didn't," he said, cheeks pinking. "Those…screens are a strange kind of magic. I wouldn't mind going back to look again."

I shot him a bemused smile before continuing. "Right. Well, he was following me because my skin is darker than yours. Do you know why?"

Simon's forehead creased as he studied my tawny skin that was lined with bandages and welts. "Ah…because it's nice?"

Laughter bubbled from my chest, tugging my stitches. "Ow." I fished out some pain pills I'd bought in a bodega and washed them down with cold coffee. "No. It's a long story with a lot of history behind it, but basically, people with skin like mine don't get treated like people with skin like yours. We're sometimes looked at as less than."

"But…but that's not on." He frowned at me. "What's the shade of your skin got to do with that?"

"Again, long story. It's like the…" I lowered my voice. "Golden Ones, persecuting the Watchers."

His cheek hollowed as he bit the inside of it. "Gods, I'm sorry, Seph. You're getting it from both ends."

"It's okay. Well, not really. But that's kind of my point. My world is different than Canhaben, but that doesn't mean it's better." I hated to take the stars out of his eyes, but as long as we were going to be here—hopefully not too long—I wanted him to know. This, too, was part of me, just like my Watcher heritage and lightbringer magic. Well, lightbringer magic might be a past tense, I thought, the meatloaf sitting heavy in my stomach.

"Anyway, we should have enough cash to stay somewhere tonight, and I can call Constance." I didn't know what we'd do after, but I promised myself to worry about it later. Our top priority was to remain hidden, and I felt more sense of purpose in carrying out these next few steps than I had in weeks. They were tangible, something I could put my finger on.

We took more pie to-go—Simon got lemon meringue, and I went with chocolate silk—and checked in at the dingy hostel our waitress recommended. It was cheap enough, even with the private room I booked. But given the dark stains on the floor, walls, and even ceiling—I decided I'd sleep on top of the bedspread, fully clothed.

What I really wanted to do was fall unconscious and sleep off the pain from my wounds, but we'd wasted enough time. After the diner, we'd had to buy a set of new clothes for each of us, plus first aid supplies. Simon's questions during our shopping trip had been incessant, and I'd had to stop him from wandering off and getting lost more than once. Supervising him in this city was a full-time job.

While he showered, I punched in the number to Constance's psychic shop and listened to the tinny ringtone. My stomach dropped when her voicemail picked up. I left a brief message, hoping she would call back soon.

Hands trembling, I dialed another number. One that I knew by heart. I chewed my lip as I waited for the call to connect.

A busy tone beeped, then a robotic voice said, "We're sorry. You have reached a number that is no longer in service. Goodbye."

Bri was unreachable, then. *Fuck.* Fighting the wave of disappointment, I curled up on top of the bed, pillowing my head on my arm. What would I have said if she answered, anyway? *Hi, I know we haven't talked in months, but turns out I have superpowers and am running from both a magical mafia and demons, and I need some money. Anyway, how are you?*

The bathroom door opened with a cloud of steam. Simon emerged wearing his new clothes, pink-cheeked and damp-haired. Good, a distraction.

I sat up. "Wow. You look...modern."

"For you, maybe," he said, tugging at the hem of his navy button down. I couldn't convince him to buy a T-shirt. "Is all clothing so... scratchy, here?"

I laughed. "We bought the cheapest they had to offer, so no. It'll soften up."

"It's so strange. All of it, not just the clothes. I'm having a lot of sympathy for your adjustment to Canhaben. It seemed so easy for you."

"Well, I was stuck in your house, not roaming the streets of one of the most populous cities in the world."

He smiled ruefully. "True enough." He sat next to me on the bottom bunk, smelling of cheap soap. "You all right?"

"I'm okay." Which was true, in the sense that I wasn't dead yet. I'd witnessed murder and been attacked, along with having my entire world upended for the second time in six months upon finding out the Diurne wanted to trade me in a devil's bargain. Losing Alex and the group of friends I'd let into my heart, the anguish of leaving Bri behind in my old life, and Durl—I squeezed my eyes shut against the memory of his small body lying on the ground next to the other Knerls. He'd paid the ultimate price for helping us. I'd never forget that, never forget that my actions had led to his death.

I was nothing short of an utter disaster.

We faced each other for several long seconds, and I saw the exact moment Simon decided it would be better—easier—to accept the lie.

"We'll have better luck tomorrow," he said, and laid his hand over mine, giving it a gentle squeeze.

"Sure," I answered, squeezing back. It was easier to accept the lie.

5

Early the next morning, my pocket buzzed just as I knocked on the door of our room. I juggled a coffee for me, tea for Simon, and a bag of donuts for both of us. When Simon opened the door, I thrust the drinks into his hands and dug the phone out, stabbing the answer button.

"Hello," I said breathlessly.

"Oh, my dear, it is so good to hear from you." Constance's drawl was unmistakable, thick like honey and twice as sweet.

I covered the phone, then whispered to Simon, "I'm putting it on speaker. You can't talk, okay?" He nodded, putting a finger to lips that were already coated in powdered sugar. "Yeah—um, thanks for calling me back."

"Well, I would've done sooner but I was out of the shop on a buying trip. There's a new set of crystal balls that—oh, never mind." Her tone shifted to concern. "You said you needed help?"

"Ah, yes." I chewed my lip, weighing my next words. Part of me hadn't expected she'd ever get in touch. Now that I had her, I was frozen with indecision. I did want—no, needed—Constance's help. But I was afraid, afraid that she was somehow connected to the Aureum, or worse, that she was innocent and they'd punish her for helping me. I couldn't be responsible for that again.

"Persephone, dear. Does this call have anything to do with the reading I gave you?" Constance asked.

"Not exactly," I hedged.

A kettle whistled faintly over the line, then clinking glasses. "Well, for goodness's sake, are you all right? What's happened?"

"I just...I have some questions I hope you can help with. You might be the only person who can."

Constance sighed. "I certainly can't help if you don't ask."

Simon raised his eyebrows in a *well, get on with it* gesture.

I remembered the day she'd done my reading. How hollowed out and desperate I'd felt, and how she'd given me comfort and kind words when I'd needed them. She'd sent me away with the necklace charm, knowing that my future would need protecting.

"I found my power," I said, sending the words out into the space between us before I could take them back. "Just like you said I would. But I lost it. I need to figure out how to get it back."

"Ah," she said, the word soft as a spring morning. "I could sense the magic on you as soon as you walked through my door. You can tell me, dear. I'd like to help if I can."

Simon sighed as I relaxed my death grip on his hand. So, I was correct—she was part of the supernatural.

I gave her an abridged and purposefully vague version of what happened in the prison world, and how I hadn't been able to access my power since.

"Oh, honey. That's just awful." I could almost picture the way her cornflower blue eyes would drop mournfully.

Anxiety was a knot in my belly, and I was glad I hadn't touched the donuts yet. "So can you help me? How do I fix it?"

Her answering exhale was heavy. "Magic isn't an exact science, dear. It's ancient and persnickety, and just when you think you've figured it out, it goes and changes all the rules on you, because it doesn't have rules. I've been a practicing witch for forty years, and I still don't know everything. But what you're tangled up in...all the creatures in town know of the Aureum. They leave the witches alone as long as we're behaving ourselves, but I can tell you for certain they've made a lot of enemies. Being the watchdogs of the supernatural world will do that to you. If you're going up against them, you'll need help."

"I don't want to go up against them. I want to stay *away* from them." For now. Revenge could come later, after Alex was safe in my arms.

She sighed. "My dear, you've gone through a terrible trauma. And only a few weeks ago at that. You need to give yourself time to process what's happened. You're blocked, plain and simple."

"I don't have time for processing," I protested, slumping onto the bottom bunk bed and raking my still damp waves.

Constance clucked like a frustrated mother hen. "I'm confident your abilities will return, dear, but they'll come back on their own schedule. Not yours."

The spark of hope in my chest guttered, threatening to extinguish. "There has to be some other way I can unblock them." I hated the way my voice had gone high and wavering, but I'd never felt so desperate and powerless in my life. Not even as a child watching my mother lay in bed for days, or when I'd struggled to grasp hold of my magic. At least it'd been there for the taking.

"If you find out, let me know. I've never known of a spell or ritual that would bring back power before it's well and ready to come."

It would be wrong to throw the phone across the room, right? My fingers tangled in the bedding, clenching and unclenching.

"However...there is still one other option, but I don't think you'll like it," Constance said.

There was another option, and she didn't think to lead with that? A six-inch tear appeared in the sheets. "Tell me."

"You don't know, then," she murmured, as if she was talking to herself.

"Know *what*?"

"You're a Siphon."

I furrowed my brow at Simon, but he looked back at me blankly. "A what?"

"A Siphon is someone who can take energy from a living being and convert it into magic. It's how you were able to send power to your friends during the battle, and why you could take it from them as well. You did it instinctually, automatically. I imagine it's part of your own particular brand of supernatural. Fascinating."

"So...I can still use power? I just have to take it from something?"

For the first time since I'd realized my magic had run dry, I felt an echo of old-me again. The me I had been while standing at the edge of Canhaben, holding the power of life in my hands.

"Well, yes. But there are consequences for the, ah, *victim* of siphoning. Only Siphons can manipulate power in this give and take. Once you draw from someone, their magic—or, in the case of non-magicals, their energy—can take weeks to replenish."

"What's the problem with that? It sounds like...I don't know, draining a battery."

"People can die, Persephone," she said firmly. "*If* you drain their energy to the point of breaking. Same goes with other living things like plants and animals. There are consequences for the Siphoner as well. You can take from them, but there is a cost to your soul."

Constance didn't know that I was already racking up sins, but I wasn't eager to add more to the list. "Well, shit," I muttered. Simon fiddled with the buttons on his shirt, staring into space.

"It's a power you must exercise extreme caution with. Siphoning can become an addiction. The power that you take from others isn't like the magic that comes from the wellspring inside of you; once you use it, it's spent, and you need to find another source to siphon from."

So I'd be reduced to some sort of leech, a vampiric parasite that sucked away the life force of my victims? That seemed...disgusting. Wrong. "Is there any other way?"

"I'm sure there is. Like I said, magic is boundless, and my knowledge is limited. This is the best I can give you for now."

"Got it. Thanks, Constance." I wasn't sure what I'd hoped to hear, but it definitely wasn't that.

"Will I be able to speak to you again?"

"Probably not," I said. "At least not for a while."

"Ah," she replied. "The Eames boy. Is that it? You're going after him."

Dead air pressed on my ears, and it might as well have been concrete pumping through my veins instead of blood. "It's better if you don't know."

"If you would just let me—"

"No. And please, don't tell anyone we talked. Trust me, it's for your own good." I didn't wait for her to answer, just hung up and started gathering our meager belongings.

"Hold on," Simon started, rising from the bed.

"We have to leave. Now. There's no time. What if the Aureum finds out? What if they're tapping the phones of every supernatural in Gravesville? God, why didn't I think of this before?" *Because you're just one powerless, foolish person*, a voice hissed. *You have no idea what you're doing.*

"Seph." He grabbed my wrist and drew me to him, then put his hands on my shoulders. We were almost at eye level, and I couldn't escape his stare. "What happened to Durl is not going to happen again."

"You don't know that." My stomach soured as sweat pooled at the base of my spine. "I'm not going to be responsible for hurting anyone else. What if—"

He wrapped his arms around my waist, holding me gingerly to prevent our stitches from pulling. "Take a breath."

I did, drawing a shuddering gulp of air into my lungs and dropping my forehead onto his shoulder. "I'm scared. But I'm going to do it. I'm going to siphon." Even if it was disgusting and morally reprehensible—what choice did I have? This wasn't a jaunt down to the park. I'd realized, too late, that it was war from here on out. Difficult choices had to be made.

Simon stroked my back, his touch almost as light as air. "Are you certain you want to open that door?"

"I won't be powerless again," I vowed, pulling away from him. "If I had magic, Durl wouldn't have died. You wouldn't have been hurt."

"Quit blaming yourself, eh? What happened happened. It's done now."

But I couldn't put it away. Durl's death was a stain on my soul, one that would be with me forever. I didn't want to spend time convincing Simon of that when we needed to get out of the Aureum's reach. Once we were safe and had some resources to our names, we could buckle down on our search for Alex.

"Then let's find a cemetery, and I can try to siphon and open a gateway. We'll go to another world and start looking."

"Where, though?" Simon asked, rubbing the back of his neck.

"I don't know," I answered truthfully. "Any place that's not here would work. I'm not sure how much control I'll have over it—I never learned properly." Gateway magic would've come during my third year of novice training, had I stayed with the Aureum. There were too many things I didn't know.

We left the hostel, making a few other stops to gather supplies with our dwindling stack of cash. After collecting the essentials, I spent the last few dollars on a notebook and pencils for Simon. "So you can draw. I know you've missed it," I said, handing them over to him.

"Oh." He stroked the black spiral-bound cover, then flipped through the pages with his long artist's fingers. "Cheers," he said gruffly, before shoving it into his satchel. "Shall we get on, then?"

We crossed the bridge to Brooklyn and made our way to 25th Street, where we ogled the enormous gothic revival gates at the entrance of Green-Wood Cemetery. It had almost five hundred acres for us to get lost in and not run into any Guardian patrols. That was the theory, at least.

"It's gorgeous." A sigh of pleasure escaped me, cutting through some of the tension that had lived in my shoulders ever since waking up in the hospital.

"They're massive," Simon observed, craning his head upward to take in the arched, brownstone pinnacles. Strangely, lime-green parakeets darted in and out of a gargantuan nest of sticks that took up most of the central spire. Their sharp chatter almost drowned out the noise from people milling around the gatehouse.

"I wish we had time for a tour."

"You can always come back."

"I thought you weren't an optimist?" I asked as we passed through one of the main archways beneath the clock tower.

He snorted, earning a look from a group of tourists with cameras slung around their necks. "You must be rubbing off on me."

After consulting the free pamphlet I'd picked up at the gates, we headed deep into the cemetery to find cover. I wanted to linger among the mausoleums and tombs we passed, to read the names and inscriptions. To let the familiar silence and beauty of a graveyard comfort me.

But there was no comfort to be found when a Guardian might be lurking around the next corner, ready to haul us off to a torture chamber. I grabbed Simon's elbow as though someone might try to snatch him away from me right that second. He shook me off, but took my hand, giving me a humorless smile and a squeeze.

We followed the smaller paths that cut through woods, passing fewer and fewer visitors until we were the only ones left amidst the trees. A dense clump of evergreens, perfect for hiding two people under cover of impending darkness, sat atop the rise of a small hill. We climbed it and pushed our way through the branches, scaring off the squirrels having their late afternoon roundtable. They chittered angrily, and I could've sworn I saw one shaking its tiny fist at me.

Once quiet descended, I took the plastic quart-sized container of live crickets out of my bag. The pet store had been our last stop to acquire siphoning material. We'd decided the bugs would be a good choice for my first experiment, given they only lived for three months anyway. I still felt terrible about it, but I wasn't sure how much power they would give me. I didn't exactly have a conversion for crickets to units of magic.

"This is disgusting." I held the container at arm's length. The crickets were going mad, thrashing against the slippery plastic walls. "We should've gotten something with fewer legs."

"It was just a suggestion," Simon muttered. "You didn't want a fish, so this was the next best option."

"Fish just seem too *alive*, you know? At least crickets are invertebrates."

"Just crunchy little goo pockets," he added cheerfully.

"Right. Thinking of them as *crunchy little goo pockets* will make this easier." I mock-gagged, then set the container on the carpet of pine needles and rocked back on my heels. Where did I begin?

Simon watched me expectantly, and I recalled the way his gray eyes had gone greenish and otherworldly while he anchored the gateway we'd escaped through. Sucking the power from him had been nothing short of intoxicating, the way my blood had felt bubbly and golden like champagne afterward.

"Erm, Seph?"

I blinked, Simon's concerned face coming back into focus. "What?"

"Your eyes," he said, peering at me. "They were, uh—glowing a bit."

"Oh." I chewed my lip. "Maybe that's a good sign?"

He shrugged, then picked up the cricket container and offered it to me. "Dunno til you try, do we?"

I held my breath and reached into the container, even though my skin crawled. But the feeling of that champagne power still echoed in my blood, and instinct took over. The crickets jumped onto my hand, then stopped moving all at once and dropped to the bottom. Energy flowed into me, racing from my hairline to the tips of my toes.

It was like the feeling of relaxation after the first sip of wine, or the sensation of slipping into a hot bath. Then there was the rush that came after; even though this wasn't nearly as much as I'd siphoned from Simon, I still felt as though I could go off skipping through the trees, a smile on my face and not a care in the world despite our many problems. The lacerations on my abdomen and wrists stopped throbbing. I lifted my shirt to see the stitches had fallen away and the open wounds had faded to white lines criss-crossing my skin.

The siphoned magic's whisper caressed my mind just as it had in the prison world, dark and alluring, full of promise and power. *You can do anything. Be anything. All you have to do is ask.* I liked that—well, broken-me did. The voice was a balm against everything I'd been trying to forget, and suddenly the pain buried beneath my bones lightened. My heart crashed against my ribcage. The line between terror and euphoria seemed dangerously thin, and I wasn't certain which side I fell on.

Simon gave a sharp intake of breath. And damned if his gaze didn't hold a little more weariness than it had before. "I'm ready," I told him, my voice tight.

"Right, then. Sun's going down."

The patch of darkening sky above our heads had my stomach clenching. The Guardians would begin their patrols soon.

I centered myself, sliding my mind over the siphoned magic. The power swirling just under my skin was glorious, like a sun-drenched afternoon after a week of rain. But it didn't feel quite like *mine*; it was similar to wearing secondhand shoes that had years of forming to someone else's feet.

On an exhale, I took the stance I'd watched other Guardians do so many times. I spread my hands in the air and let my fingers trail through it, waiting for the catch that would indicate I was touching a gateway.

Let me find a safe place. Let me find somewhere we can get the answers we need. Let me find him.

I repeated the mantra in my head as precious moments ticked by, but there was no snag on which to open a door between worlds.

"Is it...is it working, then?" Simon ventured.

"Just give me a second." Damp hair stuck to the back of my neck, and sweat trickled between my breasts. Alex had explained that gateway magic was complex, but hadn't I opened a gateway in the prison world? *It wasn't good enough,* a voice in my head chimed in. *Magoth didn't go through. You didn't have enough power.*

"Fuck," I muttered, putting my hands into position and trying again.

And again. And again. And again.

I could hardly make out Simon's face amidst the gloom. Frustrated tears built behind my eyes. He'd given me the silence I needed to work, seated on the ground of the cramped space with his knees drawn tight to his ribs.

"We can try again tomorrow, first thing. I'm still exhausted, and I bet you are, too," he said.

"No!" I shouted, sparks flying from my fingers like fireflies lighting the evening sky. Oh, fuck, I was going to set our hiding place ablaze. I drew a deep breath, forcing my cramped lungs to expand. "Sorry. I just... I have to do this. One more try?" I pleaded.

Simon gave a halting nod. I sat beside him for a moment, thinking. The evenings this far north were quite chilly in early spring, and goose-bumps cropped up on my arms.

Magic isn't an exact science, dear. It's ancient and persnickety, and just when you think you've figured it out, it goes and changes all the rules on you, because it doesn't have rules.

My magic worked differently from Alex's. It always had. I needed to stop thinking about what he would do and think about what I would do. Instinct had always been my guide. So I opened the box that held the emotions that had been swirling inside of me since I'd brought to mind memories of the prison world, and allowed the feelings to flood me.

They wrapped around my heart and squeezed, and it was with that I searched for the gateway, not with words. My senses sharpened, and I heard city sounds, the beeping of horns and screeching tires, like I was standing in the middle of the street. The sensation of each tree branch brushing against my skin was magnified a thousand times, and without trying, energy flowed into me, rich and vital, a rush that lit me up from the inside out.

The tree whose branches had been brushing my shoulder was withered and dry. Brown pine needles covered Simon's head.

"Seph," he whispered, lips parted on a gasp.

I didn't have time to placate Simon's concerns, because the mass of magic flowing through my veins I'd unintentionally siphoned from the old tree told me that I could do this. I would do this.

When I stood and raised my hands again, my heart skipped a beat. The catch was subtle, just a slight rip that I might not have noticed if I wasn't hyper-aware of any difference. But it was there, and I hooked my fingers in and pulled.

A ribbon of midnight unspooled in the space between my hands.

"You did it," Simon said, at the same time that I heard voices not far outside our precarious shelter.

We both froze. I brought a finger to my lips, barely daring to breathe.

6

"These extra patrols are bullshit," a high-pitched voice complained. "I was planning to be off this weekend to visit my girlfriend, and now I have to stick around for Easter. It's going to be chaos."

"Better not let Captain Drews hear you saying that," said another, deeper voice. "We're all on the hook for extra patrols. If that's what the higher-ups say, then so be it."

"I know, but still. They'd better catch that damn rogue novice, and soon, because I'm already on her shit list."

A snicker. "Not saying I don't agree. Can you imagine a wanted fugitive coming to New York City, of all places?"

They shared a laugh at the utter absurdity, while the fugitive in question was about to piss herself not ten feet away.

"Whatever she gets serves her right. If she can kill one of the Diurne's kids, she's capable of just about anything."

Simon's nostrils flared as he grimaced. I went hot, then cold, then hot again. So they thought I was a killer, did they? A dark voice inside my head suggested that if they labeled me a murderer, I could *be* a murderer. It would almost be too easy to pull aside an evergreen branch and fling a dagger at their backs. In fact, I could—

No. That thinking wasn't going to get us anywhere productive. I could be enraged at their lies, but getting captured would screw us.

Keep gossiping and move away, I silently urged the Guardians. The gateway billowed, opulent black silk in the darkness of our increasingly vulnerable hiding place. The effort of keeping it open strained at the edges of my control. We had to go now, or our opportunity would be lost.

I pointed at Simon, then jabbed at the gateway. He cocked his head at me, and I made a shooing motion. We needed to move so silently their supernatural hearing wouldn't catch it. Simon slowly lifted his bag from the ground. So far, so good. I did the same, holding my breath as my hands quivered. The voices seemed to be fading away, hopefully off to patrol another area of the cemetery. I let out the breath I was holding, then placed one foot down carefully, ready to launch myself through the gateway.

That was, of course, when all hell broke loose.

The squirrels I thought we'd run off earlier began an unholy ruckus, chattering and squeaking and growling as though preparing for war. They jumped from tree to tree, flitting angrily around our heads.

"*Fuck*. Go!" Our hiding place had been revealed, so it didn't matter if we were louder than a brass band.

"Not without you," Simon said, pushing me toward the gateway.

If only he'd just gone when I asked him. His chivalry cost precious time, and a Guardian emerged from the dense wall of greenery just as we reached for the unending dark.

"Holy—Kate, it's her!" In the same breath, the Guardian grabbed my arm, forcing it behind my back, and toppled Simon to the ground with a wave of his hand.

No, no, no, this is not happening. It would be Orrm all over again.

Before the Guardian got another hand on me, I sent a wash of flame racing over my skin. He yelped and let go, and I punched him in the face. My knuckles sang, but the man staggered back a step before regaining his footing. Using strength powered by magic and fear, I yanked at Simon and tossed him through the waiting gateway.

Power flickered, and the borders of the gateway shrunk. *Shit.* I'd almost used up all the energy I'd siphoned from the crickets and tree, and the second Guardian was there, trying to fight her way through the trees to get to me. A whipping branch narrowly missed my eye.

More, a silken voice whispered. *Take more.* "You don't mind if I borrow some of this, do you?" I asked the man, and when he struck out again, I latched onto his forearm.

I opened myself to the power, and watched his brown eyes widen in shock as I siphoned. The surge was so powerful it almost knocked me off my feet. His magic was strong and robust, like a full-bodied red wine. *Delicious*.

The taste of the Guardian's power distracted me from the other threat who had now forced her way into the confined space of the trees. She didn't speak, just moved like a goddamn lightning strike. Before I knew it, I was on the ground with her forearm on my neck and her knee in my stomach.

"What did you do to me?" the man choked out, terror ringing in every syllable. I couldn't answer, given his partner was slowly crushing my windpipe. Black spots crowded the edge of my vision, and my feet kicked, trying to find purchase on the ground.

Through the vague realization that I was being strangled to death, I heard an echo of Simon's voice in my head. *I would be supremely annoyed if you died on me.*

"Don't kill her," the man panted. The Guardian didn't give any indication she'd heard, just pressed down harder as her teeth bared in a snarl.

I covered her hands with mine and siphoned. This time, I did it too hard, and too fast. Her power had an acidic tinge, and the burn of it overwhelmed me. I felt engorged, and when she released me, her eyes wide as she coughed and spluttered, I turned over and vomited.

The Guardian lunged at me, the shock on her face turning to murderous rage. "What the fuck are you?" she hissed, her fingers scrabbling around my collar again.

But she was scared, too, and fear made her sloppy. I went for the dagger at my waist, stabbing her in the side. The blade slid along something hard and bounced off. Fuck, was she wearing Kevlar?

I shoved the Guardian hard in the throat. She fell back again, and I sprang up. Then I spotted the dead tree in the grove, and it reminded me: I had power now. I'd been operating without it for so long, I kept forgetting.

Drawing more power into my hands, I sent a wave of energy blasting toward the Guardians. They bowled over like ninepins and landed in a tangled heap. I grabbed my bag and jumped headfirst through the shrinking gateway.

For once, I felt comfort as the familiar blackness enveloped me, and the sensation of everything and nothing took over. Then the dark receded, and I was hurled into something solid and prickly while the scent of rich soil filled my nostrils.

"Ow," I grunted, attempting to extract myself from whatever held me.

A pair of hands pulled me off what I could now see was a...well, I wasn't sure what it was. The closest comparison was a cactus, but it was black and towered above my head. I appeared to be in a grove, pale gray grave markers interspersed between the spiky plants. The bare ground under my feet was buckled and pitted, like it had shifted a great deal over time.

I grabbed the edges of the gateway and slammed it shut.

The most important part, other than being alive, was that the Guardians hadn't followed. But would there be some kind of magical residue that told them where we went?

"You bloody idiot!" Simon gave me a hard shake. His hair was mussed, the collar of his shirt half-turned up.

"If you keep calling me that, I'm going to start thinking it's my new name."

"Why did you send me through?" Every plane of his face was rigid, and his already sharp cheekbones became deadly.

"Because it was the right thing to do. I handled it." I cracked my neck, stepping out of his grasp. The stolen magic patted me on the back for a job well done, reminding me I'd kept us safe this time. It proved that siphoning was the right choice, whatever the consequences might be. "See? No new injuries. Not dead. Speaking of." I brushed a hand lightly across Simon's stomach, and felt an echoing jolt of pain while I healed him. Holy shit, this magic was powerful.

His full mouth became a thin slash, and he took a deliberate step out of reach. "We either go together, or not at all. That's the new policy."

I hardened my jaw. Why couldn't he see that I'd done what I had to do to keep him safe? That I would make the same choice again and again if it would make me strong. The effervescence of the siphoned magic was weaker, but I still felt lighter than air. "Oh, you're making rules now?"

"I shouldn't have to." We stared each other down for a few moments, then I relented, crossing my fingers behind my back. "Fine. If we are in a life-threatening situation and I have a chance to save you, I won't. I'll let you die with me, then we'll both be no good to anyone. Happy?"

"No. But shake on it."

Rolling my eyes, I put my hand in Simon's. "Ow." I pulled out a spine that was lodged in my forearm, then glared at the offending plant. "What is that thing? And where are we?"

Behind the black cactus-like plants was an old growth forest. Fertile, verdant farmland spread out before us, ending on the edge of....

"A city!"

"We were just in a city," Simon grumbled.

"A city where we are not suspected murders and there's no manhunt happening," I amended.

"True," he admitted. "But what if there's no magic here?"

I grinned at him. "Then we'll make our own."

We trudged down a wide dirt road just on the other side of the wood. Snow-tipped mountain peaks framed a sprawl of buildings that were arranged in a bell curve. The morning air had a bite to it that signaled the change of seasons, and part of me relished the feeling of a new start. Our journey to find Alex was finally beginning.

Other folk appeared on the road, traveling on foot like us, or in carts pulled by beasts of burden. No one paid us much attention, but I kept my head down and peeked furtively at them through my lashes. Their clothing was a variation of simple tunics and pants in muted colors. I noted with relief that the women wore a mixture of leggings and skirts, so I wouldn't stick out too much in my black denim.

By the time we reached the gates, there was a crowd of at least fifty people around us. More waited by a guard post to enter the city. My nerves jangled, but I had to trust the gateway hadn't opened to a world that would lead to our untimely deaths.

"You don't suppose there's another way in, do you?" I muttered in Simon's ear.

He shook his head. "That wall is as thick as I am tall. This is it."

The mass shuffled along as the line progressed slowly through the wooden gates. They weren't as grand as those flanking Green-Wood Cemetery, but were tall enough to stop the average pole-vaulter. A slice of the city beyond was visible through the opening, displaying more people swarming like a school of a fish.

"Er, Seph," Simon said in an undertone. "D'you know what language they're speaking?"

I cocked an ear at the low buzz of conversation around us. It was staccato, almost rhythmic, but nothing I recognized. A problem to be dealt with later. "Don't worry so much," I told him. "Just look pitiful and non-threatening. We can join this group ahead of us. They'll never know the difference."

A sizable group of wagons rolled in front of us amongst the barely contained chaos of the gate. Their uncovered beds were full of the same types of produce—leafy green and cruciferous vegetables. My fingers itched to grab one, just to see if I could take it.

"Come on." I dragged Simon close behind the nearest wagon. Their drivers were engaged in some sort of negotiation with the pair of guards that occupied a booth to the left of the gates. We stooped, keeping our eyes on the wagon wheels as we followed the road. I felt the guards' eyes alight on us, hesitating, but then we were moving forward and out of sight.

The outskirts of the city teemed with noise and activity. A vendor selling aquamarine beads grabbed my elbow as we passed, trying to loop a strand of them around my neck. I waved her off with an apologetic smile, and continued on through the throng. Children darted underfoot, one almost taking Simon out at the knees as they sped past in a cloud of giggles and screams.

"Canhaben used to be like this," Simon said, raising his voice to be heard over the vendors hawking their wares. The savory, fatty scent of roasting meat went straight to my empty stomach, and it growled angrily.

"Really?" It was hard to imagine the cold, dead world we'd left behind had ever been as vital as this place. "Maybe it'll get there again, now that the edge is healing."

He shrugged, but I saw the ghost of longing in his eyes before he blinked it away. "Let's find a place to stay, then we can get our bearings."

We found the inn by resorting to pointing and miming. Simon's pretend snores almost had me doubled over with laughter, but in the end, we got our point across and made our way to the building of stone patched with whitewashed plaster. A teenage boy hung washing out of an arched window on the third floor, sheets billowing in the breeze and framed against a bright blue sky.

Luckily for us, the innkeeper didn't seem to mind that a couple of weirdos offered her a varied assortment of goods to pay with instead of local currency. She ended up taking a few quarters left over from our cash stores, looking at us with furrowed brows but pocketing the coins in her faded blue apron all the same.

We ambled along behind her up a winding staircase dotted with frameless windows that brought in the scent of lemon and fresh air. I trailed a finger along the rough stone walls, their surface cool to the touch.

"*Ti staza,*" the innkeeper said in a sing-song voice, gesturing to an arched, mosaic-tiled door off the landing. She smiled sweetly, then ducked her scarf-covered head and went back down the stairs.

Simon held the door open for me. "Home sweet home, eh?"

I shuffled through and tossed my satchel to the floor, relieved to have it off my aching shoulders. The room contained two beds that were neatly turned down and smelled of more lemon and vinegar. Paintings hung on white walls depicted forests and mountains, similar to what we'd seen on our walk into the city.

"For now," I answered, collapsing onto a bed. A yawn built from deep within my chest, and I stretched my arms overhead. The adrenaline from the fight at Green-Wood had long since evaporated, and so had the golden feeling of siphoned magic. My muscles were rubbery, and exhaustion tugged at my eyelids.

Simon sat on the other bed. His brow furrowed in an expression that was growing familiar, like he was trying to discern my reflection through a dirty mirror. "You feeling all right, then?" he asked.

Heat prickled the back of my neck. I'd been sharp with Simon earlier, glib about the fact we'd almost been caught by the Aureum twice now. I could blame my attitude on the buzz I always felt during a brawl, or on broken-me—but if I was being truthful, those weren't solely responsible.

"I might have siphoned too much," I admitted. "I think all that magic went to my head after not using any for weeks."

Simon kneaded his forehead, smudging dirt across it. "I'm not certain siphoning is the way to go. Believe me, I'm not complaining you saved us. But you were a little…"

"What?"

"Different."

Insults rose to the tip of my tongue, about how Simon didn't know what he was talking about—that he had no idea what it felt like to be powerless after he'd had the world at his feet. I froze with my mouth half-open, and swallowed the words. That wasn't fair to Simon, to either of us. He'd already lost his entire family. He only wanted to protect me.

"Do we have a better alternative?" I asked, softening my tone.

Uncertainty played out in Simon's wandering gaze, frustration in the downturn of his mouth. "Maybe we should discuss a plan first before making a decision, eh? How exactly are we going to track down Magoth?"

"Well, it's me he wanted," I offered. I'd known this conversation was coming. It should've happened earlier, really. But every time I lay awake at night, trying to think of a way to get Alex back, I always ran into the same problem: my missing magic. "Maybe Magoth can come to me, instead of me going to him."

Simon's knuckles whitened on the edge of the mattress. "I knew you were going to say that. Why must you always run headfirst into danger?"

"It would be the fastest way," I argued. "What's stopping us?"

"The fact that we'd most likely get killed right out of the gate? Your power wasn't fully stable to begin with, and now you want to fight one of the most powerful demons of all time using unfamiliar magic?"

Ouch. I folded my arms over the empty space beneath my ribs that rang with the truth of his words. If anyone knew the extent of my abilities, it was Simon, who had mentored me in Canhaben. "What's your bright idea, then?" I asked, fixing him with a stare.

"Since you ask," he grumbled, "I have given it some thought. We should find a back door."

I blinked at him. "A back door."

"Aye." He shifted forward, the bed's sunshine quilt rustling beneath him. "Find out where that demon bastard is—covertly—and sneak up on him. Observe. Plan. Deliberate. You know, all the things you're terrible at."

Rude, but not entirely incorrect. I sighed, all the fight draining out of me. "I want to throw something at you, but I'm too tired."

His smirk faded. "I know you want Eames back as soon as possible. But think about it—Magoth knows he has the bait, and he will be ready and waiting for us. That is, if he hasn't already sent his minions out looking for you. And you think the Aureum is going to stop searching for us? We've fucked them twice, Seph. Those power-mad nutters aren't going to take that easily."

The weight of just how screwed we were squeezed my lungs, my breath coming shallow. Simon was right. Our enemies were powerful, and they were many. Our allies were few, and we had no idea where they were. Sage, Sylvan, Casey, Davina, and Hollis could be anywhere in the worlds. I missed them so much, their steadfastness and their power—the way being around them made me invulnerable. It was just me and Simon against the worlds right now, two half-broken people stumbling along and trying to help each other hold our pieces together.

We needed help, but the only person I could trust was sitting across from me.

"You're right," I said. Simon's shoulders dropped, and he released his death grip on the sheets. "We can try it your way. But I'm still going to siphon."

"Seph—"

I held a hand up to stop him. "I will do whatever it takes to protect us, even if that means draining half this city dry. I'm not going to lose you." I didn't have to add, *like I lost Alex*, because it was hanging in the air between us. Alex's ghost was always between us.

Simon looked like he'd been walloped by a two by four. "I—well, that's...nice. But no more than strictly necessary."

"I know the limits now. Siphoning from people felt different than the crickets, and even the tree. It was much stronger." I flexed my fingers with the remembrance of all that power rushing into the void under my ribs. "I'll stick to a vegan diet."

"A what?"

"Plants," I explained. "So, fill me in on your covert plan, spymaster."

Simon narrowed his eyes. "Funny. I was thinking we can start with asking the locals—find out who knows what about magic, and if they've heard of a demon prince who's kidnapped a mortal Guardian."

"What about that is covert?"

"Not in those exact words, obviously," he muttered.

"It's not going to be in any words if we don't figure out how to speak the language."

He thumbed an empty button-hole on his shirt. "Well. I had a thought about that. There is a demon, Hael, with the power over languages—every language—and can transfer the knowledge of them to a summoner."

"Oh. Right," I said, sucking my teeth.

"What's wrong?" he asked, eyeing me.

Just that the last time I'd summoned a demon I got involved with a side quest I hadn't been counting on. Which Simon didn't know about yet.

"There's something I need to tell you," I began. And tell him I did, not sparing a detail.

He took the news about how I expected. "Asael's bloody wounds, Seph!" He jumped up from the bed, hands on hips as he stared out the window. "You've made a bargain with a trickster demon. Why didn't you come to me instead?"

I winced. Because we'd just been in a fight, and I was angry and impulsive and afraid. "It was the only option. We were stuck. You know that."

Simon whirled to me, his expression murderous. "For one, we don't know where bleeding Aundirne is, or what world it's in. And for two... angel's bloody arse, you're using blood magic now?"

What was he talking about? "I didn't, I just summoned how you taught me—"

"No." Simon shook his head, chestnut hair flying. "When you washed your hands in that water, you gave a blood sacrifice. Gamori wouldn't have shown up for anything less, I'm certain."

I bit my lip to stop the tremor that wanted to take over. That was a supreme fuckup I hadn't even realized. "I used my blood to heal the edge in Canhaben. Why is this bad?"

"You still have so much to learn," Simon muttered. "I shouldn't have taught you to begin with."

The hollow sensation inside me spread, threatening to plunge me into numbness. "I'm sorry. I—I didn't know."

The harsh lines around his mouth softened. "No, I'm sorry. I shouldn't be so hard on you. Look, I'll take care of summoning Hael. After this, we'll steer clear of demons for a while, eh?"

I drew my knees into my chest and rested my forehead on them. I wanted the release of crying, but my eyes were dry and hot. Then I felt a hand on my shoulder, and Simon's weight dropped down beside me.

"I, er, didn't mean to upset you. You're all right. We'll figure it out, hey?"

"Will we?" I sat up and pushed the tangled mass of waves out of my face. "Everything is fucked, Simon." *In no small part because of my mistakes*, I added silently.

"No it's not. It just feels that way. Trust me, I know." He gave me a sad smile. "Let's get this over with, then we can move on. Everything leaves a trail. We'll find Magoth's. Chin up." I nodded, pasting on a tight-lipped grin. "If you want to, er, take a walk, I can summon Hael then."

"Oh. Right." I was redundant, untrustworthy to even be in the same room as a demon. The door's latch clicked softly behind me as I left, and I leaned my forehead against the corridor's cool stone wall.

Stay focused, I reminded myself as Simon's muffled voice struck up a low chant. *Just keep moving.*

7

The Viren Tree Tavern did a roaring trade in the evenings. Patrons, young and old, clustered around low tables with glowing coal braziers, smoking viren leaves and playing a complex game involving several pairs of dice. The leaves' tangy, citrus smoke tickled my throat, and I coughed into the sleeve of my embroidered tunic.

Since arriving in the capital city of Paltara four days ago, Simon and I had gotten a crash course in its culture. This continent was called Soretia, and it was a world of mountains, farmland, and wide, winding rivers. The people were kind and fairly indifferent to the odd ways of strangers, as we'd learned while haunting the city from dawn to dusk each night.

We were compiling a list of magic users to seek out and question about Magoth's whereabouts, if they had knowledge of demons. I'd discovered The Viren Tree two nights ago, and through eavesdropping had learned magicks were accepted as fact in Soretia, if somewhat of a subculture. There were clearly people who wanted nothing to do with it, and those who swore by their local enchantress. Darra, the Viren Tree's barkeep, was one of those who steered clear.

"So, your cousin got a love charm from a witch?" I prompted Darra. My lips tried to cling to the foreign Soretian words as I spoke, my brain still not used to thinking in one language and talking in another. Simon had managed the negotiation with the demon Hael just fine on his own, so the language barrier was no longer an issue.

Darra scrubbed a hand through his shock of black hair, his wide mouth curved into a playful grin. "He surely did, and what did it get him but a punch in the eye from the girl he was after? I warned him not to fool around with magicks, but he takes after his air-headed mother, the silly bastard."

I forced the laugh Darra was expecting, but it sounded hollow. "Clearly he should've listened to you. Have you ever used magicks?"

"Nah, I don't bother. People who seek it are asking for trouble." He slid tankard after tankard along the bar to a large group of giggling women who were casting flirtatious glances his way. He winked at them, making no secret of enjoying the attention.

I sipped from my mug of ale to wet my throat. "Say someone wanted a charm. Where might they find that witch?"

Darra sidled over to me, resting his forearms on the bar and leaning in close. I forced a smile instead of recoiling.

"Why would a woman like you need a charm?" His eyes flicked over me, settling on my lips. He smirked, no doubt thinking it was flattering to be sized up like a hunk of meat. "I imagine you don't have any trouble in that area."

"Not for love, for luck."

His brows drew down as he studied me. "I know you're not from around here, that's obvious enough. But you speak like a native."

Damn. I must not have been flirting as well as I thought if he was getting suspicious. I traced a finger through the condensation on my glass, then pressed the coolness to my lower lip. Darra's gaze dropped to my mouth again. "I have a gift for languages. Now, about the witch?"

He blinked several times before answering. "She's the crone of Evinia. Like I said, it's nonsense. She's a charlatan."

Now we were getting somewhere. "Even so, where might I find Evinia?"

"To the west. Follow the trade road through the valley for three hours by horseback, and it's right there at the foot of the mountains. But no one goes there anymore. It's—"

"Thank you, Darra." I pushed to my feet and drained the rest of my ale in a single swallow. "I'll see you around." Or hopefully not.

Ignoring his dissatisfied mutters, I left the tavern and made the trek back to the inn.

"Steph," Starya, the innkeeper, called as I passed through the doors. "Cup of acquora for you?"

Just like with Durl, we'd given the innkeeper false names as an added layer of precaution. I wasn't quite used to it yet, and almost blew right past her. "Ah, sure. Thanks."

Starya slid a steaming mug of brew over the green-tiled desk she sat behind. It fell somewhere between tea and coffee, but was more chocolatey. I couldn't get enough of the stuff.

While Starya was friendly, she hadn't asked questions when all of a sudden we were able to understand her and drop the miming act. I was learning that a discreet innkeeper was worth her weight in gold.

"Should I make some for your husband as well?" Starya asked, reaching for a second mug.

"Husband?" I laughed. "No, Simo—er, Sam isn't my husband."

"My apologies," she said, ducking her scarf-covered head. "You seem very familiar with each other, so I assumed."

"He's my...cousin," I said, taking inspiration from Darra's story.

"Oh," she replied, lifting a shoulder. "Well, none of my business, of course."

"It's okay. But no, he shouldn't be back for a couple of hours. Just the one is fine." It wasn't beyond me that a man and woman traveling together might be mistaken for a couple. I hadn't exactly thought about the issue coming up, but then again, most of my brainpower was spent on more important things. Like, say, keeping us alive. Simon and I bickered like siblings, and he was starting to feel like the brother I never had.

After returning to our little room, I drew a bath and lit a fire to heat the water. Despite Soretia's rudimentary transportation, they'd mastered the science of simple plumbing.

Once the bath was hot enough, I sank down to my chin and let the warmth soothe my tired muscles. I'd walked miles and miles each day since we'd been on the run—far more than I was used to, especially after our mandatory confinement in Jupiter's. I took the time to wash my hair and scrub my skin, wishing that I could heat the cooling water with power but not wanting to waste any on something so frivolous.

I'd siphoned small amounts of magic each day—just a few drops here and there, and had kept it to plants like I promised Simon. It was getting easier to tolerate, and that golden, bubbly rush faded quicker each time.

Goosebumps sprang up on my skin when the water cooled, so I rose from the bath and reached for a flannel cloth to dry myself. Cheerful humming sounded, and a second later the bathroom door burst open.

I shrieked and rushed to cover myself, while Simon clapped a hand over his eyes. "Sorry!" he said loudly. "Sorry, sorry, I'll go!" He slammed the door behind him, while I cringed into the flannel.

Living with Simon had been easy so far, and I was usually too tired to care about any awkwardness that inevitably arose. But him seeing me naked was a step too far. I toweled myself off and dressed, taking particular care with my hair and not at all delaying the moment when I had to face him. Sighing, I pushed open the door and found him sitting at the little desk in the corner, facing the wall as though he was in time out.

"Um, hi." I leaned on the windowsill at the very furthest point of the room from him. "How'd it go tonight?"

He slowly turned and peered at me out of the corner of his eye, like he was prepared to whip back around should I have chosen to drop my towel and dance the tango nude. When he found me clothed, he gave me his full attention. "Sorry about that. I should've knocked, but I didn't think you'd be back, and...yeah. Sorry again."

"It's fine. I'm sure it's nothing you haven't seen before. Let's just forget about it. And yeah, maybe knock next time." Heat crept up the back of my neck, belying my nonchalance.

Simon tensed, his whole body going still while a muscle in his jaw flickered. What was going on with him? Perhaps I'd offended his sensibilities. Despite living together these past few weeks, I still had to remember that I didn't know everything about him. "Are you okay?"

He cleared his throat and snapped out of the rigid posture. "Fine. Er, right. So it was a load of the usual rubbish tonight. Lady Magia couldn't tell yarrow from henbane."

"Wonderful. Well, I might have a lead." I told him what I'd gleaned from Darra about the crone of Evinia.

"Should we try for Evinia tomorrow, then?"

"At sunrise. That leaves us plenty of time to go back out into the city tomorrow night if this crone doesn't know anything."

"Don't you think that's overdoing it a touch? I mean we're out from morning til midnight every day, and we've covered the whole damned city by now. Nothing's panned out. Maybe it's time to move on."

I chewed the inside of my cheek. "You're right. If it doesn't work out tomorrow, we'll leave. Somebody somewhere has to know *something* about where Magoth could be."

"There's always a trail, remember?"

Preparations for bed were awkward. Simon was overly courteous and deferential, pointedly looking away from me. After we'd extinguished the lamp, I noticed the absence of his deep, even breathing, and knew that he too was lying awake in the dark.

I couldn't sleep because I felt the vastness of infinite worlds pressing down on me with a numbing weight. All of the possibilities circling overhead of where Alex might be were simply overwhelming. Paralyzing, even.

I counted backward from one thousand in my head, and by the time I hit five hundred the tightness in my chest had eased. When I finally closed my eyes, all I could see were winged monsters and hellfire, and a horrible, never-ending dark.

———

We left the inn at daybreak, taking our belongings as a precaution in case we had to stay the night in Evinia. We caught a cart at the city gate that was heading west, seated atop wooden crates and surrounded by the pungent but not unpleasant scent of leather goods. The other passengers were a pair of Soretian natives, a couple who chatted with us as the miles and mountainous backdrop rolled by.

"Where are you headed?" asked Elio, the blond. His partner, Arman, was dark as Elio was light. Their smiles were open and friendly, just two people wanting to pass the time on a long journey.

"Evinia," I answered.

The pair traded a glance, eyes widening. "What brings you there? It's not a tourist spot."

"Information," Simon said shortly. He'd also noticed the couple scrutinizing us, and stared back equally wary.

"Ah," Arman said. "What are—"

Elio cut him off. "Your business is your business. Right, Arman?" Arman nodded, chastised. "We're headed home to Vennara, on the Aggea River."

They chattered about their lives in Vennara for a long while, not allowing either me or Simon to get a word in. I suspected this was purposeful. They didn't want to talk about Evinia for some reason, just like Darra hadn't. Why didn't people go there? Surely not just because of the crone? A tingling, restless sensation rolled over me like low-lying fog, one that I couldn't seem to shake for the rest of the journey.

We disembarked in Vennara with Elio and Arman, and they bid us farewell and good luck. I tried not to dwell on their ominous expressions. After paying the driver, Simon and I set off at a brisk pace, continuing west toward the mountains. The fine weather was beginning to turn, thunderheads mounting on the horizon. I hoped we'd make it to Evinia before the rain.

"I have a bad feeling about this," Simon said, voicing my fears. The road was not well traveled. It was so overgrown in places that we had to split up and scout ahead to find where the path picked up again. The grass on the side of the road was yellowed, and the few trees that dotted the land were gnarled and stunted.

"A bad feeling is probably a good sign," I rationalized. "Violence has preceded all of our progress so far."

"Hell," he said, raking a hand through his hair.

I couldn't help but agree. I opened my coat, checking that the daggers sheathed in my weapons harness were all accounted for.

We didn't pass a single soul for hours, and by the time we reached the edge of Evinia I understood why.

It was a ghost town. Cottages with decaying flowers in window boxes were shuttered, and their roofs sagged. Front doors were ajar, as though the occupants fled so quickly they hadn't bothered to look back. Wagons lay abandoned in the streets and waste bins were knocked over, their refuse long decomposed.

Then, I realized what had been nagging at me, apart from the obvious—it was completely silent. There was no birdsong, no bleating of farm animals or even the sound of wind rustling leaves. The air was heavy and thick with the impending storm.

"A very bad feeling," Simon repeated, surveying the wreckage.

The fog of dread thickened. "I wonder if the crone is even still here." Please, let her be here. This would be a monumental waste of time if she wasn't. Desperation drove me down the road and into the heart of town.

More destruction greeted us. Glass windows were shattered in shop fronts, and from a hasty look inside, most appeared to have been looted, the goods picked over for what was valuable and the rest left to rot.

"Gods, what happened to this place?" Simon asked, crouching and running a hand over cracked cobblestones. Weeds sprouted between them, the only thing thriving in this dead place.

"Does this remind you of something?"

His expression turned bleak, and I knew we'd come to the same conclusion. Canhaben's streets had been the same, lifeless and derelict. "We don't know that."

"There must be an edge here. That's why no one travels this way. It's the end of the world."

Simon rose from his crouch. "Then the crone is gone. Looks like everyone else cleared out, so I can't imagine why she'd stay behind."

Another dead end. Frustration and hopelessness vied for dominance, clawing at my chest. I rubbed a hand across it to soothe the ache. "Let's at least search as much as we can before we have to leave. Just to be certain."

We worked our way toward the end of the village that abutted the base of a mountain. Sharp peaks loomed overhead, threatening to block out the already meager light in the stormy sky. We checked houses, businesses, barns, but all that remained was the specter of what had been.

A path at the edge of town led from the last street up into the mountains. The wind had picked up and kept tugging on my braid, as if trying to force me onward. Just what was on the other side? As I had the thought, a low, magnetic pulse started up in my chest. It beat in time with my heart, each thud urging me toward the mountain's ridge.

Simon watched me survey the path. "Don't even think about it. The only direction we're headed is back to Vennara."

Logically, I knew that was the best option. But I couldn't make my feet turn away, back toward the town and safety. "Do you feel it?" I asked as a shiver raced down my spine, lighting me up from the inside out. My siphoned power responded, little bubbles racing beneath my skin to join the magnetic thumping. The wind that whipped across my face carried a damp scent of ozone.

"No," he said shortly. "Let's go. Now."

My pulse was thick in my ears, and I couldn't tear my gaze away from the ridgeline. If I followed the path up the mountain, I was sure an edge would be on the other side. And just over it would be paradox, that deepest black that was both nothing and everything, sucking the land into its void.

In my head I saw the edge of Canhaben, felt the biting gale and the heady flow of power rushing through my veins. Felt the same siren's song that had called me to the graveyard in that world which was in its death throes.

"I have to see the edge. Simon, I have to try to heal this." I turned to him.

"Why? Why can't you leave it bloody well alone?" His jaw was set, arms folded across his chest.

"Because if there's a chance I can save Soretia, I will."

He exhaled hard through his nose. "How can there even be an edge here, if we were able to come through a gateway?" With the Aureum closing the borders of the worlds, the ability to travel between them was cut off. We'd only been able to get in and out through seams before.

"Maybe this world isn't as far gone as Canhaben. From what we've heard and seen, Evinia is the extent of the damage. Canhaben was the last piece of your world left."

The look in his eyes told me he knew that I had a point, but didn't want to admit it. "Maybe."

"If the edge hasn't taken as much, it could be easier to heal."

At that, Simon let out a humorless laugh. "Easier? Gods, Seph. You really want to do this?"

"I want to try."

He stared at me for a few long moments. "Right. But when I say it's time to go, we leave. No questions asked."

I nodded as the siphoned magic roiled through me. "No questions asked."

Hiking up the mountain wasn't easy. The terrain was steep and rocky, and a misplaced step could mean a rolled ankle. But we made it up to the ridgeline with an hour of diligent, sweaty work.

I hauled myself up and over the last rock, Simon only a few paces behind me. "That was rough." I chugged from my water skin, then offered it to Simon. He took a few greedy gulps, draining it.

"I can't believe you would do that for fun back home."

"There's more of a sense of accomplishment when you know you're not headed toward something that could kill you." Theoretically. I wasn't actually sure what would happen if someone fell into the void, but I assumed it would be a swift death. "Plus, look at the view. Isn't it beautiful?"

The valley stretched out to the horizon, transforming from desiccated earth to verdant fields. We could see Vennara from here, nestled in the bend of a winding river, and I even thought I glimpsed the outskirts of Paltara.

"I suppose."

"Oh, come on. You just don't want to admit it."

"I'll ooh and ahh over the pretty fields once we're out of this place. Happy?"

I snorted, but stood and walked farther down the ridge toward the blackest of the storm clouds. The wind was really gusting now, and I had to squint to keep flying dust out of my eyes. "I see it! Down there."

And there it was. The black chasm stretched past the ridgeline as far as the eye could see. As if the world had been sheared in two and half had simply fallen away, leaving nothing behind.

I expected the endless void, and the battering wind, and the storm. What I hadn't been anticipating was the tiny old woman who stood so close to the edge her toes were almost hanging over it, brandishing a staff and mouth open in a silent scream.

8

"I think we've found the crone," Simon yelled over the howling wind. He clutched my shoulders as the gale buffeted us.

"What the hell is she doing? She's going to kill herself." As if to prove my point, a chunk of the mountain further down the ridgeline fell into the blackness of paradox.

"Perhaps we should let her."

"Simon!"

"Oh, all right, I was only joking."

"Not the time," I muttered as I fought my way down the ridge toward the woman. She looked tiny and helpless, stuck between the chasm on one side and charcoal gray storm clouds on the other. Pulsing energy swirled in the air, so thick I half expected not to be able to breathe.

When I was as close to the edge as I dared, I shouted, "Get back from there!" My words were taken with the wind, carried and tossed into the void. The woman didn't turn around, and in fact seemed to double down on her efforts. I needed to get closer.

Sweat beaded on my upper lip as I inched along the thin layer of scree, the sheer drop just feet away. Simon was right behind me, looking like he very much regretted this whole endeavor. I motioned for him to stay back as I approached the edge.

Up close, the woman didn't appear as old as I'd initially thought. Her face was lined and her hair gray, but she practically glowed with power. It emanated off her in waves, creating a gravitational anchor against being swallowed whole by paradox.

I didn't want to scare her and send her plunging over the edge, so I waved my hand in her peripheral vision. She finally noticed me, and didn't look surprised or confused; instead, she gestured to me to join her.

"Step back!" I put power into my voice to amplify it.

She shook her head and gestured again. *Join me, lightbringer.*

I flinched with surprise, because although her mouth was still compressed into a hard line, I heard the words loud and clear.

Come. I've been waiting for you.

Oh, god. She was in my head.

"It's not safe. I can do it, but get back." As soon as I said the words, I wondered if they were a lie. I had done *something* in Canhaben; the world appeared to begin healing, but I hadn't actually stuck around to find out what happened afterward.

The woman didn't budge an inch. There was nothing to do but go fetch her myself. I shuffled along, barely daring to pick up my feet.

I tugged lightly on her billowing sleeve. She snaked her hand around and gripped my forearm with a strength that belied her diminutive stature.

"Come on," I yelled again.

She shook her head, then sent jets of blue light into the void like she was trying to douse an inferno. But the storm only became stronger, as if it wanted to prove that it could.

This needed to end. Now.

I gently extricated myself from the woman so as not to push her off balance, and unsheathed one of my blades. Holding my breath, I scored my palm and watched the red stain of blood spread over it and drip to the ground in rivulets.

The woman finally turned to me. Her gaze was startling, one eye a fierce blue and the other ruined, clouded and shot through with milky white. I wanted to shrivel under that stare but focused on healing.

Blood pooled darkly at my feet, but didn't race along the edge like it had the last time I'd done this. In fact, nothing changed at all. The wind tore at the mountain, and the chasm was as empty as ever.

I looked at Simon, who was several feet behind us and crouched low. He met my wide-eyed stare with his own. More blood spurted out of my clenched fist as I squeezed harder, palm stinging. Perhaps what I'd shed wasn't enough?

The woman pushed my hand down and opened it. She healed the wound with a tingle of power across my skin, then sighed, her chest heaving with the movement.

Her voice flicked across my thoughts again. *Ah. I see.* She shook her head, then motioned for me to step back from the edge with her.

No. No, this wasn't right. Why hadn't it worked? When I looked down, I saw faint yellow flowers instead of bare rock, but I knew it was an illusion, a memory of Canhaben. I blinked hard, dispelling the flashback.

An immense crack, like a hammer shattering a mirror, rang out even louder than the howling wind. A chunk of the mountain calved away mere inches to my right, and fissures radiated from the epicenter. One zigzagged under my feet, and I staggered atop the shifting rock as it began to separate and sheer off. The scream caught in my throat, then came out garbled with terror. Gravity caught up to me, and I was falling.

Power shot from me like an erupting volcano. I managed to spin around toward the rock face and clung on, shredding my fingertips. I tried to claw my way up, but this wasn't like the movies; I wasn't going to suddenly pull myself up at the last second, narrowly avoiding death. Magic drained from me like water down a sink, and there was nothing in this dead land that I could siphon. My heart slammed against the walls of my chest. The mountain and stormy sky, blending together in a wall of ruthless iron, would be the last things I ever saw.

The old woman and Simon appeared in my field of vision and reached for me. Their hands dangled too far above my head, and I couldn't risk grabbing for them in case I fell off the cliff face. The woman lowered her staff over the edge, but it was still a handbreadth too short.

Grab hold.

I'll pull you down with me, I thought, not daring to speak.

Somehow, she heard me. *I'll make sure you won't. Take hold, girl. Quickly.*

I met Simon's eyes. Their color was identical to the dark clouds that gusted overhead. I couldn't hear him, but watched his lips form the words I needed to hear. "You're not allowed to die on me!"

I set my feet against the rock face and pushed off, throwing myself at the staff. My sweaty fingers latched on but instantly began sliding down the polished wood. My fingers cramped, but I clung to it. Simon and the woman braced their feet, heaving backward.

Jagged rock scraped painfully against my stomach as they pulled, my shirt snagging and tearing. But it was working, and soon the cliff ledge would be in reach.

The mountain shuddered again, knocking the crone and Simon off balance. The staff jerked, and while they were able to maintain their footing, my damp palms slid all the way to the end.

"Simon!" I screamed.

He lunged forward, throwing his torso over the edge and grabbing me under the arms. I locked my hands around the back of his neck and would have thrown power out to help him, but I was entirely empty. Simon was stronger than I gave him credit for, because even with my dead weight he was able to drag me up and over the ledge onto cracked and barren ground.

The earth quaked beneath us, an angry god bent on throwing us into paradox. While I wanted to lay there, immovable and spent, I forced my feet to move as all three of us ran like hell back over the ridge. Only after we were halfway down the mountain, skidding and sliding on rocks, did we stop and catch our breath.

"Bleeding angels, you're heavy," Simon panted. He'd collapsed in the middle of the trail, head thrown back as he gulped air. "Feels—like —both my arms've—come out the socket."

"Shut up," I gasped, equally as winded. Nausea rose in my throat, and I heaved spectacularly onto the side of the path.

"Come with me," the old woman said. I'd forgotten she was there for a moment. She veered off the trail and led us across the mountain-side. Eventually she stopped in front of a patch of sheer stone wall, too smooth to belong in the pock-marked and pitted landscape. She tapped on the wall three times with her staff, then a wooden door materialized and swung inward.

The interior was a witch's cottage straight from central casting. It was as if the room had been carved out with a spoon, its walls curved and smooth. Dried bundles of herbs hung from wooden beams, and above them was the bare rock of the mountain. The old woman set her staff by the door, then marched to the hearth and set to lighting a fire.

I collapsed into a chair next to a scarred wooden table with a cauldron sitting atop it, too drained to wait for an invitation. Simon followed suit, the candles that flickered on every surface in the small room wrapping him in a warm glow.

"So," the old woman said, leaving the snapping fire to settle across from us at the table. Even in stillness she maintained her otherworldly aura. "You've come at last."

"Er...were you expecting us?" Simon asked. He fidgeted with his sleeve as his gaze flitted around the room.

"Not you." She narrowed her mismatched eyes at Simon, then flicked them to me. "But you, child. You have been in my dreams, the lightbringer who can call the shadows or cast them out."

"Are you the crone of Evinia?" The weight of my limbs and acid taste in my mouth leftover from vomiting precluded tact, along with the discomfort that anyone had seen me in their dreams. It felt like exposure I'd never consented to. A violation.

"That is one of my names," she answered with a curt nod. "Mellandra is what I was called before I became the crone." The crone searched my features, but for what I wasn't sure. "In the dreams, I saw you come from a faraway land to heal the rift of the world with power and blood alone. This was meant to be. You are a daughter of the goddess, destined to help restore balance to the worlds who are taken by darkness."

"So we're just jumping right in, then," Simon muttered.

The goddess Iznir had in fact charged me with saving the worlds—with saving her chosen, she'd said. I'd only learned she'd meant the Diurne's corruption after they tried to sell me to Magoth. But she'd appeared to me, and me alone, during my Aureum initiation ritual. So how did the crone know? I hadn't told anyone about that, not even Alex.

"Why would you think that?" I asked.

"I have the Sight." She tapped the side of her gray head. "I Saw many turns ago that you would arrive, that you would meet me at the rift. It has been a year and a day since the darkness came with its perpetual storm. Evinia was abandoned once it became apparent that nothing I did, no enchantment or incantation, would save us. I've been waiting for you."

I studied a black burn mark on the table. Despite being crammed into the small room with the crone and Simon, I felt more alone than ever. More useless than ever, with my siphoned magic run dry and the storm still raging outside. "Then you've been waiting all this time for nothing. Your vision was wrong."

Mellandra shook her head. "Something must have changed to alter it. What befell you?" She didn't look angry that I was leaving her and everyone in her world to die. She seemed curious, and a little sad. Meanwhile, I was fighting a lump in my throat and the urge to disappear beneath the table.

"Long story," I answered. At the same time, Simon said, "She's heartbroken." I shot him a hot glare, which he countered with a look of wide-eyed innocence.

"I am sorry for it."

"I did everything the same as before. It's not like I don't have power, it's just...." I paused, trying to find the right word. "Borrowed."

"Hm," the crone mused. "Then it's not really yours. Not all power is created equal. That which is generated from your spirit, the root of all magic, is what gives you the power over life and death. You will not be able to mend again until it returns to you." Her aura of power flickered then, like a switch had been thrown. "It's a tragedy for us all. Our world will be taken by the darkness, like so many others."

I swallowed the lump and cleared my throat. "Do you have any idea how I can get it back?"

Mellandra gave a doleful smile, then shook her head slowly. "If I could help you, child, I would. For all our sakes. But I am not a god to give and take power at will."

Suddenly, I wanted to scream, to tear my hair out, to beat my fists on the table until they were black and blue. But it would be pointless. My rage would do nothing to save Alex, so long as I was powerless. So instead, I calmly folded my hands and placed them in my lap, then smoothed my face until it became a hard mask. "I'm sorry to disappoint you. But I didn't come here to heal the edge."

"Then why did you come?" she asked, her milky eye staring through me.

"You didn't see?" Simon's voice dripped with derision.

"I can only See what I've been shown," the crone said sagely, immune to our impertinence.

"We were hoping that you could help us find someone."

Mellandra sighed, then rose to take a pot off the fire. She fetched a vial containing blue liquid from a tall, glass-fronted chest that also held several brooms. "This is a restorative draft," she explained, adding a few drops of liquid to three earthenware cups, then pouring the pot's steaming contents into them. Aquora, by the chocolatey scent. "It will ease your aches."

Simon narrowed his gaze at the concoction, but I drank deeply. The crone didn't have any reason to hurt us. I was supposed to be some sort of savior, after all, and she had plenty of opportunity to shove both of us over the edge only moments ago. Though if there actually was some nefarious plot, I couldn't bring myself to care at the moment.

"Tell me whom you seek," Mellandra ordered.

I explained about Magoth, and how he'd taken Alex in my stead. What I didn't share was the horrible pain that snuck up on me when I wasn't paying attention, and the hollow feeling that had taken up residence where my heart should be. How guilt mingled with gratitude whenever I thought about what Simon had given up to stay with me.

When I'd finished, the crone was quiet for several long moments. "This is a dangerous road that you travel, but a necessary one, I fear. This demon—Magoth—I do not know his realm, nor how to find it. However."

She went to the door and laid a hand on it. I heard the click of a bolt being drawn, then the light hum of power. When Mellandra returned to the table, she leaned in and dropped her voice to a hoarse whisper. "There is a book which could help you, one that resides in myth and legend. But I can assure you it is very much real."

"What book?" I'd gone very still, hanging on her every word.

Mellandra's eyes flitted to the door again, as though ready for someone to come barging through. "It is said to be the first grimoire ever recorded, written by the hand of the Great Mother—the goddess who created magic. It contains the secrets of spirits and immortals, and speaks to the origin of power itself. It is called—" Here, she hesitated again, before moistening her lips. "The Book of Shadows."

"Book of Shadows?" Simon repeated with barely concealed skepticism. "How do you know it's real?"

"I have seen it. Long, long ago, when I was but a child myself. My mother was a very powerful witch, far more than I, and made searching for the Book her life's work. She found it eventually, though she lost herself in the process—she was consumed by learning the secrets of our kind. She guarded the Book jealously, but one night I snuck into her practice. It was...more than I could bear."

"What do you mean?" I said.

"The Book holds so much power that even gazing upon its pages can cause mortal harm to the untrained." She tapped her ruined, milky eye. "I paid for my curiosity."

I drew a sharp breath. "What happened to the Book, then? You don't still have it?"

"No, nor would I want it. It has somewhat of a tradition of being stolen, and disappeared from our home the very next day. My mother was inconsolable and driven to insanity by its loss, so obsessed was she. That book killed her, surely as if it had taken a dagger to her breast. It...it is cunning. It likes to play games, to elude capture. The Book does not wish to be possessed." Mellandra's face was tight with old pain, and I felt a pang of sympathy for her.

"You talk about it like it's alive," I said softly.

"It is," she answered. "In a way. It has become imbued with the very secrets, the very power it contains."

"Well, that all sounds terrible," Simon declared. "Why would we want this book if it's got some evil agenda and is going to turn us blind and mad?"

"It is not evil," she stated. "No more than power itself is evil. That depends on the hands who wield it. Now, I believe you will find the answers you seek within the Book's pages, for where to find your friend —how to save him, and defeat the demon prince." She turned to me, her one blue eye pinning me to my seat. "This will be a near impossible task. You have no idea the strength of the powers you will be up against, among them the most ancient wickedness that has ever walked the worlds. If you are to have any chance of staying alive, you will need to restore your power and find the Book. Of that, I am certain."

Well, *fuck*. I chewed on my lip as my thoughts spun in a thousand different directions. The true weight of Mellandra's words settled around my neck like a hangman's noose. At the end of the day, I was just a person: fallible and mortal, without my power, and caught up in the tides of forces much greater than myself. I was in over my head, and the only thing I could do was keep treading water. And now, I had another decision to make. Would finding the Book be a piece of the puzzle we needed to rescue Alex, or just another useless stopover on a breadcrumb trail to nowhere?

If *you can save him*, a voice of defeat whispered in my head. *You haven't even thought of what comes next, have you? Because you know you won't succeed. There will be no after, no saving worlds or reuniting with your friends. This road only leads to failure.*

The chasm behind my ribs opened again, squeezing the air from my lungs. I gripped the table's edge and gasped through gritted teeth.

Simon's muffled voice sounded in my ear. "You're all right. Come on, now." I commanded my fingers to relax, one by one. "That's it," he encouraged. "You're okay."

I shook my head, heat flashing over my skin. "Sorry." For something to do, I drank more of the crone's tincture. Ease slid through me, and I sat back in my chair. Simon hovered at my elbow, gray eyes tight with worry.

"Do you know where the Book is now?" I asked.

Mellandra pursed her lips. "I couldn't tell you, other than magic as ancient as the Book carries a signature. All creatures with power would be able to sense it if—" Her good, blue eye clouded over, going as milky as her ruined one. Goosebumps erupted over my skin as she stared at me with two blind eyes.

"Hello?" I asked, waving a hand in front of her face. She didn't respond.

"What the bloody hells," Simon muttered, just as the crone blinked.

"Now, child." She turned to me, picking up as though she hadn't gone full petrification a few seconds ago. "There is a grove of rowan trees past the village where it will be safe for you to sleep tonight. Do not step outside of the circle until first light. If you go east from there, you will find a burial ground after a day's walk."

What the fuck? Simon and I traded a look, his eyebrows climbing halfway to his hairline. "Er—you all right?" he asked Mellandra.

She gave him a knowing smile. "I am well, son of the Fallen. This is not the last stop on your journey, and you must be within the rowans by moonrise."

More alarm rang through me, and I jumped up. "Did you see something? What was it?"

"That you must go," she urged, beckoning us toward the door. "But first, a blessing for you." She retrieved another jar from the cabinet. "For protection. May I?"

"Ah...o-okay?" I agreed, still bewildered at the sudden change.

The crone murmured unintelligibly as she anointed the center of my forehead, then the outer corners of both eyes. The oil was warm on my skin and smelled of rosemary and honey.

She repeated the ritual with Simon. "Take care, now, and bright blessings be upon you." She scooted us outside and the door vanished instantly into the mountainside, becoming one with the granite.

9

"Right, then." Simon shook his head at the stretch of bare rock where the crone's door had disappeared. "Walk east, sleep in the rowan trees, and find the first grimoire. Seems bloody simple."

I choked out a laugh and craned my head back. Storm clouds hid the sky, but the horizon was fading to a deep purple-gray. "She could've said instant death and destruction, so I'll take it." I hooked my thumbs in the straps of my pack and leaned forward, stretching my aching back. "But why didn't the crone tell us what she saw?"

"Dunno," he answered, starting down the mountain path that led to the abandoned village of Evinia. Loose gravel crunched beneath his boots, some skittering over the side. "But we better get cracking. S'probably an hour til moonrise."

"Wait." The crone's blessing had inspired me, reminding of another sort of protection I'd received from a different witch. I pulled my tiger's eye pendant from beneath my shirt, then unfastened the clasp. "Take this."

He glanced over his shoulder at me. "Nah, that's yours."

"I want you to have it. Please. Just think about it as a backup. It saved my life once already." And if it could save his, I was happy to give it up. I'd grown to care for Simon more than I thought possible with my brokenness. He'd stuck with me this far, and that mattered to me.

"All right, then," he muttered after a brief hesitation. "If it'll make you happy."

"It will." When I caught up to him in the middle of the path, I reached forward and deftly looped the chain around his neck. The feathery ends of his hair tickled my fingers, and I drew back quickly.

"You know, that color really works on you," I said with a smirk. I dodged Simon's elbow, and we took off down the mountain path.

Simon spotted the grove of rowans first. Their leaves were a deep green and crowned with clusters of red berries, their spindly branches tapered into slim trunks. They stood out like an oasis in the desert amongst the other shriveled vegetation.

We shouldered aside branches that carried a tart, cranberry smell, and pushed our way inside. The grove's center was hollow and hushed with darkness, forming an almost perfect ring.

"Huh," Simon said, hands on hips as he turned a circle. "It's a Faerie ring, isn't it?"

Thanks to the Library at Aureum headquarters, I knew exactly what a Faerie ring was. And I wasn't thrilled at the idea of sleeping in one. "In my world, there are myths that Faerie rings are dangerous. That if you enter one, you might disturb the Faeries and be punished." In a myriad of sneaky and torturous ways, I neglected to add.

"Nonsense." He grunted in dismissal. "We'll leave an offering for them and that should sort it." He dug around in his bag and pulled out some hard cheese and bread, leaving it on a square of cloth at the edge of the circle.

"Are you sure?" These trees had to be magic, otherwise they'd be dead like everything else in Evinia. "I don't—"

"What other choice do we have? Walk back to Vennara in the dark? At least there's some cover here."

That's exactly what I was about to suggest. We'd purchased a rudimentary canvas tent and sleeping rolls in Paltara, but I was out of magic. Some instinct told me not to even think about siphoning from the rowans, lest I disturb something best left alone.

We could take our chances on the road, powerless, or follow the crone's mysterious orders.

I sighed, then knelt to untie the bedroll from my pack. Simon was already tucked inside his, blanket pulled up to his chin. "We should take shifts to keep watch. I'll go first," I offered.

Simon rolled over to face me. "Cheers," he murmured. There was no reason to whisper, other than that the clearing's gloom seemed to demand it. "Where in the name of Asael are we even supposed to begin looking for this Book of Shadows? It sounds like it could be anywhere in the worlds."

For one mad moment, I wondered if Alex and the Book might be in the same place. What if they were in a world of the lost, of unpaired socks and misplaced keys and bygone hopes and dreams?

I shelved that absurdity before my imagination could spin another story about it. My mother had succumbed to her melancholy and daydreams when my father broke her heart. I wouldn't follow in her footsteps.

And yet, I drew my knees in tight, wrapping my arms around them to keep the vacancy beneath my ribs from leaching into the rest of me. "I guess we just keep doing what we're doing. Finding people along the way who can help us."

Simon responded with a soft snore from his bedroll. God, he could really fall asleep anywhere, any time. Whenever I woke in the middle of the night from a nightmare, he always seemed to be sleeping like the dead.

The hard ground made it impossible to get comfortable. I found myself staring up at the pitch-black sky framed by the circle of treetops, trying not to succumb to the devouring emptiness and the awful voice of failure that came with it.

I would've given anything to feel powerful again, to have answers. To be with the friends who had become my family. I thought back on the night I'd gone to Gold Cay, the Aureum's private island, with Alex and his unit. That was the first time in my life I'd ever felt close to true belonging.

A new ache replaced the hollowness. I stuffed the space with memories of salt on my skin and the briny scent of ocean as laughter split the humid air. With moonlight painting the sea silver, and Alex's strong, lithe body cutting through the waves. When he'd looked at me, his green eyes had blazed with what I now recognized as hunger. It almost matched the insatiable desire I felt for him, the one that made me burn as surely as the flames that used to erupt over my skin.

The scene changed, and I was no longer on a beach, no longer digging my fingers into old bruises that refused to fade.

A waterfall crashed into a turquoise pool, sending a fine spray of rainbow mist arcing through the air. Flowers that sparkled like brightly colored gems climbed the overhanging rock and perfumed the air with sweetness. I seemed to be alone but for the cheery warbling of birds.

This place was nice. Safe. I didn't question the overwhelming peace seeping into me with each breath, and lay down in the springy grass. Sunlight kissed my face and warmed all of my cold, dark places.

Someone called my name over the thundering water. "Persephone! Oh, I'm so glad you came." The voice was soft and musical like the notes of a harp, and I sat up to see a strange woman approaching me. Her hair flowed to her waist in hues of purple and gold, the strands as silken as a spider's web. She had long, pale limbs, and moved with a dancer's grace. Her tunic and pants were the colors of the forest, and she wore leather greaves on her forearms. Her ears...her ears tapered into fine, lengthened points.

"Hello," I said, pulling myself into a seated position. Calm flowed through me like a river, and somehow I knew that this beautiful stranger meant me no harm. "Who are you?"

"I am Flora, of the Weald Fae." Her honey-colored eyes were rounded and wide-set, and she fluttered a pair of delicate wings the same color as the purple in her hair. I wondered at the trepidation I sensed in her voice; didn't she know that nothing bad could touch this place?

"What is it?" I asked, placing a gentle hand on her arm. She felt as solid and real as I did, not like a creature of myth.

"I have a gift for you, *Lihta*." The unfamiliar word sounded like the wind whispering through an orchard laden with lush fruit in high summer. "Something to aid you on your journey." She opened her hand to display a small, round gadget nestled in her palm.

The object shone silver, its edges intricately etched with flowering vines. "What's this?" I asked, mild curiosity tempering the words.

"The Desidarian compass, an ancient relic of my people. It points the holder in the direction of what they need." She placed the compass in my hand, folding my fingers around it. The metal was smooth and warm, like it'd been laying in the sun for hours. "I wish I could do more to help, but they cannot know I was here."

"They?"

Flora's face contorted with fear as she looked over my shoulder. Then, she dragged her gaze back to me and spoke with fierce urgency. "They're coming, the demon prince's soldiers. I cannot stay with you, but do not leave the protection of the rowans until first light. Do you understand?" She shook me lightly. "Do not leave the rowans. They wish to take you before you finish your journey, but you are not ready. You must not fall to them. The fate of the worlds hang in the balance."

"Yes, I understand." Her fear was beginning to cut through my state of drowsy tranquility, and my pulse quickened.

"Then wake!"

It was as if she shoved me through the dream and back into reality. I jolted upright, breathing hard with a fist of fear clenching in my belly. Something was digging into my palm, and I looked down to see that I clutched the compass from my dream. In the dark, my grasping fingers found my dagger. Simon lay beside me, still snoring softly.

A rustling noise sounded from just beyond the rowan grove. I concentrated on slowing my breathing as I lifted into a crouch. With my dagger thrust out in front of me, I crept to the edge of the trees, taking care not to step over the threshold even a millimeter.

What I saw lurking outside the branches was enough to make my heart skip a beat. Then it slammed into my ribs, so loud it was a wonder Simon didn't wake.

Half a dozen coal-black, slavering, red-eyed hellhounds paced outside the rowan grove. They were bigger than horses, and somehow, their long, curved teeth gleamed in the weak light of the yellowed half-moon. The beasts snapped their jaws and growled, but didn't approach the barrier of the trees.

I glanced back at Simon, and remembering our pact, woke him with a hard shake.

"Wot?" Simon slurred, burrowing deeper into his blankets.

I bent close and whispered in his ear, so low I could barely hear myself. "Don't freak out, but we have visitors."

"Eh?" He lifted up onto his elbows, then squinted into the night. "What the bloody—"

"No, don't," I hissed, holding on tight to him as he tried to scramble upright. "They can't come inside the circle. We're safe."

"Get off," he growled, shoving me. I clamped my arms tighter in a bear hug, his back pressed to my front.

"Only if you promise to calm down," I gritted out. His chest rose and fell rapidly against mine.

He stopped struggling, but his spine was rigid. "All right."

I released him, and Simon held himself stiffly as he watched the hellhounds pace. There was murder in his eyes, but his voice shook when he spoke. "Where did they come from?"

"I didn't see. I, uh, fell asleep." I recounted my dream in a hurried whisper. "The Faerie said we can leave the trees at daybreak. Like Mellandra warned."

"Old bat," Simon groused, but not without appreciation. "Why couldn't she have just bloody told us?"

"Hell if I know."

Both of us flinched as one of the hellhounds gave a particularly vicious snarl, like it didn't want us to forget they were ready to tear out our throats at the first opportunity. As if we needed reminding.

Something sharp and barbed lanced my gut as I wondered if my father was among their number tonight. If he'd been sent here to kill his only daughter. I searched the hellhounds' ember eyes for any sign of recognition, but all I found was vicious, animal rage.

I'd been over the memory of our first and only meeting so many times that it was soft and worn, like a letter handled too many times; the shock of seeing my same eyes in his face, the rich timbre of his voice, the unnameable feeling I got when he told me the truth about who I was. It was pure torture, and my guess was that whoever had sent the hellhounds had exactly that in mind.

I could only imagine what Simon was feeling. After receiving a bite from a hellhound, his twin would've been sentenced to a lifetime of soulless evil if Alex hadn't given him a humane death back in Canhaben. The fact that the hellhound in question had been—was—my father, only added an extra layer of torment.

"Simon," I started cautiously. "Are you—"

"Peachy," he snapped, jerking his shoulder.

Okay, then. No feelings talk. That suited me just fine. "We think Magoth sent them, right? It has to be him."

Simon scrubbed his hand over his face. "Maybe. Probably. How d'you think he found us?"

Maybe the same way the Faerie had found us. "No one should know where we are. Either someone we talked to in Paltara got suspicious and blabbed. Or...."

"Or, it was Hael," Simon said, finishing my thought. "For all we know, Magoth has put a bloody price on our heads and every demon in the known and unknown worlds is out for us."

Silence spread inside the grove as that very real possibility sank in. We'd lingered in Soretia for too long, and our enemies had caught up with us. *Stupid, stupid, stupid.*

I thumbed the Desidarian compass's engraved edges, the bite of metal on my skin an anchor amidst the part of me that wanted to simply float away. I did not want to be the daughter of a monster, did not want to have a father who'd turned into the very thing he'd tried to protect me from. I did not want to be defined by my inadequacies, but they haunted me at every turn.

"What's that there?" Simon asked.

"Oh." In my haste to explain about the hellhounds, I'd completely left that part out of my retelling. I latched onto it, tripping over the words. "The Faerie—Flora, gave it to me in the dream. It's supposed to help us find what we need."

Simon swore softly. "Finally, something good happens. It's about time."

I handed him the compass. He turned it over, studying every facet. The needle looped in a lazy circle. "There's something familiar about this," he said, thumbing the etched vines and flowers. "Like I've seen it before."

"Hopefully you would remember seeing a magic compass," I said with a wide yawn. Fatigue was beginning to catch up with me, despite the danger lurking just a few feet away. Simon shrugged, then handed the compass back to me.

"Perhaps I'm mistaken. Anyway, now that we have this it should be easy, eh? We won't even need that grimoire anymore, don't you think?

We can just find a graveyard, ask the compass where Eames is, and there you have it. Mystery solved."

My stomach muscles clenched while my heart leapt. "Maybe." Somehow, I didn't think it would be so simple. I shook the compass, but the needle didn't waver.

The hellhounds vanished as the horizon began to lighten in the east. One moment they were there, and then I blinked and they were gone, as if they'd only been a vivid hallucination. I released a held breath, although the tension in my stomach didn't disappear along with the beasts.

"D'you think it's safe?" Simon asked as he peered through the rowan branches.

I ran my hands through the dirt until I found a small stone. Cocking my arm, I heaved it through the trees. Twigs cracked as the stone hit them, but when it landed there was only silence. No creatures, hellhounds or otherwise, appeared.

"Safe enough, I guess." I took the compass from my pocket and opened the cover to expose its face. The black needle bobbed aimlessly, as if it didn't answer to any magnetic poles. I supposed it didn't, after all—it abided by whatever magic animated it. "I guess we start walking east."

We broke our meager camp and headed into the pastel dawn. I forced some stale bread down my throat, even though my stomach actively revolted at the thought of eating. But I needed to keep my strength up for whatever came next.

The dead grass turned greener with each mile, and by the time the farmland was lush again we'd reached the graveyard. It was little more than a field with trim grass, but spread far into rolling foothills that disappeared behind gentle sweeps of forest. Simple black grave markers dotted the landscape like pockets of shadow.

"This must be it," Simon said, his pale skin red with the rapidly warming day. I wiped sweat from my brow and shed my sweater.

"I need to—you know," I told Simon, wiggling my fingers. "Siphon."

"Oh. Right. Erm, carry on." He turned and wandered into the graves.

I chose a midsize tree with needle-like leaves, pressing a hand to its polished yellow bark. Magic flowed into me, strong and almost fibrous. Warmth curled around my bones. I closed my eyes and sank into it.

"Seph! Oy!"

I flinched and my eyes snapped open. Simon was behind me, gaping at something over my shoulder. I turned to see the tree I'd been siphoning from was gone, replaced by a pile of...ash. Magic sloshed inside me like liquid in a too-full cup, and for a moment nausea flooded my throat.

"Shit," I muttered, as my stomach sank like a runaway elevator. "I didn't realize."

"You don't say," he muttered darkly. "Well, maybe it's for the best. If we're walking into a demon's lair, we need to be prepared."

"Fair point," I replied. I checked in with my stomach, which was practically on the basement level of hell. Maybe we were headed there anyway.

No, damn it, I did not need this level of hysteria right now. I took a deep, calming breath, and touched the hilts of my daggers. This was really happening. I might be moments from seeing Alex, and I needed to get a grip. "Here, take this." Reaching into my pack, I handed Simon two short-bladed throwing knives.

"Right, then." He nodded, face ashen. "Let's go."

The compass needle spun randomly, as it had during the entire walk. I held it aloft, waiting for something to happen.

"Er—how does that thing work, anyhow?" Simon asked.

"If I had any idea, do you think we'd still be here?" I bit my lip, cursing myself at the flare of hurt in Simon's expression. "Sorry, I'm nervous. I don't know, except that it's supposed to point the holder in the direction of what they need."

"Then focus on what you need. Hold it in your mind."

I almost laughed. There was never a second when Alex wasn't on my mind in some way. The emptiness where our tether had been was a constant irritant, a pebble in my shoe. I wasn't allowed to forget his absence. But I did as Simon asked, and brought my need to find Alex into the forefront of my thoughts.

"There." Simon's voice was excited. "Look."

The needle picked up pace, and in another second it spun so fast that it became a black blur, like a penumbra. The silver back of the compass burned in my hand, and then almost as suddenly as it had begun the needle stopped over north, then began to shiver with excitement. Its heat traveled from my hand, up through my arm, and finally rested in my sternum, tugging me like I was a fish caught on a line.

I lurched forward a step. Simon latched onto my free hand, pulling me back toward him. "What's happening?"

I gasped. "It's inside of me. It wants me to...I can feel it—let go of my hand, no, it's okay—I need to open a gateway." Simon reluctantly released me, and held on to the hem of my shirt instead.

Knowing flooded through me, strong and sure, guiding my hands until I easily found the snag in the air we needed. I drew it open, and a slice of midnight undulated in the light of day.

My heart was beating a thousand miles a minute. "Ready?" I asked Simon. He swallowed, then gave a short nod.

I took his hand again and pulled him through the gateway after me, falling into the unknown.

We emerged from the darkness into snow and ice. Heaps of the white stuff covered every landmark and were blown into tall drifts by a steady wind. We were perched atop a cliff, and below us an iron-black sea raged, the waves racing onto the snowy beach to savagely pummel the shoreline.

Nothing sinister attacked us except for the frigid air stealing the breath from my lungs. We appeared to be alone, for now. And good thing, because opening the gateway had blown through a good portion of siphoned magic.

Simon wrapped his arms around his shivering torso. "Is this some kind of j-joke?"

The compass's needle spun languidly again, not pulling in any certain direction. "I guess this is it," I said, raising my voice over the crashing sea. The certainty I'd felt upon opening the gateway was fading fast. "Let's get out of this wind."

We trudged through snow that was up to our knees, away from the beach and toward a stand of pines that were so far off they were little more than a smudge on the white horizon. I used power to blast some of the snow out of our way, but my boots became waterlogged and my feet frozen. Pins and needles started up in my toes, which I knew was one of the first signs of frostbite. By the time we arrived at the dead pines and sheltered from the worst of the wind, my magic was down to a bare trickle.

"S-s-start the fire, and I'll set up the tent," I said through chattering teeth. We moved as stiffly as wind-up toys. Simon got a weak fire going, but the wood was damp and let off more smoke than heat.

"This wood needs to dry before it'll burn. And if it starts snowing, we're buggered," he said.

"O-okay, th-then."

"Blimey, your lips are turning blue. Get that damned compass and see if it'll take us somewhere else."

I held the compass aloft, giving it a shake. There was no spark of heat, no sure knowledge that guided my hand. "I th-think we n-n-need to stay."

Amidst Simon's stream of curses, he bundled us into the tent, removing our boots first. He had to undo my laces and tug them off my icy feet. "You need to get warm or you're going to lose those toes." He helped me layer on all of my warm clothes, which wasn't much, then bundled me into my sleeping roll so that I resembled a mummy more than a person.

Simon worried his lower lip as he watched me shake like a leaf in a storm. The walls of the tent billowed against the wind. "Right, then. Budge over," he announced.

"Wh-what are you d-d-doing?"

"Saving your life. Now shut up." He made quick work of piling our bedrolls together, then lifted the hem of his shirt and tugged it off.

My eyes widened. "What the f-f-fu—"

"Body heat," he said shortly, kicking off his trousers. I took a moment to wonder how someone who didn't lift anything heavier than a paintbrush for a living could have hard muscle wrapping his torso. "It's the quickest way to get you warm. Don't be a prude."

I allowed him to remove my layers until I was down to my bralette and underwear. It was about survival, I reminded myself. Nothing more, nothing less. I couldn't save Alex if I was dead. And anyway, there wasn't much to see.

Simon snuggled in beside me, wrapping his arms around my quivering body until we were skin to skin, cheek to cheek. He winced as I drew my knees up and pressed them against him. "Asael, you're like ice."

Mint and spiced black tea filled my nostrils as I buried my face into the curve of his neck. He didn't let go of me even though I was certain the chill of my skin caused him pain. He felt scorching, like a blazing star that had fallen to earth. Slowly, I began to warm, and a prickling sensation took over my feet and hands.

"Ouch," I said, flexing my fingers against Simon's chest where my hands were tucked between us. He stilled for a heartbeat, then drew me closer.

"Defrosting hurts, eh? Shall I distract you?"

"H-how?"

"Hmm...I'll tell you a story."

"What about?" I hadn't been able to read for so long, and hadn't read for pleasure even longer. Being told a story while the wind howled outside and we were warm inside the tent sounded luxurious.

"About a hero who is set with an impossible task, and has many obstacles to overcome before he can win his prize."

"Not a love story, then," I whispered. "Good." I couldn't bear to listen to one, maybe not ever again.

Simon paused, then settled his grip around my waist more securely. "Oh, no. Not at all. Lots of blood and gore, not a hint of romance whatsoever."

"Carry on," I murmured, sinking deeper into his heat. My eyes fluttered shut as he spun the tale, the vibration of his voice against my cheek lulling me to sleep.

10

If I felt a sense of emptiness, it didn't have anything to do with waking up alone. The place where Simon had slept next to me was chilled and bare, blankets tumbled. I unlaced the tent flap and stuck my head out to see that the ground was blessedly free of new snow. The morning was frosty and bright, and I felt more optimistic than I had the previous evening when I was half frozen to death. Although, it was probably difficult not to feel better when the bar was so low.

Simon was nowhere to be seen, but there was a neatly stacked pile of wood next to the tent. I slipped into my clothes, not allowing my thoughts to stray to the state of undress we'd been in last night. Together.

Heat flushed my cheeks, and I busied myself with pulling on boots that were mercifully dry, but still cold. Simon had been so matter-of-fact about the whole situation that it was silly to feel awkward…right? But I hadn't imagined how he'd clung to me those few times that I'd woken in the middle of the night, far after I'd regained the feeling in my hands and feet.

I settled on the conclusion that we were both lonely and devoid of human touch. It was natural that we would find some comfort in each other, and it didn't mean anything other than that. I mulled this over as I teased the heap of kindling into a semblance of a fire.

Crunching snow alerted me to Simon's return. His pack dangled by his side, and I noted with some alarm that it was moving.

"Morning," he said. His cheeks were pink with cold, but his eyes were clear. They roved over me, assessing. "You look like you're off death's doorstep. Still pale, though."

I scowled and folded my arms, even as the back of my neck grew warm. "Not as pale as you."

"There she is," he said, giving me a cheeky grin. "If you've got your snark back, you must be all right."

He didn't look at all like he was having thoughts of being glued together while mostly naked. So, neither would I. Nope. Absolutely not.

"I'm fine. I appreciate having the use of my appendages." I wiggled my fingers. Idiotically.

"Anytime," Simon said, and it might have been my imagination that made it sound like he would be more than happy to do it again. He thrust his pack at me. "Got you a present." Whatever was causing the pack to lurch scrabbled and squeaked.

"Gee, you shouldn't have. Dare I ask what it is?"

He reached inside the bag and compressed his mouth in concentration, feeling around for something. "Ouch, little bugger bit me. Gotcha!"

Out came a creature with glossy fur the same color as snow. Its body was long and sleek, its legs short but lithe. It had liquid black eyes and long, twitching whiskers, reminding me of Durl. Simon had it by the scruff, and it wriggled and squealed in an attempt to escape his hold.

"I prefer a set of first editions, for future reference."

"Ha. This is much more useful. You can siphon from it, *and* it can be breakfast."

My heart sank. I knew what he suggested was practical—necessary, even. But I didn't want to kill a creature whose heart I could hear thundering just a foot away. "What happened to the vegan diet?"

"D'you see any live plants around here?" Watching my face fall, he softened. "It's going to happen either way. We need to eat."

I stroked a hesitant finger down the animal's back. It squeaked again, and I felt an answering pang of heaviness in my chest. The least I could do was make it quick. I held my breath, then touched the creature's downy head. Power gushed through me like a roaring river as I absorbed its life force. The light went out of its eyes, and it stilled. A euphoric rush thrummed through my veins.

Fighting the sudden raw feeling in my throat, I turned away and busied myself with bulking up the fire. Simon headed some ways off to process the animal with efficient and practiced moves.

"I didn't take you for a Boy Scout," I said, adding a few sticks to the already blazing fire.

"Boy Scout?" he asked, looking from where he knelt on the ground, surrounded in viscera and blood.

"Never mind. Just that you know how to do that," I said, looking away quickly. I had lived in peace up until this point not knowing how the sausage was made, per se. Perhaps I really should consider going vegan.

"Ah. Well, back home, sometimes it came down to hunting or missing a meal. The world ending will teach you surprising things about your abilities."

"Huh. I always thought if there was a zombie apocalypse, I'd be in the first wave to die."

Simon's brow knit. "Zombie?"

"Animated corpses that want to eat your brain," I clarified. "I didn't have any survival skills—I wasn't fast enough to outrun a threat, or strong enough to fight."

"And now you can fry someone's brains just by looking at them," Simon finished. "You didn't need those skills. Maybe you weren't meant for them."

I scoffed. "I was weak."

"Weak?" Now Simon shook his head. "You've never been weak. But if you were, who gives a toss? Not everyone can be the knight in shining armor. Some of us are damsels in distress, and we're fine with it. I think I'd have liked to know that version of you."

"I don't even know that person anymore. The one who thought magic only existed in fairytales and had a—" The words *whole heart* were on my lips, but I swallowed them back.

Any wounds I'd incurred when my father left were shallow, the marks long since scarred over. The hole that Alex left was different; it was raw, oozing, and still leaked blood whenever it stretched too far. I knew Simon carried the same pain, saw it in the way his lips compressed and jaw tightened whenever we got on the edge of discussing what we'd lost. Though we'd gotten near it, neither of us had crossed that boundary yet.

"Anyway," I said, standing abruptly. "Let's get to it."

Simon nodded, but I saw a flash of something faraway in his eyes before he ducked past me.

After waterproofing our boots to avoid a repeat of the previous day's problems, we set off into the dazzlingly white land. It had an austere beauty, with frost and icicles that glittered on bare rock, and drifts of snow heaped like clouds. Silence reigned despite our proximity to the beach, and our footsteps were muffled by the thick layer of snow. Animal tracks crisscrossed the ground, frozen in place.

I held the Desidarian compass at the ready, but the needle only spun in languid circles. The silver backing was as icy as the rest of this world. There was no trace of human existence, supernatural or otherwise. Snowflakes began to fall, and soon we were also covered with white, blending into the landscape.

"It's empty. Only bloody snow and ice as far as the eye can see," Simon said, throwing his hands up at the great white nothingness. "I thought the compass showed what you needed. What could we possibly need here, other than an extra jumper?"

"A safe place to land?" I suggested, while tension steadily seeped into every corner of my being. Why *were* we here, if Alex wasn't? There had to be some sort of purpose, some reason the compass sent us that was connected to finding him. If I didn't hold onto that, I'd have to admit the truth: that we'd run into another dead end.

For the thousandth time, I closed my eyes and turned inward, searching for the end of the tether where I used to feel Alex's presence. It was limp and lifeless, and a fresh wave of pain engulfed me as the emptiness pressed up against my ribcage. The flame of hope that had sparked back in Durl's world was little more than a dying ember now. I wheezed involuntarily, the start to a hitching sob, but swallowed it back.

"What the hell?" I hissed, shaking the compass. "What's the point of having this if it doesn't. Fucking. Work!" Anger blistered my skin, and I heaved the compass. It sailed through the air and landed in a drift, sinking through the powdery snow.

"Seph!" Simon admonished, run-trudging through the snow and plucking the compass from the drift. "Tell me you are not trying to get rid of our only bloody lead!"

"Fuck," I muttered, burying my face in my hands. I couldn't believe I'd just done something so stupid. Forcing a breath of freezing air into my lungs, I tried to release bottled up fear and frustration.

"You don't want to get too cold again," Simon said, looking on with barely veiled worry. "There's clearly no threat here, unless you count the damned snow. Shall we go back and get warm for a bit?"

It was better he thought my rage issues were from the cold getting to me, and not because the strings stitching my broken pieces together were finally fraying.

I agreed to turn back, but I had to be more careful about losing control. I didn't want to scare Simon, and moreover I didn't want him to try and force me to give up because I couldn't handle myself.

Thanks to a boost of power, the fire back at camp crackled merrily and the flames were hot enough to cut through the chill that had settled in my bones. We were seated on logs around the campfire in some parody of a sleepaway camp. I tucked my hands into my pockets and leaned closer to the blaze, enjoying the woodsmoke.

"So, what now?" Simon asked, poking the fire with a stick. Sparks shot into the air as a branch collapsed. "Doesn't seem like the bloody compass is going to sprout a mouth and tell us where Eames is."

The voice of failure in my head was prepared to respond for me, but something in Simon's words tugged at a hazy piece of information in the corner of my brain. I stilled, fearing it might vanish. "Say that again."

He edged closer to the fire, warming his bare hands. "What?"

"About the compass," I urged. "What about a mouth?"

"That it's not going to tell us where Eames is?" Simon offered, brows raised.

Yes. A click of recognition, then an idea was materializing rapidly. "What—" Simon started, but I held a hand up for silence.

Pieces fell into place as my brain sorted through everything that had happened so far: finding Durl, his death, escaping the Guardians, siphoning, opening gateways, Mellandra, the Book of Shadows, the compass, the hellhounds. And now, being stuck in this abandoned, snowy world, huddled around a fire while Simon leaned in closer, giving me that familiar, furrowed-brow look. It was as if I saw it all happening from a bird's eye view, and through doing so had found sudden clarity.

"I might have something."

"Go on, then. Spit it out."

"We have more questions than answers, right? And we—*I*—feel like I'm flailing in the dark, trying to find a light, except I've lost my sense of touch. We have the compass, yes, but maybe it's not going to point us directly to wherever Alex is being held. Case in point, look around. And until we either learn to use it more effectively or it decides to show us the way to find him, we're at the mercy of forces beyond our understanding. We need to take control."

Simon nibbled on cold meat. "How do you suggest we do that?"

"I—" I licked my lips, then started again in a firmer voice. "I think we should summon demons and question them about where Magoth is keeping Alex." They could be the mouths who told us where he was. "We could be hopping around for months, years, even, while he's...." I trailed off, emotion choking me at the thought of what might be happening to Alex. At my helplessness to stop it. *Fuck.* What was it about this place that was making me come unglued? I lifted my chin and cleared the knot in my throat.

Simon stared into the flames like that's where he might find the solution to all of our problems. "What about the Book of Shadows?"

Okay, so it wasn't a no. "I get that Mellandra believes we need it, but think about it. It's an extremely dangerous magical object that apparently no one understands. Why would we waste time chasing it down when our goal is to find Alex? It's a distraction we don't need."

"And all that about it helping to defeat Magoth and save the worlds?"

I didn't want to defeat Magoth. I didn't want to save the worlds. I just wanted the man I loved back in my arms. Because if he was safe, then maybe I would be, too.

"Alex first," I answered. "Then we can put saving the worlds on our agenda. My siphoned magic is strong enough to defeat Magoth now, I know it."

Firelight reflected in Simon's eyes, turning them to embers. "If there was a way to save Penn, I would have done. There's nothing I wouldn't do for him. Even though we were at odds some of the time—well, most of the time, if I'm being honest—he was still the most important person in my world. I miss him every second of every day."

This was the first time Simon had spoken of Penn aloud since he died. My throat was tight again with unshed tears. It seemed the moment had come to cross the line and talk about something real.

"I'm so sorry," I whispered. The apology was inadequate and useless, but I pushed on. "If I'd known what was going to happen in the graveyard…if I'd known what my dad was, I would never have gone. I would have told Penn to run."

"He wouldn't have, even if you'd hurled lightning at him. Penn was going to fight that beast no matter what you did or said. You're not responsible, Seph. I'm sorry I made you feel that you were." His Adam's apple bobbed as he swallowed.

I nodded, even though Simon was wrong. The cold, shadowy truth of the matter was that somehow, I hurt everything I touched. The emptiness behind my ribs clenched as another stitch unraveled.

"We'll summon, and we'll learn what we can to get Eames back. Plus, you're not the only one with a score to settle." A muscle flickered in his jaw. "Magoth has to answer for three souls."

"Thank you," I said, head still bowed. "If we do this, we'll need to move around, probably every couple days or so."

"I've always wanted to see more of the worlds," Simon said airily.

"No, you haven't. You wanted to sit inside your decrepit mansion until both of you crumbled into dust."

"Then you came along and ruined it all," he said, widening his eyes in jest.

"I don't deserve you," I answered.

"You don't, yet here I am. Anyway, I'm the damsel to your knight in shining armor. I cannot resist your heroics and chivalry."

Simon's smile fell slightly when I didn't laugh. "Chin up, you. We'll find him. Everything leaves a trail, remember?"

Including us, I wanted to say, but instead looked upward toward the brilliant sky. The stars glowed bluish in this frozen world. I wondered what the sky looked like wherever Alex was being held. It made me feel closer to him somehow.

"You know," Simon said, "I realized what the compass reminds me of."

"Hm?" I asked, mind still half on the stars.

He pointed. "Your ring. It's got the same vines, see? And those flowers could be roses."

I took the silver ring off my thumb and compared it to the compass. Simon was right. The design was the same, twisting vines adorned with flowers. They were too similar to have been created by different hands.

"What the hell?" I murmured. "Where would my dad have gotten this?"

"Stands to reason it's the same place that compass is from, then. Faeries."

"What would my dad have to do with Faeries?"

"Perhaps you'll be able to ask them someday."

"Yeah, right." I stared at the ring and the compass again, wishing for all the worlds they really could grow mouths and tell me their secrets. "I wonder if there's a way I could contact Flora again from my dreams."

Simon shrugged. "We could give it a go. Let's see, we'd need mugwort for clarity, yarrow for protection and as a conduit for the dream realm. Vervain for awareness...."

He chattered about herbs and astral projection and dream theory, while I gave occasional nods or noises of encouragement. But my mind was far away, imagining what dangers we might encounter in other worlds.

Darkness had fallen quickly, and I hoped the sun would return just as soon. We retreated to the tent, deciding to start off at first light. The space suddenly felt far too small to fit two people, whereas last night it had been cozy. I realized with a twinge of awkwardness that our bedrolls were still piled together. I tried to make quick, nonchalant work of separating them. *This will not be weird. This will not be weird.*

It was, of course, weird. There was nothing to dance around, but we were both doing a tango of avoidance, keeping our distance in the confined space. Before last night, I hadn't really thought about Simon as a member of the opposite sex. He was just a friend, a confederate in rescue and revenge. But now that I'd seen him—almost *all* of him—I couldn't unsee it.

"Well...night," I said, once I'd yanked the blanket up to my chin. I faced away from Simon, trying not to breathe his scent.

"G'night, Seph," he said softly.

For once I didn't hear Simon's snores start as soon as his head hit the pillow. I closed my eyes, and before long succumbed to my usual nightly turmoil. The prison world with the rust red sun always waited for me behind closed lids, and I watched the scenes flash by like frames in an old film strip.

It was always the same. The roiling, infernal lake. The serpent's barbed tail. Alex. The moment of fear on his face, and the most horrible part of all—when the fear turned to acceptance. My heart shattering over, and over, and over again.

As soon as the nightmare finished, it would start all over from the beginning. I gave in to the torturous memories and was ready for it to start, but the dream changed.

I still stood on the edge of the sheer cliff, but I was alone. There was no Alex, no Simon with his glowing eyes, no demon in the form of a winged beast. Choking smoke came off of flames that danced on the lake's surface, suffusing the air until it formed a dirty gray wall of smog. It burned my eyes, and I tried to wave off the smoke to get some relief. It kept coming, pressing on my nose and throat, choking me. I collapsed to my knees, clutching my neck, when the unnatural smoke cleared.

A form approached me, crossing the pocked granite ground with inhuman strides that took two for every one a man could make. The creature was vaguely person-shaped, but it was clearly something *other*.

It didn't occur to me to feel more terrified than I already was. I had no more room for fear or panic or even the will to survive. I stayed on the ground, at the creature's mercy. In fact, there was a small part of me that wondered if the thing would just smite me and get it over with.

Then the haze parted, and its outline solidified. It was a man, or wore the form of a man, tall and broad with long, dark hair. His face was handsome but vicious, and his angular jaw was clean-shaven. He wore a sword at his hip and a pair of night-black wings at his back. His fine raiment was the same black as his wings, and the gold circlet across his brow indicated this was a demon of high rank.

I wasn't able to hide the tremors that wracked my body. I couldn't speak, could barely breathe. We waited in the silence and watched each other.

The demon finally spoke. "You are well protected, even in dreams. I wonder who you have to thank for that." His voice was compelling, but harder than a diamond. I flinched at every word.

"Who are you?" I asked in a hoarse whisper.

"I have many names from many places, most of them lost by now. Your kind made sure of that." At this he sneered, curling his lip. "You would call me ancient, but I existed before time, when the worlds were young and men fell at my feet to worship. I was known as the flying god then. Now I am called Beelzebub."

Five heartbeats passed before I ran. I wasn't sure where I was going, just that I needed to get as far away from the demon as humanly possible. But Beelzebub wasn't human, so I fled even knowing that my best efforts wouldn't be enough. He was worse than Magoth, more powerful, and if grimoires held any truth, then he sat at Lucifer's right hand. My footfalls landed in a staccato beat, ringing in my ears along with the sound of blood being pumped furiously to my extremities to fuel my flight.

A low laugh sounded in my ear, and Beelzebub appeared in front of me. I skidded to a halt inches from him, then tried to dart in another direction. Each time I pivoted, he was there, his icy blue gaze holding me in place.

Then I reminded myself that this was just a dream—a dream I visited nightly. I knew this place far better than the demon. "What do you want?" I demanded, doing a passable job at steadying my voice.

Beelzebub tilted his head, dark hair falling across his face. "I have a message for you, from Prince Magoth."

I released a harsh breath. "What, was he too embarrassed to come tell me himself, or too scared?"

Was that amusement that passed through the demon's eyes? "The prince says he will grant you leniency if you come to him now. That he will not harm your...Alex."

There was no way to stop the adrenaline and fear that raced through me after hearing Alex's name on the demon's lips. "If Magoth touches a hair on his head, I'll destroy him slowly."

Beelzebub didn't break his unblinking stare. "You are brave, for a mortal. Rest assured, your lover has come to no harm. Well, no mortal harm."

"Why should I believe you?"

"Because *I* have a message for you, too. A warning."

"A—a warning?"

In a flash, his hand was on my arm, squeezing. "Stay on the move. Do not allow yourself to be caught. Do not ally with any of my kind. Give up your foolish plan of saving your lover, and hide somewhere you cannot be found."

He could've knocked me over with a feather. "But you just said—"

"I know what I said, foolish girl. Delivering that information was a ruse for the real message that I am sharing with you: run, and run far."

I moistened my lips before I spoke again. "Why are you helping me?"

"Child, I am not helping you. I am helping myself. If he catches you, there will be hell to pay." He gave a mirthless laugh. "Heed me, and keep your distance."

Beelzebub released me abruptly, stepping back into the smoke. "And if anyone asks—you never saw me." He laughed again, the sound caressing my ears, then disappeared.

An ear-rattling snore from Simon pulled me out of the dream like I'd been electrocuted. My chest heaved, and I fought the sweaty tangle of my blanket. A demon—a king of hell—had just given me a warning. Why? And what was going on amongst the demons in order to require that kind of subterfuge?

I lay back down, turning the questions over in my mind. But I couldn't find logical answers for either. The only thing I knew for sure was that I wouldn't take Beelzebub's advice.

I would come for Alex, even if the devil himself tried to stop me.

11

"Why is it so damned hot?" Simon complained, wiping sweat from his face. It was pink from both warmth and sunburn. His pale skin hadn't seen the likes of the sun in this island world before.

That morning we'd traded snow and ice for more tropical climes, the gateway spitting us out onto a rocky outcropping that was the site of several shipwrecks. The debris caught on the rocks and reef signaled that this was a graveyard made by circumstance rather than design.

As it had in the snow world, the Desidarian compass's needle bobbed aimlessly after we'd arrived, its warmth cooling. I'd fashioned a sort of necklace by attaching it to a drawstring, and vowed to wear it all the time so I'd be alerted whenever the backing grew hot.

I yawned from my place in the sand where I was stretched out like a lizard basking in the sun. "Put this on, it'll help." I took off a hat I'd fashioned from fallen palm fronds and tossed it to Simon. Muttering curses about getting cooked inside your own skin like a sausage link, he tugged it low over his brow.

"How can you stand wearing those sleeves?" he said. "I'd be bloody boiling."

I touched the spot on my biceps where long sleeves covered a purple, hand-shaped bruise.

I'd chosen not to tell Simon about the dream. I reasoned with

III

myself it would just worry him, and I hadn't actually been hurt—not mortally, at least.

"You live in a place where the sun hasn't come out for over a decade. In my world we have hot weather. I'm used to it."

The mistruth rolled off my lips too easily. I'd also managed to convince Simon that we needed psychic protection while we slept, so we now had sachets of dried rosemary and lavender to wear at night—the best Simon could produce given the constraints of our travel supplies. He wasn't suspicious about my request, and if he wanted to assume my regular nightmares were getting worse, that was fine with me.

"Hmph. I s'pose it's nice, for about ten minutes." He retreated under the shade of a palm tree. "You all right?"

If I was becoming a more accomplished liar, Simon was getting more observant. In truth, I still felt deeply unsettled by the encounter with Beelzebub. I was more jumpy and distracted than usual. "I'm grand," I answered. "Ready to get out of the heat? We should prep for tonight, anyway."

We retreated into the canopy of the jungle. Though still humid, it was several degrees cooler than the beach. Home for the next day or so was a clearing in the bend of a crystal-clear stream. The trees weren't as dense in this area, but they were strange. Some had bark of orange rust, others deepest purple. Red flowers as big as my head hung from vines, their petals curved to form a bowl-like shape. I pulled one toward me and drank deeply from the cool, refreshing water held within. It was almost sugary, although I wasn't sure if that was my nose and my taste buds getting confused.

Simon slapped the side of his neck. I jolted, and he displayed a squashed bug in his hand. "Don't tell me you're used to these," he said.

"Bugs don't like me. My blood isn't sweet." At Simon's horrified look, I laughed. "It's just a saying."

"Barbaric, that is," he said darkly. "Anyway, we've got our whole summoning kit here: candles, salt, herbs, offering, bowl. Hopefully, we'll catch ourselves a demon."

"Right," I said. Nerves jumped under my skin and swirled in my stomach. When the moon rose, we would summon and interrogate a demon. Theoretically, we were prepared. Theoretically being the key word.

The first surprise of the night came after sunset. When the violet and pink clouds gave way to darkness, two moons rose in the east. They were pale crescents that were a mirror image, twins turned to face each other.

"Er, do we think this is going to be a problem?" Simon asked.

"We'd better hope not," I said. "If anything, it might help us...don't you think?"

"Not necessarily. Whatever demon we summon will be tied to the hours of the night. The two moons might give them more strength than just the one."

"Well, fuck," I muttered. "What should we do?"

"The compass brought us here for some reason. If we're choosing to trust it then we should proceed as planned, I suppose."

I wasn't sure if I wanted to trust it. It hadn't brought us to Alex, and yet we didn't have any other sort of direction to follow. The compass was better than nothing, but not *much* better.

Once the altar was finished, I siphoned from one of the smaller trees in the forest. The glossy leaves turned dull and its bark shriveled, but I stopped before I killed it entirely. I didn't like doing that, though there was another part of me that was already whispering in the back of my mind: *more, more, more.*

"Are you ready?" Simon asked, breaking me out of the trance.

"As I'll ever be. You?"

He nodded grimly, armed with a dagger and a pouch of salt. We laid the circle, then began. I worked from memory, picturing demon's names listed in the pages of ink-stained grimoires. Chanting low under my breath, I called forth the demon Ethiel, who was supposed to aid in finding hidden things.

Ethiel appeared to be busy with other matters, because by the time the moons had reached their zenith he still hadn't shown. The effort of summoning made sweat drip down my temples.

"Shall we try another?" Simon suggested.

I agreed, although it felt like another defeat to give up on Ethiel. A feeling that I would soon get used to, as we called two more demons with no response. I'd thrown power into the summoning, thinking that would help. But the circle within the salt line sat empty of everything but sandy soil.

"Are we doing something wrong?" I asked, wiping my face with my shirt hem. My body was heavy, like I'd just trekked through a foot of dense, sucking mud. I leaned on the nearest tree to stay upright. Everything felt itchy, suddenly, the compass weighing too heavy around my neck. I ripped off the necklace and flung it onto my pack.

"I don't think so," Simon answered. The wrinkle between his eyebrows deepened with every demon that failed to show. "They're just...not coming."

"Maybe they're all at the same infernal conference. I should've penciled myself into their schedules." I strongly considered visiting harm upon the altar. Destroying it wouldn't matter, for all the help it had provided. "I'm going to try again."

"Seph," Simon said with a warning tone. "Don't. You're barely able to stand up."

I pushed away from the tree, seeing stars. "I'm standing fine. See?" I knelt back down in front of the pentacle that was inside the altar space, blinking hard to clear my vision.

"Stop. You're putting yourself in danger."

I gave a humorless laugh. "I've been in danger my whole life, apparently. It's a little too late to care about that now."

Simon knelt next to me, and I caught the anger flashing in his eyes. "This is different, and you know it. Why are you punishing yourself? It's not your fault that Eames was taken. But I watch you day after day pushing to the point of a breakdown. And mark my words —one of these times, you won't be able to put yourself back together."

"Whatever you say," I answered, and readied for another summoning attempt.

"No," Simon ground out, grabbing me by the shoulders and pushing me away from the altar. I must have been weaker than he anticipated, because I fell over.

For a moment, I couldn't make sense of how I'd ended up in the dirt. Then I saw Simon's shocked expression. I threw myself at him, battering with my fists until my vision went red. The fact that he was able to hold me off with one hand, then pin me to the ground, should've told me that he was right. I was going to burn out, but I kept on wriggling like a fish on a line anyway.

"Get off!" I screamed, bucking my hips as he leaned his full weight against me.

"I am not going to let you kill yourself," he said, his breath warm on the shell of my ear. "Tell me what's going on."

"Fuck you," I growled, my spittle landing on his cheeks.

"Tell me," he demanded.

"No."

"I'm not letting you up until you answer me. Why are you acting like this?" He'd switched tactics, adopting a calm, soothing tone. I hated him for it. So I told him.

"I hate you."

"I'm not feeling too keen on you at the moment, either. But I'd rather have you hate me than be dead."

"I should be!" The confession wrenched the empty place beneath my ribs, and pain wracked my bones. The rift between old-me and broken-me stretched a mile wide. "If I had just let Magoth take me like he was supposed to, Alex would still be here. *That* was my fate, and Alex took the bullet for me. I've been marked for death since the day I was born, and everyone who has tried to help me or hide me has suffered and just prolonged the inevitable. My dad left because of what I am, and my mom spent years acting half-dead because of it. I abandoned Bri, and the Guardians tried to protect me, but all it got them was being hunted by the Diurne, too. Fern betrayed them in the first place because of me. Durl's dead. *You've* nearly died a bunch of times. If I had never existed, then the people I love would be much better off. Something about me is *wrong*, and I can't outrun it or change who I am."

Exposing the truth felt both wonderful and terrible at the same time. Wonderful because the knowledge that had been digging its claws into my skin was now exposed, spoken into the air and impossible to take back. But it was terrible for the same reasons—that I no longer held the secret and could pretend to be normal.

Simon released me, but I stayed on the ground, unable to even cry. I felt like a dead thing. I couldn't bear to look into his eyes and see a monster reflected back at me.

"Why would you think that?" he asked, voice raw. "How could you? Everyone's life is better off with you in it. For Asael's sake, you saved my *entire world.* I owe my existence to you. If you hadn't come when you did, I would've moldered away and died in the stacks of Jupiter's, friendless and alone. Thanks to you, I get to have a life, a real one with meaning and adventure, and—and love."

"And I got Penn killed," I said, barely hearing Simon.

"We've been over this—"

I cut him off. "Yes, we have. Please, don't say another word." On a burst of fury, I stormed out of the clearing. Simon didn't follow.

The jungle became an endless blur of smooth bark, dark leaves, and tangled vines as I plunged further into its heart. I wasn't angry with Simon, but with myself. I was spiraling out of control, blind to everything but my own pain. I wanted to be alone with it. To revel in it. To seek pleasure from the feeling of wanting to burn.

I might have kept going until dawn if I hadn't fallen.

One moment I was running, then the next I was suspended over a gaping maw in the ground, wide and toothless. It seemed like I hung in the air, gravity be damned, until my body realized that it was meant to be falling and plunged downward. Humid air whistled around my ears until water swallowed me and everything went quiet.

The cenote's turquoise water was lit from within. Bioluminescence, I realized. My falling into the water must have disturbed the organisms that lived there, exciting them into a chemical reaction. The effect was almost hypnotic in its beauty.

The water was cool but not uncomfortably so. My clothes became heavy and clinging, dragging me down to the bottom of the underground pool. I didn't fight it, and felt a sudden serenity, like the water had doused the fire that propelled me out of the camp and away from Simon.

It would be so simple, so easy to just stay. Like none of my troubles on land could reach me in the watery world of the cavern. My chest felt tight, signaling that I was running out of air. And yet, I took another languid stroke that propelled me further down.

The concave bottom of the cenote was illuminated now. What I saw there had my mouth opening in a silent scream and swallowing water.

Skeletons. Small ones, big ones, ones with grinning skulls and empty eye sockets leering at me.

Panic set in, and I kicked to the surface, pulse pounding in my ears. My arms became lead and my muscles burned with exhaustion. I scraped bare rock when I tried to pull on strings of power to propel me upward.

I didn't want to die. I didn't want to end up as one of those grinning skeletons, condemned to a watery grave. What had I been thinking, letting myself go so deep in my exhausted state? It was like there was some force in the water along with the bioluminescence, trapping me.

The water around me frothed and lit up, then there was a hand reaching out, blindly grasping.

Simon.

His hair floated around his face, otherworldly. He grabbed me around the waist, then struck upward, and we finally breached the surface.

Sweet, sweet air filled my lungs, painful but delicious all the same. I coughed and spluttered, clinging to Simon with my last remaining strength. He held onto a vine, using it like a rope to tow us to a rocky ledge.

"Can you pull yourself up?" Simon panted, water dripping into his eyes.

"I—don't—think so."

"Right then, stay here and don't move." Simon looped the end of the vine around me, then levered himself onto the ledge. He reached down and hauled me over it. We both collapsed, breathing as heavily as if we'd run a marathon.

The strange weight I'd felt while in the water sloughed off, like I was shedding an old skin. I didn't feel powerful, exactly, but closer to being alive than dead. "How did you find me?" I asked, after I'd caught my breath.

"I went after you almost as soon as you left. Took me some time to find your trail, but you weren't exactly being subtle."

I squeezed my eyes shut on the tears that wanted to erupt. "Thank you."

"Anytime," Simon said. Then he sat up, turning to face me. "I'm worried about you, Seph. What you said back there...it scares me."

I stared up at the brilliant moons framed by the mouth of the cavern. "It scares me, too. But that's how I feel, and I don't know how I can change it." Or if I even wanted to change it.

"I thought you...well, I wasn't sure what I'd find. Were you trying to..." he cleared his throat, "jump? On purpose?"

"Do you mean was I trying to kill myself?" I said bluntly. Simon flinched, then I sighed. "No, I wasn't. I don't want to die." I just felt like there were parts of me that were burned and ruined, twisted and ugly. My selfishness, my weakness, my shortcomings. I was terrified of looking at them, at the thought that other people would know what a failure I was.

"I see," Simon said slowly, studying me with knitted brows. He brought a slow, faltering hand to my shoulder. His grip was warm and steady. Unshakeable. When I didn't pull away, he drew me into an embrace. I leaned into him, wrapping my arms around his soaked form. He rubbed soothing circles on my back, and I counted his breaths until the rise and fall of our chests were in sync.

"Anything I can do to help, love?" His voice was a deep rumble, vibrating into me. After one last breath, I pulled away.

"I think you're already helping, just by being here. You're keeping me alive." I injected some lightness into my voice. "What is this, the second or third time you've saved my ass? And you think *you're* the damsel in distress?"

Simon shook his head, sending droplets flying. "Can we agree that we are both mutually heroic and leave it at that? We can take turns. Next time, you save my life."

"Deal." I paused. "There's something wrong with that water, you know," I said quietly. The cenote was dark and opaque once more, hiding its secret.

"What do you mean?" Simon asked.

"Well, for one, there are a bunch of dead people at the bottom." I explained about the skeletons littering the cenote's floor, spread like an augury of bones. "And, I had this feeling of peace when I was in the water. Almost like I was in a trance. I knew that I was drowning, but I didn't really care. Like it was easier to just give in, even though I wanted to live."

"That's fucking terrifying," Simon said, casting a wary eye over the water. "Seems like some kind of evil burial ground."

"Or a trap. I don't think those skeletons ended up there of their own accord, if you know what I mean." I wondered if they had come across the cenote by accident, like me, or if something had lured them there. "We should go back to camp." I stood, wanting to get as far from this haunted cave as possible. Or better yet, to leave this world altogether.

"There are notches cut into the wall over here, kind of a ladder. That's how I came down." Simon pointed to the rock wall behind us that rose at least fifty feet in the air. The hand and footholds were shallow and slick with moisture, a death trap in and of itself.

"Fabulous," I muttered. "Lead the way."

We secured ourselves with more vines that would presumably stop us from plunging into the ensorcelled water if we fell. I clamped down on the urge to siphon from them, although the empty well of my magic was clamoring to be filled. Maybe just a little bit?

No. If I sucked the life out of these vines, they'd be no use at all. *Get your head on straight, Seph.*

"You go ahead of me," Simon said. "That way I can coach you up if you get stuck. Just don't look down."

"Right. Perfect. I'll go, then." I reached for the first handholds, curling my fingers into claws around stone that had been polished smooth over time.

Prickly anxiety cut through my exhaustion, propelling me through the climb. After a while, I got into a rhythm of reach, hold, pull. Reach, hold, pull. The only sounds were the slow drip of water falling into the cave and labored breath.

"How much longer?" I asked. My legs shook and my feet were beginning to cramp. I climbed one more length, then stopped. "Simon? Can you hear me?" I chanced a look down, expecting to see Simon's chestnut head. But there was only a swath of bare wall.

Ice cold panic gathered inside me. "Simon? Simon! Where are you?" I peeled myself away from the wall as far as I dared. There was no sign of him anywhere. The water below was unnaturally still and reflected the twin moons. Surely I would have heard if he'd fallen?

"Fuck. Fucking goddamn *hell*." I reversed and climbed down, falling the last several feet. I searched the rest of the cavern, holding hope that Simon was playing some kind of joke, that he'd pop out from behind a rock and yell, "Surprise!"

My fear became its own entity, with thoughts and feelings and pooling dread. "Where are you!" I screamed. My voice reverberated through the cenote, the plea echoing back in my ears. "Okay, you know what? Don't panic. Panic is bad. It's not going to help you, or Simon. Think." *And do not by any means allow yourself to believe that what happened to Alex might happen to Simon.*

I gathered the facts. Simon had vanished into thin air. This cenote almost certainly had some kind of sinister presence that lured people to their deaths. Ergo, there must be a demon of some sort living in this cave. I could deal with demons. I *had* dealt with them.

Now, what did I know about a demon who might inhabit a cenote? I racked my brain for anything, any hint of an idea that could tell me where Simon was. In my world, cenotes were famously associated with Mexico and Mayan gods. If I could only remember who those Mayan gods were....

I paced back and forth, focusing on the steady beat of my steps. I repeated the information I knew: demon, cenote, death, possible Mayan-like connection. I knew I'd read some mythology about them. Something like—

"Oh," I said softly. "Oh, no."

PART II

12

I was fairly certain of two things. One, that this cenote was a seam, a gateway to an underworld. And two, that Simon had been taken by a death demon.

But the question was, was the seam underwater, or somewhere else in the cave? I only had time to explore one option, if there was any time left at all. I traversed the perimeter, exploring every crevice for some evidence of a passageway. My heart leapt when I alighted on a dark streak that I'd previously taken to be slime. I touched the stain, and when I held my fingertip to the light of the moons it was crimson. *Blood.*

This had to be it. I pressed my palm against probably-Simon's blood. The rock didn't shimmer, or disappear, or change in any way. Hellfire and damnation. I pressed harder, and my hand went through the wall. With adrenaline spinning through my veins, I walked into the rock and out the other side.

The passage sloped down at a steep angle, but the floor was rough enough that my sodden boots didn't slide too much. I followed it at a run, twisting and turning as the tunnel narrowed, the walls brushing my shoulders. My breath came shallow, but there was no room for claustrophobia to compete with the rest of my panic.

I eventually spilled through a door into a cavernous room that was dimly lit by torches mounted high on the walls. The torchlight glimmered on an inch of standing water that covered the ground. There were four doors in the room—one that I'd just come through, one directly across from me, and one each to my left and right. Strange symbols were carved into the rock atop each door, an *X* with three curving lines above the one I'd just come through.

It was a crossroads. The power of the liminal space lifted the hairs on the back of my neck. But which way was the underworld? I spun a tight circle, eyeing each of the doors. They were identical, hewn from the same stone as the walls, with no helpful drops of blood to tell me where Simon had gone. Why the fuck had I been foolish enough to take the compass off earlier? Oh, right, because I was holding a grudge against a hunk of metal.

I sprinted to the lefthand door, splashing through the water. "Please, leave me a sign. Where are you?" There was no indication that anyone had been here before me. I checked the others, finally ending with the far right door. Something crunched underfoot. I moved my boot aside. A metallic, sinuous shape was visible through the few inches of water.

Stooping, I snatched it up. The tiger's eye pendant hung on a cheap silver chain; it was my charmed necklace that I'd given Simon after our visit with the crone. "You freaking brilliant genius. I'm coming for you." I shoved the necklace into my pocket and wrenched open the west door, barreling through it into an utter nightmare.

I stood atop a hill that gave me a good vantage of the valley below. The sky was an unending sheet of bruised storm clouds, lightning jumping between them. Thunder boomed, reverberating in my chest. Massive bats swooped and whirled on a foul wind that stirred withered ivory trees. A blood-red river wound sluggishly across the landscape, and just beyond that was an immense palace the color of old bone that jutted up into the horizon.

A trio of cloaked figures were on a road between the river and the palace. Two of them held the third between them, who struggled against his captors.

Part of me sagged in relief that I'd found Simon. Another part of me knew that I had to get to him before they entered the palace. I had a feeling that not many who went inside came back out again. I raced down the hill, the maddeningly hot air singeing my lungs with every inhale. A stitch developed in my side, but I ignored it. I needed to focus on how I would cross the river that was too wide to jump.

The river wasn't as sluggish as it appeared from afar. The red water —or more likely blood, based on the iron-tinged smell—coursed with a strong current, creating eddies and whipping up pinkish foam. I slipped a tentative hand in and recoiled at the burn, hissing in pain. Blisters sprang up everywhere the blood touched. Swimming clearly wasn't an option, then.

I scanned the riverbank for anything that could help me cross. Maybe I could use branches to create a raft and float to the other side? I dismissed the idea. It would take far too much time, time I didn't have.

"Think, Seph. *Think.*" What did I have on me? A necklace charmed with a protection spell, a Faerie ring, two daggers strapped to my thighs —make that one dagger, I'd lost one somewhere along the way—and my own scattered wits.

One of the eagle-sized bats wheeling overhead released a harsh screech, diving for the river. It skimmed some liquid off the surface before taking to the dark skies again.

Of course, they had to be *vampire* bats. But if they were, that meant they'd be attracted by blood.

Gritting my teeth, I yanked up my sleeve and sliced the dagger down my forearm.

The bats changed their flight pattern and began to circle me. The intermittent lightning flashes created a strobe effect, so that they appeared to lurch forward. It would be almost impossible to grab their clawed feet, but I had to do it anyway.

They were getting closer now, just about within jumping distance. I glanced at Simon; he was almost at the palace. My heart hammered against my ribs painfully, urging me on. Then, one of the bolder bats swooped low, screeching. I made a grab for its claws.

The bat did not appreciate its meal jumping on it. I did not appreciate having to dangle midair like some kind of fucked up children's mobile. And I especially did not enjoy it when the bat dipped precariously over the river and boiling hot blood coated my boot. But it also gave me an opportunity to siphon, and I used power to direct the bat across the river.

As we closed in on Simon, I had the horrifying realization that the immense palace wasn't just the color of old bone—it *was* old bone. Skulls, vertebrae, and femurs were stacked together to create the building's soaring arches and domed roof.

Simon would not be joining their ranks.

I let go of my trusty steed and tumbled to the ground, tucking into a roll and flinging my dagger before I'd even regained my feet. The blade found its mark in one of the demons, who hissed and released a garbled wail. Its hooded cloak slipped and revealed a skeletal face with sunken, waxy skin the color of a corpse, and.... Horror washed over me when I saw the demon's empty eye sockets.

"Take him," the skeletal demon rasped to its fellow. It removed a bone-handled whip from the folds of its cloak. "I will deal with the human."

"That's not going to work for me." I thrust the tiger's eye necklace into its face, then aimed a kick at its kneecaps. The death demon stumbled. I bowled past it, grabbing for Simon, who was still being held by the second demon.

Unfortunately, this one had learned from its compatriot and was ready for me. It struck me with a staff that looked to be carved of bone but felt like iron. I doubled over, grasping for power, and shot blue flames. The demon's robes caught fire, and it threw Simon to the ground. A cloud of ash fell as the fire went out.

Shit. I blasted more flames as the twin skull faces advanced on me, but the demons extinguished the fire before it reached them. I reached for more power and came up empty. I needed to siphon, but nothing in this deathly wasteland was alive. Except for the bats, but I didn't have one of those handy.

I ducked and dodged the demons' attacks, drawing them away from Simon. They moved like smoke, and my vision grayed at the edges. My strength was fading fast. I wouldn't be able to distract them for much longer.

"Run!" I yelled, as the demon with the whip sent licks of flame racing down its length. It circled the whip overhead like a lasso, then brought it down, lashing my back from shoulder to hip.

I dropped to the ground on a cry of pain. After summoning tonight and nearly drowning in the cenote, I had nothing left to give. But maybe, just maybe, Simon could make it out.

The staff-wielding demon appeared in my range of vision. "She will please the god-king," it said, nudging my leg with its staff. The demon pulled its hood up, throwing its horrible face into shadow again.

So their aim was to capture, not murder. I supposed I could be grateful for that, in a way, because if they had wanted to kill me then I would certainly be dead already.

I watched the demon warily, only now catching the stink of decay emanating from it. The whip demon retrieved Simon, who still struggled but with slow, slack movements. His eyes were dull as well, the color of a mud puddle.

"What did you do to him?" I demanded.

The demon lowered into a crouch. I forced myself to look into its face as disgust pooled in the back of my throat. "We are the bone demons, human. We feast on the suffering and fear of your kind."

"I–I have things I could trade you for him. Please."

"Nothing you can offer would replace the value of your human soul." The demon grabbed me, its long fingers of exposed bone surprisingly strong. I couldn't resist, just let my head loll onto my chest like a ragdoll.

It was true that there was no life in this desolate underworld. But— there was power. Power I could steal for myself to save us from becoming the god-king's sacrifice. No matter how repugnant it seemed, I had to try.

We would not die tonight.

I came to life in the demon's arms, drilling an elbow into bare ribs. It loosened its grasp, and as I dropped from its embrace I spun around and latched my hands around its shriveled neck. I opened myself to the demon's power and siphoned.

This was so different from that first time in the prison world. If that power had been limned in gold, this was made of ash. Instead of the glorious, heady rush, I felt char and smoke and decay filling my veins, pumping through my heart and burrowing into my bones. It was a magnificent and terrible thing, and I knew once I started that I wouldn't be able to stop until there was nothing left for me to take.

The demon's skull began to crumble, chipping away as it collapsed in on itself. I released my grip and watched as the bones became dust, then the dust was carried off by the wind. It swirled into a funnel before dissipating, and just like that, it was as if the demon never existed.

A grin lit my face when the second demon dropped Simon and disappeared behind the palace gates. It seemed like this should have been the order of things all along; that demons and mortals alike should fear me, because I had a power they couldn't hope to understand.

Simon looked on, nonplussed. I was counting on getting him out of this world to shake his strange lethargy.

"Come on," I said, slinging his arm around my shoulders. I supported him, half pulling, half dragging him back to the riverbank. Infusing siphoned power into my muscles, I gathered Simon into my arms and got a running start, jumping and clearing the bloody river easily. It was faster to just carry him, so I did until we reached the top of the hill. The door wasn't there until I willed it into existence, and it appeared as if it had been waiting for us all along.

The hour-long return journey only took half that with my magic-enhanced speed. Simon had fallen asleep and seemed almost childlike in my arms, with his long sweep of lashes and tumbled hair.

I felt extraordinary. Strong, ruthless, and most of all, indestructible. No one, mortal or supernatural, could touch us while the death demon's power flowed through me.

When we arrived at camp, I laid a still sleeping Simon down gently while I packed our things. Even if our initial goal of interrogating a demon hadn't been met, we'd found something so much better. With this kind of power, I could summon any demon and destroy any foe. Something like real confidence warmed me for the first time in a long while.

Holding Simon under one arm and our bags under the other, I let the compass point us to the next world.

———

The world of Kusu was straight out of a sci-fi movie, what I imagined my world would be like in a few hundred years. Yet, it felt disorienting in the extreme to interact with technology so seamless it was difficult to tell how it worked. Even though we'd only been there for a day since fleeing the death demons, I couldn't wait to leave.

I'd just returned to our hotel—I suppose that's what it was, although it seemed more like a beehive with a cell for a room and coffin-like beds that retracted from the wall—when Simon began to stir. I rushed to his side, my muscles going slack with relief.

He murmured something unintelligible. "What did you say?" I asked, bending closer.

"Hungry," Simon said in a cracked voice. His eyes fluttered open, and I noted that they were back to their normal gray.

I smiled, holding up the bag that contained hot fries and some kind of plant-based burgers and nuggets. Apparently fast food was a multi-universal concept. "Already ahead of you."

Simon sat up, groaning, then reached for the bag. I watched as he systematically annihilated the food until there were only a few crumbs left, and even those he licked from his fingers.

"Where are we?" Simon stretched his arms overhead, the muscles of his bare torso pulling taut. "And where's my shirt?"

"It had death demon stink on it. Here, I got you a new one." I tossed him a shirt that matched his eyes. He caught it and pulled it on, then gingerly lifted the blanket off his lap and peeked underneath.

"What?"

"Just checking if you took my trousers, too."

"No, although those also smell. There's a replacement pair in there," I said, pointing to a second bag I'd left by the door. I was also wearing brand new clothes, their material sturdy but softer than water. The robot at the store I'd stolen them from had assured me they were sweat-proof, rip proof, and wouldn't stain. They were unlikely to live up to their reputation, given how hard we were on our wardrobe.

"Thanks," Simon said. Then he gave me a measured, assessing look. "You seem chipper."

"Why shouldn't I be? We're both still alive. And since I saved our asses this time, the ball's in your court."

Simon's eyes widened. "Gods. What happened?"

"What do you remember?"

He scrubbed a hand over his face. His jaw was shadowed with several days' growth of reddish beard. "Those skeleton things coming out of nowhere and taking me. And then that place with the storm and the bone palace. They said...." he trailed off, his lips rubbing together.

"They said what?" I urged.

Simon grimaced. "That my blood was sweet."

A shiver swept through me as my earlier words came back to haunt me. "We got away, and we'll never see them again. That's the important part."

"Right," he answered. "So, tell me about the rest."

"Well... I'll give you the CliffsNotes. The shortened version," I explained at his look of confusion. "I followed the sign you left me, which was genius of you, by the way, and managed to reach you right before the death demons were going to take you into that palace. But I was out of power, and I...I discovered something amazing." I explained to Simon that I'd learned I could siphon from the demon, that I had taken all of its power and killed it, or whatever counted for destroying an immortal being.

"Please don't take this the wrong way," Simon said, wetting his lips, "but I don't think that was a good thing you did."

My mouth fell open, even as I felt a twinge of hurt. "Of course it was a good thing. Weren't you listening? Simon, the power I have now is so much more potent than what I was able to siphon before. And it's going to last longer, I can already tell. I won't have to hurt living things anymore, I can just siphon from demons. This solves all of our problems."

"Does it? Or is it going to end up hurting you? I have to say I'm not thrilled with you having demon bits in you."

I rose angrily from the bed. "I already have demon bits in me." I put air quotes around *demon bits*. "All Watchers do, including you. And you're the one who said that not all demons are bad."

"They're not, of course they're not. But...this doesn't feel right, Seph." Simon drew the quilt back and stood so that we were at eye level.

I took his hands. "It's going to be fine. I'm still me, see?"

Simon peered into my eyes as though looking for some trace of the demon whose power I'd stolen. It felt like he was putting my soul under a microscope, examining every facet. I wondered what it would look like to him. Did he see a powerful lightbringer? Or the lost girl who'd fallen into his world?

I cleared my throat. "See any red?"

"No." A hint of a smile played around the corners of his mouth. "But be careful, will you?"

"I'm always careful." At his sound of disbelief, I amended my words. "I think about being careful, at least. And I'll check for signs of horns every day. Promise."

That got me an outright grin. "You're mad, you know that?"

"Oh, Simon." I sighed, rising to look out at the congested streets. "We all are."

13

We moved on to another world that evening, then another the day after. Always, the compass went still after we went through the gateway.

Three days after fleeing the island, we were in a town that teemed with people and creatures I'd thought to find only in fairytales. There were goblins and cloaked men riding pale horses, elves and wary warlocks, and jewel-colored birds the size of my thumbnail that flitted around the eaves of houses, gossiping with each other.

A castle made of pale blue stone with fanciful turrets and spires stood at the rise of a hill, where real life kings and queens made their home. Knights in shining armor patrolled the gates that circled the castle, their swords honed to sharp points. I made an effort not to catch their eye.

The clock had just struck midnight, and Simon and I were headed to a graveyard that lay adjacent to a temple where the townsfolk worshiped their deities.

The burial ground was hushed and still but looked the same as any cemetery in any world; the dead were one thing they all had in common. Grave markers ranged from simple plaques set flush with the earth to multi-family mausoleums with elegant facades. The night was chilly and our breath came out in puffs of vapor. Seeing in the dark was no problem for me, but Simon's steps were slow and awkward. I reached for his hand and towed him along behind me until we were out of sight of the candlelit temple windows.

"Okay, I think this is good." I stopped behind one of the larger mausoleums that may have been more square feet than my apartment back home. It was made of rust-colored stone polished to a mirror shine, and had brilliant stained-glass windows.

"I can't bloody see anything," Simon whispered, letting go of my hand and immediately running into the wall of the mausoleum.

"Here," I said, stifling a laugh, and called a small sphere of light to hover in my open palm. Simon's face flared into relief, throwing sinister shadows across it.

"Thanks." He began to pour the salt circle, while I set up the altar facing west. When we were finished, he gave me a hesitant glance. "Seph, wait."

"What is it?" Power was slick under my skin, pooling like hot oil. I wanted to begin.

"Just...have a care. If you can," Simon said, harking back to our earlier conversation.

"You know I will," I replied, even though the time for caution was over. He gave a final nod, then took his place beside me with his salt pouch and dagger held close.

I lit the candles with a wave of my hand, then fed the parchment on which I'd drawn the demon Ethiel's seal into the flames. As it burned, I called for the demon to appear.

A form manifested inside the circle within moments. It looked like a man, if men had been shaped from the night sky.

"Who calls me?" Ethiel's voice was the soft beat of a bat's wings.

"We do," I replied. The demon locked its starbright eyes on me.

"Mortals?" His gaze flicked warily between me and Simon. "I sensed the power of my own kind."

"That would be me," I said.

Ethiel made a sound akin to a scoff. "Impossible."

"Do you want a little show and tell?" I snapped my fingers and flames raced around the salt circle.

The demon didn't flinch, but his starry eyes narrowed. Then he began to shimmer, and his edges bled into the darkness.

"Where do you think you're going?" I extinguished the flames, and power lapped at my feet, urging me toward the demon. I crossed over the salt circle, ignoring Simon's sharp intake of breath, and snatched the demon's blurry arm. It was like touching a shooting star, so hot it was cold, but that didn't hinder me. My stolen power roared in approval, egging me on. "I didn't say you could leave."

Ethiel began to rematerialize, and it might have been fear that made the stars in his eyes burn brighter. "What do you want, mortal?"

"For you to help me find someone. A gods-touched mortal who was taken by the demon Magoth a few months ago. Alex Eames, a Guardian. Where is he?"

"I know not."

I tightened my grip on Ethiel's arm. "You know the location of hidden things. Tell me where he is."

Ethiel shook his night-dark head. "I can reveal where treasures are buried on this mortal plane, but on no other. I cannot help you."

Instantaneous rage crashed over me like a wave, and I whipped a dagger from my belt. I bent, still holding onto Ethiel, and traced it along the salt line that enclosed the altar. Then I pushed the salted tip into the demon's neck. He hissed as whatever passed for his skin began to sizzle. My heart thrashed in my chest, and my brain felt like it was boiling.

"Seph, stop this," Simon pleaded, a note of disgust threaded through his fear.

His voice could have been a whisper carried away by the wind for all the attention I paid him. Nothing was going to stop me now. Hatred welled deep inside me—hatred for demons, and the Aureum, and everyone and everything who was keeping me from Alex.

I scored the blade further along the demon's neck. "Don't lie to me," I said in a whisper colder than a winter's dawn, staring into Ethiel's flashing eyes. "You won't like what happens if I find out you have."

"If you know so much about my kind, you understand that we may not tell outright falsehoods," the demon reminded me, thunder lacing his words.

"Let me rephrase that. If you are not telling the truth, then I will fucking end your existence. I've done it before. Just ask him." I jerked my head toward Simon.

"It is true," Ethiel insisted. "But I know who could help you."

"Tell me."

"Gorsyar. He has power over the knowledge of hidden things." The demon leaned away from the knife, eyes wheeling. "He will help you."

The death demon's power screamed for me to run Ethiel through with my dagger. It wouldn't kill him, but it might hurt.

Then, I felt Simon's furious presence behind me. He hadn't crossed into the salt circle, but tugged at my belt loop, trying to pull me back across.

Dark fury roiled in my gut, and I released a harsh breath through clenched teeth. Who the hell did Simon think he was, trying to stop me? He'd been holding me back from the beginning, always second-guessing my decisions and slowing me down. It was like he didn't even want to find Alex, like he wanted to be on this fucking endless merry-go-round forever.

Still holding tight to the demon, I thrust my other hand back at Simon and shoved him. Heat grazed my palm, then I heard a soft yelp. The pressure on my belt loop vanished.

Leaning in, I lowered my voice to a whisper. "Okay. Just one more thing."

I siphoned some of Ethiel's power. It was like drinking moonlight, fresh and bright and pure, but with an undertone of malice. Then I shoved the demon away, and he vanished into the night.

With two demons' power coursing through me, I was euphoric, higher than the clouds. The night seemed to glow, the stars turning so bright I had to squint. The air was velvet on my skin, a sultry caress beckoning me to take more, more, more. Whispering in my ears that I could do anything—be anything.

Then my gaze landed on Simon. He leaned against a crypt, cradling his arm against his chest. The fabric of his sleeve was singed in a stripe from forearm to wrist.

Something tangled with the bliss running through my veins. A voice, or maybe an echo of a voice, shouting words that I couldn't comprehend.

"What in Asael's name do you think you're playing at?"

Simon's tone was quiet fury, but his eyes had the old, haunted look from months ago. The voice in my head grew louder, but then my power pulsed, sending little swirls of pleasure along my skin.

"Relax." I smiled, putting a chummy hand on his shoulder. He batted me away. "It's just a little blister. I'm sorry, but you shouldn't have gotten in my way."

"Shouldn't have gotten in your way?" he repeated, brows drawing down.

"Exactly. Now we have another lead. This is so much more efficient than just closing our eyes and pointing."

"No, it's reckless. Seph, you *burned* me."

Rolling my eyes, I snatched Simon's wrist and sent a healing shove toward the burn. "There. Better?"

Repulsion twisted his features as he wrenched out of my grasp. "Not really."

"Come on, don't be naive. We have been miles behind ever since the prison world. This can finally give us an advantage." Why couldn't he understand, when it was so obvious?

"Promise me you won't do it again," he pleaded.

I shook my head. "This power, it's like nothing I've ever experienced. I can be as strong as Magoth, stronger, even. When we find Alex, we can take him out for good." That's what the power told me, anyway. It purred in my ear, hypnotic, whispering that this was the reason why both the Aureum and the demons wanted to be rid of me; because my power was greater than any they had ever seen. "Think of it like a shortcut. The sooner this is over, the sooner you can return to your life. And I can get back to mine."

Simon blanched, his lips parting as if on a silent gasp of pain. A second later, he arranged his face into careful, blank lines. "Right. Of course." Then he walked away into the darkness, leaving me behind.

"Where are you going?" I called. He didn't answer, just kept picking his way through the now quiet cemetery until he faded from sight.

Simon didn't return to the inn where we were staying that night. Part of me was worried, wondering where he'd gone and why he'd stayed away. The other, larger part of me, the part glowing with demon magic, said that Simon would be fine. He was an adult who could do as he pleased, and it wasn't my job to worry about his hurt feelings if he couldn't grasp common sense.

I made plans to leave the following morning, sure he'd reappear at first light. But when Simon didn't return by the time I was up and packed, I went out looking for him.

The immediate thrill of siphoning had faded from my blood, and shame began to trickle in. Okay, maybe I'd taken things too far last night. The power had momentarily overcome me, but I could control it. My will was iron, stronger than their magic.

Soft light gilded the cobbled streets while birds trilled their morning songs, and the village began to wake. Aromas of fresh bread and sizzling meat scented the air, and vendors uncovered their market stalls. Working folk scurried to and fro, either on their way to their employers, or already having been sent out on errands.

There was no sign of Simon in the busy streets. My chest tightened with the first ripple of panic. Where could he have gone? What if something happened to him? I approached a portly man who was sweeping the front step of a bakery.

"Excuse me, I'm wondering if you can help me. I'm looking for a man, about my age and height, brownish-red hair. Have you seen him?"

The man paused, leaning on his broom. "I haven't seen anyone like that. Is he a friend?"

"Yes. He was...upset with me yesterday, and has been out all night."

"Ah. You'll want to check the Golden Cauldron."

"I'm sorry?"

"The Golden Cauldron alehouse," the man clarified. "Down the high street and take a left. Your...*friend* may have sought comfort in the bottom of a bottle."

I turned to leave, not wasting time on disabusing the man's assumption that Simon and I had a lover's quarrel. "Thanks."

"He'll come around, I'm sure." The man winked and resumed sweeping.

I set off for the alehouse at a jog, and after a few moments found the crooked sign with a gold cauldron painted on it. The cauldron bubbled over with what I assumed was foamy beer.

The pub was closed, as even the most hardened drinkers were likely still abed. I rapped on the scarred wooden door with iron bars set into its center. Several minutes of pounding later, an irate voice called through the door, "We're not open yet."

"I don't want to drink. I'm looking for someone who might have been here last night."

Wood scraped against wood, then a pair of bloodshot brown eyes were revealed through a window behind the bars. "I'm not responsible for wayward husbands. Now get gone, before I put a hex on you for getting me out of bed before luncheon."

My power reared its head at the threat. "Or I can put one on you," I said, and touched a finger to iron, superheating the metal. When it turned orange and began to melt like candle wax, a bolt clicked and the door opened to reveal a woman of middling height and age with tanned skin. Her eyes were wary.

"All right, fine. Say your piece," she said, folding her arms over a substantial bosom.

I described Simon, down to the clothes he was wearing. The woman nodded, and her expression turned even grimmer. "Aye, he was here. The idiot drank his weight in spirits, then started a fight. I had to throw him out. I don't allow troublemakers in my place."

Fuck. Simon, starting a fight? "Where did he go?"

"How should I know? I just leave them at the door." She sniffed. "But you could check the field across the way. Sometimes they end up there to sleep it off."

She wasn't sorry to see the back of me. I was drawing too much attention, and annoyance crept in to mingle with worry for Simon. What the hell was he thinking, getting that drunk? If he thought that summoning demons in the graveyard would get us in trouble, what did he think would happen by starting bar fights?

The field was a wildflower meadow, colorful and rich with the scent of honeysuckle. I started to cut a path through the flowers when I heard an almighty snore. I looked down and saw a pair of feet, one bootless, sticking out of a ditch. I recognized that boot.

I stormed over and found Simon slumbering peacefully in the muddy ditch. I kicked his leg. He snorted, eyes shut, then turned over and squished his face farther into the mud. "Hey!" I kneeled and shook him hard.

Simon slurred something, still asleep. I turned him face up none too gently, pinching his nose shut and covering his mouth. His eyes flew open and he shoved me away, gasping. "Bloody hells! What the fuck d'you think you're doing?" His accent was thicker and rougher than usual.

"Bloody hells!" I mimicked in an unflattering voice. "You have some fucking balls. What are *you* doing?"

"Minding my own business," Simon muttered. He cradled his head in his hands. "Someone turn the lights off."

"Hungover? I don't feel sorry for you. You made quite the impression on the pub owner, who had to throw you out after *starting a fight.*"

Simon got to his feet slowly, squinting. "I don't recall that."

"Do you recall passing out in a ditch?" My hands were on my hips like a lecturing school marm, and I quickly clenched them at my sides. "Ugh, you smell like the carpet of a bowling alley."

My angry resolve weakened. Simon was covered in muck and had mud plastered in his hair. His shirt was torn and there was a rip in the knee of his pants. A bruise bloomed purple over his jaw. He was pitiful, really.

He groaned. "I'm sorry. Please help me."

"Wait there. I'm going to see if I can find your shoe." After fishing Simon's boot out of the weeds along the ditch, I took his arm and ushered him through the town, trying to keep to side streets. I didn't want to catch the attention of a palace guard and their inconvenient questions.

"Look, about last night...I got carried away. It won't happen again."

He was quiet for a long while. "Won't it? You turned into someone I didn't recognize. You weren't brave, or kind, or compassionate. You were just cruel. Vicious, even."

I didn't slow down, although I wanted to. I wanted to stop in the middle of the street and apologize, to throw myself at his feet while I begged for forgiveness. I had *hurt* Simon, something that I never wanted to do. He was my sole ally in this, the only one remaining out of my friends.

But my power wouldn't allow it; it sizzled and popped like an angry fire, maddened at Simon's accusations.

"That *is* me. I can't change those parts of myself just because you don't like them. I'm not always sweet and kind and nice. You either accept all of me, or accept none of me."

"You were never sweet," he shot back. "And I wouldn't want you to be. But you are kind. You are *good*. I know you, and it's those demons' power that's making you this way."

We'd almost reached our room at the inn by this time, and I stomped up the stairs before whirling around to face him. "We barely know each other. I lived a whole life before I met you."

Simon reared his head back like I'd slapped him. "Barely know you? I—no, forget it. You can think whatever you want, Seph. You don't listen to me anyway." With those parting words, he walked into our room then slammed the door behind him, leaving me with a face full of solid wood. I tried the knob, but it was locked.

I leaned against the wall, sliding down until I hit the floor. Shit. That was not how I meant for our make-up chat to go. Instead, the threads of our conflict had become even more tangled.

After a while, Simon emerged, mud-free and smelling much better. He had his bag slung over his shoulder and walked past me without looking back. "Shall we go?" he asked, his voice coated with frost.

This was a Simon I hadn't encountered before. He could be grumpy and waspish, but never cold. "Do you want me to help with your head—"

"No." He finally looked at me, and I saw that his eyes had turned to shards of flint. "Let's just go before I do anything else stupid."

"Simon, I didn't mean—"

But he didn't hear me, because I was speaking to his rigid back. I shoved down the gnawing sense of guilt as I followed him silently to the cemetery. It wasn't my problem if Simon was in a bad mood. He'd come around. Eventually.

14

Our salt was running low. I reached into the pouch and scraped the meager amount covering the bottom. There was probably only enough to lay one more circle, maybe two. Dropping the crystals into the pouch, I sat back on my haunches and let a sigh whistle through my teeth. The sounds of a tent being raised behind me ceased for a moment, then resumed.

"We're almost out of salt," I called. Simon grunted, but didn't say anything. That was about as much as we were speaking these days.

I dusted my hands off on my pants, then stood. We were camped at the edge of a wood. The trees were tall, so tall that when I peered upward the tops of them soared far beyond my enhanced vision. I'd heard sounds coming from above our heads, and had thought I'd seen a flash of a furry tail. The tree bark smelled spicy and warm, reminiscent of Christmas. It certainly wasn't the worst place the compass had brought us. I'd need to find some salt the next time we traveled, which would be at first light.

Simon and I ate a silent meal of some kind of dried jerky we'd picked up in the last world. It was stringy and coarse, but it was something. A few nights we'd gone to sleep with our stomachs emptier than the space between us.

My sleeve slipped as I reached into my pack for a canteen, revealing my wrist with the silvery scars I'd received in Durl's world. Both of our bodies had turned into hollows and bones stretched tight under skin. I'd always been naturally thin, but now I could count each rib and felt the knobs of my spine digging into the ground every night as I slept. Simon was almost as bad.

Simon, it turned out, was a master at holding a grudge. And I'd never felt more alone in my whole life than I did as we traveled the worlds. Together, but apart. It had been easier before I'd let him in. Let them all in, rather—Bri and Alex and Fern and the rest of my friends. Because once you let people be part of your life, they could just as easily disappear from it, even when they were sitting right beside you.

So, I'd hardened my heart. Simon and I stayed at a distance, always cordial, but the knowledge of what we'd lost bit like frost on bare skin. I'd long stopped trying to bridge the divide between us and burrowed deeper into myself. Deeper into the power of the demons that flowed through me like a river of ash.

I cleared my throat. "I'm going to start."

"Fine," Simon said. He stood up and walked off into the trees. He always left when I summoned, ever since that first night I crossed the salt circle while questioning Ethiel. It had been weeks since then—maybe over a month—and I was still no closer to finding Alex than when I'd started. Demon after demon had given me names, but no matter how... convincing I was, they didn't give up the information I needed.

The compass had brought us to some incredible places. I saw things I'd never imagined in all my wildest dreams. An abandoned city whose buildings were made of pure gold. A world of sightless creatures that lived below ground because the surface was a cloud of poison gas. I saw statues of gods as tall as the Empire State Building that flanked a river-city built upon stilts. Had stood in pale moonlight while clouds of moths descended upon a haunted town, and watched butterflies take their place as the sun rose.

But everything still felt empty as the days passed and my life became an unending cycle of move, summon, question, sleep, repeat. I became emptier still as I filled myself with demons' power.

Simon was right. It was changing me, this absorption of power from beings who held their own incomprehensible magic. The more I siphoned from them, the stronger I became, and the more I became a stranger to myself.

It was a short walk to the burial ground through which we'd arrived. There were no obvious graves, but I'd soon discovered that each tree planted in the circular area was its own tomb. Strange letters marked each one, just like an epitaph on a headstone.

I poured the salt circle, emptying the bag and creating a hasty altar. Shutting my eyes, I flipped through the catalog of my memory, remembering the required words to call on the demon Cazul.

As I began to speak the words, there was a rustling sound from inside the circle. My eyes snapped open and I saw that it wasn't a stray animal who had crossed the salt line, but a demon. A familiar one.

Gamori stood in its center, corporeal and glowing with beauty. A crown perched atop her raven hair, and her dark eyes were obsidian pools that beckoned me closer. The haughty line of her chin was more apparent now than it had been when she first appeared to me in Orrm. She wore robes of deepest wine embroidered with gold, and her sleeves were bell-shaped, so long they brushed the ground.

"Well met, daughter," Gamori drawled, tilting her head to study me.

I took a step back, heart jumping into my throat, then belatedly inclined my head in a short bow. What was she doing here, coming when I hadn't called her? Whatever it was, it couldn't be good. "Gamori. I, uh...didn't expect to see you."

She gave a humorless chuckle. "Cazul is busy at the moment, waging war on some faction or other. Besides, I thought we needed to have a chat. Just between us girls."

The hairs stood up on my arms, and my palms turned clammy. I flicked a glance toward the salt circle to confirm it was still intact. "Really?"

"Oh, yes. You have been busy, haven't you? Questioning demonkind about your lost lover. Word spreads, you know. You surely didn't think it would go unnoticed?" She smiled at my stony expression. "You are blazing a trail through the worlds like wildfire through dry lands. Creating quite a reputation for yourself. *Lightbringer.*" Gamori hissed the last word, and her cruel beauty morphed from delicate to virile.

"I'm doing what needs to be done," I replied. The demon power flowing through me swelled at Gamori's challenge, like recognizing like. *Hurt her*, it whispered. *Make her feel pain.*

"I have no quarrel with your aims. But I did not know *you* are the mortal who the prince seeks," Gamori said.

"What does that have to do with anything?"

"Daughter, it has to do with *everything*." The demon approached the edge of the salt circle, looking down at it in disgust before meeting my eyes. "Your power is—"

"Yeah, I know," I interrupted. "Too dangerous for mortals or demons. I'm a freak of nature, an abomination, a threat to all the worlds. I've heard it before." My fingers twitched by my sides, itching to act.

"Do not behave like a petulant child. It is not an attractive trait." Gamori tapped a finger to her lips. "So you don't know, then."

"I'm sure there are a lot of things I don't know. Are you going to tell me what you came here for? Because I'm busy."

"I should smite you where you stand."

Blood roared in my ears, and I gave my own cruel smile. "Try it. I dare you."

Gamori's jaw tightened. "I did not come to argue with an ill-tempered mortal, though you do test my patience. I am here to check on our bargain. Clearly, you have not yet retrieved the stone of Vadyron from Aundirne."

"I have time. A year, you said."

"Well...yes, I did, didn't I?" Gamori pouted, then snapped her fingers. "But I can give you a little incentive to finish it sooner. Light a fire under you, as the mortals say."

Wind rose, blowing tree branches and whipping hair across my face. When I brushed the tangled waves out of my eyes, I saw Simon next to the demon, just outside the salt circle. He was trapped inside a lattice-work of sharp thorns, his expression bewildered.

"Simon!" I cried, racing to him and ripping at the bars of the cage. It was like grasping knives, and my hands came away bloody and torn. His eyes were wide with fear. He also grabbed at the thorns, but released them with a gasp of pain.

I turned to the demon, cupping blue fire in my blood-soaked hands. "Let him go." Power raged across my skin, sparks snapping.

"Go ahead. Burn it down," she said almost lazily. "But you'll burn your friend, too."

"You fucking bitch," I snarled.

"Yes, I am." Then Gamori snapped her fingers again, and the cage disappeared. Simon dropped to his knees like a stone, and I ran to him. He was trembling, but pushed me away and stood.

"If you don't get me the stone of Vadyron in a fortnight, I will take your friend. Then I will torture him slowly, until you return the stone to me." Gamori's teeth glowed unnaturally white when she smiled, and the angles of her jaw hardened again. "How does that sound?"

Blood drained from my face in a rush, and I fought not to stagger. "Fine. I'll get you the damn stone. Just leave Simon out of it."

"That would be up to you, wouldn't it?" Gamori said. "Call me when you have it, and I shall come to you."

"Where am I supposed to find Aundirne?" I asked.

"Ask your compass. I daresay it will lead you in the direction that you need, in order to save your...Simon, you said? The listener." Gamori chuckled again. "Perhaps you should have listened to him."

I blinked and she was gone, the salt circle deserted.

"I told you, you shouldn't have done it." Simon's mouth was drawn in a hard line, his eyes tempests of fury.

"It's a little too late for I told you so."

Simon kicked at the circle, sending grains of salt scattering. "I've had enough."

"Look, I'm sorry. How many times do I have to apologize? There's nothing we can do now but find the stone. Everything will be okay. Gamori said it would be simple." And I was frantic to believe that was true.

"You believe that demon? Just because you've leeched from their kind doesn't mean you understand them."

I stilled, and my head began to pound. "I'm siphoning from them so that I don't have to suck the life from living things. You know that. Demons have so much power—so much more than an animal. I'm barely taking a drop." A lie. I was taking so much more, needed more to sustain me. I'd tried backing off a few worlds ago. But the headaches, the feeling like fire consuming my bones, was too much to bear.

"Keep telling yourself that," Simon returned.

"You don't know what it's like." My voice cracked, and I slowed, taking a breath. Not only was I exhausted from running and hiding, moving to a new world every other day, but I was hardly sleeping—maybe only an hour a night. My dreams had begun to change.

They were torturous, even more so than my nightmares. Because while I was in the prison world, I knew what was going to happen, the steps choreographed like I'd been dancing them my whole life. The agony of that final moment with Alex, the hope of a better world shattered like a rock through a windowpane.

But in these new dreams, I was remembering some of the best moments of my existence. Nights in Canhaben spent with Alex's touch bringing me to life, laughing with Sage and getting stronger with Fern. Reading grimoires and learning about the fascinating world of magic that had changed my life. Coffee dates with Bri, who was the best part of my old world and the person I missed the most other than Alex.

I was filled with so much regret. The dreams made me ache with pleasure and pain, and above all, love—which cut the deepest. And I didn't know how much more I could take, but I had to carry on. Misery had finally consumed me, boring into my marrow until I was nothing but a gaping, infected wound. The only thing that made it better for a while was demon magic.

Simon no longer looked at me; he couldn't see any of it at all. He'd turned his back on me, just like he promised he wouldn't. He was a liar, but so was I.

"Why are you still here?" I asked.

"Beats me," Simon answered, folding his arms over his chest. "I'm sick to death of watching you become some kind of torturer."

"Then go. If I disgust you so much, you can leave. I'm fine on my own."

"I will. Soon as we get that stone. I don't trust you to finish the job. Likely you'd just ignore it like you do everything else."

I wanted to say, *I would never. Not when it comes to you.* Instead, I turned my back on Simon and walked into the forest. My power felt oily and thick, a coiled serpent ready to strike. "I'll find somewhere else to sleep tonight."

———

The night passed, cold and empty. I felt outside of myself, which was better than touching the sickness that had grown inside me like a cancer. How had I ended up here? Bereft and hating myself. I tossed and turned on the bed of damp pine needles, unable to sleep. Then I realized it was because the night was too quiet; I had grown used to falling asleep to the sound of Simon's breathing next to me.

Furiously, I rose, deciding that I would wander the forest until first light. There was no chance of getting any rest until we'd found the stone, anyway, not with the threat of harm looming over Simon.

Wrapping my arms around the vacant cavity in my chest, I stumbled around the seemingly prehistoric forest. The loamy ground felt like it was much older than anything in my own world. I saw no animals or creatures who made their home here, but that wasn't surprising. Ever since I'd begun siphoning from demons, the living avoided me. Apparently, I was repugnant to everyone, not just Simon. So I walked on in a vacuum of my own making.

The night was the inky black of the witching hour when I sensed it —that draw of darkness that stirred feelings I didn't have names for, and whipped them into a wild frenzy. I ran through the wide gaps between trees until I came to the edge of the world.

The familiar void stretched in front of me, the same as it had been in most places we'd traveled through. The wind grabbed my hair and tossed it about, tugging at my clothes. I shivered, affected more by the cold with the weight I'd dropped.

Sometimes I thought I could feel the worlds that had already died when I used the compass. When I brushed my fingers through the air to open a gateway, I sensed their ghosts, fading into nothingness.

It was strange how this world with its ancient vitality could feel so alive, while the very thing that was killing it was right in front of me. I stepped up to the chasm of paradox, my sense of self-preservation long gone.

The thoughts that I'd been trying to keep at bay tore into me like the howling wind. What if I couldn't do it? What if it was already over? What if this whole thing had been a pointless mire of suffering that could have been avoided? Why had I dragged Simon along with me to his ruin?

What if...what if I jumped?

I wondered what the void would feel like, that paradox of everything and nothing all at the same time. Would it be painless? Or would it be like jumping into a black hole, my body compressing and stretching until my bones snapped and my organs turned into pulp?

Simon can't find the stone without you, a voice in my head reminded me. *You can't leave him alone. Not yet.*

I backed away from the edge, resisting its siren song, then sprinted away as fast as my weakened muscles would carry me. I raced the rising sun back to camp, wondering exactly how many hours I'd lost to the void. It had seemed like only a moment, but time had been distorted lately. Like every movement would either take a year or a second, and I never knew which.

Simon was packing up the tent when I arrived back at camp. His head snapped up, then he quickly averted his gaze. His mouth was pinched, like he wanted to say something. But he didn't, and when the tent was folded and strapped to his pack, he finally turned to me.

"Are you ready?" I asked stiffly. I hauled my pack over my shoulder, ignoring the clenching fist of hunger in my stomach.

"Aye," Simon said. "Seph—"

"We'll have to work out a plan once we get there," I cut in, not strong enough to take any more criticism. "I won't talk to you more than necessary."

Simon looked stumped for a moment, then nodded. "Fine. Good."

"Great," I said, rounding off the horrific parody of pleasantries.

The corner of Simon's mouth began to pull up before he deepened his frown. "Let's get on with it, then." He led the way back to the tree graveyard, and once we arrived, I pulled the compass out of my bag.

I brought my desire to the forefront of my mind, hoping the compass would listen. *We need to go to Aundirne. I need to keep Simon safe.*

The needle began to whir, then slowed and pointed due south. I turned around and felt through the air, grabbing the fabric of the world and tearing it open.

15

I always felt more human when we rejoined civilization after weeks of hiding in the wilderness. Aundirne seemed to have the opposite effect.

We arrived inside the city gates in a cemetery that was the embodiment of Bedlam. Headstones were vine-choked and crowded together like rows of cracked teeth. The ground dipped and buckled so that coffins speared out of the ground like weeds. Some were missing their lids, and the yellowed bones of the disturbed dead were laid bare.

Simon and I took off through cramped and twisted streets, covering our noses with our sleeves; the air was thick with the smell of smoke and something sour. Buildings that rose several stories above the muddy streets were sooty and stained, and I noticed something peculiar about them.

"Simon," I said, nudging him. "What are those?" I inclined my head toward the graffiti that marked every building. It was the same symbol, a white infinity sign that was pointed at the ends and had a circle inside each loop.

He stopped and squinted at them, then after a moment drew in a harsh breath. "I think...well, they look like eyes, don't they?"

Apprehension rippled down my spine. I couldn't unsee the stark, unblinking outline of the eyes that watched our every move as we dodged trash and wastewater being tossed from upper windows of over-crowded houses.

Most everyone we passed was dressed in gray rags—whether that was by design or due to the smoke—and carried the marks of destitution in their haggard faces. But there were children playing in the street, hiding behind mounds of rubbish, their laughs and screams of delight cutting through the nightmarish mood.

I pointed up the hill toward houses that hadn't been stained by smog. "I think we should head up there," I said thickly, trying not to inhale the polluted air. Simon nodded his agreement, also not daring to waste precious breath on speaking.

The road was steep and marked with potholes and cracks, but improved after the homes began to space out. We stopped a little over halfway up, both panting.

"Gods, that was horrible," Simon said, sounding like his old self.

"Those poor people. How can they live like that?" I asked. Even though we were back in clean air, I still felt like a layer of ash coated my lungs.

"Because they don't have any other choice," he said shortly, eyes shuttering again. "Worlds like this haven't even invented the word equality yet. You're born poor, and you die poor. Don't judge them. They're living in the only way they're allowed, and making the best of it."

I ducked my head, reprimanded.

We traveled on until we saw a sign for a public house off the road. We entered to find a young man with tight curls wiping down a table with a rag. He didn't look up as he began to speak.

"Welcome to the White Iris. It's a bit early for the evening meal, but the cook might be able to rustle you up a loaf of bread and some cheese." He still had the soft jaw of adolescence, and was more of a boy, really.

"Smashing," Simon said, and started forward eagerly.

The boy finally looked up. His mouth fell open and he dropped his rag, taking a step back. "O–oh, well. Actually, er, I just remembered. We're all out."

Simon looked askance at the boy, then I looked at Simon. It didn't register when we were in the slum, but I realized just how frightful we must seem. Compared to this shiny-cheeked teenager, we were like wraiths: both thin and dirty, our hair long and unkempt. And, just as I had predicted, our clothes hadn't stood up to the hardships of travel. I gave my shirt a subtle sniff and almost recoiled. Not only did we have the reek of garbage on us from the city, but weeks of accumulated sweat and body odor.

"It's all right," I said, raising a quelling hand. "We're not usually like this, I promise."

The boy blanched. "Downdwellers are not allowed in Updweller establishments. It's the law." He sounded like he was reciting something from a book, or at least a mantra that had been drummed into him.

"Okay," I soothed. "We're not Downdwellers." The look on the boy's face clearly said that he didn't believe me. "I'm Steph, and this is Sam. We just need a place to stay for a few days."

"I could be arrested," the boy said, shaking his head. "No, you must go back to the Downdwelling. I should've never allowed you in."

"Please, just listen," I protested.

The boy approached us, holding the rag aloft like a weapon. "I don't want any trouble. There's not much that's valuable here, anyway. Go on, shoo!" He swatted at us as if we were mice that had broken into the pantry. I jogged out, with Simon hot on my heels. The door slammed behind us, and I heard the decisive click of a lock.

"It's off to a great start, then," Simon grumbled, rubbing his stomach. "I suppose it's back to the *Downdwellers*."

From our vantage point, the whole of the Downdwelling was visible. It was a stain spreading out from an ink-black lake whose shores abutted the city. Near one end of the lake was a sort of fortress that was half sunk into the water, its black stone covered with pale green slime. There was a tower on one end with a raised platform that jutted toward the center of the lake, with an enormous fire burning in a beacon tower. Hugging the fortress from the other side was a dense forest. Behind us a sleek white building curved in a semicircle, perched on top of the hill like a bird poised to take flight. The city resembled a piece of half-charred wood—part whole, and part burned.

"I wonder what that's for," I said, nodding to the fortress.

"Nothing good, I'm sure," Simon said darkly.

Goosebumps spread over my arms, and I repressed a shudder. I had to agree with him. The lake gave me a sinister feeling, all that stagnant black water with garbage floating on its surface like flies trapped in honey. Even the pristine building on the hill seemed off—it was too quiet. My throat closed, and I could almost imagine I was choking on the great plume of oily, black smoke from the beacon fire.

"Maybe we should go camp in the forest," I offered. "It's bound to be more comfortable than the Downdwelling."

"Can't argue with you there," he muttered. "But I'm bloody starving. The sooner we get the stone and leave, the better."

"Food first, then."

We headed back down the hill, my heart sinking further with each step. There was no real way to keep the smell at bay, so I gave in and breathed normally, turning to my thoughts for distraction. At least Simon seemed to be on speaking terms with me again. Our tenuous alliance was worth the difficulties we faced, even if it was only temporary. And, he was right—the sooner this was done, the sooner I could get back to my search. The thought of parting ways with Simon was unthinkable, but guilt and desire to find Alex drove me further.

The pub's stained sign that read *Dreya's* was hanging on by one rusted chain. It seemed like the next stiff breeze would send it crashing to the wet cobblestones below. I pushed the door open on creaking hinges. A woman was on her hands and knees by the fireplace, scooping ash into a bucket. She didn't look up as we entered. "Special's mutton," she said, her voice gravelly. "Two?"

"Erm—yeah," Simon replied, looking nervously around the dank space. "Lovely."

The woman stood, wiping her hands on a soiled apron. Gray streaked her hair, though her face was only gently lined. One of her eyeteeth was missing. "Coming right up."

We sat down, and she returned in short order with two plates containing grayish lumps of meat. The plates clattered on the table. She stood back, hands on hips.

I stared at the mutton. Maybe it was the special because it went bad three weeks ago. Simon gamely picked up his fork and took a bite. "Mm," he said, compressing his lips against what I was certain was a gag. "Delicious."

Putting my fork down, I scooted away from the table. "Is there anywhere I could wash?"

The woman shook her head. "We don't drink the water or use it for washing. But I've got some milk set aside in the back. It'll cost you extra."

"Um, that's okay. Thank you, though," I said, trying not to cringe.

"Suit yourself." She left us, disappearing behind the bar.

Simon leaned over his plate, spitting out the bite he'd taken before pushing it away. "Gods, that was bloody awful. Even I'm not hungry enough to eat this slop," he said quietly, casting a glance over his shoulder.

"Should we ask her about the stone?" I hissed. The room was too quiet, and it seemed like every word I spoke was magnified a thousand times.

Simon shook his head. "Better to find somewhere more crowded. And with drunk people."

I tilted my head. "Why drunk?"

"Easier to confuse if we've got to scarper," he mumbled, just as the woman came back around the bar. Her gaze was far too scrutinizing for my liking.

We traded her the last of our cotton fabric for the meal, and she ran her fingers over the soft material like it was silk. "A word of advice," she said, not taking her eyes off the fabric. "You're clearly not from around here. Make sure you're safe indoors before nightfall. You look like nice folks."

"What happens after nightfall?" I asked. Gooseflesh appeared on my arms.

"Nothing good, love." She turned without another word, and a moment later a door slammed.

"The sun is about to set," I said, picking the skin around my thumb. "Maybe we should wait."

"No way." Simon stood, hooking his pack over his shoulder. "We need to get that stone, then get the fuck out of here. Besides, what are you afraid of? You've got the power of demons inside of you. *You're* the scariest thing in the dark."

There was silence for the space of two heartbeats as my insides caved in, then I cleared my throat. "Right. No problem." Shouldering my own pack, I followed him outside.

The last rays of sunlight coated the Downdwelling in a hazy glow, casting long shadows over the already dark pall of the city. The beacon fire atop the fortress was still visible, an orange smear amidst the black. Maybe that's why they seemed to keep it lit at all hours.

It was cold, and I pulled my hood low both for warmth and anonymity. Fires flared in braziers, with people huddled around them like moths flocking to a lantern. The light they gave off reflected in puddles and created the effect that the ground was aflame. It was almost like we were walking through hell.

My brain was telling me that there was something unusual about the gloom, and I realized it was splotches color. Men and women in long, purple robes with shaved heads and eyebrows walked the streets. Patrolling might have been a better word for it, given their vigilant expressions.

We found a tavern not far from Dreya's. A smoke-stained sign swung drunkenly, though there was no wind. It didn't have any words, just an illustration of a man pouring a drink into his mouth. One of the eye infinity signs was graffitied over it.

I pressed into the shadows of the building as a purple-robed figure passed us. The man held a brutal chain that swung with the motion of his steps. "Let's start here," I muttered. More importantly, I wanted to get off the streets.

Inside was almost as dark as outside, and held the pungent odor of sour milk. Conversation died and heads turned from all corners of the room to peer at us as we entered. I wished my hood obscured more of my face, and tugged it down again. It wasn't out of character with the place, as almost everyone was hooded.

We took seats at a wooden bar that had about an inch of grime on it, and the low murmur of conversation picked up again. The barman ignored us, wiping a glass with a stained rag. Simon rapped a knuckle on the bar, and he sidled over.

"Can I get for you?" the barman said. He was soft-spoken, which contrasted starkly with his appearance. My heart jolted when I saw that his otherwise symmetrical features were marred by a crescent scar running from the corner of his mouth to his eye. The skin was puckered and purple, pulling his lips into a half-grin.

"Erm—the usual," Simon said, trying to sound confident and failing. His gaze flitted between crates filled with brown bottles that were stacked to the ceiling and the barman's scar. I had a feeling that Simon was regretting his foolhardiness in coming out after dark.

The man flicked shaggy black hair out of his face and poured the contents of a brown bottle into two short glasses. The liquid was white, but seemed thicker than milk. Simon and I exchanged dubious glances. The barman stared at us until we picked up our glasses and sipped tentatively.

It tasted like sour, rotten yogurt, and had to be responsible for the smell in the tavern. I choked on the drink, forcing myself to swallow it down even as I gagged. Simon hadn't fared any better than me, and was cycling through several shades of green.

"Sweet Asael, what *is* this?" Simon spluttered.

The man tilted his head, peering at us through narrowed eyes that were more gold than brown. "Fermented grunea milk." He crossed his arms, leaning his elbows on the bar. "You're not from Aundirne, are you."

"How could you tell?" I muttered dryly, still feeling nauseous from the dregs of fermented milk coating my tongue.

"The Downdwelling doesn't get visitors," the barman said. "Unless you two are priests, which I highly doubt."

"Us? Oh, no. Not at all," Simon said in a rush. "We're, ah—visiting family."

"Our Aunt Dreya," I added swiftly. "She owns a pub."

"A pub," the man repeated. His golden eyes flicked between me and Simon, and for a moment I could've sworn that something sparked in them. Something that wasn't entirely human.

"Yes," I said, daring him to contradict me. My power raised its head, scenting the air for a threat. I quashed it back down; I didn't need an outburst when we were trying to stay inconspicuous. "A pub."

Perhaps the barman saw the faint glow that emanated from my skin, or maybe he was just bored. He straightened and nodded, picking up another glass and wiping it with the same stained rag, then moved down the bar. "Enjoy."

The relieved slump of Simon's shoulders matched my own, but just then, someone else appeared next to me.

"'Ello, love." A wave of unwashed flesh and fermented milk floated over me. I turned slowly to see who was assaulting my nostrils.

The woman's hair must have been fiery red once, but was now faded to a grayish orange. Grooves were dug into her forehead and bracketed her full mouth. The shadow of the woman's former beauty still lingered in her light green eyes and high cheekbones. She smiled, revealing blackened stumps of teeth.

"Hi," I said thickly, holding my breath.

"I seen you come in from across the way." She jerked her head toward the corner of the tavern, where two other women sat nursing glasses of fermented grunea milk. "I'm Cilla. And who might you be?"

"Stephanie," I said, pressing my knee into Simon's thigh.

"Funny name," Cilla remarked, crossing her legs on the stool. The movement made her cloak fall open, which revealed an ocean of cleavage. "And your friend?"

"Sam," Simon answered gruffly.

"Steph'nie and Sam," Cilla said, rolling our fake names around on her tongue like they were a fine wine. "Well, it's a pleasure to meet you."

"Likewise," Simon said, as he was farther from Cilla's halitosis. "What do you, eh...do, Cilla?" If this was how he picked up women, it was no wonder Simon was single. I barely restrained myself from an eye roll.

She laughed, low and raspy, and the barman plunked a glass on the bar harder than necessary. "Oh, you know. A little o' this, a little o' that. You know, Steph'nie, you've got lovely skin. Just be-yoo-tiful."

I drew back a fraction as a frisson of unease ran through me. "Oh... thank you?"

"I was thinking to meself, how does a soul get such smooth, shining skin? Tell me your secrets, girlie."

"Leave them be, Cilla," the barman called. He was moving wooden crates between stacks.

"Oh, come on, Fane," Cilla said, licking her lips. "Don't ruin my fun."

"No, it's fine." I gave Cilla the most dazzling smile I could manage, which was to say, not at all dazzling. This was my chance to steer the conversation. "I use a special blend of herbs in my washing wat—er, milk. I'll give you some."

I almost regretted it, because Cilla smiled broadly and more of her ripe fragrance wafted over me. "Tha's a girl, I knew you was a kind soul. We Downdwellers don't have much, but we have each other."

It was a surprisingly sweet sentiment, and I softened toward Cilla. "Of course."

"They're not Downdwellers," Fane murmured, too low for human ears.

I ignored him and leaned toward Cilla, effectively blocking him out. "So, Cilla. Tell me all about Aundirne. We're only visiting here for a week, and I'm just so curious about...well, *everything*." I smiled again.

"I lived here all me life, so I know more 'bout this place than a priest does 'bout the Watching God." Then her eyes turned sly. "But I could get thirsty during the telling."

"Fane, a drink for my friend," I said. It may have been my imagination that Fane huffed while he poured Cilla's drink and slid it down the bar to her. She caught it with a practiced hand and took a long draft, smacking her lips.

"Ah, tha's nice. So, my darlings, what can ol' Cilla tell you?"

"Well." I lowered my voice conspiratorially, then looked past Cilla's shoulder at Simon before bringing my attention back to her. He was all the reminder I needed of what was at stake. "I've heard some things about a certain stone."

Cilla's already pale face drained of all color, and she shoved back from the bar. Through the buzzing of panic in my skull, I heard the room quiet again.

"What're you playing at?" she whispered through clenched teeth. Then, with her eyes wheeling, she ran out of the bar, ragged cloak swirling behind her.

Simon's eyes were wide with shock and something else, something that I felt the twin of in my own chest. Others in the bar began to talk again, and a dull roar of muttered accusations and chatter ricocheted around the room.

"You look like strong folk," Fane said, tapping the bar to get our attention. "Help me move these crates." We both stared at him, dumbfounded, until he said under his breath, "If you don't want to be murdered by a mob or arrested, get your asses behind the bar, now."

We scrambled up and accepted the crates Fane thrust into our arms. "Follow me," he ordered, and led us through a back room that was lined with wooden casks, then through another door. Fane stopped when we were in an alley, and dropped his own crate into the mud. Then he removed a rolled paper from an inner pocket and lit it, inhaling deeply. The smoke curled around our three silhouettes, binding us together for the moment.

"I suppose your idiocy is understandable, given you're not from around here," Fane said, blowing a stream of smoke through his nostrils. "But the priests won't care about that if they find out. They'll nail your corpse to a wall and stick your head on a pike faster than you can blink."

Power hovered over my skin, ready to fight, but I gritted my teeth and reigned it in. "Who are these priests? And why did Cilla run off when I asked her about the stone?"

"Keep your fucking voice down," Fane said mildly. He looked over his shoulder, then turned back to us. "The priests run this city. They worship at the temple of the Watching God on top of the hill. And to answer your question, anyone would have reacted the same way. Perhaps not as extreme as Cilla, but she has reason to fear the priests."

"Why?" Simon asked. Nervous energy was coming off of him in waves, and I clamped down further on my power that wanted to bolt like a spooked horse.

"Cilla trades in sex, which is punishable by disfigurement or death, even in the Downdwelling. I don't tell the priests as long as she doesn't make trouble in my bar, but she wouldn't want to do anything that calls attention to herself," Fane said. "So she won't tell the priests that you asked, and neither will I."

It figured that I had managed to ask the worst possible person for information. "Why wouldn't you tell?"

Fane's golden eyes seemed to glow in the darkness. "That would be none of your business. You have no reason to trust me, but I won't say anything all the same."

You can kill him where he stands, my power cooed. *Then he'll never talk again.* "I need the information enough that it doesn't matter if we're arrested or killed, because we'll be dead anyway if we don't find that stone."

The cigarette paused halfway to Fane's lips. "Interesting. So, you want me to tell you about the stone of Vadyron."

"Aye," Simon said. "Like Seph—Stephanie said, it's a matter of life and death."

"Then you're dead," Fane replied, flicking ash onto the ground. "But that means it's no concern if I give you the information anyway." He took a deep drag, blowing smoke from his nose. "Vadyron was a mage who ruled Aundirne for centuries in ancient times. He made bargains with spirits of the shadow worlds to maintain his unnaturally long life, so that he could stay in power. And he was a paranoid bastard. Long story short, he decided to place all the power he'd amassed inside a stone for protection—so his enemies couldn't get at it, even if he was attacked. It's said the stone was once a star, plucked from the heavens."

Fane smoked silently for a moment, then resumed his story. "All was well and good, for Vadyron at least, until the followers of the Watching God came to Aundirne. Power changed hands, as power does. All magic was wiped out after that, and any caught doing it were killed on the spot. The priests of the Watching God keep the stone under strict guard at Festborg Fortress, on the other side of the lake. It's sacrilegious in the extreme to discuss the stone at all, but more than that, it's treason punishable by death."

Simon cursed in a low voice, then turned to me. "What have you done, Seph."

"We've been up against worse odds," I said with false bravado. *Do not let the fear take you, because if you do, you'll die.*

"Wait," Fane said, staring at me. Then he started laughing in disbelief. "Do you think you can, what, steal it?"

"That would be none of your business," I replied. "But thanks for the information."

"Come to the square tomorrow at midday," Fane said. He tossed the cigarette to the ground, crushing it under his heel. "Then you'll see what you're up against."

16

The central square in the Downdwelling teemed with people. They were all acting as though Christmas had come early, or perhaps that their water had suddenly turned potable. The air of celebration, coupled with the blood-stained block that was centered atop a wide stage, made nausea churn in my gut. That, plus the heavy scent of unwashed bodies.

Fane was easy to pick out as he stood head and shoulders above the crowd. He saw Simon and I coming, and inclined his head. "Glad you could make it."

"It seems like every Downdweller in the city is here," I replied, dodging a sharp elbow from the milling crowd.

"Just about," Fane murmured, ducking his head toward us. "The priests will make sure of it, anyway. The combination of fear and frivolity works wonders when you're subjugating the masses."

"Why don't the Updwellers come, too?" Simon asked, gazing at the shining purity of the city that climbed the hill like stepping stones before the white, crescent-shaped temple.

Fane gave a wry smile, but his scar turned it into more of a grimace. "You really have to ask that?"

"Point taken," Simon muttered.

"These priests," I said. "What exactly are they in charge of?"

"Apart from being both judge and executioner? Everything. They're religion and the law and the hand that feeds us. Look, now, it's starting."

The bald, purple-robed priests filed onto the stage, along with a black-hooded executioner and his ax. The curved blade glinted dully underneath rusty brown spatter. Two more priests joined, holding a young woman between them. Long, dark hair blew around a heart-shaped face. She was dull-eyed and had about as much life in her as the bones in the cemetery.

This woman...she bore more than a passing resemblance to Bri, but her skin was far too pale. Simon didn't shrug me off when I felt for his arm and held on.

A priest wearing white robes approached the front of the stage, and the crowd quieted, their attention rapt on the bald man. A thick golden chain bearing the infinity eye symbol hung around his waist.

"People of the Downdwelling! May the Eyes bless you," the priest with the golden belt called, raising his arms to encompass the crowd. His voice warbled like an out of tune instrument. "The priests' quorum has passed judgment on the accused that stands before you today."

The crowd roared, and the priest basked in their approbation. He gestured to the woman being held at the side of the stage. The Downdwellers shouted abuse, but she gave no sign that she could hear any of it. I noted with horror that her bound hands were completely engulfed in iron mittens.

"That's the high priest in the white robes," Fane muttered, bending to reach my ear. "Olker Geist."

Geist spoke again, and I could tell by his wide grin that he loved having command of the crowd. My stomach gave an ugly twist. "This woman is guilty of using magic inside our city gates. She cast curses on her neighbor, but was turned in by the faithful of this city." Then Geist's voice turned paternal, almost loving. "It is you, the steadfast flock of the Watching God, who will be rewarded in eternity for your good deeds. But the Watching God does not ignore your earthly needs; no, his benevolence is *mighty*. He has commanded me, his worldly vessel, to provide extra rations for all of the Downdwelling tomorrow!"

The high priest was triumphant, a god himself with the praise and shouts and applause of the penurious crowd. Sick bastard. I looked at

Simon and saw everything I felt reflected in his storm cloud eyes: disgust, rage, and helplessness.

But I, of all people, wasn't helpless. My stolen power had woken the moment we joined the crowd in the square and I'd seen the executioner's bloody block on the stage. After listening to that speech it felt molten, nuclear, hotter than the sun and twice as large. It frothed and sloshed and rushed like a flash flood that was going to sweep me away at any moment, and I was powerless to stop it.

Simon knew. He grabbed my hand and squeezed hard enough to make me yelp. "Seph, don't," he warned. "I hate it too, but *do not do anything.*"

Fane's golden eyes flicked to us with mild interest, as though he was watching a play. I supposed it was, in a way; there was the stage, with the priest as the star of the show and the execution the supporting actor. Because Fane was right. All of this was a sick bit of theater, performed so that the Downdwellers remained complicit in their own oppression.

The hooded executioner stepped up to the bloodstained block as the priests holding the woman forced her to kneel before it. The crowd roared.

No. I couldn't accept this. But I also couldn't endanger Simon or Fane by doing anything about it. I was torn, turmoil stretching me like I was on a torturer's rack. I felt myself coming apart at the seams and knew that I'd lost the battle of wills. Simon was right. The demons' power was too strong for me.

Blue sparks flew from my fingers, and an acrid burning filled the air the moment I lost control. Panic burst from every orifice, and I turned and pushed my way through the crowd, running from Simon and Fane. I didn't want them to be tainted with the brush of my magic. If the priests thought a woman cursing her neighbor was bad, they were going to be blown away by what was about to happen. Perhaps literally.

People shouted and called curses after me as I jostled them in my attempts to break through the throng. Their faces all blurred together. I felt hotter than lava, sweat pouring down my back in rivulets with the effort of holding everything in. The clear space beyond the edge of the crowd was in sight, but I wasn't nearly close enough. I closed my eyes as electricity jolted through my bones, jerking me like a marionette on the end of a puppeteer's string.

Angry voices buzzed in my ears, but one rose above the cacophony. "What's she doing? Oy, girl!"

Unseeing, I turned rigid as fire overtook me, racing along my skin and transforming me into a living column of flame. The voices of a dozen demons shrieked at me to burn the entire place to the ground, to slash and kill and corrupt until there was nothing left but ashes and the echo of screams.

I wanted it. In that moment, I became everything Simon dreaded. Dark, triumphant power spilled from me, vicious and powerful and violent, a fucking supernova of disaster aimed straight for the priests who executed the supernatural because they feared us.

Well, I'd make those fuckers afraid and drink their terror like wine.

When robes of purple emerged from the sea of gray and black, I lunged at them, a tiger going after her prey. Power consumed me, and as I wielded it amongst the blur of screams and pain and flames, I knew it was *right*, this ruinous justice.

The onslaught only stopped when I reached for power and found nothing. The magic had burned out like the embers of a dying fire, the fine powder of ash coating my tongue.

I came to, gasping for air, standing in the center of a burned-out circle. Scorch lines radiated from me like the spokes of a wheel. The bodies of priests were on the ground at my feet, their faces slack and eyes open but unseeing. Their bald heads and utter stillness made them look like sleeping infants.

I'd killed them. The knowledge of it dug deep into my bones even while I tried to shrink away from it. The square had been deserted, but people began to filter back in when it became clear that my murderous rampage was over. They circled me, then struck up a chant.

"Witch! Murderer! Kill the witch! Kill the witch!"

The remaining priests had naked fear on their faces, but they edged closer to me, poised to take flight at any sign of movement. The part of me that had short-circuited felt nothing, but the other, lucid part wondered how the hell I was going to get out of this. I'd had so many close saves that escape had become routine, but I couldn't see any options. I was surrounded on all sides and had nothing left to give.

I searched for Simon's face in the crowd, hoping that he'd stayed far away from me. Maybe he'd still have a chance to get Vadyron's stone. He was smart and capable, and as long as he didn't get caught in my calamitous net, he should be okay.

So, of course, when the priests rushed me, Simon shot out of the crowd. The priests were on him instantly.

"No!" I yelled, but found that my throat was bone dry, so it came out as a harsh whisper. I yanked on purple robes and pulled priests off of Simon, landing a few well-placed punches and kicks. Whenever I touched bare skin, I siphoned drops of power. But I was so exhausted, and my muscles were heavy and sore. I felt like I was moving underwater.

Simon and I ended up back-to-back in the middle of a circle of priests who had violet bruises blooming on their faces to match their robes. I reached behind me and found his hand.

"I'm so sorry," I said, and my voice hitched on a sob. This might be my last chance to tell him. "You were right all along. Why didn't you leave me?"

"I could never," Simon said, squeezing my hand. "I was a right fool, wasn't I? And Fane told me—"

He was interrupted by the high priest Olker Geist. The golden chain belted around his waist clinked as he walked toward me and Simon. The other priests parted, then flanked him.

Geist was nearing old age. His face was creased around the eyes and forehead, but had an energy that made him seem like a younger man. Although, his shaved head and eyebrows gave him an unfortunate resemblance to a hard-boiled egg.

The head priest wet his lips. "More witches in our city, revealed to us by the all-seeing Eyes of the Watching God!" He reached around his waist and unbuckled the golden chain. It clanked loudly, the crowd having gone silent as soon as the priest spoke. "You will pay for your crimes at the hands of the God, you and all of the traitorous magic wielders in this city who seek to usurp Him."

The priest swung the chain over his head, turning it into a gilded blur. I grabbed Simon and backed away, but the crowd closed ranks and there was nowhere to go.

I shoved out with power, sending a jet of blue flame arcing through the air. When it hit Geist's chain, it vanished. What the hell?

Hands reached out and shoved us forward so that we were stumbling when the chain flew through the air and hobbled us like horses. We tumbled to the ground on harsh cries of pain, and the priests fell on us, punching and kicking until someone's boot connected with my head and everything went black.

———

I heard the steady *plink* of water droplets falling on stone. The ground was cold and hard along the length of my body, and there was a smell of mold and damp and something else entirely that my brain refused to acknowledge. Goosebumps dotted my arms, and when I pushed off the ground every joint and muscle screamed in protest. My head throbbed like I'd been on a three-day bender, and my tongue rasped against the roof of my mouth. Fuck, even my bones hurt, like they were bruised. I lifted my hands to probe my face, but balked as smooth metal touched my cheek.

My hands were enveloped in iron mittens up to the wrists. Immediately I shrieked and tried to tear them off, pinning the metal between my knees and yanking. My hands were curled into fists inside of them, and claustrophobia set in at my inability to spread my fingers. My chest tightened and my head buzzed, panic engulfing me in a wave as I slammed the mittens repeatedly on the ground. The din rang in my ears, and maybe I passed out again because when I came back to the room, I was lying in a heap on the ground.

This time, I didn't panic or scream. I tried to breathe through the trapped feeling and remain aware of my surroundings. I lifted an iron-mitted hand and saw that there was a long chain attached from the wrist to a ring in the wall.

The room—or cell, rather—was small and cramped. The door was a heavy metal grate that I noted with disappointment didn't appear to be rusted. I would have bet my freedom that I was in what Fane had called Festborg Fortress, at the edge of the lake. The symbol of the Watching God was drawn in chalk all over the black stone walls, countless eyes staring at me.

There was another cell across the way, and in it I made out a shadow slumped in the corner. Was it Simon? There were no windows, but light pooled in the corridor just past the door. A torch must have been burning somewhere. As if remembering the utter absence of heat, my body began to shiver and soon I was wracked with tremors, the chains rattling with every movement.

Despite my jerky gait, I made my way to the door of my cell and kicked the bars. They didn't budge. I peered past them as far as I could, which wasn't far at all. To my right I thought I saw the suggestion of a small room or alcove, but it was difficult to tell with the shifting light. It seemed that there was another torch on the other side of me. The light stopped short of illuminating my cell.

I wet my lips and tasted blood. "Simon?" I called, as loud as I dared. "Is that you?"

Silence. I kicked the bars again, and was satisfied when they clanged loudly. "Simon?" I called again. The lump in the other cell didn't move.

I needed to master myself, to stop the quivering and crying and start thinking. *Be strong and smart and stay alive.* What would Alex do if he was in this situation? Well, he wouldn't have been in this situation in the first place. No, that line of thought wasn't helpful.

I still had my supernatural senses and strength. They'd fallen by the wayside because I hadn't needed to use them since I'd been siphoning from demons, but they were still there. I knew how to fight, even though at the moment I felt as weak as a newborn kitten. It would have to be enough.

A click like nails on stone had me reaching for siphoned power. I hit an impenetrable wall, thudding against it as my head reverberated with an ache. I reached again, more gently this time, seeking a way around the wall. It wouldn't budge, and nausea echoed through me as I pushed harder.

Then, a large shadow plodded into view. I relaxed my clenched muscles when I realized what it was.

A sweet, sad looking hound stopped in front of my cell and sat close enough for me to reach out and touch him. I would have, if my hands hadn't been bound. The dog was large, his head as high as my waist, and his ears were long and floppy. His head drooped beneath the weight of a vicious iron collar. Was he some sort of guard dog? He didn't look very ferocious. I crouched in front of the bars and poked my nose out.

"Hi, buddy," I whispered. "What are you doing down here?" The hound didn't answer me, of course, but he licked my nose. Despite myself, I smiled. His fur was patchy, and he had scars crisscrossing his hide. The skin under his neck was raw and crusted. "Poor thing. What do you say we break out of here together, huh? Wouldn't that be nice?"

"Seph?" Simon's voice was faint but steady, coming from my left.

Relief coursed through me as I stood abruptly and flung myself at the bars, closest to where I'd heard his voice. The dog scampered away into the darkness past my cell.

"Simon! Are you all right?" It struck me as a ridiculous question as soon as I asked. Of course he wasn't all right; he'd been beaten and taken prisoner by a bunch of religious zealots.

He coughed. "I've felt better, I won't lie to you. But nothing's broken."

I released a sigh and leaned my forehead against the grate. The knife-sharp cold soothed my headache. "I'm so sorry. I'm going to get you out of here."

Simon coughed again, a hacking noise I didn't like the sound of. "I was trying to tell you before those maniacs jumped on us. Fane is a magic user. He said he'd try to help—then again, that was before we got thrown into this shithole."

"I knew there was something about him," I said, remembering the way his golden eyes had flickered in the tavern. "How can Fane help us?"

"Dunno. He figured the priests would take you here if they didn't kill you first. Actually, he said—" Simon stopped short, and I strained for any further sound.

"What?"

"He said we'd be better off dead than in here."

The air grew thick, and I realized it was because I'd stopped breathing. Sweat broke out on my hairline. "Why would he say that?"

"Apparently, this is where they...well. Doesn't do any good talking about it."

Fear had white hot claws around my throat. I squeezed my eyes shut and pressed my lips together in a hard line. When I could speak again, I asked, "What kind of power does Fane have?"

"He wouldn't say. He ran off as soon as you had the crowd distracted."

We didn't speak for a while, because there was nothing to say. I'd dragged Simon into this utter disaster with me, despite that being the last thing I wanted in the world. And now we were trapped inside of a seemingly impenetrable fortress by people who beheaded magic users and their associates.

A fresh frisson of panic raced through me. I said I'd get him out of here, but that was another lie. The reality was that I couldn't keep Simon safe. I couldn't even keep myself safe. And we were going to die in this dank fortress, far from everything we both loved.

Except for maybe each other.

Every horrible thing I'd said to him in these past few months ricocheted in my head. Regret was a living thing, clawing at my guts and crushing my lungs.

"Simon?" I said in a clear, loud voice. I wanted to be sure that he heard me. "When you said you knew me, after that first night we summoned Ethiel. What were you going to say?" I didn't think I could stand another second in this horrible cell with my hands encased in iron without knowing. That I could die without knowing. It was selfish of me to ask him for this. To ask what I was both hoping and dreading to hear, for a fragment of goodness that might soothe my ravaged soul.

After a long while, he answered.

"I know that you hate getting wet but love the rain. I know that you're happiest with either a good book or someone to make you laugh. I know that you love your mother, but it's difficult because you feel disappointed in her, too. I know that your heart is bigger than all the worlds combined, but you trust few with it. I know that you claim not to like people, but you're fascinated by them. And...above all, I know that your greatest ambition is to find a place where you belong, and people you belong with."

I was stunned into silence, and my nonexistent heart squeezed. Pain tangled with tenderness, or maybe they were just two words for the same thing.

"Seph? Are you still there?"

"Yes," I whispered. "Yes, I'm still here."

17

We languished in our cells for days. Or, I thought it was days. Time was difficult to keep track of when there was no daylight, and the stillness was only broken by a priest bringing moldy bread and stale water at irregular intervals.

I had to be fed, of course, given I was still chained in the iron mittens. I nearly choked as the priest—a tall, meaty man—shoved bread down my throat, then slopped water into my mouth so that half spilled down my torn shirt. My hands had long gone numb, and I would have feared they would sustain permanent damage if I thought I'd ever use them again.

Our cellmate from across the corridor also sported the iron mittens. The light didn't reach into his cell, so he was always cast in shadow. He hadn't spoken a word, even though Simon and I talked to him every once in a while. The only sounds that came from him were the clank of chains and occasional moaning while he slept.

Simon and I hadn't been idle. We spent most of our time brainstorming escape plans while wondering if Fane would come to our aid. But we were growing weaker with each passing hour, as was intended from the rations that just held starvation at bay. And I was even worse off, with the headaches and shakes and constant nausea, the cravings for demon magic clawing at me. Withdrawal might kill me before the priests of the Watching God did.

"And you're sure you can't get out of those gloves?" Simon asked. Our most recent idea was that we could overcome the priest while he fed us, then steal the keys and escape. But I didn't think I could manage it with my hands incapacitated as they were.

"I've tried," I said for the hundredth time. "But if he gets in range, I might be able to knock him out." I sat cross-legged on the ground near the crack we'd discovered in the wall between our cells. It was no thicker than a fingernail, but the sound traveled better there. Plus, the cold stone against my forehead soothed the pulsing soreness.

Simon blew out a breath. "There's no other choice. It's that, or wait for whatever Olker Geist has in store for us."

"It won't work." The silvery voice came from across the hall, from the cell with the shadowed form. I jerked my head up and saw a man standing in the corner, mittened hands resting against the metal grate. He'd spoken in English, not Aundirne's guttural tongue.

"Did you hear that?" I asked Simon, putting my lips close to the crack. It was always more difficult for him to hear me, given his lack of heightened senses.

"Hear what?"

I rose, swaying as queasiness roiled in my gut, and walked to my cell door. "Why won't it work?" I called.

Our fellow prisoner was slender and maybe slightly shorter than me. His skin was pale with yellow undertones, like he'd been sun-kissed in the outside world but had succumbed to the gloom of the prison. His hair was some indeterminable dark shade, and stuck up everywhere in spikes. But I discerned the color of his eyes even in the darkness. The irises were a bright robin's-egg blue that were ringed in navy, the most striking I'd ever seen. Other than—

"I've tried it," he said. "And tunneling through the rock, which was your idea from yesterday, I think. And using magic." He rattled the chains attached to his mittens. "They call this ferronite. It stops magic users from accessing their power, which you've obviously figured out."

By this time, Simon had heard the man and walked to his own door. "If you don't have any ideas to contribute, then you can bloody well shut your mouth," Simon growled.

"I am not trying to dissuade you, only save you time," the man answered coolly. "I estimate I've been here for a month, which is twenty-six days longer than you have."

Well, that answered one question. "How did you get caught?" I asked.

The man swiped at his long nose with his shoulder. I empathized, and would never again take for granted being able to scratch and itch at will.

"Trying to get the stone of Vadyron, of course. Isn't that what you were doing?"

A cold sensation spread through my stomach. "Why would you think that?"

"I assume that's what everyone wants. It's immensely powerful." The man scrutinized me for a long moment.

"I heard that the stone is guarded here, in Festborg Fortress." I was too exhausted to attempt finesse.

"Oh, did you? It seems your source is out of date. The stone is with the high priest, in that gaudy belt of his. The fraudulent fuck uses its power but says it comes from the Watching God. Idiots, all of them. I doubt there ever was a real god to begin with."

It was as though I'd been struck by lightning, every nerve in my body tingling. We had been so close to the stone while in the square. So close, and we hadn't even known.

"How do you know that?"

"Maybe the question you should be asking is, how didn't you?"

My silence was answer enough.

"What's your name?" the man asked.

"Seph. And this is Simon." Stephanie and Sam had gone out the window with the rest of my sense. I was still reeling from the fact we'd been within inches of the stone before I'd gotten us thrown into this hellhole. "And yours?"

"Alder. I would say pleased to meet you, but given the circumstances, I assume we would all rather not have met in the first place."

Simon huffed. "You're not wrong."

"You must have a sense of their weaknesses by now if you've been here for a month," I said to Alder.

"Weaknesses? Sure. The priests are as fallible as any mortals. They're not stronger than us, except that they're drugging the water to make us weak."

"How'd you know?" Simon asked.

"I can smell it. But I also don't want to die of thirst, so I drink it anyway. We're under several floors of stone blocks that are each thicker than three men, inside a fortress that's crawling with priests of the Watching God. Below us is a fetid lake that would probably melt the skin right off your bones. I haven't been able to figure out how to get these mitts off without cutting off my hands, and I'm not keen on that, either."

We all stiffened as footsteps rang down the hall, but I relaxed when the hound came around the corner. He'd made a habit of visiting me, and would lay on the ground placidly while I chatted to him about the sun and green things and everything else I didn't want to forget about before I died in the darkness.

"Hi, buddy," I cooed, and he flopped on the ground in front of me. I poked my nose through the bars, and he raised his head with a clink of iron collar against stone and licked me in greeting. His long ears were puddles on the floor.

"That dog likes you," Alder stated. "He's never hung around me before."

The hound laid his head back down. "I don't know how anyone could hurt him. He's just a defenseless animal." Burning anger exploded in my chest, but it had nowhere to go. If I'd had access to my power, I would have branded anyone who had a hand in it. And maybe cut off their balls for good measure. "You're a good boy, Folly." The dog gave a single wag of his tail.

"Folly?" Simon said. "Why Folly?"

"Because he doesn't belong here. He's no one's pet, but he doesn't seem to be much of a guard dog, either."

Alder shook his head. "The dog—er, Folly—was here when they imprisoned me. He does seem out of place, I'll admit."

"Can you help us, Folly? Want to break us out of here?" I asked.

To my surprise, Folly got to his feet and came close to the grate, staring straight at me. His eyes were a warm amber. There was something behind them that was intelligent beyond a regular animal.

"What is it?" The dog scratched at the bars of my cell and whined, then turned toward the door at the end of the hall where the priest always came from.

"Where are you going?" I called.

He loosed another whine, returning to my cell and pawing at the grate. Human footsteps thumped down the hall. The dog turned and ran, but shot me another look before he disappeared.

I backed away from the grate and stood in the corner so that the wet stone wall was at my back. Alder did the same, and we stared at each other through the bars while the priest approached.

The clink of metal on metal made me fear that Olker Geist had returned with his golden chain, but it wasn't him. The same tall priest that always came to feed us stopped in front of my cell, but it was too early for a meal. He selected a key from the ring hanging at his waist and inserted it into the lock at the very top of the cell. The door swung open, and I pressed into the corner, ignoring the seep of damp through my clothes.

The priest approached, holding a bundle of white cloth. He reached for me and I lashed out with my mitted hand. He grunted when I grazed his shoulder, then shoved me back into the wall. My head struck stone, and I saw stars.

"Seph!" Simon yelled. "Don't touch her, you bastard."

The priest unsheathed a short blade from the folds of his purple robe and held it against my throat. "Don't move, or I will slit you from nose to navel."

My heart skipped wildly beneath my ribs as I tried to keep my balance and catch my breath. I nodded, the blade scraping my skin lightly, while wondering if I should just let him do it. If whatever was to come was worse than being mutilated. Over the priest's shoulder, I watched Alder study his feet.

Holding one hand to my throat, the priest sliced my already shredded clothes with the dagger. He made me lift my legs when he pulled my pants off, and then I stood naked before him, shaking with shame and humiliation and sickness. His lip curled in disgust, and the man looked at me like I was nothing more than an animal—a rabid, diseased one.

The priest unfurled the white bundle and yanked it roughly over my head. The dress was designed to lace up each side so they didn't have to remove the iron mittens to jam my arms through its sleeves. Waves of repulsion made my stomach cramp as his thick fingers brushed my skin, tightening the laces. When he was done, he spun me around, slamming my front against the slimy stone wall.

"Face the wall until I leave," the priest commanded. The door squeaked on its hinges, then the lock snicked and his lone set of footsteps faded away.

"What did he do to you?" Simon demanded, his voice was tight with rage.

"He made me put on a dress." The fabric was rough against my skin and appeared cheaply made. Either that or someone was in a hurry, the stitches uneven and the hem slightly jagged. "A white dress."

Like a virgin sacrifice to appease the gods. My knees gave out and I dropped to the cold ground, wrapping my arms around my waist in an attempt to stop my fear from spilling out all over the floor and infecting Simon.

I felt with unerring certainty that I was going to die. The priests would kill me, perhaps by their own hands, or maybe they would throw me to a mob of angry Downdwellers. I wondered dully what Simon's fate held. If he would be left to rot in this fortress like the garbage in the lake, or be put to the executioner's block.

The thunderous beat of my heart was a clock ticking down the remaining seconds of my time in this world. *Thu-thunk, thu-thunk, thu-thunk.* I covered my ears, trying to block out the noise.

"Seph," Alder said. He was standing at the door of his cell, and on his face was a look of such compassion that my jaw worked against tears that wanted to spill. "We're going to get out of here."

"How, exactly? You said it yourself. This place is impossible to escape from."

"Not impossible," Alder corrected. "Just extremely difficult. But there is always a way."

Something in his voice reminded me of Alex. Alex, who needed me. Alex, who could be undergoing torture in a cell just like mine, waiting for—

I pushed up with numb hands and got to my feet. "The next time they come, we're doing it." The next time they came, it would be for me.

"I'm going to get those keys. Don't drink any more water. We have to be ready."

———

As much as I hated the prison, I found myself hoping Folly would visit one more time before our escape attempt. But he stayed away, wherever he went when he wasn't in the cell block. I wondered what he'd meant earlier, whining at the stairs. Although, he was only a dog—maybe he just smelled something weird.

Hours passed before the sound of keys clanking on a ring interrupted my thoughts. Alder gave me a slight nod, then I rapped on the wall that Simon and I shared. It was time.

Luck was on our side. Only one priest came for me, a testament to how pitiful I appeared. It was the same man who had forced me into the dress. For the first time in days—weeks, even—I felt animated, like a wooden doll come to life.

After the priest swung the latticed gate open, meaty hands clenched at his sides, I swooned. Or, I gave an approximation of a swoon. I'd never done one before, but I counted on some form of sexist chivalry to force the priest to lower his guard and come to my aid.

The man knelt over my crumpled form, then sent a swift punch to my kidneys. Pain shot up my spine, and I wretched. "Get up, witch," he hissed in my ear. "Or you'll get worse than that." He stood, looming like a dark cloud.

I would definitely get worse than that, if the public execution I'd almost witnessed was any indication of what the priests of the Watching God had in store for me. I rolled over, stifling a moan, and pushed onto my knees.

"Please," I begged the priest. "Please, don't hurt me." Hunching my shoulders, I made sobbing noises and covered my face with ironclad hands. It wouldn't have been too difficult to produce real tears, but I needed my vision clear.

"Seph!" Simon yelled, the panic in his voice clear despite the thickness of the walls. I forced myself to block him out.

The priest grabbed my elbow to wrench me to my feet. In the moment we were both bent over, I snapped my head upward into his nose. There was a crunch and a searing ache in my skull. I threw all my weight onto him, and we careened into a wall. He roared, throwing a clumsy punch. I dodged, but he grazed my jaw, then I stumbled, the chain that bolted me to the wall straining. The priest reached for the knife inside his robes, and more shouts sounded from Simon's cell.

This was it. My last chance before he skewered me. I feinted, wobbly though I was, and when the priest was focused on slashing my throat, I found my target. My foot met his crotch with a resounding *thwack*. But the priest only smiled at me, then yanked the chain and threw me off balance. I toppled, then slammed into the icy stone floor.

"Whore," he hissed, then the dagger was arcing toward me.

Until it wasn't.

I heard screams and growls, then the scent of blood hit my nostrils. The dagger spun away, out of the open cell door.

The priest was on the ground, Folly's teeth clamped around his throat. The dog shook his head, and a chunk of something covered in blood went flying. The priest no longer struggled, but Folly continued to ravage him.

Simon was shouting something incoherent, and Alder stood motionless at the bars of his cell, those bright eyes peering through the gloom.

"Stop," I implored. "Please, Folly. Stop." The hound lifted his head, muzzle covered in blood. He let out a soft whine and ran out of the cell.

"I'm okay," I called to Simon, fighting numbness. I couldn't afford to float outside of my body right now.

Folly had dragged the priest's corpse into the doorway, and it lay halfway in and halfway out. I crawled over to it, because I wasn't certain that my legs would support me. The body was mangled and covered in blood and gore, but the key ring was still attached to his belt. Just out of my reach.

Holding my breath, I pincered the priest's leg between iron-mitted hands and dragged him until the ring was in range of my chain. I tried the same move with the key ring, but my bonds made me too clumsy and they slipped over and over again.

"Use your teeth," Alder called, speaking for the first time.

I winced. "I can't." The dark red coating the ring being inside my mouth wasn't worth thinking about.

"You have to," he urged. "When he doesn't show up with you in a few minutes, they'll know something's wrong."

Fucking hell—Alder was right, and I was working on borrowed time. I leaned over the body, and ever so gently, closed my teeth around the ring. Hot copper suffused my mouth as blood coated my tongue. Willing myself not to gag, I maneuvered a key into my mouth. It took three tries before I was able to find the right one, then fit it into the lock. When the left restraint sprang free, hope tickled my sternum. One more.

"Hurry!" Alder's voice was laced with something that might have been panic. I realized why when steps rang in the corridor.

My freed hand was numb to the wrist, and my fingers wouldn't move. With a bloody key in my mouth and crouched beside the body of a dead man, Alder's warning shout came just as the shadow fell across me.

18

"You're a fucking mess," Fane barked. He loomed above me, his tall frame blocking out the light. "Give me that." He snatched the key from my mouth, then unlocked my other hand.

"What the hell are you doing here?" Tears of pain lodged in the corners of my eyes. My left hand was on fire as it regained circulation.

"Saving you," he answered.

I followed Fane out as he unlocked Alder's cell, then Simon's. I marveled at being able to walk more than six feet.

Simon pulled me into a crushing hug. I clung to him, feeling every hollowed place and sharp edge hunger had claimed. He smelled of dirt and sweat, and fear.

"I hate to break up this touching reunion, but we need to go." The shiny skin of Fane's scar stretched tight.

"Who are you?" Alder demanded, flexing his wrists and fingers.

"The person who's saving your life," Fane drawled.

"But why?" I asked.

"You had the poor luck to stumble upon a revolution." Fane's eyes glinted. "This just moved up the timeline."

"How do we know he's not working with the priests?" Alder said to me, as if Fane wasn't standing right next to us.

"You can question me and die, or follow me and live. Well, you might live. Your choice."

Fane strode down the hall past Simon's cell and stopped at the door at the end of the corridor. Folly was there too, alert and wagging his tail. Dark streaks of congealed blood covered his fur.

"Folly!" I kneeled to embrace him. "You came for us," I whispered into his neck.

He gave me a gentle lick. "His collar! Give me the keys." I inserted key after key, and finally the last one fit the lock. The iron collar fell off him, revealing a seeping, crusted wound. Folly gave a full body shake, flopping his long ears and giving a doggy smile.

"Help me shift this," Fane ordered, slapping one of the stone bricks that made up the wall. "It's loose, and there's a passage running behind here." Alder and Simon joined him, heaving with their shoulders. The stone was stuck fast.

"Stand back," Alder entreated, raising his hands. They hung limply at his wrists. His face screwed up in concentration. The stone scraped and shuddered, but after a few tense moments it crashed to the ground.

Fane gave Alder an appraising look. "That's handy."

"Elemental magic," he replied brusquely.

The hole left in the stone's wake wasn't ordinary darkness. I grabbed one of the flickering wall torches and thrust it inside. Light revealed a polished tunnel, no more than three feet wide, that sloped downward at a sharp angle.

"Is that a slide?" I asked, my voice hitching.

"Yes. Get in," Fane commanded.

I backed away, my chest tightening. Might it be better to face the wrath of Olker Geist than wedge myself into that tight, unforgiving space where I could become trapped for eternity?

"You go. I'll take the stairs," I breathed.

A shout echoed from somewhere above our heads. "Decide quickly, because they know something's wrong. Come on, dog," Fane snapped. He climbed into the slide and pushed off, whizzing into the darkness. Folly clambered up, sliding down on his belly, tail wagging all the way.

Alder shrugged. "See you at the bottom." Then he, too, was gone.

"Simon, you know I can't do that," I said, eyes glued to the opening.

"You bloody well can, and you will. Now get in there before I toss you inside. You couldn't knock over a bug in your state, so don't test me."

I threw a glance over my shoulder. Was it just me, or was the corridor brightening?

"I'm not going without you," Simon said in a low voice. He grabbed my shoulders and turned me to face him. "You've battled demons. You can do this."

"Because I'm the scariest thing in the dark?"

He cupped my cheek. "Yes."

Now I knew what he'd meant before. That to be feared was its own kind of power—if I wanted to claim it.

I broke away and shuffled toward the opening, when pounding footsteps clattered around the bend and two priests in purple robes flew toward us.

"Go, now!" Simon shouted.

He pushed me in, following half a step behind. If there were any blocks in the tunnel, he would crush me and we would be trapped. The thought of not being able to move, to breathe, made my chest tighten painfully.

We hurtled downward smoothly enough, and I shut my eyes even though it was already pitch black. Nothing could have made this better, not even magic.

After an eternity, I shot out of the tunnel and landed in an inch of standing water. Alder pulled me to my feet as I heard Simon splash behind me. The air held the most foul odor I'd smelled so far, even in the Downdwelling. It was like rotten remains mixed with raw sewage.

Alder snapped his fingers, and a spark rose from them to hover above our heads.

"The priests saw us," I said, gagging on the smell.

"Run!" Fane called, and we all took off behind him, splashing and sliding while Alder's spark lit the way. Fane was the only one with shoes, but Folly with his four legs was faster. They both seemed to know where they were going, and guided us through the maze-like halls in the bowels of the fortress.

I couldn't tell if the priests were behind us, because the splash of us dashing through water drowned out everything else. I risked a glance backward, not sure if it was a good or bad sign that no one was there.

The water deepened as we ran, slowing us down. It was at mid-calf now, brownish and murky. Debris floated on its surface, and there was something bloated on the bottom that squished between my toes. I covered my mouth with the crook of my elbow, stifling a gag.

We eventually came to a partially submerged passageway with water climbing toward the ceiling at its end.

"It's a dead end," Simon said, anger lighting up his voice. I realized this was why the priests hadn't followed us—all they had to do was wait for us to come back up, or drown in the fetid lake. Like rats fleeing a sinking ship.

"We swim," Fane declared. "It only takes a few moments."

"In *that*?" I asked. The light still hovered above us, but I found myself wishing it was pitch dark again.

"Yes. This was the boathouse before the lake rose. There's a way out if we swim through there."

"How d'you know that?" Simon said.

"My aunt was a priest. Before Olker Geist had her put to death," Fane replied softly. His golden eyes were hard and cold, showing no sign of grief. Not for the first time, I wondered how Fane had gotten his crescent scar.

"We'll be poisoned," Alder asserted. "This water is toxic."

"I've been through it before. Just don't swallow."

"Don't swallow, he says," Simon fumed under his breath. "Bleeding Asael's pants. Say we survive this swim. Then what's your genius plan?"

"We flee into the wood on the other side of the fortress."

"But what will you do afterward? You'll be caught," I said. And we needed to get the stone from the belt hanging around Geist's thick waist.

"Don't worry about me. The right people are in the right places. All I ask in return for rescuing you is one small favor."

There it was—the price of our freedom. I steeled myself. "What do you want?"

"The stone of Vadyron, of course."

The only sound was water dripping into the murk. I had to think fast, but my brain was foggy and numb. There was no way I could give Fane the stone, not when Gamori had threatened Simon's life. But we might not be able to survive this without his help, either.

"What do you need it for?" Alder asked, folding his arms. He looked at Fane with suspicion in his bold eyes.

"That stone is immensely powerful. We'll use it to knock the priests out of power once and for all. And, you should know this—I won't rest until I have it." His tone was almost casual, except for the iron beneath it. "Either we make a deal, or I leave you here. Your choice."

Fucking hell. Simon caught my eye, giving me an inscrutable look. I stared back, hoping to convey that he could trust me, even though he had no reason to.

I addressed Fane. "Fine. You'll get the stone."

He shook shaggy black hair out of his eyes and smiled. It was almost lupine, the way he showed his teeth. He extended a hand. I clasped it briefly, feeling his calluses press into my palm.

Then, he transformed into a black wolf.

"Holy—" I stumbled, startled at the sudden change. The wolf standing where Fane had been had a scar curving from snout to golden eye.

"He's a wolf," Simon bleated. "A fucking wolf."

Fane bared his teeth, then nosed a rope out of his pile of discarded clothes. He bit the rope, then shook it.

"I think we're supposed to take it," Alder said. Fane gave another growl, which I interpreted as canine for *yes*.

Fane dove into the water, doggy paddling. Folly lumbered in after him, splashing merrily, and the rest of us had to sprint to grab the end of the rope before it disappeared.

Swimming through that lake was one of the worst things I'd ever done. I thanked any deity I could think of that Fane was guiding us, because we surely wouldn't have survived otherwise. Eyes shut tight and mouth clamped, I kicked as icy water engulfed me.

My chest burned, and I fought the reflex to breathe. The urge was unbearable, and just when I thought I couldn't take it anymore, we breached the surface. A cold wind blew over my head and I heard a low growl.

I opened my eyes, gasping and gulping air while treading water. Simon was next to me, shaking the hair out of his face.

The sky was milky blue, the horizon growing lighter by the second. The fortress hovered behind us, wholly backlit by the dawn.

Something niggled in the corner of my brain as I took in its imposing darkness. Maybe it was seeing the fortress from a different angle, but that wasn't all. I began to shake, from the cold—and something else. We struck out for the shore, the skirt of my dress tangling around my legs.

"Simon," I said, touching his arm as we trudged onto the muddy bank. We were the last to come out, with Alder and the canines already shaking themselves dry. "Something isn't right."

"I can think of a few things myself. Blasted pants are all twisted up from the wet, not to mention this *thing* touched me—"

"No, not your pants," I interrupted. As we reached the others in the safety of the treeline, I surveyed the black fortress. It hit me like an avalanche, starting slowly then snowballing into panic as I finally realized what was wrong. "Why isn't the beacon lit?" The great bonfire atop the fortress was always lit, the oily black smoke that billowed a constant throughout the day or night. So why was it extinguished?

Fane whipped his head around, then bared his teeth, a growl coming from deep in his throat. Six forms emerged from the shadows of the trees.

Olker Geist was as imposing as I remembered, larger than life and twice as horrible. His shaven head was so shiny that I could've seen my reflection in it if there had been more light. The chain around his waist clinked with every step, the insignia of the Watching God swaying. The insignia that Alder claimed held the stone of Vadyron.

Alder stared at the priest, hands raised in a defensive posture. Folly let out a low whine, then scampered into the trees. No one stopped him.

"One of you heretics is attentive, I see." Olker Geist held the chain around his waist, feeding the links through his hand until he held the insignia with its double eyes. "We extinguish the beacon when we prepare for sacrifice. Your sacrifice."

"Seph, run," Simon whispered out of the corner of his mouth. "I'll cover you."

"No." I raised my hands aloft, prepared to siphon from the first person who touched me. It was worth the cost. And further, I wanted to. The priests accompanying Geist held chains of their own, with ferronite mittens dangling from the ends. I recoiled. I would die before they put those on me again.

Geist laughed, wheezy and whistling. "You cannot escape the reach of the God. He sent me to capture you, to make you our offering. And He will not be denied."

"If you touch me, I will rip your fucking throat out," I threatened. Apparently, Fane agreed, because a deep snarl rippled through his bared teeth.

"Wicked, wicked girl. And your accomplices, too." Geist snapped his fingers, and the other purple-robed priests moved toward us. "Seize them!"

They swung their chains, advancing on us in a half circle so that we were cut off from the woods, the water at our backs. One of the chains made contact with Alder, and he grabbed onto it, yanking it from the priest as it lit up like a glowing ember. The priest cried out, dropping the chain and whimpering over his blistered hands.

"See how you like it, roach," Alder growled.

He swung the chain so that it became a red-hot whip, slicing down on the priests. They jumped out of the way, and Fane leapt on one of them, tearing into her calf with razor-sharp teeth. I grabbed the one that Fane was mauling, making contact with her skin and siphoning her life force. Sticky and vile energy flowed into my hands. When she lost consciousness, I yanked her chain away and threw it to Simon.

We all panted, gasping through gritted teeth. Only one priest remained between us and the woods, along with Geist.

"Let us pass," Simon thundered.

On a high-pitched laugh, Geist swung the insignia on his chain, blinding us all with white light that left stamps on my vision before my knees buckled.

———

Cold wind bit my face, and I smelled smoke and rot. White-hot needles of pain lanced the soles of my feet. Then a bloodcurdling scream ripped through my throat.

"Ah, she's awake," Olker Geist cooed. He removed the burning torch from beneath my feet. I tried to buck away, but was tied at my elbows, knees, and waist with heavy rope. Someone had also bound my wrists together, but thankfully they were free of iron.

We were atop Festborg Fortress, on the tower beneath the unlit beacon. A platform to my left jutted out over the lake like a high-dive board. Simon, Alder, and Fane, naked in his human form, were all tied to their own wooden pilings to my right.

"What did you do to us?" I coughed. The inside of my throat burned, as though I'd inhaled a roomful of smoke.

Geist patted his belt, mouth twisted into a sick smile. "I did nothing. It is the Watching God's light that shone upon you. I am just His humble servant."

"I already heard that bullshit, you prick." I looked at the others from the corner of my eye. None of them were conscious. "Does your god know you're tricking people with the stone of Vadyron?"

Geist's eyes glittered. "My God is a benevolent master. He has entrusted me with divine power. He thanks you for showing him your magic." He patted the insignia. "With every magic user we find, the power of the stone—of the God, grows."

I dug deep for my siphoned power. It lay just out of reach, like there was a clinging film covering it. "What did you do to me?" I demanded.

"The light of the God, only given to the truest believer, has stunned you. Your heretic magic will return, but you needn't worry. By that time, we'll have fed you to the deep." Geist nodded toward the platform. "I only thought to have one sacrifice today, but the God has given us four. What a bounty." His grin stretched wide, taking up most of his face as he leered. Fucking hell, he really was insane with power. Or maybe it was the stone he wielded that had twisted him so.

"What benevolent god demands sacrifice?"

"It is what He demands as payment to halt the encroachment of the darkness that eats at the land. He has sought to punish us for our wickedness, the wickedness of those who do not follow his path," Geist said with practiced reverence, like he'd used this sermon many times.

I stilled. There must be an edge in Aundirne. And the priest was using it to justify his slaughter of innocent people. Or, maybe he actually believed it. But I wouldn't be joining their ranks.

Burrowing into my bones, I clawed for the siphoned magic. It stirred feebly, responding the harder I pushed. Sweat beaded on my forehead.

Someone coughed beside me. "I'll see you dangling at the end of a noose before you throw me into that lake," Fane growled.

"It is not your choice, unnatural beast." Turning to me again, Geist reached inside his white robes. "Tell me about this object." He held aloft the Desidarian compass. Its silver glittered dully in the light of the sun spilling over the horizon.

"It's nothing. A trinket," I lied.

Geist examined it, opening the face. Then he shrugged, snapping it closed. "No matter. I will plumb its secrets later. The time has come for the sacrifice, as the new day dawns!"

Pulling a short-bladed knife from his robes, he sawed at the ropes tying me to the piling. I imagined drilling through the barrier between me and the borrowed power. I was so close. So, so close.

As he yanked me toward the platform, I saw movement. Simon was awake, too, his eyes like the dark bruises of storm clouds. *Forgive me*, I thought. As if he heard me, he shook his head, hair falling across his face.

I dragged my feet, stumbling as Geist pulled me by the elbow. The insignia swung from the end of his belt in time with his gait. Every muscle in my body ached with the effort of hacking away at the internal barrier.

A few feet away from the end of the platform, the priest shoved me to my knees. They stung painfully as I hit stone. He pushed my neck, forcing my head down into a bow. "Oh, Watching God!" he cried to the dazzling rays of light that bathed us in a wash of gold. "See me now, your servant, as I give the lives of those who would see you vanquished to the depths!"

As if on cue, the center of the black lake rippled. Icy terror rolled down my spine, freezing me in place. A black tentacle thicker than a sapling breached the surface.

"No," I whispered hoarsely. I wasn't the scariest thing in the dark anymore. That was the creature with ten suckered tentacles, followed by a beaked mouth that rose above the lake, clicking open and shut.

"Seph!" Simon cried out.

Geist gave an exultant laugh, his pleasure at my murder turning my stomach. "Any last words for the God?"

"Yeah." I met his eyes. They were black as the lake below, as the creature who lurked there. "Fuck him. And fuck you, too."

His lips pulled back in a snarl, and I toppled forward as he shoved me. I pitched over the platform, but managed to cling to the edge with my fingertips. I'd finally broken through to my siphoned power, and it was the only thing keeping me from falling.

Geist stomped on my hand, and pain blasted through me as a bone snapped. Grunting, I hauled myself up and over, rolling onto the platform.

He raised the insignia, but I shot a jet of blue flame at his hand. Hissing, he withdrew his grasping fingers. I launched at Geist, taking him to the ground, battering his face with punches. An electric shock jolted through me, and I gasped, rolling away. Then his hands were around my throat, squeezing as I clawed his meaty fingers. Geist smiled, and I hooked a finger into his cheek, pulling until flesh tore.

He released me, choking, blood seeping from his mouth. I reached into his robes, snatching the compass, then grabbed the dagger hanging from his belt and slashed him in a diagonal from eye to mouth. Shoving away from him, I tripped over the hem of the goddamn dress.

"Watch out!" Alder cried.

Geist was screaming and grasping for his chain while blood slicked his face. I struck him in the throat, then kicked him in the chest so that he slammed into the piling I'd been tied to. The move should have knocked him out, but he snapped back like a rubber band, rebounding toward me.

A black and tan blur came from behind and tackled Geist. *Folly*. He snapped and snarled, pinning the priest. "Untie the others," Folly growled. I blinked. I must have really been losing it if I thought the dog was talking.

"I said, untie them!" He turned a bloodied muzzle toward me, yelping as Geist struck him in the flank.

Swaying on my feet, lightheaded, I staggered to Simon. "Gods, Seph. Hurry," he urged. Blinking away dark spots, I sawed through the ropes, but when that took too much time, I just burned them off. Simon struggled out of his bonds, then ran to the others, using his small pool of magic to burn through their ropes, too.

Fane and Alder advanced on Geist just as the insignia shot brilliant light again.

"Get down!" Fane yelled, grabbing the back of my neck and slamming me to the ground. A jet of air stirred my hair as the light just missed us. Folly squealed, and a bolt of fear arrowed into my gut.

Shoving Fane off, I rolled to stand. Folly's prone form was on the ground at Geist's feet, unmoving. The priest held the insignia aloft while unraveling the golden chain from his waist.

"Heretics and heathens," he choked through a spluttering cough. Blood poured from the cut across his eye, from his mouth. "You will die screaming."

Alder raised a hand, lighting the torch that Geist had used to burn my feet. With a whoosh of flame, he sent it rolling toward the priest. The bottom of Geist's robes caught fire, and he screeched as he stamped out the flames.

"We need that stone," I told Simon. "I'm taking it, then we're running for the forest. Can you get Folly?"

"Hold on," Fane started. I turned toward him, baring my teeth in a snarl. He flinched, eyes wide at whatever he saw in mine.

"Take this, use it to find any magic users you can, and stay out of my way." I shoved the compass into his hands, then scraped the bottom of the barrel on my power. Slashing a hand at the flames to quell them, I launched at Geist where he stood at the end of the platform. I punched him hard in the gut as I ripped the golden chain from his fingers.

"No!" he choked, doubled over.

The chain burned hot in my hand, the feel of it silky and molten. I stopped, staring at the insignia that seemed to pulse like it had its own heartbeat. It had some unnameable feeling that was filled with power, chomping at the bit for release. The stone called to me, and I grasped it, raising it to eye level.

"Seph, watch out!"

Simon's warning was too late. Geist's knife swept down on me, stabbing through the joint in my shoulder. The chain clattered to the ground. The high priest stood over me, knife dripping blood, a mad smile on his face. A shadow moved behind him—Simon. Simon brought his joined hands down on the priest's neck, sending Geist to his knees.

I snatched the chain off the ground, swinging the insignia at Geist's face. It connected, and he snarled, then whirled on his knees and plunged his knife into Simon's gut.

"No!" I screamed, raw horror tearing through my throat. Simon's face went slack, and he staggered, hands going to the hilt of the knife. As I reached over Geist's head, he shoved me backward off the platform's edge—into the jaws of the beast.

I hurtled towards the black lake, sending a last burst of blue flame toward Geist as I did. Dark satisfaction curled through me at the blood-curdling scream he emitted.

It was a long fall, the wind tearing at my hair and making my eyes water. Time slowed. I had the stone, but it didn't matter. Simon was dead, a knife through his gut. And Alex—I'd failed the man I loved, the man I was leaving to suffer in the hands of demons. Salty tears streaked my cheeks, as the heart I thought I'd lost ripped wide open again.

Then there was a yell—more of a shriek, and three bodies plummeted toward me. Alder, hands reaching. Simon, limp and pale, with blood soaked through his tattered shirt. Folly, long ears flapping in the wind. *No*, I mouthed.

As if borne on a jet stream, they reached me far sooner than the laws of gravity allowed for. Alder curled his fingers toward Simon and Folly, pulling them into an invisible net. He grabbed my wrist then jerked me sideways, out of the reach of the creature's grasping tentacles.

Lake water rushed up to meet us, swirling in a spiral pattern and creating a funnel. The last thing I saw was the creature's milky, blind eyes before the four of us plunged into the water.

My mind reeled, unsure why I hadn't been eaten by the tentacled beast. Or perhaps I had, and this was all some sort of dream induced by its gastric juices liquefying me.

After an indeterminate amount of time that could have been a year or a second, we fell out of the water into a courtyard. I landed painfully on my shoulder, rolling face up.

The sky was brilliant blue, filtering through trees covered in purple buds. The air smelled sweet, and a light breeze caressed my face. I had the impression of voices, someone screaming, then an utterly lovely hallucination—Bri's heart-shaped face looming above my own, her amber eyes wide in shock.

"Seph?" she breathed.

Everything went black.

PART III

But it's no use now, thought poor Alice, to pretend to be two people! Why, there's hardly enough of me left to make one respectable person!

— LEWIS CARROLL, *ALICE IN WONDERLAND*

19

I was back in Jupiter's Books, the moldering mansion that was Simon's ancestral home. The halls were dusty, as usual, cobwebs adorning the corners like festive tinsel. My footsteps echoed through the stacks.

"Hello?" I called. No answer. Not only did the home have its habitual air of decay, it felt abandoned, like not even the ghosts of memories remained.

I wandered aimlessly, climbing the stairs and eventually ending up in the kitchen. It was the heart of the home, where we'd often gathered back when the Guardians were hiding out at Jupiter's. It felt like a hundred years ago, and just yesterday.

A man sat at the scarred wooden table, his back to me. His hair was dark like mink, the muscular line of his neck flowing into broad shoulders. My heart thudded. I knew that back.

"Alex?" I whispered.

He turned toward me. His green eyes flashed, and the corner of his sensuous mouth pulled into a half-smile. He looked whole and beautiful, not as I'd left him on the edge of the pit in the prison world, but as he had the nights we'd spent together in Canhaben.

"Seph." His deep voice caressed my name and sent slow warmth through my chest.

I ran, throwing my arms around him. He smelled like cedar, like the forest and everything good in the world. "Oh, my god. I've missed you so much. How did you get here?" I burrowed into his neck as he crushed me to his chest.

Alex stroked a hand down my waves, resting his cheek against my forehead. "Why did you leave me?"

Loathe as I was to draw away, I peered into his eyes. The corona of gold circling his pupil was warm like sunshine. "Magoth dragged you into the pit. Don't you remember? I've been searching for you."

His brows knitted, and his dimple showed when he frowned. "What are you talking about? I've been here the whole time."

My stomach clenched. "No, you haven't." Had he? There was no way. But here he was, lithe and strong in my arms. "It doesn't matter." I shook my head, unable to tear my gaze away from his face, that pirate's grin and shadowed jaw.

Alex cupped my cheek. "I love you, Seph. I love you so much, and I wished I'd told you more often. Every single second of every day." He bent to kiss me, his lips soft, then firm, claiming my mouth. Licks of heat raced over my skin, but he drew back gently.

"It's fine," I assured him, clutching the fabric of his shirt between my fingers. "You're here now. Everything's okay. I love you, Alex." It felt so good to tell him, so right. I regretted not saying it more, too.

He frowned again. "I'm fading."

"What? No!" But Alex was right. He was disappearing in front of my eyes, as though his very atoms were uncoupling and floating away. "No! Please," I begged. "Don't leave me again."

I was left standing in the kitchen, alone. So damn alone.

"I think she's waking up," a familiar voice said. "Go, fetch the healer."

Healer? My eyes fluttered open, and I wasn't in Jupiter's. The ceiling held large rectangular skylights with sunlight streaming through, the walls made of burnished wood planks. I was lying in a bed that was softer than a cloud. My lungs ached as I drew a deep breath that hitched. I wanted to go back to Alex, back to the unconscious dream world, or wherever it had been. I didn't want whatever awaited me in this room.

"Seph," Bri said. She held my hand, her skin impossibly soft and warm. Her eyes were wide, her tanned skin pale. "Thank the Mother you're awake."

It must have been another dream. Because there was no way that Bri, my best friend from my old life, sat next to me, wearing a pale green gown that floated over her like a leaf riding the wind. White flowers were braided into her black hair that was half pulled up, exposing slightly pointed ears.

I sat up, scooting away from her as panic shot through me. Those were wings at her back, delicate and gossamer with each apex trailing into rounded points. "Where am I? What are you doing here? Where's Simon?" Everything came rushing back in a deluge, battering my senses. Olker Geist's terrible gaze, the ferronite mittens, the insignia's hypnotic power, the creature from the deep, Fane in wolf form, Simon getting stabbed, then, finally, Alder, Simon, and Folly plunging toward me, falling into a whirlpool.

Bri held out her hands like she was approaching a wild animal. "Simon is...healing. Alder and the hound are fine. We have the stone of Vadyron, too. Everything is okay, Seph."

Everything was not okay. Simon might be on the brink of death, and Alex was still gone. I felt the ache of losing him all over again, reverberating in that hollow place under my ribs. A wash of pain rolled through me, stealing my breath. And Bri—how the hell was she here?

"Are you real?" I asked, hovering on the far edge of the bed. Bri seemed corporeal, but I'd seen stranger things. "Where am I?"

Bri hesitated. "I am real," she finally said. "You're in the Faerie realm. Alder brought you here. This...this is my home. My true home."

"No it's not." The denial rose automatically to my lips. Bri, in a Faerie world? It didn't make any sense. Nothing made sense. I reached a tentative hand out to brush her arm and met solid flesh. She took my hand and squeezed.

"I wasn't honest with you." She lowered her gaze. "I didn't know what you were. If I had, I would've helped. Brought you here, where it's safe. By the time I figured it out—and got over myself—it was too late. I've been trying to track you down ever since. Flora was finally able to reach you in the rowan circle, but after that...I just had to hope you were okay."

I shook my head and jerked my hand out of her grasp. "I don't believe you. I want to see Simon."

"He's not well enough for visitors yet."

My blood ran cold. "Is he...is he going to die?"

Bri shook her head, eyes soft. "It's too early to tell. But we have our best healers tending to him, and he's responded positively so far." She leaned toward me, then stopped. "He needs rest. The demon, too."

"Demon?" I said absently, the dark pit of guilt in my stomach rapidly expanding.

"The hound," she clarified.

Sweet, brave Folly was a demon? I remembered how he'd commanded me to untie the others while he ravaged Geist. A shiver crept down my spine.

Bri's wings fluttered open and closed as we spoke, like a butterfly's when it rested on a flower. She saw me staring at them. "When I'm in Faerie, I can't hide my true nature like I did in your world." She sounded almost regretful. "I know this is a shock."

I gave a humorless laugh. "To learn that my—" I swallowed down *best friend*. "You aren't even human? You could say that." But the truth was, I could believe it. Bri had always been different from the rest of us —a little too polished, too perfect to be completely human. I'd discovered over the course of my time with the Aureum and traveling the worlds with Simon that people saw what they wanted to see. Back then, I really had believed that magic only belonged in stories. Now, of course, I knew better.

"What the hell were you doing in Gravesville?" Boring old Gravesville, which I was rapidly realizing wasn't quite so boring with demons, demon hunters, witches, and now apparently Faeries running around.

Bri examined her hands. "I wanted a different life. Something that wasn't so constricting, where I could be free."

"Free from what?" I asked incredulously.

Her shoulders slumped. "I am a Lady of the Weald Fae. Part of the royal court. My life here was politics and service to the royal family. Not that those aren't admirable duties, but they're not for me."

I blinked at her. "You're a fairy princess."

"Technically, no. I'm Fae nobility."

A headache sprang up in the center of my forehead, and I kneaded it with stiff fingers. "How did you keep this a secret?"

"I have magic, Seph. And to be fair, you never asked. You didn't want to know about my life before we met." There was hurt in her voice, and I remembered the last conversation we'd had. *I left the damn door wide open*, she'd said. *But you won't step through.*

"I guess we're both liars, then."

She nodded stiffly. "I guess so."

Perhaps she wondered what else I was keeping from her—that's what I was thinking, at least. What other secrets did Bri have? We weren't close enough anymore to share them. Our friendship had been destroyed, another cost the Aureum had exacted from me.

There was a soft knock on the door, then it swung open. A Fae man with downy blond hair and white wings lined with brown entered. His ears tapered into subtle, fine points, and in his long-fingered hands was a leather case. "Lady Bryony," he said, sketching a short bow.

Lady *Bryony?* I shook my head, like that would dissipate the anger that pierced my shock.

"Catkin is here to assess you," Bri explained. She sounded different, more formal than I'd ever heard her. "He is an accomplished healer."

"I'm fine." My throat still burned, and my body ached like I'd been dragged behind a truck for twenty miles. Maybe fifty. My feet throbbed from where Geist had burned me, my shoulder from where he'd stabbed me, my finger from where he'd broken it. The scars around my wrists left from the Aureums' burning ropes now had a new wound overlaying them from the iron mittens. The lily birthmark on my wrist, the sign that marked me as a gods-touched Guardian, had long been scarred over from injuries.

Okay, I was a mess.

"It will only take a moment," Bri said, gesturing for Catkin to come forward.

I allowed the healer to poke and prod me, ignoring the way his eyebrows inched higher as he assessed my myriad wounds and scars. In addition to the silvery skin around my wrists, I had a scar that ran underneath my collarbone from shoulder to shoulder—a relic from my encounter with the demon Ventusiel—along with the raised line on my back from shoulder to hip, courtesy of the death demons from the cenote, and countless other marks scattered across my body. At least my protection tattoo was unmarred by injury. I kept my head down and eyelids half-shuttered.

Catkin re-bandaged my wrists with green, gauze-like plant material soaked in something cool, then pulled a glass bottle containing purple liquid from his case. "A tincture for your pain, Mistress Persephone. Drink the whole thing."

I shot it back, bracing for it to be disgusting, but the taste was a mild lavender essence. "It's Seph," I returned.

"As you wish." He stood and snapped the leather case shut. "I'll have more sent for you. You may take the whole bottle, twice a day. It will speed your healing as well." Catkin bowed to me, then Bri, and left on silent feet.

"Bryony?" I questioned when he'd cleared the door.

"You're not the only one who doesn't like her name. It's Bri to my friends." She gave me a small smile.

"So you are actually rich in real life. Nobility," I murmured, shaking my head.

Bri shrugged. "I can't help what I am, Seph."

Begrudgingly, I acknowledged the truth in her statement. "I want to see Simon."

"I'm not sure that's a good idea," she said slowly.

My fingers clenched the silken sheets. "Let me rephrase that. I'm going to see him. Now."

"Fine," she acquiesced, "but you can't wake him, or stay long."

Bri, or any other Fae for that matter, wasn't going to stop me. But I nodded. "How long was I out for?"

"Five days."

"*What?*" There was no possible way. Wouldn't it have...*felt* longer, if I'd been unconscious for that long?

"Time works differently in Faerie than it does in the mortal realms. Your body is still adjusting to the transition, but it wouldn't have been more than a few hours for you back home." Her full lips thinned. "You weren't well, Seph. Not at all." Bri stood. "I'll leave you to dress. There are clothes in the wardrobe." She gestured to an armoire carved of light wood, then left the room, gauzy dress trailing behind her.

I tested my legs before I rose from the bed. Light filled the entire space, illuminating the white furnishings so they appeared to glow. A canopy was draped behind the bed's tall headboard. A desk, also made of light wood, sat in the corner. I found a full complement of clothes in the armoire, everything appearing roughly my size.

Shucking off the white embroidered shift I'd been wearing, I caught sight of myself in a full-length mirror with a gilded frame. Air caught in my lungs.

When was the last time I'd used a mirror? Months ago, probably. The woman staring back at me was unrecognizable.

I was gaunt, skin stretching tight over bone. My brown-green eyes looked huge in my head, wild, like I was more skeleton than person. Hanging to my waist, my wavy curls were matted. Bruises of all colors marred the roughened texture of my tawny skin. Two of my fingernails were black, and a sliver of new growth showed from where I'd lost one entirely.

I didn't want to see this stranger I'd become. Broken-me. The one who'd led her friend into danger, who might have gotten him killed. Who'd hurt him, and other people besides.

Turning away from my reflection, I tugged a long-sleeved, high-necked green tunic over my head and paired it with brown pants. The fabric was softer than butter, lighter than air. After pulling on thick socks, I chose brown leather boots. I gave my hands a good scrub with lavender-scented soap in a washbasin with gold curlicued taps.

There, that was better. Wearing these fine clothes hid the wrecked woman beneath them. I found a leather strap to bundle my hair up so the mats weren't as visible.

Bri waited outside my room. She gave a hesitant smile. "You look lovely."

I jerked a shoulder, looking past her ear. "Thanks for the clothes."

She nodded slowly. "This way."

We walked down a set of spiral stairs, the banister curved like the long stem of a flower. The rest of the house was spacious and simple, light suffusing everything. The air smelled clean, like a breeze coming off fresh water. I felt stiff and achy, but my mind was clearer and sharper than it had been in months. Maybe something in Catkin's tincture was responsible.

"Simon's room is through here," Bri said, ushering me through the main level to the very end of the hall. She knocked on the door, then opened it.

A Fae woman with yellow wings and long, strawberry blonde hair bent over the bed, obscuring Simon. I only saw the outline of his legs beneath the white bedclothes. She turned to face us, pale pink lips puckering. "No visitors, yet. Lady Bryony," she added belatedly.

Ignoring her, I went to Simon's other side and knelt. His eyes were closed. His face was pale, his lips bloodless. If I hadn't seen the steady rise and fall of his chest under the covers, I'd have thought him dead. I took his hand, squeezing cold fingers.

"Extenuating circumstances, Rosemallow," Bri said, her voice ringing with authority.

The woman stood, fluttering her wings once, and huffed. "Five minutes." Then she left, Bri following. The door clicked shut.

"Simon," I breathed, touching my forehead to the center of his chest. "I'm so sorry. This is my fault. All of it." He gave no indication he'd heard, no flicker of the eyelids or hitch in his breathing. "Please be okay. If you're not...well. You have to be okay." If he didn't get better, then I'd have another scar to add to my soul. Another loss slowly crushing me. I wasn't certain I could survive it.

I was silent after that, content to count Simon's breaths. The door opened again, and Rosemallow entered the room. "I need to get back to work," she told me, not unkindly.

Bri was waiting at the end of the hall, and we walked through a set of wide arched doors. Outside, everything was soft and green.

Stone pathways branched through a meadow of grasses and wildflowers that came to my hips. Fat bees droned, flying lazily, and butterflies winged from blossom to blossom. Trees, their leaves the bright green of early spring, dotted the landscape. The air had the same fresh scent imbued with flowers, and the sun caressed my skin. Buildings of all sizes made of light wood and stone perched in the treetops or upon the ground. They had peaked roofs, their lines curling and fanciful.

"Welcome to the court of the Weald Fae," Bri said. "We're in the capital city, Medwë. This is a residential district on the outskirts of the city, where the courtiers and nobility make their permanent homes. The queen's castle is this way," she pointed down a path to her left, "and the city is this way." She pointed to the right, along which a river ran. "Do you want me to show you around, so you can get your bearings?"

I nodded, though I honestly didn't care. The only things that mattered to me were in the room I'd just left, and in the hands of a demon.

We descended to the dock and boarded a riverboat along with some other finely dressed Fae. It slipped downstream, and after an hour we disembarked onto a teeming city wharf.

The architecture in the city center looked the same as the residential district, but the buildings were closer together, some sharing walls. The river—Bri said it was called the Mona—split the city down the middle into two halves, with arched stone bridges spanning regular intervals. Fae meandered along the cobbled streets as well as the air, flying between shops that were set high above street level.

Underneath the English that reached my ears, I heard the Fae's true tongue. They spoke in the language of wind in the trees, the sounds of flowers unfurling their petals, of bees buzzing. Of water rushing in the river and the soft footfalls of deer in the forest. It was magic and music all at the same time. The language stirred some emotion beneath my numbness, but it wasn't strong enough to break through.

We stopped in front of a building facade that spanned the length of three townhouses. "This is the queen's city residence. Sometimes she'll stay here if she has city business, but she mostly uses the main castle," Bri explained. Her brow furrowed when I didn't answer. "Are you hungry?" My stomach rumbled, but I had no desire to eat. "Come on, have something. Healer's orders."

She bought us the Faerie equivalent of street food, roasted mushrooms tucked inside warm bread with melted cheese. Once I took a bite, ravenous hunger tore through me. I finished the sandwich, then realized I could've eaten five more.

"Your color is better," Bri observed. "Do you want another?"

"I should take it slow." I sat on a stone wall by the river, watching the comings and goings of boats on the water. The scene was so peaceful. Normal. It was hard to believe goodness still existed in the worlds after leaving Aundirne. As if in answer, my wounded wrists throbbed.

"What happened to you all?" Bri asked quietly, keeping her eyes trained on the water. "Alder told us about the escape. But before that. How did you end up there?"

Through my own selfishness and stupidity. I just shook my head and pushed off the wall. "I'd like to go back now."

Bri took her time rising, brushing out the folds of her gown. "I'm here to talk, you know. Whenever you're ready."

Looking away, I strode past her and boarded the boat that would take me back to Simon.

20

I knocked softly on Simon's door, prepared to hear Rosemallow's clipped voice permitting me to enter. She and I hadn't taken to each other—I imagined it was difficult to concentrate when there was a hollow-eyed woman always lurking around.

A voice I hadn't heard for days called out, "Aye?" I shoved the door open, almost tripping as relief threatened to buckle my legs.

Simon sat on the side of the bed, shirtless. A thick bandage wound around his torso just above his navel. His chestnut hair waved to his shoulders, his beard full. None of it should have come as a shock to me, but I felt like I was seeing him for the first time all over again. Sudden shyness gripped me. "You...look better."

He grunted, not meeting my eyes. "We could've done worse than landing in Faerie. Least they've got plenty of food here."

I didn't know why, but that made me want to cry and laugh at the same time. A strangled noise worked its way up my throat, one I wasn't able to swallow down.

Simon looked up at me, gray eyes soft, not punishing like I thought they'd be. Like I deserved.

I perched next to him, trying not to shift the mattress. "How are you feeling? I didn't know you were close to waking up."

"Truthfully? Best I've been in a long time. They know their stuff, the Fae." He stretched, pulling a soft gray tunic over his head. "Barely even feel like I was gutted in the first place."

An oil slick of guilt coated my insides. "You will never know how sorry I am. For Aundirne—for everything. For all the times I've almost gotten you killed, for leading you into danger, for Penn—" I broke off, swallowing another sob, then cleared my throat. "If I spend the rest of my life atoning, it won't be long enough."

He didn't say anything, just looked at me. "Is that all?"

"Now that we have the stone of Vadyron, I'll give it to Gamori. You'll be free and clear of me. When that's done, I'm leaving."

Simon's brow furrowed. "What d'you mean?"

"I can't do this to you any longer." I breathed deeply through my nose. "I'm broken, Simon, and I—everything I touch goes to shit. You were right about siphoning from the demons, too. I—I'm an addict." I still felt the echo of where the invincible torrent of their power used to flow, and clenched my fists. "It's best if I continue on alone."

Simon shook his head. "No."

"How can you say that? After what I've done to you?"

"You're daft if you think you're leaving here without me," he shot back.

"I'm not arguing about this." Dull acceptance throbbed at the base of my skull. I stood to leave. Simon grabbed my elbow, yanking me down onto the bed.

"Like hells you're not. We're having it out properly this time."

He should yell at me. Be angry. I met his eyes, ready to take his scorn.

"I spent too long not talking," Simon started. "I stayed silent, minding my business when I should've been watching out for my family. If I'd been braver, I would have been out there with Penn, with Diana, with my mum and dad. All of them had courage, like you. I'm spineless, and what have I got to show for it? A fat lot of nothing. Except for you." His burning gray gaze took me in. "You're my family, Seph. The only one I've got left. I'm not leaving you, and you're not taking off without me."

My throat ached. "Simon—"

"Hush." He put a finger to my lips. They parted in surprise, and he left his fingertip there for a heartbeat, then two, then three. Heat rushed to the spot, but he dropped his hand and continued. "Even with siphoning, I should've said more. I should've made you stop. I won't bury my head in the sand again. If this is what my fate is, so be it. We've both fucked up, monstrously. But family forgives each other. *We'll* forgive each other."

Tears pressed against the back of my eyes, but I blinked them away. Simon's face was set in resolute lines, his belief so strong I almost felt it shining on me. I wondered, just for a moment, what it would be like to lean into his warmth. But—no. I couldn't do that. Could I?

The air between us stilled, and his gaze slid to my mouth. Breath catching, he listed forward ever so slightly. I bit my lip where his fingertips had brushed it. The skin was still hot.

Three sharp knocks sounded on the door. Simon blinked, the tips of his ears coloring as he rose from the bed.

I leaned back and drew a deep breath. I felt exposed and too warm, my heart fluttering a rapid beat that I put down to anxiety over the intimacy of our conversation. Simon considered me family, and he was like the brother I never had. He wanted to protect me, to save me like he couldn't save his own family. I was confusing emotional closeness for something entirely different, just like I had when we were trapped in our cells in Aundirne.

Hovering just inside the entryway was a Fae woman dressed in a green and gold tunic and pants, a sword sheathed at her hip. Black wings poked over her shoulders. Her eyes were cobalt blue, her hair almost the same color. "Master Simon and Mistress Persephone? The crown requests your presence at the palace. I'm here to escort you."

Simon looked over his shoulder at me and raised a finely arched brow.

Bracing myself, I stood. The sooner we could get this over with, the better. "Lead the way."

The palace was as much a part of the forest meadow as the tufty green sedge and purple cones of foxglove surrounding it. Its outer walls were covered with twisted bark and vines that flowed into large arched windows. I wasn't sure if a tree grew inside the structure, or if the whole thing was a tree itself, all of the wood and glass and stone twining together to create a masterpiece. Hanging rope bridges spanned some of the larger branches, leading to other small structures embedded within the tree's limbs.

"Gods," Simon muttered as we passed a gatehouse surrounded by more Fae in green and gold uniforms. The Fae escorting us, Indigo, nodded to the other guards. They raised long wooden-shafted spears to let us pass.

We entered the castle through a living gate, the wood covered in—or made of—vines and flowers. Ivy and yellow climbing roses scaled the inner walls, and the ceilings were like the sunlit canopy of a forest. Despite Indigo's heeled boots, she walked soundlessly, while my and Simon's footfalls clattered like gunshots on the polished floors.

I'd pass on my thanks to Alder for rescuing us, then we'd be on our way. We no longer had the compass to guide us, although it didn't seem to have done much good, anyway. Momentary guilt flashed through me at tricking Fane out of the stone. Perhaps I'd get it back to him one day, but until then, it belonged to Gamori. I wouldn't risk Simon again.

Indigo approached a wide set of doors made to resemble the thick boughs of an oak. She rapped sharply on them three times. They swung inward.

My lips parted in silent surprise. Trees wider than barn doors supported the roof of the massive room, their branches intertwined to form an arched canopy. Twinkling lights hung from them like scattered stars.

Directly across from us, a Fae woman sat on a raised dais upon a throne of white tree boughs. They were set with a rainbow of flowers that sparkled like jewels. Gold rays speared from the top of the throne, as if the sun rose behind it.

The woman had dark brown skin the color of rich topsoil, and wore a crown woven from gilded leaves atop her braided hair. Her violet and cream dress flowed in the same gauzy style as Bri's had, with long, bell sleeves. Wings the same color as her dress fluttered at her back. She had proud features, with high cheekbones and a pointed chin. It was currently raised as she looked down upon me and Simon.

She needed no introduction. This woman was, undoubtedly, a queen.

Several Fae arrayed themselves around the queen at the bottom of the dais. Alder was one of them, his robin-egg blue eyes gleaming. He nodded to me. I lowered my gaze to the queen's feet, noting Indigo had moved out of the line of fire after issuing a sweeping bow.

The queen spoke, her voice deep and melodious. "Mistress Persephone, Master Simon. Welcome to the realm of the Weald Fae. I am Queen Calytrix Rosa, the ruler of these people."

I felt Simon's confused glance on me. How did one greet an actual Faerie Queen, the stuff of fable and legend? I jerked my head in a shallow bow. "Thank you. We appreciate your kindness, and for letting us stay here while we were...unwell. Please, call us Seph and Simon."

"Of course," she replied, nodding so that the gold of her crown winked in the lights. "You returned Lord Alder to us. You have our deepest thanks. And, Simon, I am glad to see that you are back on your feet." Simon gave a deep sort of nod, cheeks coloring.

I finally looked at Alder. His wings were the same color as his eyes. I wondered how he'd managed to hide those in Aundirne—probably the same way Bri had. "*Lord* Alder?"

"My nephew," Calytrix clarified. "All Fae in our realm are precious to me, but I will not deny that having him gone was like an arrow in my side." Her dark gaze beheld me and Simon. "He tells me that you were searching for the stone of Vadyron when you freed him."

I nodded, tensing. There was something foreboding about the way she said that last part.

"If I may ask, Mistress—Seph," she corrected, "why do you seek the stone?" The queen gripped the arms of her throne. Gold chains hung from her many rings, meeting at a central point to wrap around her wrists.

I slid my gaze to Simon. Yellow freckles in his eyes were stark against the storm gray, like lightning strikes. They didn't hold any answers.

"Please don't take offense, but we've learned to keep our own counsel," I hedged. I wasn't quite brave enough to ask her the same question in return. Not yet.

There was an intake of breath amongst the Fae surrounding the dais. A smirk played around Alder's mouth, giving him a stronger resemblance to an imp than Fae.

Calytrix pushed up from her throne, revealing what had been hidden beneath the folds of her gown—a distended belly, bowed outward in a graceful curve. The queen rested a hand on it.

"Please, walk with me." It wasn't a request. Alder took the queen's hand, escorting her from the dais. I glanced at Simon, and he shrugged.

We passed the dais and continued through a set of French doors that sprang open of their own accord. After several strained moments, we ended up in a courtyard with ivy-covered walls and a round dining set. Water burbled from a stream that wound lazily between tufts of wildflowers and smooth stones, then flowed into the castle.

Alder pulled out a chair for the queen, and she seated herself in a fluid motion. "Please," she said, switching fluidly from the Faerie tongue to English as she nodded to the other seats. With a snap of her fingers, servants appeared from the palace, filling crystal glasses with pale liquid and laying out plates and trays of food. "Help yourself," she encouraged, as the winged servants disappeared into the castle.

Simon immediately reached for tiny sandwiches and cookies and piled them on his plate. I watched Calytrix watching me.

"The Fae are your friends, Persephone," she said, both hands folded atop the bulge of her pregnant belly. "We seek to help you."

I didn't bother to correct her use of my full name. "How, exactly?"

"We are tied in ways you may not understand." She looked pointedly at the silver ring on my thumb, the leaves and vines so realistic it was hard to believe they weren't alive. "Your father, Ezekial, came here after your birth. He asked me for a ring forged of Faerie silver, so that we would recognize you as a friend to the Fae if you had need. To seek sanctuary."

A low buzz filled my ears. "My father?" I touched the silver ring, hard and skin-warmed. I wanted to remember my dad as the person he'd been, not the creature he'd become.

Echoing my thoughts, Calytrix said, "Ezekial is a good man. The Watchers and Faerie have long been allies, given our common ancestry."

"What—what common ancestry?"

"We are made of the same stars. From that primordial crucible in which magic was poured in, and we came out. Nephilim. The Fae are but one race of creatures bearing Watcher blood." She shifted in her seat, arms curling around her belly as if to shield it. "I hoped the Desidarian compass would lead you to us. It shows what you need, which is not always the same thing as what you want. And we, Persephone, very much need you."

My cheeks flashed with unbidden heat as Simon asked the next question for me. "What do you want with Seph, then?" He dropped a half-eaten sandwich to his plate, brushing crumbs from his fingers as he sat forward.

Alder inclined his head toward Calytrix. "Shall I explain, Aunt?"

She waved a bejeweled hand. "Please."

Alder settled back in his seat, running a hand through spiky brown hair. "Despite the abundance you see in the Weald Realm, there is a plague lurking amongst the worlds. It eats the land, taking until there is nothing left but a void of darkness." His voice dropped. "The Weald Fae have taken precautions against it with wards—old magic that our ancestors foresaw we would need some day. The wards have kept the darkness from encroaching upon Faerie. Until recently."

"So you've an edge here," Simon asserted.

Alder shook his head. "Not in the Weald, but in Fyrian lands to the east. However—" He looked at Calytrix. The corners of her mouth tightened infinitesimally. "We feel its presence knocking at our wards. These last fifty years, more and more Fae have fled our world to seek harborage elsewhere. The other Fae realms—the Water Sprites, Sylphs, the Fyrian and Mountain Fae—have suffered more than we have."

"What does this have to do with us?" The knot in my stomach hinted that I knew exactly where this was going. I wanted to stop it, to turn the conversation around from what I would be forced to reveal.

"What it has to do with *you*," Calytrix corrected, sipping from a crystal goblet. "There is a prophecy about the *Lihta*. The Lightbringer who can drive back the darkness." She took a breath, then recited, "She wields the sword of stars and ash; she holds life in her hands, and death in her eyes. She swings the blade, and worlds burn; worlds rise." Her liquid, dark gaze bore into mine. "You are the Lightbringer, are you not?"

She said Lightbringer like she would King or Queen—a title to be bestowed. My hands flexed in my lap as the absence of my power rang empty. "Not anymore."

"What does that mean?" Alder asked.

"Exactly what it sounds like," Simon said, holding Alder in a narrowed stare. "Seph isn't in the business of saving worlds at the moment."

"Impossible." The diamond drops at Calytrix's ears swung as she shook her head. "Our seers have seen this. They have seen you, Persephone."

I grimaced. Just like at Mellandra's, the idea that anyone had seen me in a prophecy made me want to fall into a sinkhole. "Simon's right. I lost my magic. Whatever I have has to be...borrowed." I sat up straighter, taking a breath. "I still don't see how the stone of Vadyron fits into all of this. We need the stone for something else. And if I'm not able to help you, then I think it's best we take it and be on our way."

"The stone fits into the pommel of the sword from the prophecy. The Fae sword that we have in our possession," Alder explained, giving what I assumed he thought was a charming smile. "United, they make the Soulstone Sword of legend."

I clenched my jaw, refusing to allow his hypnotic stare to distract me. "If we don't get that stone, Simon's life is forfeit. You can either give it to me, or I will take it from you."

Alder inched his chair backward. "I think we can work this out to our mutual benefit."

Standing, I shook my head. "There is no mutual benefit. There is only us taking the stone of Vadyron and leaving this world. I'm looking for someone, and I'm not going to stop until I find him." Something echoed through me, a pebble thrown into an empty cave.

"The Aureum captain?" Calytrix posed, a challenge in her eyes.

I swallowed back the urge to growl at her. Queen or no, she wouldn't intimidate me on this. "What do you know about him?" I bit.

"Persephone, we have spies everywhere. It is not only our wards that protect the Weald Fae. Sit, and I will tell you."

I lowered into the chair and crossed my arms, setting my jaw for good measure.

"We know about what happened in the prison world—the fight between your faction, the Aureum, and the demon Magoth. Your other companions are searching for you."

I surged forward, almost lifting out of my seat again. "You found them? Where are they?"

Calytrix shook her head. "Your friends were spotted in the Sylph realm, but have since disappeared again. We have eyes out for them."

Disappointment washed away the fluttering in my belly. But—they were out there somewhere, alive and together. That dying ember of hope sparked a little.

Simon grinned at me. "Maybe we can find them, Seph," he murmured. "They can help us get Eames."

"As can we," Calytrix replied, businesslike. "I believe you will find our interests in this matter are aligned."

"I told you, I'm not—"

The queen raised a hand to silence me. I bit back a retort, though I wanted to roll right over her. "I will help you get your captain back." She narrowed her gaze and canted her head, her next words measured. "For a price."

I paused. The Fae clearly had resources—lots of them, judging by the city's wealth and the number of guards I'd seen around the palace. The queen practically dripped with jewels. With their power on our side, we could find Alex and take on Magoth. I would be a fool to refuse, or at least not to hear her out. And I was done with foolishness.

"What price?" I ground out.

"You will remain in the Weald Court, training while you recover your powers. When they return, you will retrieve the Book of Shadows for us. Once you have the Book, we will send our forces with you to liberate your captain. Afterward, you will return to the Weald."

She listed it all out like items on a restaurant menu, like it was that easy. Too many thoughts clamored in response, all vying for attention. But the Book of Shadows took top place. I'd barely given it a passing thought since dealing with the death demons.

"The first grimoire," Simon said slowly, shoving back an errant strand of chestnut hair. "What d'you want with that?"

"You know it? Good, that saves time," Calytrix said. "And what I want with the Book, in no uncertain terms, is to ensure the safety of my people. We are fighting a war on two fronts, Master Simon. The death of the worlds, and the rise of forces who would like nothing more than to plunge the rest of us into a hell of their own making."

Trilling birdsong and the trickle of running water were the only sounds in the courtyard. Simon looked as stunned as I felt, his features frozen into a mask of shock.

I broke the silence. "What forces?"

Alder cleared his throat. "Demonkind. Or, more specifically, Magoth."

My jaw worked, but nothing came out as I felt a tugging sensation in the pit of my stomach. Perhaps there actually was some deity who wove the threads of fate, jerking on my string as they had a laugh.

So, Magoth was connected to this situation in more ways than one. He wasn't just the demon the Diurne had bargained with to slow the flow of his kind coming into their world, in exchange for handing over Lightbringers. If the Fae were to be trusted, then he was also plotting, what...the downfall of the worlds?

"How do you know?" I asked. "And why should I believe you?"

Queen Calytrix rubbed her brow, her only concession to anything less than tranquility since we'd been speaking. "I told you, we have eyes everywhere and friends in most places. Your father trusted me, Persephone. Is that not enough for you?"

"Frankly, no."

"Then you will need to take it on faith alone, and my word as sovereign that I speak truth. Surely, it should not be difficult to believe that Magoth is planning something more sinister. He is a demon, after all."

"Oy," Simon interjected. "Not all demonkind is like that monster."

Calytrix dipped her head. "My apologies. I did not mean to offend. But I implore you to understand the gravity of our position."

"Okay," I said, rubbing my temples. "Let me get this straight. You want the Book of Shadows to get rid of Magoth. Why do you need me to get it?"

"You are the only Lightbringer I currently have at my disposal," she snapped, her studied calm vanishing. "With your magic, you can sow life and beget death. The Book has unimaginable power, with the added benefit of being able to reveal where Master Eames is being held." Her chest heaved in a sigh. "Moreso, it's not about what I need, but what you want. And if you want our assistance retrieving your captain from the very forces who would destroy everything you hold dear—yes, your Guardian friends, Lady Bryony, your own human family—you will retrieve the Book of Shadows. You will wield the Soulstone Sword. And you will be our weapon."

A knife wouldn't have been enough to cut the tension between us.

A chainsaw, maybe. "I'm no weapon." *Not anymore.* All I wanted was to get Alex, then get Simon and I out alive. That was it. What Calytrix demanded from me seemed impossible to give.

"But you will be. That grimoire contains the knowledge of the first magics. Without it, we will all perish. With it, we will end this blight once and for all. And I aim to end it, Persephone." Her eyes shone fiercely, her jaw set.

I turned to Simon, his eyes flicking between the queen and Alder. "We need a minute."

Calytrix didn't break her stare for another few seconds. Then, she rose. "Of course." Alder took her elbow, escorting the queen back inside the palace. She glanced back before they disappeared. "But don't take too long."

Simon let out a harsh breath once they were gone. "Gods' teeth. She's a bit ferocious, isn't she? Doesn't seem like it at first."

I'd seen it all along, in the lines of her face and the set of her shoulders. From one woman with savage purpose to another, it was obvious. Queen Calytrix would stop at nothing to protect her kingdom.

As for me, I would stop at nothing to get to Alex. Calytrix had gathered that in an instant, and was using it to her advantage. Clever queen.

I leaned back in my chair, sighing deeply. The gentle warmth of sunlight on my skin and the fragrant scent of blooms in the courtyard were so at odds with talk of death and war. "I think she has us over a barrel," I told Simon.

His mouth twisted into a grimace. "You're right about that. No, er —offense, but I think their help can turn the tide on this. And if we're having a showdown with Magoth, I'd rather have them on our side, given the whole 'sending everyone to hell' bit."

"So you believe her, about Magoth taking over the worlds?"

"Until there's reason not to, I suppose," he answered. "Maybe that's why he wanted you so badly."

It made a certain kind of sense. Everyone wanted a piece of the Lightbringer, apparently. Lucky me. "Everyone seems to think I'm some insanely powerful being, but I really don't know shit." And it felt like a farce, especially since I still didn't have any magic at all right now. The only thing I'd managed to achieve so far was hurting both myself and Simon in a collection of increasingly terrible ways.

"Maybe the Fae can help," he offered. "Calytrix seems to know a thing or two about Lightbringer power."

"Maybe," I echoed, twisting the ring on my finger. All of this was supposition. We had no facts. "I don't want taking on this mission to slow us down." Though I couldn't even trust time anymore, given what Bri had told me. "But...." I had to admit that Simon was right—what we were doing to find Alex wasn't working. We needed to change tack, and the Book might hold the answers we needed. Perhaps I should've listened to Mellandra in the first place, but had instead been so wrapped up in impulsive urgency I didn't know what to do.

"My dad trusted them," I said, more to myself than Simon.

"True enough," he agreed.

"I'm also not making the mistake again of ignoring you. You can have the last word on this. I promise." Even though broken-me's desire to flee this place, to hold Alex in my arms, was like fire racing through my veins.

Simon's lips quirked into the semblance of a sad smile. "Thanks, Seph."

I wondered if we were having the same thoughts, remembering all of the times in the past months I'd selfishly gone forward with what I wanted, starting at Durl's house in Orrm.

"What do you think?" he asked. "Honestly."

"I think...that I'll do whatever it takes to find Alex," I said slowly.

Nothing was more clear than the fact that we needed help. We'd gone it alone, and gotten nowhere. But if it was the smart choice to stay, why did this feel like a betrayal? That it was becoming *us* over *him*— Simon and me over Alex? I pressed a hand to my stomach, desperate to rid myself of the dismal weight lodged there.

Simon nodded. "It seems like the Weald Fae are our best bet. And if it doesn't work out, we'll leave." His eyes tightened. "I don't know how we're going to sort Gamori, though."

"If the Fae want us to stay with them and keep the stone, they'll have to protect us from her."

"We can." Alder came back through the doors, bright wings undulating. "None but the Weald Fae, and those granted permission, can cross our wards."

"What happened to privacy?" Simon growled.

Alder grinned, showing sparkling white teeth as he adjusted his blue brocade vest. "I knew you'd say yes."

"You know, you're a lot more annoying now that we're not both locked in cages," I sniped.

He laughed, but his grin faltered. "I wanted to properly thank you for helping me escape."

"It was really Fane and Folly who saved us. Actually, where is Folly?" I wanted to see the courageous hound, but was a bit nervous—given the use of human speech, and all.

Alder rolled his eyes. "With some of the ladies in waiting. They're fawning over him. And while he had a part in it, you were brave enough to attack the priest in the first place. I admire courage."

Simon shot him a sour look. "Why don't you admire it from farther away?"

Chuckling, Alder asked, "Shall I inform the queen you're accepting our offer?"

I turned to Simon, and he nodded once. His eyes shone with certainty that I didn't feel, but I agreed anyway. "Yes."

Alder extended a piece of parchment and a short-bladed knife from behind his back. "For you."

"What's this?" I asked, although the sight of it jogged a memory.

Simon stayed my outstretched hand, mouth grim. "A blood promise?"

"It's a standard contract. That you will fulfill the obligations of the bargain with Queen Calytrix, in exchange for her protection and aid. You cannot depart from Faerie without her leave until the terms are met. And if she fails to protect you...well, there is a consequence for that as well."

"Deal's off," Simon said instantly. "She's not signing that."

"Simon," I warned. "You wanted to do this."

"Not if it requires forfeiting your freedom."

"If I remember correctly, you were only too happy to initiate this before."

"That's different," he answered, ears pinking slightly.

"Has Calytrix signed this?" I asked Alder.

"Of course." He pointed to a looping, rusty-brown signature at the bottom of the page. Then, his tone turned sincere. "She is the most honorable Fae I know."

"Then give me the damn paper." He set it on the table before me, and I sliced my finger with the knife he offered. Pressing it to the paper as I'd seen Alex do in Canhaben, words scrawled over the page, inked in my blood. I was surprised to find that I didn't much care about signing my life away.

"Tell the queen I want to start now. There's no point in wasting time." Alex couldn't afford for us to waste time.

"I shall convey your exact words." Sketching a short bow to me and nodding to Simon, he fluttered his wings and rose through the air, soaring into the heart of the branching castle.

"Why does everyone have to have wings?" Simon grumbled.

"Jealous?" I asked, arching a brow.

"Not at all," he mumbled, cramming another cookie into his mouth.

———

Alder had been telling the truth. Several Fae servants were in the palace's sunny atrium, lavishing attention on Folly. They cooed and rubbed his long ears, one going so far as to hand-feed him bits of meat. He looked rather pleased with himself, but lumbered to his feet when I approached.

The Fae left us alone, scurrying away with as much noise as a falling feather.

I eyed Folly, his black and tan coat dull, the wound on his neck wrapped. "So," I began, then trailed off.

"You needn't be frightened," the hound said, his voice deep and rumbling. "You weren't before. You were kind to me. The only one in that prison to not kick me or call me dog. Or worse." He wrinkled his nose, as much as an animal could.

"You looked so sad." I'd felt a kindred spirit in him, inside the walls of the dank fortress. "Were you a prisoner, too?"

"I was. For many, many years." His amber eyes drooped. "But you freed me. I owe you a debt."

"No." I shook my head and kneeled before him. "I'm tired of debts, of owing people. You attacked the priest in my cell. And Geist."

Folly bared his teeth. "It was a pleasure to taste his blood."

"Oh. Well...that's great, then," I said, trying not to grimace.

"My kind is loyal, Lightbringer. We delight in vengeance—when it is deserved."

"What is your kind? No offense," I added.

He gave me a doggy grin. "None taken. I am Eudaemon."

"Sorry, what?"

"We are guiding spirits, giving advice and protecting our masters should they fall into danger."

Huh. Handy. "So, what's your actual name?"

Folly shook his head, making his ears flop. "Folly is as good as any other. I rather like it, in fact. My previous master named me Schwartz-geneinshlengtine."

I snorted, clamping my lips together. Folly released a forceful pant that sounded like laughter. "You are my mistress now," he said, placing his chin on my shoulder.

I stroked his long ears. "Don't you want to be free? I'm sure you have a world that you belong to. A family?"

"Eudaemons do not have families. We were created by an ancient spirit, in an ancient world that no longer exists. I have had this form for a thousand years, and before that I was something else." He swiped my face with his long, wet tongue. "I choose you."

My chest ached in response to his words. I hesitantly wrapped my arms around him, and he bent toward me, humming low in his throat. It felt so good to lean into something soft and warm, and I buried my head in his neck, breathing in his musky scent.

I held onto him for a long time.

21

The training quad was on the west side of the palace grounds, past an orchard where tender blossoms unfurled on branches. High stone walls bordered the diamond-shaped field, which was part grass and part flag-stone tiles. Round targets were in one corner, while a barracks ran on the long side of the wall. Sizeable wooden poles were stuck in the ground at various intervals, and white chalk demarcated lines in the grass.

But what dominated the space was an obstacle course shaped like a spiky, spiny creature. There were climbing walls, hanging logs, ropes, platforms of varying heights, and at the very end was a brutal contraption with stumps arranged like teeth on either side of a hinged metal jaw.

Its brutality was at odds with the peace I'd come to associate with the Weald Fae over the past couple of days since we'd decided to stay. After all, the air still smelled of sweet flowers, and bright green leaves swayed gracefully in a light breeze.

I leaned against the wall as I waited to meet my new Fae trainer. Doing pushups and working with my nonexistent magic was the last thing I wanted to do, but I needed this. To be stronger, better, faster. When I faced Magoth, he would be brutal. And I had to be ready.

Hard pressure clamped down on my shoulder—a hand, yanking me backwards. Whirling, I struck out, only to have my arm grabbed and wrenched behind my back before I could lay eyes on my attacker. They pulled upward, forcing me to my knees. A whimper of pain escaped my lips even as my heart somersaulted.

"That's pitiful," a bass voice said. They released me, and I fell forward, my shoulder protesting. "Get to your feet, *Lihta*."

Scrambling up, I turned to face the asshole. And craned my head back to see his face.

The Fae man was well over six feet tall, and built like a brick wall. Brown skin encased all that muscle, and his black hair was tightly cropped, exposing gently pointed ears. His nose was crooked, as though it had been broken and never set correctly. But it was his eyes that made me quiver—they were tawny and rimmed by thick, dark lashes, practically leonine.

To my credit, I didn't turn and run. Then again, I was so winded already I wouldn't have gotten very far. "Who the hell are you?" I panted.

"Oleander. But you can call me Leander. Everyone does."

The part of my brain that collected obscure facts recognized that Oleander was a poisonous plant. Fitting. "Did anyone ever teach you to keep your hands to yourself, *Leander*?"

Parting full lips to reveal white, even teeth, he shoved my shoulder. It was more of a tap, really, but I stumbled all the same.

"Hey!" I raised my hands into a defensive position, scraping for power that wasn't there. I hadn't siphoned from anything since we'd been with the Fae. I promised myself I wouldn't, and would go without magic until mine returned. But my fingers still twitched toward all that smooth, bared skin.

"They won't keep their hands to themselves." Leander reached for me again, but I skipped out of range. "The demons, the ghosts, and the ghouls. The nightmares that sneak out from under your bed at night." The beat of his golden wings reminded me of a stalking predator.

The first shot of fear raced up my spine. "What the hell is your problem?"

Leander crossed tree trunk biceps over the muscled chest outlined by his snug green tunic. "I'm here to train you. And I don't have a problem. You do."

"Oh? And what's that?"

He was on me in the space of a heartbeat. He flipped me onto my back and held his leather vambrace against my throat. I struggled against him. Despite the gentle pressure he exerted, his arm was immovable as stone.

"Fight me off, *Lihta*. Go on."

"Let me up and I will," I gasped.

"No." His tawny eyes flashed. "This is your first lesson. Don't let your opponent take you by surprise. That's how you end up on the ground."

"If I had power, I would kick your ass," I snarled.

"Another weakness," he noted. "That must explain all the scars."

I saw red. Heat raced up my spine, and I brought my knee up between his legs. He swiveled to avoid it, smirking. I wanted to claw that smile right off his face.

"Try again," he taunted.

Bridging my hips up, I bucked, trying to roll and hook my leg around him like Fern had taught me. *Fern*. With my emotions running high, her betrayal stung like a slap. I dropped to the ground.

"Do you care about this?" Leander demanded, watching my rage fade from a boil to a simmer. "Queen Calytrix must be mistaken. You're no warrior. You'd be useless to us in battle."

Fucker. I cleared my throat, then spat in his face. The bastard didn't even blink. "Is that your worst?" he jeered.

I didn't think about what happened next. I sunk my hands into the grass, siphoning its life energy into me. It was only a thimbleful, but I used it to arc flames over my body. Satisfaction flared through me when I smelled sizzling flesh. Leander hissed and loosened his grip. I shoved fifteen feet away from him in an instant, holding blue flame for a second until the siphoned power dried up.

Shit. I hadn't meant to do that.

"Now that is a neat trick," he admitted, flexing his fingers. "Too bad you can't sustain it."

"You're a fucking prick," I panted. That little show had cost me. Pain pulsed behind my left eye, and my legs trembled.

"Yes. I'm the fucking prick who's going to keep you alive. And by extension, the rest of us." He crossed the gap between us, and I shuffled backward.

"Now run."

"Excuse me?"

"Should we add poor hearing to the list of your faults?" He enunciated the next word. "*Run*. If you can't fight, at least you can work on your fitness."

I reminded myself that I needed to do this anyway. If I walked away from Leander like I so desperately wanted to—preferably after throwing something heavy at him—I'd be giving up. Now that I was getting my head back on straight, I couldn't afford to back down. I wouldn't.

The bastard must have seen acquiescence in the slump of my shoulders. "Go until I say stop." He sprang into the air, flying to the top of the wall and perching atop it like a gargoyle. An ugly one, I thought sourly.

But I swallowed down my anger and pride, and ran around the perimeter of the training field. And ran. And ran. My legs were like lead, and the field blurred into stripes of green grass and gray wall. Last night I didn't have an appetite, so I'd only picked at my dinner—served in the kitchen of the cottage I shared with Simon, rather than the formal dining room—and now heartily regretted it. The mirror in my room had shown me just how much weight I'd lost, and I'd never be able to build back muscle if I didn't eat.

At least the burn in my legs kept my mind off the shame that had flooded me after I'd siphoned. But it felt so good, that flare of power where there was usually emptiness. *No. Don't think about that. Keep moving.*

Sweat stung my eyes, and my lungs were on fire. Surely, I had to be burning up from the inside out. Eventually, my legs failed me. I stumbled and went to my knees. When I began to crawl, Leander called, "Stop."

Black spots flashed across my vision as I collapsed onto my back. Clouds scudded across the cornflower blue sky. Then Leander's face appeared, hovering over me. Ugh.

"We're done for today," he said. "Oh, and no more siphoning. If you're using magic, it's going to be clean. Fix that." He pointed to the two dead spots of grass where my hands had pressed into the earth. "See you tomorrow, *Lihta*. Same time. Same place."

He launched his gargantuan body from the ground and flew, zooming off toward the castle. Or perhaps hell, which was where he belonged. Maybe Leander was one of Satan's handmaidens in disguise.

I crawled to the wall and braced my hands against it as I vomited. Bile seared my throat, but I let it come until I felt hollowed out. Not much different from normal.

"Are you okay?" Bri jogged toward me in a pair of loose white pants that were split to the knee, and a sleeveless tunic. Sandals laced to her mid-calves.

I wiped my mouth on my sleeve and sat back. "Do I look like I'm okay?"

She frowned, then said, "Cup your hands." I glared at her, but she insisted. "Go on."

I did. Crystal clear water appeared in my palms. I gulped it down greedily. Its icy chill washed the acid from my mouth, leaving me with the feeling that I was unsullied. Clean. "Thanks." I got up and skirted the pile of vomit, coming to rest against a patch of wall near Bri.

"I can talk to the queen. Ask her to assign someone else to train you. I saw Leander flying off. He's a general and our best warrior, but—he has a reputation."

"And no one thought to warn me," I muttered. "I'll be fine. I know how to deal with assholes." The press of cool stone against the back of my head soothed the ache put there by siphoning. That little taste had me wanting so much more. "You have that kind of pull with Calytrix?"

"Queen Calytrix and one of my dads were close friends as children. With Alder's mother, as well. His father is brother to the queen's husband, Virid."

I squinted, barely able to make sense of all the connections through my exhaustion. "Does the queen have any other children?"

Bri shook her head. "No, this is her first. She has been trying for many, many years to get pregnant. Since the darkness came, it's been increasingly difficult for our people to bear children. This child is a miracle. If she hadn't been able to conceive, the throne would have passed to Alder when the time came."

"So not only is he a lord, he's next in line to the throne?"

"Yes. Which is why the queen is so thrilled to see him returned."

I sighed. "My reward for rescuing her heir is to train with a sadist?"

Bri snorted. "She is very grateful. And now, you're doing her another service by seeking the Book of Shadows." Her face fell. "Look, I want to talk to you. To explain about all the shit that's gone down." These were the first words I'd heard of hers that sounded more like Bri, not Lady Bryony.

There were no secrets between us anymore. Bri knew exactly what I was, and I knew what she was, too. What was missing were the thousands of little moments we hadn't shared with each other that had gotten us to those places. Could I give her that? When I looked into Bri's eyes now, I saw a stranger. The distance between us—who we'd been and who we were now—was more vast than an ocean.

"I'm not up for that." I straightened, pushing off the wall. "It's still sinking in that you're..." I gestured to her wings. "Not human. You could be a thousand years old, for all I know."

She scoffed. "Hardly. I'm 130. But, um, much younger in human years, of course," she added quickly.

My teeth clicked together as I snapped my jaw shut. Bri, who looked the same age as me—younger, even—was 130 years old? It only added to the sense of betrayal, to the lies she'd fed me. "Christ," I muttered.

"You're not human either," she said softly.

"I only found out less than a year ago! You've known what you are your entire life. And you lied to me about it. I mean, you're old enough to be my great-grandma. Great-great grandma? Whatever."

She bit her full lip. "I'm sorry, Seph. Truly, I never meant to hurt you. But I was living as human—fully human, no wings or magic or any of it. Even if you would've believed me, I didn't think it would matter."

"It does matter. It did." I scrubbed my hand over my face, wiping away a crust of dried sweat. "You could've said something when I—that last time." Old pain filled her eyes, and I knew she was also remembering our last phone call.

"As could you," she said softly. "Maybe I would've tracked you down sooner if you had."

"Tracked me down?"

"I came back to the Weald after you disappeared. I tried to contact you a million times, even went to your mom's house a few months ago.

She didn't know," Bri added hastily at my look of horror. "When I found no trace of you, I returned home and asked for help. I didn't know that your father had a relationship with the Weald Fae. That you are a Watcher."

So that's how Calytrix had caught wind of me, apart from the fact that my father had once upon a time been in Faerie. Had gone to them after I was born, for help. To ask them to give me sanctuary, should I require it. He'd given up his life, his love, his home. Everything that mattered.

Was I wasting it? Squandering the life he'd given me over petty disagreements with people who cared about me? Bri had gone looking for me when I disappeared. No matter what happened between us—the Bri I once knew was still my friend. Was still in there somewhere under the facade of Lady Bryony.

Bri worried her bottom lip, the skin under her eyes tight. Her long, black hair blew around her heart-shaped face.

The friend I'd known, not the Fae Lady, was who I spoke to next. "My life changed, so completely," I began, tucking an escaped lock of hair behind my ear. "It was hard, but good. In a lot of ways, it was the happiest I've ever been. And now...." Now almost everyone who'd become my family had been swallowed up by the vastness of the worlds, and I didn't know how to find them. "I just feel lost."

Her brows knit, and a sheen of tears filled her eyes that she blinked back. "I'm sorry, sweetie. Do you...do you want to talk about it?" she offered.

I took a deep breath, pain whistling through the hollow place in my chest. "I'm not sure I can. Yet."

"I think I know someone who might be able to help with that."

———

I may have taken longer in the bath than strictly necessary as I prepared for a meeting with a Fae healer called Val. The hot water soothed my aches and pains from the awful training session, but did nothing to quell the churning in my stomach.

Val wasn't a healer of the body—she was a healer of the mind and spirit. Bri assured me she was the best, having helped Queen Calytrix through her grief over multiple miscarriages.

I was willing to try anything to get my magic back, which was the only reason I'd agreed to let some stranger inside my head. That didn't mean I had to like it.

Dressing in the same style of loose clothing Bri had worn earlier, I left my hair down and descended the spiral stairs to the cottage's lower level. When I entered the living area, I found an old woman sitting on one of the overstuffed couches. She was framed by a pair of sapphire wings, and lines were carved in the corners of her bright brown eyes. They shone with quiet compassion that calmed some of the tension in my shoulders.

"Hello, Seph." Her voice was as clear and deep as a lake. "That is what you prefer to be called?"

"Yeah." I took a seat on the couch across from her, twisting my hands in my lap. "Val, right? Er—thanks for coming."

"It's normal to be nervous." Val's lips curved in a gentle smile. "Why don't we get to know each other before we begin?"

"Um...okay." I traced the silver leaves of the Faerie ring on my thumb. "Well, you know my name, obviously." She nodded, tucking her hands into the sleeves of her loose yellow dress. It matched the sunny rug on the floor. "And...." How to tell her about myself? There was too much to sort out, like sifting through a mile-high garbage heap for the grossest piece of trash.

"What do you like to do in your free time?" she asked.

An easy question. I breathed a sigh of relief. "Read."

Val smiled again, the folds in her face deepening. "How wonderful. I love a good book myself. Any favorites?"

We talked about books for a while—not that we knew any of the stories outside our respective worlds—but it was nice to chat about something other than demons and death.

I relaxed into the tufted couch, smoothing a hand over the sage green velvet. "It's never been easy for me to talk to people," I admitted.

"Oh?" Val raised a white eyebrow. "You appear to be quite the conversationalist."

"I feel...comfortable around you."

"I appreciate that. I hope I will continue to earn your trust." She shifted. "I wonder if you would tell me about your power?"

I stiffened. "Oh—sure." I explained about the twin power sources behind my mental door, how the riverbeds were dry and crumbling.

"Hm," Val said, considering me. "It sounds like you need to make some rain."

Make rain? As if it was that simple. "Right," I answered. "I'll try."

She smiled. "Good. Now, if I have your permission, I would like to sense you."

"Sense me?"

"I am not just easy to talk to," she said with a gentle smile. "I'm sure Lady Bryony told you I work in the healing arts. Part of that includes assessing my patient."

My throat closed, and I cleared it. I'd battled demons, for Christ's sake. This would be nothing in comparison. "Okay."

Val had me lay on the rug, face up. "You don't have to do anything," she assured me. "And I promise you, it won't be painful. Although, you may experience some mild discomfort."

Oh, shit. I nodded, staring up at the arched, exposed beams in the ceiling. Val knelt over me, palms facing down.

"I'm going to begin now," she stated. I swallowed hard.

She started at my feet, hovering her hands several inches above me as she worked her way up. I didn't feel anything at all until she reached my left hip, where the slash from the death demon ended. A ghost of pain echoed there. It didn't hurt, but there was some uncomfortable pressure.

"Shall I continue?" she asked. I nodded again.

The scar tingled all the way up my back, until Val's hands reached my chest—the hollow area beneath my ribs that had emptied when Alex was dragged into the pit.

The ache increased until it was a hot, dull throb, like an open wound that wouldn't scab. I grimaced, and a feeling rose in me that had tears pricking the back of my eyes.

Without hesitation, Val moved up my chest, over the scar from the demon Ventusiel, and finally finished at my head. She paused there for several minutes, before sitting back onto her heels. "You can sit up."

I sat on the ground and pulled my knees into my chest, trying to shield the ache. Val's soft gaze held mine.

"You have deep wounds in your soul," she finally said. "Layer upon layer of them. Some old, some new."

All I heard was *damaged, broken, weak.*

"That's what's blocking my magic?"

"I believe so. Although, I cannot say with certainty."

"So how do I get rid of them?"

Val shook her head. "There is no getting rid of. There is only living with, and in time, healing."

"What if I don't have time?" I couldn't afford to wait years to get my power back. Alex needed me now.

"You cannot rush these things. But you need to touch your pain, Seph. Avoiding your emotions helps no one, least of all you. When you are able to look your grief in the face and welcome it with open arms—that is when your magic will return. Accepting this will begin the healing process."

"Alex isn't dead," I said through a tight jaw. "I don't have to grieve anything."

The old woman gazed at me with those bright, all-knowing eyes. It made my palms itch. "Grief is for the living, my dear. It is for anyone who loves deeply, and loses. It is a part of life if you're really living it." She continued at my slight head shake. "What is light, without shadow? Love, without loss? Joy, without pain? Neither can exist without the other."

How was this New Age mumbo jumbo supposed to help me? I needed actionable steps, something I could hold in my hands and reshape until it looked the way I wanted it to. "I'll keep that in mind."

Val rose, sweeping the skirt of her dress aside. "It may help if we continue to meet and discuss this. If you're agreeable, of course."

"Fine," I said through a clenched jaw.

"I'll see you again soon, then." With a short bow, she swept out.

I sat there numbly until a door opened down the hall and Simon strode through the arched doorway into the living area, a cup of tea in hand. He stopped, staring at me. "What's happened? You look like you've seen a ghost."

I released a bitter laugh. That's what Val wanted—for me to see the ghosts of everything I'd lost. But if I did, I feared I'd get stuck in the past with them. I'd watched my mother fall prey to the specter of my father's memory—how it had kept her bedridden and far away for years. *Keep moving.*

"I'm fine," I said, getting to my feet. "You're looking chipper for someone recovering from a stab wound."

Simon waved his mug. "I feel good, really. And...they've given me some paints and canvas." He grinned broadly.

Simon's art had been all over Jupiter's, but I'd never seen him paint before. I was getting to know a new side of him in Faerie, one that wasn't visible in Canhaben nor when we were on the road. Instead of his usual snark, he was humorous without the bite. Not as reclusive, either. "That's great. Can I see what you're working on?"

"Later. I have a process, you know."

"The temperamental artist." I rolled my eyes, and he grinned again. It was good to see him smiling. I was glad one of us was.

"Who're you calling temperamental?"

I laughed, as he expected me to. "I'm going out. Be back later."

I left him there, in his happy little cloud. If I didn't keep moving, I wouldn't be able to protect it.

22

It had been two weeks of Faerie time since we'd arrived in the Weald realm, battered and bloody. Gamori hadn't come to collect on our bargain, or if she had, the wards were keeping her at bay. I was able to withstand Leander's punishing running drills a little longer each day before I collapsed. My wounds from Aundirne had healed.

Yet, the memories remained unchanged. Nightmares invaded my sleep, but at least I didn't encounter any demons in them. I only saw purple-robed priests, ferronite mittens, the edge in Evinia, and my broken magic. Like clockwork, I'd wake up in the wee hours, shivering and slicked with icy sweat. Anxiety gnawed at my nerves like a dog with a bone until the sun rose and I could get outside.

Folly, who'd moved into the cottage with us, would walk with me as the early morning air washed away the stickiness of dreams. He never asked what those nightmares were about, but stayed by my side. That was much better than having to talk about them with Val, so I'd stopped bringing them up during our sessions.

Simon eyed me over the breakfast table as I attempted to overcome my lack of appetite by holding my breath and shoving food down my throat. Folly lay on top of my feet under the table.

"You know, people don't usually treat breakfast like an adversary," Simon mentioned. He buttered toast, then took a huge mouthful.

I scowled at him. "When did you become a morning person?" While we'd been traveling, I always had to shake him awake right before we left.

"It's these Faerie beds. You think they'd tell us how they make the mattresses?"

"For you? Probably." My grouchy, irascible friend had unwittingly become a darling of Faerie nobility. Perhaps they found his attitude charming, because Simon was inundated with invitations to dinners and events. I wondered if it was the beguiling artist side of him that attracted their attention—he spent his days painting until dusk fell.

I'd seen some of his work, inspired by the bucolic countryside of the Weald Fae. It was exquisite, the lines graceful and colors so true they seemed like a photograph.

Simon transformed when he painted. I'd watched him a few times now, working by the riverside or in enchanting meadows. The way his gray eyes focused so intently on his subject, like the rest of the world just faded away; how he bit his bottom lip, wielding the paintbrush like it was an extension of his hand, the hair skimming his collar paint-flecked and in disarray.

"What's on the agenda for today?" he asked, taking a long draught from his tea. I'd resigned myself to not having coffee—I didn't even miss it anymore, it had been so long.

"Calytrix wants me to ride out to visit the wards with the guard." I was almost grateful that I wouldn't have to see the prick—what I'd taken to calling Leander. But I knew that any day off wouldn't help me improve. He'd agreed to lay off the magic and only work on physical training, by order of Calytrix. I was certain that Bri had whispered in her ear about it after our discussion at the training field.

"Wards, eh? Sounds interesting. Should I come?"

"I thought you were going to some luncheon—that lady who's a few houses down. What's her name?"

"Ivy," Simon reminded me. "And nah. How these folk can have so many parties, I've no idea. What have they even got to celebrate? There's always too many of them around, I tell you. It's hard to find a moment of peace."

I stifled a laugh. "You know, every time you refuse, they're going to work even harder to get you to acknowledge them."

He flicked his wrist in dismissal. "Eh, I say yes to a few. Anyway, shall I join?"

I surveyed Simon over the rim of my mug. He'd put on weight, and had the robust glow of someone who spent time outdoors. He looked... content.

"No, that's okay. I'm sure it'll be boring."

"If you say so." He dipped his head. I took one more bite of porridge, then stuck an apple in the pocket of my tunic.

"Gotta go. See you tonight?"

He nodded, waving me off. "Enjoy your wards."

I pushed up from the small breakfast table, walking under the arched opening toward the foyer. Folly scrambled to his feet and lumbered after me. The day was bright and sunny, as every day had been so far. Warming temperatures signaled that we were about a month away from the summer solstice.

"Mistress Persephone." A green and gold liveried Fae man with pale blue wings and blond hair approached. "And Master Folly."

"Hi. It's Seph," I reminded him. As I'd been reminding everyone for weeks now. Folly snuffled.

The liveried man only gave a short bow and escorted me the rest of the way to the stables. I'd never ridden a horse before, but now was as good a time as any to learn, I supposed.

Except there was no equine presence waiting for us just beyond the stable at the edge of the forest.

Ten sleek foxes the size of small horses sat back on their haunches. Most had red coats, but a few were gray and black. Their eyes shone yellow, green, and brown, flicking back and forth between me and my escort.

Their curious eyes weren't the only strange things about them. Atop each fox's head grew a pair of antlers perched like a crown, ranging from snow white to ebony to silver.

I drew a sharp breath. "What are those?"

The Fae man smiled. "The *deor feya*. The wild ones from the Bearu-Glom, our forest. Or rather, their forest. *Deor feya* have been in these lands long before Faerie came."

A black fox with deep green eyes looked at me and flicked its tail, as if to say, "What are you staring at?"

I blinked and averted my gaze. A retinue of Fae guards approached from around the side of the stables.

Alder was among them, walking with a swagger in his step and a mocking smile on his face. Calytrix was just behind him, on the arm of a pale-skinned, light-haired Fae man. She wore brown leather pants and a long-sleeved tunic, with a matching leather vest loosely laced over the mound of her belly. Her braided hair was swept up into a knot, and she wore a thin crown of silver daisies.

The man escorting her was handsome and also wore a simple crown, like Prince Charming but a little rougher around the edges. He looked at the queen with such devotion, I knew this must be her partner.

"Persephone," the queen said. "Nice to see you again."

Inclining my head to the queen, I bit my tongue. "Queen Calytrix."

Alder flashed a smile at me. I settled for raising my brows in my response.

"Allow me to introduce my husband, the king consort. Virid, this is Mistress Persephone Hart."

"An honor," he intoned in a deep voice, bowing from the waist. His green eyes were brighter than new spring leaves. They missed nothing as they scanned me.

I nodded again, hoping that my expression conveyed the appropriate reverence. These courtly greetings were confusing at best, and a mine-field at worst.

"Thank you for agreeing to come," she told me. The queen approached the largest of the giant foxes, a red one with yellow eyes and white antlers. "And thank you for escorting us, Rua."

The fox blinked once, then stretched, lowering its shoulders and neck. Virid held the queen's hand as she swung gracefully onto Rua's back. Calytrix patted the animal, then beckoned to me. "Come. Time is wasting."

I exchanged a glance with Folly. "They will not harm you," he said, jowls quivering. "The *deor feya* are guardians of the forest. Only those who they permit walk amongst the shadows of these trees."

The forest seemed different than any I'd encountered so far in the Weald Realm. These trees were larger, their trunks thick as ten Fae men standing side by side, their rough bark deeply furrowed into grooves. Dark green leaves, almost black, budded from their branches.

One of the foxes—the black one with the green eyes who'd caught me staring earlier—approached me with silent strides. It stopped a few feet away, watching me with a boldness that had me shrinking back. I pressed against Folly's shoulder, reassured by the hound's sturdiness.

Hello, Lihta. The voice sounded like shadows at midnight, dark and sinuous and female.

Startled, I looked over my shoulder.

The fox barked a laugh. *No, girl. That was me. I am Sceadu. Climb upon my back.*

"Um—" I turned back to stare. "Are you sure?"

Sceadu narrowed her eyes then bowed, tail lifting into the air. Folly nudged me forward with an encouraging headbutt to my knees. I clambered onto the fox's back none too gracefully.

By this time, the others were mounted and already turned toward the forest. "You'll stay with me?" I asked Folly.

"If I have permission," he answered.

You may enter our forest, eudaemon, Sceadu said. *But do not stray from us.*

Folly let out a melodious howl of agreement, then we set off into the Bearu-Glom. I couldn't help but think about hounds hunting foxes, but decided to keep that to myself.

Sceadu moved so smoothly underneath me I felt like I was floating above the ground. Still, I wove my fingers into the dense thicket of her shiny black fur for security.

The trees were spaced far apart, but their colossal canopies cast overlapping shadows so that we were almost plunged into a twilight. Silence descended on our party, the only sounds the rustle of clothing and clearing of throats.

Alder sidled up beside me on his *deor feya,* a red with eyes that had turned liquid black in the gloom.

"Fine morning, isn't it?" he asked in English, voice a hushed murmur. As opposed to most of the Weald Fae, who tended to wear more muted tones, Alder dressed in saturated hues. Today's outfit was a white shirt with tangerine trousers and matching vest.

I gave him a sidelong glance. "I suppose."

His eyes, that brightest blue, sparkled even amidst the shadows. "If I knew it would take going to the wards to spend time with you, I would've asked Aunt Caly and Uncle Vir much sooner."

My back stiffened. Alder had come to the cottage a few times to "check in on me." So far, I'd politely refused all his requests to accompany him into the city for evenings of merriment and revelry. I wasn't sure if it was misguided gratitude that led to the invitations, or if he genuinely wanted to spend time with me. Either way, I didn't need him underfoot.

"I'm not here to play," I reminded him. "I have a job to do." A job that was going very poorly at the moment. I still hadn't recovered my power, despite meetings with Val. Leander continued to wipe the floor with me during training. Yesterday, the damned sadist made me run for the full two hours. My hamstrings suddenly ached as if in remembrance.

"So serious," Alder commented, smirking. "Lighten up, Seph. We survived Festborg and Geist. You should be celebrating the win."

All I could do was stare into his laughing eyes as I battled with the rage burning my sternum. Folly let out a low whine from where he trotted on my other side. Then I heard Sceadu's voice in my head. *Breathe, Lihta. Else you will faint and fall off my back. And if you do, then I will leave you for the beasts who are not so friendly as me.*

Her midnight voice was like a thick layer of ash thrown over a fire. It quieted the flames of my anger to a dull crackle.

I shifted my attention to the mossy ground as I answered Alder. "We have very different definitions of what it means to win. That battle may be over, but there is a war ahead of us. One that you would do well to prepare for."

After a beat of silence, he spoke. "I do not mean to belittle your hardship. It is in my nature to be somewhat...brash. I apologize." There was real contrition on his face, his bright eyes sober.

"No harm done," I replied.

"I do hope that we might be friends," he added. "As I said, I greatly admire you."

He should find something worthy to admire, not a ravaged, burnt husk of a woman. But I nodded anyway, knowing that such a thing would never really be possible. "I've been meaning to ask you something," I started.

"Yes, of course," Alder answered swiftly, perhaps eager to change the subject.

"When we were on top of Festborg, after I...fell, and you came after me. How did you manage to open a gateway in the water?"

Alder scrunched his forehead. "A gateway?"

"The whirlpool we went through." I mimed the swirling motion of a spiral. "I thought they were only able to be opened in cemeteries." I'd thought a lot about it during my early morning ramblings with Folly.

"Ah," he said, the light of understanding coming into his eyes. "*Fealdplethe*."

"What's that?"

"As you said. A portal, an opening between worlds. We have no need for a burial ground to open them, although that would work. Fae can open *fealdplethe* in any place of..." He searched for the word. "In-between. When we fell, I opened one between sky and earth. Or, sky and water, rather."

Curiosity flickered amongst the ashes. "Any space of transition?"

Alder nodded. "All you need is a middle space. That is what the borders of the worlds are, anyway—neither here, nor there. Both, and nothing."

Something he said tickled my awareness, like a half-forgotten memory. I brushed it away. How useful would it have been to open a gateway during some of our narrow escapes?

"Can you teach me?"

His brow furrowed again. "Perhaps. I don't see why not. You are Nephilim, after all. But you would need this, I think." He held his palm out to me. On it was a line of dark, swirling ink. A tattoo of a spiral.

I'd never noticed that before, but then again, I didn't usually stare at people's hands. "What's that?"

"It concentrates power. We take advantage of the in-between nature of the portal and instruct it where to go with our will. Portals like being told what to do. Magic likes direction."

I glanced at him. "Really?"

Alder seemed like he wanted to say something else, but the convoy slowed. The trees ahead thinned, light penetrating the gloom to shine on the forest floor. Soon, we were back in the open, and Folly broke away to trot ahead into a meadow pocked with orange and red flowers.

Stately trees with broad, sweeping boughs arced over us. And then there were the wards.

Great cairns made of mounded black stones rose into the sky. They stood in formation like straight-backed soldiers ready to defend, spaced at intervals in an unending line. Power rippled from them, enough to make my heart beat unevenly.

Calytrix dismounted Rua and laid a hand upon his shoulder. He turned and walked back into the forest, waiting in the shadows.

The rest of us slid from the *deor feya* with varying amounts of grace. *I will be waiting for you, Lihta,* Sceadu said. She joined her folk, almost invisible amongst the trees. The guards in our entourage began walking between the cairns, stopping at each to check for...well, I wasn't sure what.

"Our wards, Persephone. They defend us by keeping our magic in, and everyone else's magic out." Calytrix stood with her back to them and faced me. She spread her hands wide. "These have been standing for thousands of years, since the time of ancient Faerie. Their power is tied to the earth itself—the elemental magic that the Fae wield. We renew the magic on the summer solstice, the day that we celebrate the abundance and fruitfulness of the land." She gestured me forward. "Come. See for yourself."

Folly loped around us to sniff at the base of one of the great cairns. The structure was as wide as the trees we'd left behind in the Bearu-Glom. The air surrounding the cairn seemed thick, catching in my lungs.

"The protection is strongest here where it comes from the source. These wards defend all of the Weald." Calytrix's dark eyes met mine. "All of my people."

I knew she wanted to impress upon me the severity of my mission to retrieve the Book of Shadows, wherever it was—to regain my strength, so that I could beat Magoth and save the worlds.

But under the weight of her stare and the umbras of the wards, I felt small. So very, very small.

I simply nodded, gazing at the verdant grassland beyond the ward-line. "What's out there?"

"The Sylph Realm. This is our shared border. Past the Sylphs is the

Mountain Realm, then the Fyrians. On our other side are the Sprites, although they live all across the Silver Sea."

"They don't have wards?"

Queen Calytrix compressed her lips. "They have their own protection, but none so powerful as our wards. Though the Weald Fae are a peaceful people, we have a sizable army. I have sent soldiers to their borders for reinforcements."

I didn't need her to tell me they hadn't been successful. The drawn look on her face said everything. Her hand went to the curve of her belly, stroking.

"These are dangerous times we find ourselves in, Persephone. But," she looked to where Alder stood, circling the base of a cairn with Virid, "we take our joy and pleasures where we can. For they may soon be few and far between."

"Your Majesty—" I broke off at Folly's low growl.

A shape flickered into being in the grassland. It was a tall figure, with long, raven hair and crimson robes. Dusky skin and black eyes, a glittering crown perched atop her head.

Gamori had found us.

23

Ice gathered in my sternum. Folly howled, blaring the alarm. I grabbed the queen's arm and backed us away from the wards without a word, retreating toward the forest. Calytrix didn't protest, just followed my gaze past the ward-line.

She rattled something out in Fae language too fast for me to follow. Her guards drew their swords and surrounded us at once, Virid pushing past them to get to Calytrix. Alder appeared at my elbow, Folly underfoot.

Gamori approached the line of great cairns, trailing her fingertips through the high grass. It blackened at her touch and left a path a rot in her wake. "Hello, my wayward daughter. You are a slippery one, aren't you?" Was that a grudging ounce of respect I heard in her tone?

I couldn't force words past my dry throat. Part of me had wanted to believe that she'd give up the stone when we didn't show—but of course, that was a child's magical thinking.

"Leave, demon. You cannot cross these wards," Calytrix stated from the center of the ring of guards. Unafraid, unbothered. I wished I felt the same.

"Perhaps not." Gamori scowled at the wards. She stood about six feet beyond their line. "But I came to remind our dear Lightbringer that the moment she or her darling little friend steps outside them, I

238

will be waiting." She smiled, her white, pointed teeth glistening in the late spring sun. It was a predator's smile, hungry and eager for the taste of blood. "Oh, and there's one other tidbit I wanted to share. You have a contingent of Guardian friends, yes? The ones who don't want you dead. Well, I am more than happy to track them down and pick them off one by one if you don't fulfill the terms of our bargain."

Heart straining against my ribs, I shoved through the guards until I was free of them. Folly came after me, nipping at the hem of my tunic. "If you touch a single one of them—" I began.

Gamori laughed. "You'll what? You cannot do a single thing if you are behind that ward-line, my dear. But if you want to come out to play, I'm more than happy to entertain you."

In that moment, I wanted to. The rage surging through my blood compelled me forward, and had Calytrix's guards not surrounded me again, I would've. Except—as I had the thought, there was a strange sensation around my ribs. A crushing, binding feeling that put pressure on my heart and caused it to slow from a sprint to a hobble. I gasped, clutching at my shirt. Was it the magic from the wards, or something else?

Calytrix's gaze flicked over me before returning to Gamori. "I am not interested in threats, and neither is the Lightbringer. Your trip is wasted, I fear."

"Wasted?" The demon seemed to grow taller, and her waist-length hair rippled in a breeze. "If you say so, pixie queen." She locked eyes with me again. "So be it."

Gamori flicked her fingers and sent an inferno blasting through the grassland. It raced in all directions, burning up swathes of land in an instant. Black smoke billowed from the flames and blew toward us in a thick cloud.

Sulfur rushed into my lungs, hot like I'd inhaled the fire itself. Everyone was swarming and shouting orders, rushing toward the forest where the *deor feya* still waited. I watched it all happen like I was standing outside myself, frozen. Instead of the burning grassland, I saw sheer cliff walls with a bubbling pit at the bottom. Yellow eyes and a scaly, barbed tail. The love and sorrow in Alex's eyes as he disappeared.

Then I felt something warm and wet on my hand, and looked down to see Folly licking me insistently. Someone grabbed my arm and pulled me toward the forest. "Come on," Alder urged.

"Stop." Calytrix's voice rang out, and everyone immediately ground to a halt, coughing and wiping streaming eyes. "Air users, blow this vile stench away. That demon will not distract us. We will continue conducting our business until I deem it finished." She scanned the crowd of Fae, their wings held rigid. "What are you waiting for? Go on."

Three Fae assembled at the ward-line, raising their hands toward the sky. A strong wind tugged at my braid, then the cloud of smoke reversed toward the burning meadow past the wards. Someone thrust a canteen into my hands, and I took two hard swallows before passing it on.

I wanted to slump to the ground and curl in on myself. Davina, Hollis, Casey, and the twins, were out there somewhere. And now Gamori would be hunting them, because I'd failed to deliver. Because I was bound by another promise to an obdurate queen who would use me for her own ends. The powerlessness that was my constant companion stung, a knife finding its target and twisting.

Virid came forward, his pale face ash-streaked. "Myself and the other water users can put out the fire."

"No," Calytrix barked. "That demon is waiting for you to do exactly that.

"You would let it burn?" he demanded.

"I would have you live," she replied.

Virid held her gaze for a moment longer, and the look that passed between them was so intimate that I turned away. "Come," he instructed, and the rest of the guards followed, dispersing back to the wards as the fire raged on.

Calytrix approached where I stood at the edge of the woods with Folly. A scattering of gray ash covered her shoulders. "Are you well?"

I narrowed my gaze, unsure how to articulate the anger and fear and desperation all grappling for dominance. "Gamori is going after my friends, but I can't do a damn thing about it because of the blood promise—which is what I assume stopped me from going after her just now. She firebombed your meadow to make a point." And in doing so had scared me brainless, thinking about the possible consequences for

Simon should he leave Faerie. I released a long breath. "No, I'm not well."

"I will not apologize for protecting my people. You would do the same if our positions were reversed, would you not?"

I wanted to tear my hair out. Because I would, of course I would. That didn't make it an easier pill to swallow. "You're just going to let her loose, then? To let all this burn?"

Calytrix's high cheekbones sharpened as her face went diamond-hard. "Virid will alert the Sylph Queen of both the fire and the demon. I have already told you we have Fae looking for your friends. If they are anywhere in Faerie, they will be found and offered sanctuary. That is as much protection as I can offer." She took a half-step toward the cairns, then paused. "Do not accuse me of not caring, Persephone. For I do, and deeply."

I searched her gaze, and found nothing beyond what I always did—enough determination to light up a whole city. I gave a sort of head jerk. Apparently accepting that as good enough, she headed for the group of Fae circled around Virid and Alder.

"The queen has good intentions," Folly said in his low grumble once she'd gone. "I can scent them on her. She means no harm."

"Right," I muttered. Like I didn't intend to lose the only person who made me feel whole to a demon prince, but it happened anyway. A few moments later, the queen returned with Alder and a handful of guards.

"We are returning to the city. There is someone you need to meet," Calytrix stated matter-of-factly.

I scoffed. She wanted me to have a meet and greet now? "Sorry, but is it the time?"

She studied me for a long moment before turning to mount Rua. "Fire is nothing compared to the danger we face. And I see no other recourse but to show you, since you have not yet grasped the severity of our situation." She dismissed me with a flick of her gaze, and headed into the forest.

Alder threw me an apologetic grimace and swung onto his own *deor feya*. My cheeks burned from the rebuke, but I followed when Sceadu appeared and lowered her shoulder for me.

No one dared attempt conversation on the journey back. Folly stuck close to Sceadu's side as the fox creatures navigated the shadows. The forest almost seemed like another world separate from the rest of the Weald, as though time was suspended here in the perpetual hush and gloom. So when we passed a glade that hadn't been on the route to the wards, I was thrown off guard.

The trees were taller here, forming a ring around a dolmen in the middle of the clearing. Weak sunlight filtered down to dapple the ground in places, although the dusky atmosphere remained. A shiver of awareness ran down my spine, and I thought I felt the ghost of something stirring in my veins. I tried to snatch it, but it slipped away like falling water.

"What is this place?" I murmured.

Sceadu slowed to a halt, as did Rua and Alder's mount. *This is our relick, where we bury our kind. Where we worship trees and air, animals and earth, water and flame. Nature, she who nourishes us all. When we die, our bodies return to the earth to nourish her. And so goes the cycle.*

The flat rectangular slab of rock was laid atop four other upright rectangles, so that the whole structure looked like a massive table. Though the stones were still, some kind of power vibrated from them that resonated deep inside my chest.

Do you feel it, Lihta? I wonder. You have the mark of death upon you.

My stomach gave a little flutter. "What do you mean?"

That was not a threat. Just an observation. You feel at home amongst the dead, do you not? This is a sacred place of power. You have my permission to visit whenever you like.

I wasn't sure how to respond, so I gave Sceadu's withers a hesitant pat and a murmured thanks. She started off into the trees again, steps falling soundlessly.

We fight together, Lihta. Or we will all fall.

———

To my surprise, Simon was waiting for us inside the palace. After we ascended the fourth flight of stairs—the Fae walking with me instead of flying to be polite, I assumed—I spotted him lounging in a window seat in the corridor. Folly trotted over, and Simon gave him a rub before standing. The smile of welcome on his face dropped when he saw me. "Bloody hells, what's happened to you?"

"Long story," I said, making the split decision to save the bad news for after whatever Calytrix wanted with us. "What are you doing here?"

"I requested that Master Simon join us," Calytrix interjected. She stood in a half-opened doorway, shadows spilling from it. "I believe it will be helpful for you to have support for this conversation."

Both thoughtful, and ominous. Great.

Alder filed into the room behind Calytrix, and Folly ambled in after him. Just as I was about to enter, Simon caught my elbow and pulled me back into the corridor. "Er, just a sec. You've got." He swiped at his cheek. "Just here."

I had to be covered in all manner of things—sweat, dirt, ash. There was an acid taste in my throat, too, a remnant of fear. I scrubbed the spot. "Good?"

He shook his head, then hesitantly reached out and pressed his thumb to my cheekbone. "There."

My skin tingled beneath his touch, and the back of my neck grew warm. His gaze traveled down, perhaps tracking the flush spreading over my face.

"You all right, then?" he asked, rubbing small circles over the spot.

If I allowed my neck to go boneless, he'd be holding me in the palm of his hand. Part of me wanted to let him, to know how he would handle taking my weight. But there was only one person I wanted to do that, and he wasn't here. I bit my lip, tasting salt. "Not really."

His lips pursed as he let out a breath. "Didn't think so. You'll tell me about it later?"

I nodded, then stepped away. Simon's hand dropped, and we hesitated another moment before heading into the room. I breathed through the flutter that had sprung up in my belly. Before the prison world, I didn't like being touched by anyone other than Alex. These days, I couldn't tolerate it at all. Except from Simon, it seemed.

But I wasn't able to dissect that, because there was another pressing distraction in the form of a cloaked figure standing next to Alder. My night vision adjusted to the dimness quickly, but behind me Simon let out a muffled grunt as he stumbled over a piece of furniture.

A low, husky laugh sounded. There was a finger snap, then candlelight flickered from sconces on the walls, illuminating the figure. Folly sniffed the hem of the cloak, then raised his head. They leaned over to scratch beneath this chin, and he let out a soft dog sigh. Folly-approved, then.

When the figure straightened, long-lashed hazel eyes studied us from beneath the hood. Freckles scattered across the bridge of the woman's aquiline nose, stark against moon-pale skin. "This is her?" she asked. Rolling vowels made her throaty voice even richer as she spoke in English. The way her gaze roved over me, like I was an animal on an auction block, made me bristle.

"Who are you?" I asked, folding my arms and omitting several swear words.

With the scrape of a chair against wood, Calytrix rose from where she'd been seated at the head of a long table. Her posture was erect, but her chin drooped slightly, like the crown she wore had become too heavy. "Persephone Hart and Simon Bishop, meet Vesper Duvalle."

"Charmed," Vesper replied, though the way she exaggerated the word made me think she was less than thrilled to be here.

Alder ushered Vesper along the table to Calytrix, flapping one wing at us in a way that bore an uncanny resemblance to a beckoning hand.

Simon and I sat opposite the red-haired woman, who'd moved with such supple grace she appeared to be floating across the floor. Folly went under the table and laid across my feet, apparently unconcerned enough to take his afternoon nap. His laxity was reassuring, but the hairs on the back of my neck still stood in warning. Simon rubbed his arms as though he'd caught a chill.

"What's all this?" Simon asked, staring blatantly between Vesper and Calytrix. Alder was on Vesper's other side, silent for once.

"Vesper is recently arrived from the world of Ombryterre," the queen began. "She is one of their leaders, along with being the head of a Watcher intelligence network who are allied with us. Our court has been assisting to relocate their refugees for years."

So Vesper was one of the spies the queen mentioned when Simon and I had our first audience with her. She hardly looked old enough to be the head of a country, or of a spy network. But that wasn't what I wanted to ask about first. "Refugees?" I repeated.

Vesper pushed her hood back, exposing a sheet of fiery red hair.

"The people of my land, who are fleeing our dying world. Ombryterre is almost entirely gone."

I stilled as my stomach rolled over. This was what Calytrix meant when she said fire wasn't the greatest danger we had to face. I snuck a look at Simon. His face, always such an open book, was drawn with tension. The urge was strong to smooth the divot between his brows, to tell him everything would be okay. But everything wasn't okay, and it probably wouldn't be for a long time.

"I'm sorry," I told her, and meant it. "I've been to edges before, and I know how terrible—"

"You know nothing," Vesper said, her tone sharp enough to draw blood. Those hazel eyes narrowed, and I drew back in my seat to escape the force of her gaze. "Until you have seen your home swallowed by darkness, I suggest you save your platitudes."

"That's not what I meant," I started, then paused. Maybe I should shut my mouth before I stuck my foot in it again.

"Vesper," Calytrix said with a hint of warning. "Anger is useless without direction. Persephone is going to help with that, but first she must understand." The two women exchanged a look that I couldn't decipher. "Now, let us begin with business. How is the latest evacuation effort? General Hawthorn's report has been delayed."

Vesper's shoulders lowered, like she was making a concerted effort to maintain calm. "That is because the seam has collapsed. The general is helping our forces repair it—if it can be fixed." I didn't think it was possible for her to pale further, but not a hint of life showed beneath her skin. "I fear the time for evacuations has come to an end."

Beside me, Simon made a noise from deep in his throat. "How many of your people didn't get out?" I asked.

Vesper held me in an unflinching stare. "Five thousand six-hundred and eight." Then she turned to Calytrix and Alder. "Only ten were able to get through the seam each day, by the end. If we are able to open it back up...I am not certain how to make the decision of who gets out first. The children are already safely away, thanks to you."

"We have a refugee settlement in the west of our lands," Calytrix explained in response to my confused expression. "The people of Ombryterre we haven't been able to take have gone to the other Fae kingdoms, in addition to worlds less impacted who have space for them."

Refugee camps. Collapsed seams. Evacuations. They were nightmares made real, the consequences of the Aureum's campaign to close the borders of the worlds.

I felt sick, like my insides had been scooped out. Simon's silence beside me spoke volumes. Now I knew why, when I'd asked him back in Canhaben why people weren't trying to escape, he'd said that the time for leaving was long ago.

"How can we help?" Simon asked. He'd paled beneath the ruddy complexion he'd gained over the past weeks.

Alder spoke up. "We have several organizations who volunteer aid to the refugee settlement—clothing and food collection, Fae who donate their time and materials to building homes. There is not enough infrastructure to support the amount of people who are there, but we do our best."

Guilt weighed heavy on my chest. If I had my magic back, I could save Ombryterre. Fix their edge, fix the seam. Stop people from dying. Perhaps this was what Calytrix wanted to impress on me—as if I didn't already know. As if the extent of my deficiencies wasn't in the forefront of my mind every waking moment, that I was the only one who could save the worlds. And yet I was failing them all.

If she wanted to motivate me, this was the wrong way to go about it.

Calytrix turned to me, resting a hand on the curve of her belly. "I would ask you to speak with Vesper of your experiences with the Aureum."

I met Vesper's eyes, looking past the hostility. She was a leader who'd lost her country—a woman living in fear for her people, many of whom would—had— died on her watch. I would withstand whatever disapprobation she threw at me. "What about them?"

"Everything," Vesper said. "They are notoriously difficult to infiltrate, and my information on their organization is limited to what we can observe from the outside. Getting an insider's knowledge is priceless."

I understood her reasoning, and wanted to help. Yet when I tried to speak, my throat ran unnaturally dry.

Vesper leaned forward when I didn't answer. "Or perhaps a little Faerie truth serum would loosen your tongue?"

"Oy," Simon barked, gaze sharpening. "Don't threaten her."

"Surely there is no need for such extremes," Calytrix soothed. "Persephone?"

I swallowed. "I swore an oath of loyalty to the Aureum. I don't think I can tell you anything that would betray them. Like about the e —" My tongue seemed to swell two sizes, choking me. I spluttered while Folly jumped to his feet and pawed my leg. I'd been trying to say *extermination program*, but apparently that was off limits. I gasped, finally catching my breath and massaging my neck. Simon shot a glare at Vesper, as if she was the one who'd cut off my air.

The corner of the queen's mouth dipped into a frown, but she deliberately smoothed her expression. "That is unfortunate to hear. A binding magical agreement counteracts truth serum."

"I'm sorry." My voice was low, almost meek. I hated that the Aureum still had that kind of power over me. It was a violation, when they were the ones who were twisting the true meaning of their oaths in the first place.

"There is one other reason why I wanted you and Vesper to meet," Calytrix said, looking at me not unkindly. "She is uniquely suited to assisting with your power, once it returns."

My skin pricked, goosebumps spilling down my arms.

Vesper scrutinized me, then flicked her tongue out, moistening her lips. "Are you familiar with vampyres?"

24

"Oh, bloody hell," Simon cursed. He made to push away from the table, but I grabbed his elbow to stop him.

Vesper's lips curled, revealing luminous white, pointed eyeteeth. They weren't quite fangs, but close enough. "Do not worry. I've already eaten today."

Simon made a choked noise.

The darkness of the room finally made sense. And with her snow-white skin and easy grace, I should have put it together sooner. Except that I hadn't realized vampires—or, the way she'd pronounced it, like *vampeers*—actually existed until a second ago.

Calytrix tutted and fluttered her wings. "Vesper, do behave. Master Simon, I assure you that we are completely safe here." She turned to the vampyre. "Explain."

Vesper released a sigh, drumming her fingers on the table. Light played off her hair, turning some of the reds strands into copper. "Vampyres from my world do not drink blood. Not if we can help it. We consume the nectar of our sacred flower, *sanglysse*, for sustenance. It is how we were made, just as you were made to eat plants and animals. But," she continued, giving a one-shouldered shrug, "as our world began to collapse, we had to make choices to survive. So we escaped to other worlds, some staying temporarily, some making their permanent homes there. And the only adequate substitute for *sanglysse* is blood. Now, through the royal family's generosity, we do not have to prey on the living. Some of the volunteers donate blood for us, although the supply cannot keep up with the demand. Many of our people are going hungry."

It was hard to believe that vampyres lived off nectar, of all things. Like...butterflies and bees. But when they'd been forced from their homes, they'd had to kill to survive. If the Aureum hadn't closed the borders of the worlds.... How many deaths would have been avoided, both in Ombryterre and my world?

"Okay, so you're a vampyre. What about it?" I said.

Vesper's face settled into an expression I knew well. That was grief bracketing the corners of her mouth, dulling the spark in her hazel eyes. "My sister, Seraphyna. She was...like you."

I didn't miss the past tense she used. I leaned forward, bumping the table's edge. "How do you mean?"

"Seraphyna was of two worlds. A vampyre with speed, strength, and the power of influence over others. But she was also a sorceress. She could command the powers of life and death. Her power was...perhaps too strong."

Another Lightbringer. So I wasn't alone in this...this burden I was yoked to, the mantle of responsibility and power that I no longer wanted anything to do with. "What happened to her?" I asked in a low voice.

Vesper shut her eyes. "They took her."

"Who?" Simon asked, perhaps harsher than he'd intended.

"A dark god," she answered, opening her eyes. "Someone who saw her light and stole her away. This was a hundred years ago." But the pain on her face was still fresh, as though it had happened just yesterday.

I'm sorry seemed an inadequate response to Vesper's grief. "You were close," I managed.

She let out a humorless laugh. "Four hundred years together, side by side. You see, vampyres are not made—we are born. My sister was there from the moment I entered the world. So yes, we were close." She paused. "And soon after she disappeared, darkness began to destroy the land."

The darkness that was the dying worlds from the Aureum keeping anything coming through gateways.

"So, vampyres are Watchers?" Simon cut in.

She nodded. "The Nephilim had a far reach. Creatures from many worlds have Watcher blood. There are far more of us than there are Guardians, which is one reason why they seek to murder us in cold blood." Then she gave a wicked smile. "So perhaps I should call you cousin."

Simon's mouth hardened into a grim line. "Let's keep it at Simon and Seph, shall we?"

Calytrix and Alder had been silent throughout the whole exchange, but the queen spoke up. "Vesper will be staying on to train with you once your magic returns, Persephone. She has an understanding of the Lightbringer's power that no one else in the known worlds—who we've been able to find, at least—can give you."

"I don't want to keep you from your work." To waste her time waiting for a power that I was beginning to think might never reemerge.

"The nights are long," she replied, holding my gaze. "I will have time enough."

"Indeed," Calytrix said briskly. "This will also give you two a chance to get to know each other."

Simon looked between me and Vesper, brow furrowed. "And why do they need to get to know each other, exactly?"

Calytrix gave him a small smile. "I'm glad you asked, Master Simon. It is because of the Book of Shadows."

The Book, or, as I'd come to think of it, the noose hanging around my neck. No one had discussed it in weeks—not Alder when he dropped by the cottage, nor Val or Leander when I met with them. My days had become a blur of training, forcing food down my throat, and pretending to act at least half human around Simon.

I should've asked about it already. The Book of Shadows should have been my top priority, given it was the last obstacle before the Fae would help me go after Alex. The fact that it hadn't crossed my mind nearly as much as it should've had a thick layer of guilt pooling in my gut, sloshing around like water in a sinking boat. Having a safe place to rest my head at night had lulled me into a false sense of security. But I wasn't really safe, and Alex certainly wasn't.

Because you're tired, an oily voice whispered from the back of my mind. *And you're weak. Soft. Alex can't count on you to save him, and no one else can, either. You couldn't even save yourself.*

I wanted to bleat that it wasn't true. We'd gotten this far, hadn't we? But when I turned over all the close calls we'd had, all the events that had led us to Faerie, the fact was that I hadn't done a thing except get us into those disasters. My leg twitched beneath Folly's chin. The urge to flee from the truth was strong, but I knew I couldn't run from this.

"You know where it is, then?" Simon asked. "Why didn't you say so from the get?"

"There seemed to be no rush on that front," Calytrix said. Ouch. I'd known Val and Leander were sending her reports, but to hear the hint of dismissal in her tone made me shift in my seat again. "And besides, the Book is inaccessible at the moment."

"Inaccessible?" he echoed. "What the bloody—"

"It means," Vesper cut in, "that my spies have good reason to believe that the Book is being kept on an island called Tristia. In the Vale of Sorrow."

"Well, that sounds fun," I muttered. Simon snorted.

"It will undoubtedly be a challenge. The Vale of Sorrow is only accessible by a bridge that appears during an astrological event occurring every seven years, the Lacrima meteor shower. It is due in ten weeks Faerie time."

Ten weeks? Just over two more months to train, to get my magic back, to become the person I had to be to not let anyone else down. To get Alex. I nodded, unable to speak around the knot in my throat.

"If we do not retrieve the Book on that date, we will not get another chance until the next Lacrima shower." Calytrix brought her hand to rest on the mound of her belly. "My people are counting on you, *Lihta*."

The edges of the room blurred, and I blinked hard. Folly gave a soft whine. I stroked his velvet ears, their warmth and weight grounding me. Hopefully no one else noticed the way I was fraying at the edges.

"She'll be ready," Folly answered for me.

"I—yes. I'll be ready," I said, forcing the words from my vast emptiness. They rang false, and I was certain everyone else in the room knew it.

The queen levered herself up from the table, wincing. Alder jumped up to offer her his elbow, but she waved him off. "Excellent. I'm glad to hear it. Now, good day to you all." She nodded to the rest of us, then swept from the room with Alder at her heels.

Vesper stood as well, her movements smoother than silk. She halted in the doorway, and drew up her hood. "Please do not take my words too harshly. I will do everything I can to help you."

Words stuck in my throat, but I coughed them out. "Thank you. And I won't. I can't begin to grasp how you're feeling, but...I've lost people, too."

"Then we will understand each other very well, I think." With a tight-lipped smile, she disappeared into the corridor.

I dropped my forehead to the table with a loud thunk. "Ten weeks."

Simon made a tutting noise. "Plenty of time, hey?"

Opening one eye, I squinted at him. "Not really."

"Right," he said, rising and pulling me up by the elbow. "You need to have some fun, yeah?"

"Fun?" He let go of me when Folly growled. "I don't have time for that. And since when do you like fun?"

"Since my world is no longer crashing down around my ears. And fine, if you don't want to, then I will."

I traipsed after him, surprised when he headed in the direction of the cottage. Folly loped by my side, seeming to understand that I didn't want to talk any more tonight. Or perhaps ever.

Happy yellow roses climbed the cottage's stonework, their delicate petals opened wide to catch the last of the afternoon's rays. How had it gotten to be verging on evening already? Gamori's attack at the wards seemed a million years ago. Then again, time moved strangely in Faerie.

When we entered, Folly hied himself off to bed without a backward glance. I huffed. Either he was tired from missing his afternoon nap, or he wanted to leave me and Simon alone. I guessed the latter.

I collapsed onto the first couch I encountered. My body was drained, a deep weariness settling in my bones that had little to do with actual fatigue. Worries crowded my mind in a swirling mass, and I wanted to do nothing more than fall asleep and get a break from them for a while. But they were insistent, pressing on me with cold fingers that made my pulse race.

A harsh scraping sound came from the hallway. Simon appeared in the wide arched entryway to the living area, hauling an easel and canvas. He propped them in front of me where I sat curled on the couch, then dragged a stool over.

"What are you doing?"

"Having fun," he replied, setting a glass of water and an artist's palette on the stool. "If you're determined to mope, you can at least pose for me."

That got my attention. "Pose for you?"

"I want to do more figure studies." He tucked his hair behind his ears. It was chin-length now, the ends brushing his collar. "You're helping me out, really."

His assessing gray gaze lingered on the line of my shoulders, the curve of my arm in my lap. I was used to being stared at by this point, though it never grew more comfortable. It felt like everyone I met put me under a microscope, unearthing new ways to squeeze what they wanted from me, whether or not it was within my power to give.

This was seeing in a different way. Examining form. Studying light and shadow. Not searching any further beyond what met the eye. This was a scrutiny I could withstand.

I dropped my shoulders and settled back into the velvet cushions. "What should I do?"

He shrugged and picked up a piece of charcoal. The canvas blocked him from chest to waist, obscuring the movements of his arm. "Nothing. Or, whatever you want."

"Helpful," I murmured, but propped my head on my hand and settled back to watch him work. Simon wore standard casual Fae attire of a linen shirt open at the collar, and a buttery leather vest with a watch chain hanging from the pocket. Similar enough to what he wore in Canhaben, albeit in much better condition.

But it wasn't just the clothes that made him blend in here. He'd taken to the Fae way of life like a duck to water, could almost have been mistaken for one of them except for the lack of wings and pointed ears.

"Are you happy?" The words slipped from my lips before I had a chance to think twice. "Here, in Faerie."

Simon lifted his eyes from the canvas. Fae lights nestled in copper wall sconces cast a soft glow across his face. It gave him an uncanny resemblance to his Nephilim ancestors, those children of fallen angels. "I think I'm the closest to happy I've ever been."

"Good," I murmured.

He returned his attention to the easel. "Why'd you ask?"

I told him about Gamori's ambush. He listened, biting his lip all the while as his charcoal scraped across the canvas. "So you want me to stay here forever, is that it? Not leave the bounds of the wards?"

As usual, he parsed my tacit argument in an instant. "There wouldn't be any reason for you to. You could stay here for as long as you want, I'm sure of it. Everyone likes you."

He arched a brow. "I wouldn't say everyone."

I snorted. "Right." After a brief silence, I continued. "So what do you think? Would you stay?"

Simon dropped the charcoal onto the stool, rubbing soot from his fingertips. "What do I think?" He gave a humorless chuckle. "I think we've already had this discussion. And you're not listening to me."

My forehead knit in confusion. "I am listening. You said you're happy here."

He blew out a sigh, then rounded the easel to drop down next to me on the couch. Our knees bumped together. "Sometimes you are so thick, you know that?" he said, the harshness of the words softened by humor. "One, I said I'm *close* to happy. Happiness, I fear, is a fantasy. And two, that's because I'm with you."

Silence rippled into the space between us. Not because I was surprised—we shared a bond forged of countless nights staring at the same starlit skies; of facing down death and somehow coming out on the other side, gulping the same sweet, life-giving air. No, it was down to the realization that my own happiness was now inextricably linked with his. He'd become an essential part of me during these past months, familiar as my own face. If I left him behind, it would feel like leaving a piece of me behind, too.

My lungs shuddered as I released a pent-up breath.

"Why don't you think I can protect myself?" he asked, clearly oblivious to my inner turmoil.

I blinked as I refocused on him. "I know you can. It's just—"

"Just that my magic isn't as powerful as yours? I'd say we're fairly even now, aren't we? Unless you want to start siphoning again."

"Of course not," I snapped, even as the phantom of that gilded magic throbbed in my veins. This new awareness about Simon only exacerbated the urge to fill myself with power. To obliterate all the chaos inside me with its golden touch. "I just—I can't deal with this right now. I'm tired," I finished feebly. I rose from the couch on unsteady legs, avoiding his narrowed stare.

"Running away again?" he shot, following me to the base of the winding staircase.

My fingers gripped the banister so tightly that the wood groaned beneath them. I peeled my hand away and began the climb. "Trust me," I said, guilt clawing my insides. "It's for the best."

And it was. Whatever I did or didn't feel for Simon Bishop was best left alone, for both our sakes. Truth was a luxury I couldn't afford at the moment. And though my scars had healed, I was still ruined—pathetic, empty, hopeless. If he had any sense of self-preservation, he'd move on.

25

A Fae soldier with a long brown braid and orange wings ascended the obstacle course. She made it down the beast's tail, skipping lightly across logs spaced at irregular intervals, then scrambled up a curved wall that formed the haunch.

I watched her move through the next part of the course from my vantage point on the training field. She had to climb, then swing from rope to rope across the midsection. If she fell, she'd be encased inside of four sheer walls. The only way out was to either run up the wall and use momentum to snag a rope, or go through the tunnel.

The tunnel was only three feet wide and three feet high—my chest tightened in sympathy at the absolute nightmare of claustrophobia.

She made it across the ropes, arcing gracefully through the air. Once across, she dropped onto a narrow platform, landing catlike on hands and feet.

Her next obstacle was a series of metal spheres. She had to balance on each ball as it rolled downhill to the next, where she'd then jump atop the next one before it began to roll. Four spheres stood between her and the swords swinging on counterbalances that sliced, whistling, through the air. The sound was a warning, or an invitation for a swift death.

The soldier stepped onto the first ball. It rolled, and she danced nimbly backward. But when it crashed into the second sphere, she lost her balance and dropped twenty feet to the hard ground. From what I'd seen so far, flying wasn't allowed if they were already falling.

"Ouch." I winced as the soldier slowly got to her feet and shook herself off. She staggered before being helped away by some of her fellows.

Leander had been observing as I tracked the Fae soldier running the course. "Every soldier needs to tame the beast before they're allowed to join battle ranks," he said. "Enough gawking. Back to work."

Groaning internally, I resumed my lunges. I'd already run until my legs were jelly, and was finishing up my exercises before we worked on sparring techniques. The hours I'd spent training with Leander were terrible, but I'd survived worse. No matter how harsh he was or how hard he pushed me, I didn't break. Honestly, I preferred it to talking about feelings with Val. I also preferred it to thinking about my current tension with Simon. I'd woken up this morning with a heaviness in my chest that contained every unsaid thing from last night—everything I'd fled from.

"You're sloppy, and you're lazy," Leander stated, watching me struggle through a basic punch combination. "And you're damned lucky you've survived this long."

Angry heat raced down my spine, but I kept my head down. I fought to control the breath wheezing through my lungs, punching out again at the heavy bag. *Jab, jab, hook, cross, hook.* And on, and on, and on.

My forearms and biceps ached with fatigue. But at least if I was in pain, there wasn't any room for Simon's words to echo in my mind. There was no room for the fear and helplessness and worry that haunted me as much as Alex's ghost.

"You're hunching." A gust of wind exerted light pressure on my shoulders. Straightening, my elbows dropped. I self-corrected before Leander could yell at me.

"Stop, stop," he said, uncrossing his arms. "Like this." He stood next to me, demonstrating. I nodded, a headache pulsing between my temples. "Now you try."

Muscles screaming, I mirrored his movements.

He gave a satisfied nod. "Better." He strolled around to the other side of me. "You haven't fixed the grass yet," he noted. The patches, in the shape of two handprints, remained dry and dead.

"I can't," I wheezed, still punching. "I don't have power."

"You don't need power to fix it. Get some seeds. Use a shovel. It's not difficult."

Manually fixing the grass would be giving up. It would mean accepting my magic wasn't returning, that I had failed. And, I'd realized over these past few weeks, that I was sick to death of my own failure. I shook my head, panting.

Leander sucked his teeth. "We won't move on to swordplay until you do."

Fine. He could have it his way. I didn't give a shit about swords, despite Calytrix's belief that I was destined to wield one. That I was destined for anything, really.

He let me go after another hour. I limped back to the cottage, fantasizing about sliding into a steaming hot bath, when Bri intercepted me on the path.

"There you are." A gentle wind rippled the fabric of her loose, silky pants that were the color of an evening sky. A matching top stopped just above her navel, leaving her midriff bare. She smiled at me, tucking an escaped hair from her chignon behind her ear. Compared to her breezy perfection, I felt like a drowned rat. Looked and smelled like one, too.

"Hi," I grunted, yanking open the cottage door. I didn't bother to close it behind me. If she wanted to come in, I wouldn't stop her. I didn't have the energy for it.

The lower floor was deserted, apart from Folly snoozing on a rug in the foyer. He lifted his head, then got up and trotted over to me. I bent to give him a swift ear rub before dropping into one of the high-backed chairs grouped around the kitchen table.

I heard the soft click of a door shutting, then Bri appeared in the kitchen on silent feet. She held her iridescent wings stiffly.

Things had been cordial but awkward between us since she'd arranged for me to see Val. My feelings for Bri were complex at best, insurmountable at worst. The feeling of betrayal still lingered, though it was softening as time went on. The hard spark of anger I felt toward her had eroded from a sharp edge to a worn ache.

"Lady Bryony," Folly greeted, giving her a doggy head tilt.

"Master Folly," she replied, grinning. "I've told you, call me Bri."

He gave a soft *whuff* of acknowledgement. "What brings you to our doorstep?"

Sweet Folly, fighting my battles for me. Bri's gaze flicked between us. "The queen wishes for your presence at the palace."

This wasn't Bri. It was Lady Bryony, with her courtly speech and manners. Resentment rose up in me, and I was too exhausted to push it back down. "I'm not her dog. She can't snap her fingers for me anytime she wants."

I knew it for a fact, because I'd tested the bounds of the blood promise since the day I visited the wards. I was chained to Faerie for the next nine weeks and change, whether I liked it or not. But she couldn't force me to do everything—only what was defined in the bounds of our contract, which was that I would remain in the Weald, train, and get the Book of Shadows. Nothing more, nothing less.

Folly's grumble of disapproval had me looking down where his chin rested on my knee. Oh, right. The dog comment. "No offense."

"None taken," he responded, though he stepped on my foot. "Why has she summoned us?"

"To see the Soulstone Sword. Val recommended it."

My tired brain shorted out, and I blinked at her. "Why would she do that?"

Bri's genteel mask slipped for a moment, and she chewed her lip. "Well, I believe the theory is that holding the sword of prophecy may help bring forth your magic."

Although the very last thing I wanted to do was move—preferably not for the next twelve hours—I pulled my aching body from the chair. I might not be Calytrix's dog, but it seemed a small ask for the possibility of a big payoff. *Keep moving.*

"Lead the way," I told her, suppressing a sigh.

A divot appeared between her brows as they drew down. "If you're too tired—"

"I'm not," I said shortly. "Let's just do this. Please."

The pale outline of a crescent moon was beginning to peek out from a sky gone hazy with dusk. I started in the direction of the palace's soaring tree canopy, but Bri called me back.

"I, ah, thought I could offer you a lift?"

"Oh." I stopped short and turned around. She looked cautious but hopeful, wings still.

"Since it's a long walk," she added quickly. "And you're exhausted, I can tell. When we were at Whitlock—" She shook her head. "Never mind."

"What about when we were at Whitlock?" I asked.

"Just that you always rubbed your birthmark when you were stressed. Or tired. Or hungry, under-caffeinated, pissed—"

"Okay," I said, holding up a hand. I hadn't realized I'd been engaging in my once-familiar tic. I dropped my hands to my sides, forcing them to relax.

It wasn't the flying itself that made me hesitate, or even Bri. It was that the last time I'd flown had been with Alex. I remembered escaping from Ventusiel after my potentia had come in, supernatural strength flowing through my body as I ran down the old country lane. How Alex had appeared above me, great ivory wings shining in the glow of the setting sun, and scooped me into his arms.

That night, he'd pledged his loyalty to me. Pledged to keep me safe from demon and man alike, to stay with me for as long as I'd have him. I closed my eyes, picturing the way his eyes had burned into mine with the promise of a kind of love I'd never been given before. A love that was steadfast, and true, and forever.

My heart shuddered, and my throat thickened with unshed tears. I nodded, once. Then I opened my eyes, and Bri gathered me up and flew to the palace. Folly's howl trumpeted into the twilight as he galloped after us from below.

We alighted on a wide ledge that abutted a door several stories above the ground. Bri led me through the web of the palace's upper levels, the part reachable by rope bridges strung within the expansive forest canopy.

I knew we'd reached the right place when we found not the green-liveried palace guards in front of a circular door, but leather-clad warriors cut from the same cloth as Leander. Their vambraces covered forearms corded with muscle, an array of weapons strapped from head to toe. Indigo, the Fae woman with blue hair who'd escorted me and Simon to meet Calytrix in the throne room, was there. The tip of a crossbow was visible over her shoulder. She caught me staring and gave a nod of greeting.

"Lady Bryony," the center Fae greeted, bowing his head and sweeping his wings wide. He had auburn hair and hawk-like nose, his skin dotted with freckles. His wings were black, and seemed more muscular than normal. "*Lihta*. Healer Valerian is already inside."

"Thank you, Gentian," Bri answered. The four other warriors stood aside as Gentian opened the door to admit us. She glanced over her shoulder at me. "There's an enchantment on the threshold. Just push through to the other side."

I didn't have time to ask which enchantment, because she was already stepping over the threshold. Her image refracted like I was viewing her through water. Then, she disappeared from sight, the doorway going dark.

"After you, Mistress Persephone," Gentian encouraged. His voice was surprisingly soft for such a burly Fae.

Bracing myself, I crossed the threshold. The air was somehow both solid and not. It dragged at my limbs as I pushed through, sticky and cement-thick.

I gasped for air when I reached the other side, immediately shaking out my arms. "Ugh."

Bri winced. "Sorry about that."

"The enchantment is bothersome, but necessary, of course," a placid voice chimed in.

Val shuffled toward us, a smile on her wrinkled face. Her gnarled knuckles were clasped in front of her, but she opened them to embrace Bri. The healer was so diminutive that Bri, who wasn't in danger of being chosen for any basketball teams, had to bend down to reach her.

"Thank you for fetching Seph," Val said. "May we have the room?"

Bri nodded. "I'll find Folly and wait with him." Her eyes flicked to me one last time before she vanished through the doorway.

I picked at my thumbnail as I examined the room, suddenly not eager to face Val and the Soulstone Sword. A vaulted ceiling soared above my head, lined with wooden ribs that could have come from a whale's skeleton. My gaze traveled down walls of thick, dark rock, finally alighting on a plinth made of the same type of stone. A purple velvet cushion covered it, and atop the cushion lay a long silver sword.

My experience with swords was limited—that was to say, nonexistent—but the weapon seemed almost innocuous. The hilt was made of some whitish material, wrapped with leather, and the blade long and straight, sheathed in dull grey metal. However, the stone embedded into the pommel marked the sword as far more than ordinary. It glowed faintly, sending off a halo of light into the room's dimness.

"Is it what you expected?" Val asked, arranging her thick white braid over her shoulder.

I jerked backward, looking down at where she stood beside me. Fae were even quieter than Guardians.

"I wasn't sure what to expect," I answered truthfully. I was as out of my depth here as I was everywhere else.

"The Weald Fae have had possession of the sword for a millenia now," she said, walking over to the plinth. I followed, my footsteps echoing into the vast space. "It was crafted to fit the Soulstone, knowing that when the two were united it would become a near unstoppable weapon."

"Why was it created in the first place?"

"Why is any weapon made? Push and pull, my dear. Ask, and answer. For time immemorial there has been a battle between those who would protect their peace and those who would take it from them."

By this time, we'd arrived at the plinth. The stone of Vadyron glittered with an inner light, sending refracted rainbows dancing over my skin. I hadn't been able to see its true form while inside Olker Geist's chain, emblazoned with the infinity eye symbol of his Watching God. The stone was so clearly extraordinary, I wasn't surprised he'd hidden it.

Galaxies swirled in the stone's heart, ribbons of violet and gold and black all weaving together among minuscule, white stars. I reached out to stroke its glassy smooth surface.

Val's knobbly hand appeared atop my own, drawing me back. I blinked hard, like I'd just surfaced from a dive.

"Legend says the stone was once a star, stolen from the night sky by a firedrake who sought to curry favor with the Mother Earth," she told me. "Despite the richness and beauty of her own world, she sought what she could not have."

"Grass is always greener, I guess," I murmured, still enraptured by the stone's beauty. The Fae legend matched what Fane had told me about the stone—plucked from the heavens, he'd said. But something in Val's words tickled a different memory in my brain. I reached for it, but it was like trying to catch smoke.

Val chuckled. "Indeed. However the stone came to be—most likely created from powerful magic of another sort of creature altogether—it is now our responsibility to keep it out of the wrong hands. Joined with the sword, the Soulstone has the power to smite all enemies. It is unbreakable, and the edge never dulls; the wounds it inflicts never heal."

"And Calytrix wants me to use this?" I croaked. Smiting enemies was great and all, but was I up to it? I didn't exactly have a great track record with handling that kind of power. And, as it always did in these moments, the phantom of siphoned magic scraped along the parched riverbeds where my gold and black threads used to flow. The urge to latch onto Val and suck her life force was so strong that sweat beaded at my brow. I exhaled harshly and forced myself to step away from her.

Her brown eyes peered into me, like she knew exactly the struggle I was experiencing. We'd discussed my addiction at length, and she'd taught me how to deal with cravings—distraction, reflection, substitution. And damn them all right now.

My fists clenched, nails digging into my palm and bringing a welcome sting. The pain didn't overpower that phantom feeling, but it was enough.

"You are stronger than you know, Seph," Val said quietly. "Taking the sword will be a reminder."

I automatically shook my head, but Val stopped me. "If you are so hard on yourself, your magic will never return. Saplings do not grow when they are deprived of light and water, earth and air. You will not grow if you don't believe you can."

The voice of failure in my head had been lying dormant, but at her words leapt up and snarled. Yet through the dark thoughts that had become so habitual I hardly even noticed them anymore, I recognized Val had a point. I'd let my hopelessness overcome my faith. I'd managed to stay alive, but I hadn't been strong or smart. Alex would be disappointed in me.

No, he wouldn't. He'd be worried about me, and love me through it all.

"Are you ready?" Val asked. She stood before me with arms extended, the sword laying flat upon her upturned palms.

I nodded. I was ready to move on.

I took the blade from her, the sheath cool against my skin. Its hilt was smooth, almost slippery save for the leather.

"Go to your door first, like we've practiced," she encouraged. "Then draw the sword."

We had practiced, many times. During every meeting with Val she had me go to my rust-streaked obsidian door and connect with the source of my arcana. It always left me feeling more hollow than when we began, but maybe this time would be different. The hilt was warm and friendly in my hand, and as I gripped it, I shut my eyes and went to my power source.

The sky was a soft purple-gray, clouds flowing like waves above my head. Soft grass swished against my feet as I walked toward the dry riverbeds. The scent of night jasmine emanated from the tiny white flowers that speckled the grass like flecks of paint. I inhaled deeply, the familiar smell quieting my racing heart.

Alex was everywhere here. We'd spent so much time behind my door together when he taught me at Aureum headquarters, then again in Canhaben. It was a place we could both escape to when the outside world felt like too much, to avoid talk of demons and responsibilities.

He'd kissed me against the crooked white tree with a knot like an eye in the center of its trunk. I pressed a hand to my belly where desire curled thick even now at the memory.

"What's your favorite?" Alex had asked. I was sandwiched between the tree's smooth bark and his weight. One hand was overhead to brace himself, while the other thumbed the hollow of my throat. A tingle of pleasure spread to my chest.

"Favorite what?"

"Everything."

I laughed, more interested in the way his full lips shaped the words than answering. "Why?"

"Because I want to know everything about you. And we didn't get to talk about these things the normal way."

"The normal way," I repeated. "And what's that?"

"You know. Dating. I would've taken you out somewhere, maybe had a meal. Talked about everything under the sun. And then, I'd take you home. Walk you to your doorstep."

I nodded, seeing the scene in my head as he described it. It was so traditional, but we weren't traditional people. "Then what?"

"Then," he said, settling his hips against mine and pressing me against the tree, "I'd have asked if I could kiss you."

I bit my lip, and my stomach clenched deliciously at the way his pupils blew wide. "I'd have been lucky," I whispered.

Alex dropped his brow to mine and shook his head. "I'm the lucky one."

My heart gave a long, slow roll as warmth flooded me. This, I'd realized, was happiness. No, it was beyond that. It was...joy. Profound joy that travelled down the tether between us. I couldn't stop my smile, and the corners of Alex's mouth lifted into a grin.

"Mint chip, mango, black, dogs, *The Hobbit*, hydrangeas," I said breathlessly.

He twined his fingers through my waves, softly tugging my mouth toward his. He kissed me, then murmured against my lips. "Rocky road, green apples, also black, hawk, *The Count of Monte Cristo*, magnolia."

"Great. Enough talking."

"Agreed."

He traced my collarbone, then the valley between my breasts, to the button of my trousers. He opened them with a deft flick, and I laughed into his mouth, taking his face in my hands as I kissed him soundly.

I'd loved him under this dark sky, had given myself to him so completely that our souls were now intertwined. His pulse had beat alongside mine, two hearts inside one chest. That was what it felt like to be with him—wholeness, and a love so strong and complete it was bright enough to become its own star.

My magic had always been stronger when I was with Alex. *I'd* always felt stronger. So I held tight to the memory of him as I drew the Soulstone Sword.

The rasp of metal against metal rang in my ears as warmth traveled up my arm. The sword's blade was luminous, glowing like a frosty winter moon. It was solid and weighty, but not too heavy for me to hold with one hand. Concentrated power surged up my arm, and I almost dropped the sword. A buzzing sensation rippled through my chest and into my palms where they gripped the hilt, and my heart was a trapped bird fluttering madly in my ribcage.

I held magic in my hands, but it wasn't *my* magic. Not those shining filaments of gold and black, but a tsunami of pure, raw energy.

My eyes snapped open to find myself back in the vault. Val's direct gaze pinned me to the spot, and she smiled softly. But the smile wasn't one of triumph—it was of acceptance. She knew.

"There is no reason to feel ashamed," she told me. "There is time yet."

I shook my head, unable to force words through a throat that had clamped shut. Foolishly, I had allowed myself to hope. I fought the shame threatening to drown me, and managed to croak some noise of agreement before sheathing the Soulstone Sword. The stone of Vadyron gleamed in its hilt, dormant once more.

26

True to her word, Bri waited for me outside. Folly paced circles around her, and leapt on me after I forced my way through the enchanted doorway.

"You're heavy," I grunted, running a hand over his knobby head before dropping his front legs. I kept my gaze down as I fled the vault, not knowing where I was going except far away. Bri didn't make a sound behind me, but the itch between my shoulder blades told me she followed.

"Seph, wait," she finally called out. I didn't slow until she grabbed my elbow and forced me to a halt. "Just hold on a damn minute." Her eyes glittered, and her voice was high and tight.

"What?" I spat, jerking out of her grasp. "Does the queen's errand girl have another message for me?"

The flare of hurt that crossed Bri's face should've banked my temper. Instead, it was the spark that started the inferno. I was acting hateful and terrible, but I couldn't seem to stop it. The tide of my own anger swept me away, and then I was spewing.

"I'm fucking sick of this, you know that? Getting my head shrunk isn't working, training isn't working. I'm in the exact same place I started, even after weeks here. I thought you all were supposed to help me. But so far, I'm just getting *worse*. If I wasn't bound to Calytrix, I'd be long gone."

My chest heaved as I gulped air. Bri and Folly watched me with blank expressions. The heat of my anger retreated under their stares. I dropped my chin, fighting the overwhelming tide of shame that rushed in to replace it.

"Are you finished?" Bri asked in a quiet voice.

I forced myself to meet her eyes as I nodded. "Think so."

"Good. Come with me."

Wrung out and empty, I followed her. Folly's nails clicked on the stone as he walked beside me, so close I felt the heat radiating from him.

We ended up atop one of the large platforms slotted between a crook in the massive boughs that topped the palace. Stars blanketed the night sky, and the air was cool and dew-scented. A spread of cheeses and wafer-thin crackers, honey-glazed berries, and fresh bread smelling of rosemary adorned the low table. Three inviting, fluffy ivory pillows sat around it.

"Your favorites," Bri said, dropping onto a pillow. "After the day you've had, I thought you might be hungry."

I didn't have much of an appetite, but I sat anyway. She'd gone to these lengths because she was concerned about me, wanted to help me, and I'd responded by lashing out. I was the lowest of the low. "Fuck," I muttered, dropping my head into my hands.

"You might as well eat, because I'm going to talk. I have things to say to you, things I should have said weeks ago." She took a deep breath. "You're right. I am the queen's errand girl, and I hate it. That's why I left Faerie. As long as I'm here, I have a duty to serve her and the royal house of Rosa. It's different from the human world. We operate by protocol and etiquette, and there's no room for skirting responsibility. All I've ever wanted is my freedom. Being back here has been...difficult. No, it's been shitty. I'm happy to see my dads, but I'm stuck in the same cage I've been in for the last hundred years. And I thought, having you here...I thought it would be different." Another breath, then she poured a goblet of wine and quaffed half of it in one go. "Anyway. I'm sorry I lied to you. You're the best friend I've ever had, in any world. And I miss you."

Her amber eyes were bright, and her tanned skin held a radiant glow in the silver light of the waxing moon. This wasn't Lady Bryony of the Weald Fae, nor the Bri I'd known. She was someone in-between, with one foot in each world. Like me.

"I..." I trailed off, trying to find the right words. But the right words never seemed to appear when I wanted them. "I'm sorry you feel trapped here. And," I swallowed, "I'm sorry for everything I did. Have done. Back in Gravesville, and here. I'm...I'm not right."

Her perfectly arched brows furrowed. "What do you mean?"

I swallowed, my throat gone dry. "Can I have some of that?" I reached for the bottle, not waiting for her answer. Val had cautioned against drinking until my magic came back, but I longed for the release.

"Be careful with Faerie wine," Bri warned as I poured myself a goblet. "It's potent."

"It's not going to turn me into a toad or something, is it?" To my supernatural eyes, the liquid was still ruby red in the darkness. The aroma of blackcurrant and spices hit my nose, and I inhaled deeply.

"No, but it'll get you shit-faced if you don't watch yourself. And there may be some other unintended consequences."

"Oh?" I lowered the glass.

"It doesn't make a difference to Fae—we're immune. But if humans or other creatures drink the wine, they might temporarily gain Fae powers. Small things, like perceiving lies or being extra persuasive and charming. Seeing auras. The biggest side effect is that once you've drunk our wine, you can always see Fae and the Faerie realms. Forevermore," she added, waving her fingers dramatically.

"Seeing auras is small?" If so, I hated to think what was big.

"It wears off eventually." She twirled her glass by its stem. "Our healers can read auras—helps them figure out what's wrong with you. And we have elemental magic, with minor control over all the elements, but a stronger affinity for one."

I studied my wine again. "What's your affinity?"

Bri rubbed her lips together. "Air." She lifted a hand, and a breeze caressed my cheek.

"So when you made the water appear on the training field...."

"Rapid cooling to create condensation," she answered, tucking a lock of black hair behind her pointed ear. I caught myself staring and took a slug of wine, auras be damned. It tasted of sun-ripened blackberries, dark and lush.

"Feel anything?" she asked, her tone artificially light.

"Not yet," I said quietly. We were entering dangerous territory here. These past few moments with Bri had almost felt...normal. And now, we were discussing magic. It was the secret that had laid between us for as long as I'd known her. I could shut it down, could ask her to leave and get drunk on Faerie wine alone, shrinking inside myself so that I didn't have to feel anything at all.

Or.

Or, I could be open. Could address the pain and the lies that had plagued us from the beginning. We could pick the scattered pieces of our friendship from the ashes and rebuild on a foundation of truth. I could walk through the door she'd left open for me. I could throw my own wide open and let her see everything.

"So, nice try with the subject change," Bri said casually, swirling her wine. "Spill, Hart."

Lifting my eyes to hers, I saw what I needed there. And I opened the door, giving a grim smile despite everything. "I feel the furthest from myself I've ever been. I thought I found out who I was—who I truly was—when I was with the Aureum, and back in Simon's world. But with everything that's happened, I just...I don't know."

"Is Val helping?"

"In a way," I answered. "But it's...it's hard. One of the hardest things I've ever done. She's asking me all these questions about my mom, and my emotions, and...and Alex." I massaged the tightness in my throat.

"You love him." Bri piled cheese atop a cracker, then shoved it into my hand. "Eat."

"I do. But more than that, we're connected." I told her in fits and starts, my appetite awakened, about the tether between me and Alex. About how it had gone dark, and that I couldn't feel him on the other end. I'd stopped trying, because it hurt too much.

"What was he like?" she asked, sitting forward and resting her elbows on the table. "How did you meet?"

I told her about him—everything I could remember—and we talked until the moon was past its zenith. It felt good, almost like old times. Except, now we weren't discussing our office crushes, or the books we'd been reading—now, the conversation covered topics from magic and the multiverse to a potential demon-generated apocalypse.

"So what's the deal with Simon?" she asked, stroking Folly's ears. He'd long fallen asleep, splitting the night air with whistling snores.

"Ugh." I ran my fingers through my tangled waves. "Your guess is as good as mine."

"He's charming, in a gruff sort of way," she mused.

I sighed. "He's pissed at me. We haven't spoken since last night. Or I guess, two nights ago now." Her brows crept upward. "I feel guilty. That I dragged him into this."

"Dragged?" She pursed her lips. "Did you bind and gag him?

I snorted a laugh. "Course not."

"Then you didn't drag him anywhere. Simon has his own free will as far as I know, just like you do."

"To an extent." I poured more wine, frowning when none came out. I shook the bottle.

Bri chuckled. "I don't think that's how it works. And we should go to bed, anyway. You still have training in..." She looked at the moon. "About four hours, is my guess."

I groaned and slumped back onto my pillow. "I shouldn't have stayed up so late. But...this was nice." It had been more than nice. Though Simon had been unfailingly at my side for the past several months, our relationship was different than that of old friends. What Simon and I had was an unbreakable bond, borne of disaster and, lately, fraught with tension. Despite Bri and I lying to each other, our friendship had always been easy. Tonight was like picking back up where we left off. Simple and familiar.

"Want another lift?" Bri offered. She looked down at the slumbering Folly. "He can sleep it off here for the night."

I crouched to press a kiss to Folly's velvet head, then Bri flew me back to the cottage. Memories of flying with Alex didn't hit me as hard this time, or maybe that was because of the wine. Either way, when we alighted in the cottage's wildflower meadow, I felt almost level-headed. My worries seemed to have taken the night off.

"A few of us are going to the waterfall tomorrow afternoon," Bri said. "You should come." She smirked. "Alder will be there."

I rolled my eyes, shaking my head. "Then you can count me out."

"He offered to come get you this afternoon, but I volunteered instead. Thought you might appreciate it."

Regret for my earlier outburst filled me. Bri had been taking one for the team, saving me from Alder's cringe-worthy attempts at flirting. "Thanks for that."

"He means well. So, you'll come?"

I chewed my lower lip. Spending time with Bri tonight had been a balm. But I couldn't go so far as to have fun on purpose, could I? That seemed wrong, like I was being disrespectful to Alex. "I don't know."

"Think about it. Night, Seph."

She winged off toward an eastern horizon that was turning navy, the witching hours releasing their hold on the dawn. I walked to the cottage with lighter steps, as though she'd lifted some of my burden and flown away with it.

———

After what seemed like only a few seconds of sleep, I dragged myself out of bed and to the birch glade that abutted the training field. I was counting on the cool air to clear the cobwebs and headache from overindulging last night. Also, Val strongly encouraged—some might say forced—me to meditate before training.

It had become enough of a habit that I didn't like to start my day without it. Plus, daybreak was when training started, and Leander waited for no one.

Yesterday's failure with the sword dragged on me, making my thoughts heavy. The ease I'd found with Bri last night had dissipated like morning mist burned away by the sun.

Every time I closed my eyes, I saw my empty hands grasping at the space where Alex had been, Simon being stabbed, Ventusiel flaying me open with a serrated knife, the heartbreaking but righteous look in Fern's eyes when I realized she'd betrayed us. The memories overwhelmed me, leaving my body damp with sweat and shaken.

I kneaded my forehead, trying to reign in my wayward thoughts, but then I saw Gamori's terrifying beauty. Heard her warning ringing in my ears. My breath came faster.

Every second I spent here, powerless and weak, was time that Alex was languishing in some kind of demonic prison, in pain, alone—

Breath rattled through my clenched jaw as I panted. My eyes snapped open, but I didn't see the gentle forest glade where I sat. I saw Alex's face as he fell, watched him go down, down, down into the dark.

The walls of my throat constricted, and suddenly I couldn't breathe at all. My chest was tight, my hands scrabbling at my throat, breaking skin in an attempt to get some air. Black spots appeared in my vision, and my heartbeat thudded rapidly in my ears.

Then there was warmth on my face, and the broad swipe of a tongue on my cheek. Heavy weight settled against my side, leaning into me with firm pressure. Without seeing, I grabbed hold of Folly's solid body, his fur soft beneath my hands.

I clung to him as the waves of panic subsided, leaving washed-out exhaustion in their wake. Taking a long, shuddering inhale, I turned to Folly. He said nothing, just looked at me with his soulful eyes that turned down in the corners.

"There's something wrong with me," I said in a hoarse whisper. I didn't mean just because I'd had a panic attack. That happened sometimes, when the flashbacks got too overwhelming. When I caught sudden movement from the corner of my eye, or smelled roasting meat that reminded me of the scent of burning flesh.

Folly shook his head, setting his long ears swaying. "Every being has shadows. Some are longer than others."

"No, Folly. It's not just what I've seen—what I've done." I dug my fingers into the loose skin around his neck. "Everyone thinks I can save the worlds. Get the Book of Shadows, defeat Magoth, heal the edges. But I can't. If I can't save the person I love, how can I do any of that?" I rasped. The pressure of it all, of my own shortcomings, pressed against my nose, my mouth, suffocating me.

Folly snuffled into my neck, licking my cheek again. "You are stronger than your fears." He pulled away, looking me in the eye. "You were made for the light, Persephone. And for the dark. Do not be afraid to look into your shadows. They cannot harm you." He tilted his head. "By saying these words—failure, wrong, weak—you wound yourself."

I released a long breath. *You are the scariest thing in the dark*, Simon once said. "How do I stop being afraid?"

"Fear is not the problem. Do not just look. See yourself for who you really are." Folly gave a full body shake, his loose skin flapping. "But what do I know of the minds of humans? I am only a demon, and a dog at that. Now, aren't you late for something?"

"Shit." I sprang to my feet and sprinted out of the clearing toward the training field. The eastern horizon was banded in yellow. Folly trotted at my side, tongue lolling from his mouth.

Leander was perched atop the stone wall bordering the training field. When I stood before the tall wooden gates, he jumped, not bothering to use his wings, and landed silently as a cat.

"Best of luck," Folly murmured before he galloped away. Coward.

"Sorry I'm late." The hangover from the panic attack still lingered, my throat dry and chest sore.

All six-plus feet of Leander were dangerously still. Then he shook his head, pointing through the gates. "Laps. Until I tell you to stop."

I didn't protest. The order didn't even seem like a punishment, because that's what I did every day.

After an hour, he called, "Stop." I slowed to a halt, legs shaking. He opened a shed set against the wall, then tossed me a wooden sword. I snagged it out of the air, a splinter biting into my palm.

"We're starting sword work today," he told me.

"I thought you said we weren't progressing until I fixed the grass?"

Leander's dummy sword was larger, more suited to his size. "I changed my mind. Thought it might give you some motivation." He held his sword aloft. "The first thing you'll learn is how to hold your weapon. How to maintain proper balance and weight distribution. Have you used one before?"

I shook my head. "Only knives." A memory surfaced of Davina complimenting me when we'd discovered my hidden talent for knife-throwing. If only she could see me now.

"Starting from scratch is probably better. You haven't had a chance to learn bad habits. Change your grip like this." Leander extended his arm like he was going in for a handshake, the sword moving into an angled position. "See how that's different from the upright grip? This helps to keep distance between you and your opponent, especially if they have a longer reach."

He wasn't quite smiling, but the bent of his mouth was soft instead of rigid. I was wary, but followed his instructions to the letter. By the time the sun had reached its zenith, I'd learned three different grips and walked back and forth in a line endlessly while Leander critiqued my posture.

"More core engagement," he decreed. "We'll end here for today."

Sweat dripped down my forehead in rivulets, and my arms ached. He'd insisted that I learn the grips with both my left and right hands. Blisters adorned my palms. Sticking the swordpoint into the ground and leaning on it, I wiped away sweat with the hem of my tunic.

"You did well," Leander said. His skin glistened with a sheen of sweat. He looked like a god, or at least a hero of old.

"A compliment?" I panted.

His expression turned solemn. "I saw you in the grove."

Embarrassment washed over me, heat creeping up the back of my neck. The idea that anyone had seen me fall apart was...unbearable. "Oh. That was nothing."

He crossed his arms over his broad chest. "It wasn't nothing. And you shouldn't be ashamed."

Wiping grass from the tip of the sword, I returned it to the equipment shed. "I'm not."

"Every soldier I know has battled the same thing." Leander sought my gaze again, but I looked away. "It is part of a warrior's life."

I snorted. "I'm not a warrior."

He shook his head. "You are. What you felt—I've felt it, too. It's inevitable, with the things you see. The horrors and the harm and the death. I don't have to know what happened to you in order to recognize it."

Val was always encouraging me to connect with others who experienced similar issues if the opportunity came along. I just wasn't expecting it to show up in the form of a mountainous Fae man. "How...." I rubbed my lips together, exhaustion creeping through every limb. "How do you deal with it?"

"I wake up every morning and face it. I choose to, because if I don't, it wins. What I've lived through is part of me, but it doesn't have to control me." His voice softened. "And I remember that I am not my worst moment. I am the sum of every moment, good and bad."

"What if I'm not strong enough to face it?"

"Then you learn how to. You work at it, every day."

His sincerity made my eyes ache. I cleared my throat.

"That, and lots of push-ups," he added quickly. "So many push-ups."

A harsh laugh scraped out of my throat. "Right."

"Now get going, before I change my mind and make you do a few. Or a hundred," he said, lifting a threatening brow.

There was a note waiting on the kitchen table for me when I arrived back at the cottage. I recognized Simon's neat penmanship before I picked it up.

Gone to waterfall with Lady B and others. Come!
—S

Damn it. I leaned back against the counter, thumbing the note. I'd hoped to talk to Simon in my next few free hours, somewhere in between cramming as many calories as possible into my body and napping. But if he was at the waterfall—and who knew how long he'd be there—I'd have to wait.

Or, I could track him down now. Give him the apology he deserved. Spend time with Bri and tend to our restored friendship.

Maybe there was more to life right now than training every second of the day. But it felt wrong to relax or let my guard down. I'd go to the waterfall, say my piece to Simon, then leave.

Set on my plan, I turned to grab an apple from the counter. But I paused with my hand hovering in the air, because I'd seen a flash of something familiar through the cracked door at the end of the hall. My face, in Simon's room.

"What the hell?" I muttered. I walked over and pushed the door open, fully exposing the drawing that sat on an easel in the middle of his room.

It was the sketch he'd done of me the other night, before our argument. He'd captured my likeness on the canvas in bold strokes of charcoal, but the image showed a woman I didn't recognize.

Simon had made my eyes sparkle with humor, the curve of my full lips sensuous, my stubborn chin tilted. My expression was that of Psyche waiting for Eros. In love. Eager. Full of desire.

My breath caught. Was this how he saw me? Or...was this how I looked at him? No. No, that wasn't right.

I reached a finger out to stroke along the edge of my face but pulled back. I didn't want to touch the sketch for fear of smearing the charcoal. He couldn't know I'd seen this.

One, I was certain he would be mortified. And...would he expect a response from me? A memory surfaced, of the moment after he'd woken up from the knife injury. He'd said then that I was his family. The air between us had gone honey-thick and hazy, and for the space of a heartbeat I'd considered what his lips would feel like against mine. If his smart mouth would taste as good as it looked.

I blinked at the drawing again. He had such talent. He was a good man. He was kind, and funny, and loyal.

He was—

"Snooping?" Folly asked, nails clicking on the hardwood.

I spun to face the hound, blocking the easel behind me. "Nope. I was just leaving." Walking quickly, I shut Simon's door so hard it rattled on its hinges. "I'm going to some waterfall. Want to come?"

He gave a low whine I took as agreement. "I know the place."

Folly led us toward the Wode—the friendly, open forest that lay to the south, not the eldritch Bearu-Glom.

"What were you doing in Simon's room?" he asked.

"Nothing." I kept my eyes straight ahead. "And you're not going to tell him I was in there."

Folly grumbled. It sounded something like "humans."

Soon the noise of crashing water reached my ears, then the waterfall appeared around the bend. "Wow," I breathed.

It was something out of a dream. Literally. This was the place I'd gone when the Fae woman, Flora, had given me the Desidarian compass.

Water spilled from high above the wide pool, sending up a cooling spray of mist. Flowering vines climbed the rock face, violet, yellow, and azure weaving together to create a bright tapestry. Slabs of rock, large and small, were perfect places to either catch the sun or dive into the water.

Fae flew to the top of the falls, then jumped, executing dives and flips before cutting into the crystal clear, turquoise pool. I spotted Indigo's distinctive blue hair among them, and she waved to me before leaping in. Shouts of laughter and conversation filled the air, along with a soft floral scent. With sunlight making the water sparkle like a gem, the whole scene was entirely enchanting.

Folly loped over to the waterfall, wading in up to his neck. He paddled around, splashing the delighted Fae who cooed over him. Silly eudaemon.

I spotted Simon sunning himself on a rock, arms splayed overhead. Some Fae girls a couple of rocks down from him were sending long looks his way, fluttering their lashes and giggling. He appeared oblivious, eyes closed and lips parted.

For a moment, I tried to imagine Simon not as my friend, but how a lover might.

He had a thick fall of warm, reddish-brown hair skimming his ears. His long-lidded eyes tipped up slightly toward his temples. He'd shaved the beard covering his angular jaw—that, and his cheekbones, were sharp enough to cut. The line of his throat flowed into strong shoulders and a defined chest.

He was...handsome. Sexy, even, with lean muscles cording his arms. But had I ever looked at him the way those girls on the rock were, with longing gazes and secret smiles?

I exhaled hard. This was ridiculous. Simon would never be more than a close friend. Well, a best friend.

And why was I even entertaining this? *Alex* was who I'd fallen in love with. The man who had been taken in my stead, who had sacrificed everything for me. I loved him so deeply that my soul ached for him every minute of every day, a dull pain always occupying my mind.

Just then, Simon sat up and spotted me standing in the shadow of the trees. He smiled, so brilliant and bright that I felt an answering warmth. A caress that slid down my throat and into my stomach, wrapping around my hips, pulling taut along my belly.

"Oy! Come over here," he called, beckoning me.

I mastered my breathing and clambered up the rock beside Simon. "Hi," I said, my voice rougher than I would've liked it. I cleared my throat.

"Isn't this the most beautiful place you've ever seen?" he asked, looking out at the sparkling falls. Tiny rainbows formed in the mist, arcing into the water. "I'm itching to paint it."

"It's lovely," I agreed, happy to observe the scene and not look at him. "So, about the other night—"

"Water under the bridge, hey?" he said quickly, turning his chin toward the water. "I was in a mood. We temperamental artists get that way sometimes, you know."

My brows pinched. "If you say so. But I'm sorry for what I said. It—"

"Right. Thanks." He pointed toward the top of the falls. "Look at Lady B."

I cut my gaze over just in time to see Bri launch skyward, flip three times, then straighten into a graceful dive. She emerged from the water close to our rock, climbing up and shaking her wings like a dog. Her dusky pink swimming attire was cut high on her legs, and the neckline plunged practically to her navel.

"You made it!" she cried, wringing out her hair.

"I'm not staying long," I warned.

"Sure." She grinned, then turned to Simon. "Anyway, since you're both here, I wanted to introduce you to someone. Flora!" she called, cupping her hands around her mouth.

A purple and gold head bobbing in the pool turned toward us, blinking wide-set, honey eyes. Then a smile bloomed over her face, and Flora swam over to our rock. Silken hair was plastered to her body, molding to her substantial breasts and hourglass figure. She seemed more like a mermaid than Fae, except for her pastel purple wings.

"*Lihta!*" She squealed and pulled me up into a hug, like we were old friends. Trying not to cringe, I extracted myself from her wet grip.

"Seph, Simon, I'd like to formally introduce you to Flora. She is also in the queen's service, and one of my good friends."

She curtsied. "Passiflora, technically, but only my mother calls me that. It is a delight to meet you, Master Simon."

"Just Simon," he muttered, cheeks pinking.

Flora waved a hand over her hair, drying it instantly. She tucked the lush strands behind pointed ears. "I am so pleased you made it to the

Weald realm after all this time," she said. Then she folded into a graceful sitting position next to Simon. "I hear that you are an incredible artist."

"Er, well—" I heard him start, before Bri grabbed my wrist and marched me off toward a waiting group of Fae, Indigo among them.

I glanced back, but Simon appeared enraptured by Flora. It wasn't like him to get distracted by the first pretty face that came along—a very pretty one, I thought, noting the way he forced his gaze to remain above chest-level. Well, if he—

"Seph?" Bri said. "Did you hear me?"

I turned to find her staring at me, along with Indigo and another Fae woman with dense brown curls. Was her name Ivy?

"Sorry." I grimaced apologetically and ordered myself to pay attention. Bri resumed her story, chattering on as the others burst into laughter.

I didn't hear another word they said.

27

The rising sun stained the horizon orange and pink, ushering in the summer solstice. Simon, Bri, and I had gotten up while it was still dark to watch the daybreak, finding a perch atop the cottage's roof.

Beside me, Simon was driven speechless by the view. Bri was riveted as well, her lips curving in a smile. She'd experienced many midsummer celebrations while growing up with the Weald Fae. In the weeks leading up to it, she'd chattered nonstop about their traditions and how excited she was to share them with us. This was the first of many events planned for the day.

The first ray of sunlight peeked over rolling meadows to limn the clouds in gold. "Drink!" Bri cried, holding up her glass. "As dawn's first fire blesses this day, may it always shine to light our way."

We clinked cups and sipped herb-infused liqueur. The drink left a trail of heat down my throat, tasting of rosemary and honey.

"And for your birthday, Seph," Simon toasted, lifting his cup again. "Many happy returns."

He caught my eye, and his mouth twitched. Though there was only enough for a mouthful, I downed my drink in a single swallow.

"Happy birthday!" Bri crowed at the top of her lungs. Folly bayed from where he lay on the ground below us.

"Shh!" I hissed, but it was too late. Fae from the neighboring cottages, also on their roofs to watch the sunrise, toasted me and chorused, "Happy birthday!"

"Goddamnit," I muttered, wishing for more liqueur.

"You only turn twenty-seven once! I'm going to make sure *everyone* knows," Bri said happily.

"I'd push you off this roof, if it would make a difference," I said. She only laughed, fluttering her wings.

"I'll hold her down if you want to get in a couple of shots," Simon said. She leaned across me to whack his shoulder. "Ouch, Lady B. Be gentle."

"For the thousandth time, don't call me that."

An amused smile crossed my face as I listened to them bicker. Bri had accepted Simon without question, and he'd taken the opportunity to needle her relentlessly.

We stayed a while longer, watching until the sun fully breached the horizon. The pale blue sky promised a beautiful day.

"Okay," Bri said, standing with only a slight wobble. The liqueur must have been stronger than I thought. "I have to go to the palace for the queen's personal gathering. See you at the formal celebration tonight?"

"We'll be there," I assured her.

She smiled, radiant as the sun, and vaulted into the sky.

"I'll never get used to that," I murmured, watching her shrink as she flew toward the palace.

Simon frowned. "Show off."

We climbed inside through the terrace. "I'm going back to sleep." He shook his head, turning for the stairs. "Sunrise. Too bloody early."

I waved him off, then stopped in the kitchen, wrapping a few muffins in a cloth and tucking them into my satchel. Folly fell into step beside me as I made for the training field, walking off the vestiges of the alcohol. Spring's blossoms had given way to emerald green leaves, and fat bees clustered around blue delphinium and hydrangeas.

"Happy solstice," Folly said. "And happy—"

I cut him off. "Thanks. And, uh...happy solstice to you." He took the hint, and we continued in companionable silence.

Berries on bushes gleamed like rubies and sapphires, and the boughs of trees in the orchard bent under the weight of ripe stone fruit. Just past them, the beast came into view.

The obstacle course had become the bane of my existence, something on which to focus my energy and take out my frustration. Two weeks had passed since I'd taken my first abysmal run at it during a training session with Leander. He hadn't exactly told me it was the worst attempt he'd ever seen, but it was implied. Thoroughly.

I'd conquered my embarrassment since then, but hadn't made it past the rope bridge with swords that arced in a deadly pendulum.

On its other side was another climbing wall, but this one was concave—it had nubby, worn pegs for handholds that seemed impossible to grasp. A hinged metal jaw with stumps for teeth comprised the final element. It snapped shut if touched, and would crush anything that had the misfortune to get in its way.

That first time I'd tried to cross the rope bridge, the closest sword had knocked me straight off. I'd tumbled to the ground ten feet below and managed to land in a roll. The second time, I'd gotten to the next sword down the line, and it sliced the back of my hand before flattening me. The blades were dull from lack of sharpening, but I'd collected dozens of wounds across my arms and upper body. And even worse than the injuries—I was growing fearful.

"The beast doesn't just test your physical strength and skill. It's a mental game," Leander had reminded me during our last session. Despite his claim that he wasn't a cleanup crew, he'd helped wrap my injuries after every practice.

Perhaps the power of the solstice would help me get past the bridge today.

Folly settled underneath a tree to nap in the shade. I tossed my satchel to the ground, then fetched a dummy sword from the equipment shed and strapped a sheath between my shoulder blades. I stretched and jogged a warm-up lap, getting acquainted with its extra weight.

Tail first. I leapt across the logs, surefooted, until I reached the beast's haunch. The climb had my muscles straining, but I made it to the next platform.

The ropes that comprised the beast's belly dangled above a cavernous pit enclosed by sheer walls. Pulling the first rope toward me, I adjusted my grip and swung out over the cavity. My movements became measured—breath, swing, reach, jump. I dropped atop the skinny platform at the other end, only wobbling slightly as I caught my balance. My palms stung from the rope's rough fibers.

Spheres next. I pulled the wooden sword out of the sheath and held it in front of me with both hands. The weight distribution kept me balanced, but the trick was to do this part quickly. Tightening my belly, I dropped onto the first sphere. It rolled immediately, and I shuffled backward, keeping my center of gravity directly overtop.

I made it through three of the circles, barely breathing, when my foot slipped out from under me just as I got to the fourth. My left hand scrabbled on the smooth metal as I tried to keep from dropping the sword. Remembering that my legs were stronger than my arms, I wrapped them around the sphere in a clinging grip. The metal was already hot enough to leave blisters from the powerful sun.

"Fuck," I ground out, though managed to hang on. I'd have to wait until the sphere reached the next platform to climb back up. Sweat dampened my skin, and my hands slid an inch. Then another. My thighs burned, but the end was within reach. Spearing out with the dummy sword, I wedged the tip into a crevice and used it as a handhold to climb onto the narrow platform.

Stinging sweat dripped into my eyes. My mouth was dry, and my throat ached. Wiping my brow, I faced the swinging swords.

Fear had my legs trembling, a conditioned response by now. "You can do this," I urged. "Just get the timing right."

The swords swung in three second intervals, with about a foot and a half of space between each. But even if it was timed correctly, there was still the unstable rope bridge to contend with. An uneven step would send me careening into the next sword. There wasn't enough clearance between the bridge and sword tips to slither across on my belly.

The longer I stared at the obstacle, the more impossible it seemed. How the hell could anyone do this?

"You're not getting across by just standing here," I chastised, returning the dummy sword to its sheath. I stepped forward so that my toes hung off the ledge, the first sword whistling inches from my nose. A cold fist twisted in my stomach.

I backed away.

"You know, most people take midsummer off," Alder called. I looked sharply to where he'd appeared below. His spiky hair stood on end, and his eyes, that most unique shade of blue, blazed.

"Go away," I called. "I don't need you distracting me."

"Looks like you were ready to give up anyway." His tone was bright, playful. I had a violent urge to punch him.

"Nope. Just getting a running start."

"I see." His wings fluttered, punctuating each word. "Well, by all means, don't let me disturb you."

"You always disturb me." I turned my attention back to the bridge. I was only half joking.

He laughed loudly, straightening the leather vest he wore over an aubergine shirt. "I'll make a wager with you. If you don't make it across, you have to save a dance for me tonight."

"Why would I take that bet?" I asked, stare trained on the swords.

"Because if you win, I'll owe you a favor of your choosing."

Interesting. "It can be anything I want?"

"Anything," he echoed.

I didn't have too much to lose—one dance with Alder, no matter how irritating I found him, wasn't a big deal. But I had a lot to gain. It never hurt to be owed a favor.

"Okay. Deal accepted."

"Excellent," Alder purred.

I'd been counting the rhythm of the swinging swords during our conversation. They weren't exactly in sync with each other. Maybe that was my problem. I'd been focusing too much on the timing.

Loosing a long exhale, I approached the bridge again.

One-two-three, step. The second sword's blade whistled a few inches away. I tightened my abdominals, steadying myself. One down.

I took another step on the half-beat. Two down. The wooden planks under my feet rocked, and I fought the instinct to slide forward and counterbalance my weight. *Careful, now.*

When the bridge quieted, I moved forward again. *Be still. Still like a rock in a river. Controlled.* I stepped again, then drew back as the next sword came slashing down. The bridge swayed side to side, and my breath came short and shallow.

My eyes were playing tricks on me, not quick enough to follow the swords now that they were so much closer in my field of vision. A memory popped into my head, unbidden—Alex at Gravesville Historic Cemetery, snowflakes swirling around his head. *Use your senses.*

As my heart thumped painfully at the thought of him, I let my eyelids drift shut. The blades cut through the air, singing. My enhanced hearing picked up the frequency and amplitude even better than a machine would. I'd been relying too much on my magic, or lack thereof, and not enough on what I was. A supernatural with gifts far beyond anything human.

The whistling noise grew louder as each sword fell, then softer on the upswing. I waited for a few moments, familiarizing my ear to their individual sounds.

Exhaling, I stepped.

I braced for pain, but none came. Listening for the swoosh and whistle of the next sword, I stepped again. And again. And again. And again.

Until my foot met solid ground, and I opened my eyes. Turning, I looked back from where I'd come. I fucking *did it.* My triumph helped me to breeze through the nubby climbing wall.

Now for the last element.

The platform leading to the hinged jaw of crushing stump-teeth was narrower than a balance beam. I kept my steps light and arms extended on either side, walking the long, long path. Quiet exhilaration pulsed steadily in time to my heartbeat. I didn't need magic to succeed.

Past the slope of the beast's jaw stood Alder, arms folded. I smiled. I'd wiped his grin away.

This part was easy in theory. All that was left was to pop through the roughly five-foot opening between the teeth. However, if the mechanism was triggered at all—even the slightest brush of skin or clothing—it would snap shut, pulverizing anything in its way.

I'd been thinking of what I'd do if I got to this point. And I had a trick up my sleeve.

One of the logs on the bottom row jutted inward, leaving an over-hang of about six inches. Wide enough for me to get a foot on it.

Only when I got closer to the stumps did I realize how truly massive they were. If I got caught inside, I'd be turned into jelly and shards of bone.

"You're almost out," I reminded myself. "Just go."

I thrust my dummy sword into the jaws of the beast. They snapped shut with a resounding crash before I even had time to draw breath, the force vibrating the ground and reverberating through me so that my teeth clacked together.

Just as they closed, I levered onto the overhanging log, throwing my weight against the other stumps until the jaws opened again. If my gamble didn't pay off....

The stumps sprang apart, and the momentum of the bottom jaw crashing to the ground flung me upward. I pushed off the stump and vaulted through the opening, clearing the space. The ground rushed up to meet me, and I landed on the other side of the beast's jaw in a tangle.

Folly let out a musical howl, bounding over to lick me soundly.

Panting, every limb tingling with adrenaline, I levered myself up using Folly as a crutch and met Alder's assessing gaze.

"Neat trick," he said, eyes narrowed.

"Thanks." I pushed back some loose waves that had escaped my topknot. "I'll let you know when I need that favor."

As I turned and walked away, I couldn't help the mile-wide grin plastered across my face.

I still hadn't come down from the high of beating the beast hours later when it was time to prepare for the evening's celebration. Simon had listened patiently as I recounted the whole story in intricate detail, smiling and nodding in the appropriate places. I could tell he didn't fully understand what the accomplishment meant to me, but that was okay. He didn't have to.

Besting the course had opened something inside of me that had been shut tight since last winter. I felt more connected to old-me than I had in a long time.

A knock sounded as I toweled off my hair, fresh out of the bath. Shrugging into a robe, I opened the door.

It was Flora, her purple and gold hair bundled into an elaborate updo. She wore a gown that was—well, it was mostly sheer, highlighting her long, toned limbs, but the skirt had embroidered flowering vines that matched the colors of her hair.

"Hello, *Lihta*." She smiled, entering the room without invitation. A long garment bag slung over her arm trailed along the floor.

"Um—hi," I answered, shutting the door and turning to where she'd already hung the bag in the wardrobe. "What are you doing here?"

"I'm to help you prepare for the solstice celebration. On the queen's orders." Honey-colored eyes blinked at me guilelessly.

"I was just going to wear what I normally wear." I pointed to the tunic and pants laid out on the bed.

Flora's forehead puckered. "Oh, no. You couldn't. That would be most...unusual. You and Master Simon are honored guests."

I sighed. "What's in the bag?"

She removed a dress and held it aloft. The floor-length gown was also semi-sheer, creating an optical illusion as creamy lace subtly threaded with gold climbed toward the neckline from the skirt.

I ran a fingertip along the fitted waist. The material was soft as spider's silk, baring more and more skin as it climbed so that only a sheer scrap of fabric was exposed in the deep V between the bust. Lace applique flowers covered each breast, but only just. The strapless neckline was concave, scooping downward.

It would show far more skin than I would ever have dared. I stole a peek at the back, which was just as bad. Its entirety was exposed to right above the butt, only covered by fine, invisible mesh.

"Fucking hell," I breathed. "I'm supposed to wear this?"

"Queen Calytrix had it made specially for you. It would be a great insult to refuse her."

A childish part of me wanted to say no. I wouldn't particularly mind pissing off Calytrix, but it wasn't the smart thing to do. Kneading my forehead, I folded. "Fine."

I allowed Flora to stuff me into the dress, which was almost worse than being naked. It highlighted every line, every curve of my body, baring smooth skin stretched over muscle. She messed around with my face, positioning me as she applied goo and powder.

In my head, I was in another world, going through the same motions. Allowing Sage, Davina, Casey, and...and Fern, to help me prepare for my initiation into the Aureum. I'd worn midnight black then, instead of ivory. An iron band closed around my chest, and I struggled to breathe.

"Are you all right?" Flora asked, deft fingers weaving sprigs of baby's breath into my hair and pinning it up.

I cleared my throat. "I'm fine." All I had to do was shut down the memories, if only for tonight.

"Just about done," she muttered, holding a pin between her teeth. After she secured the last lock of hair, she stepped back, nodding. "Okay. You're perfect." She took my hand and faced me toward the mirror.

Startled, I drew in a sharp breath.

My skin glowed like I'd swallowed a star, warming the ivory lace of the dress. What there was of it, anyway. It showed miles of bare skin that had been bruised and cut just seconds ago, but was now smooth and unblemished. The long scar running below my collarbones was still visible, along with the protection tattoo on my inner forearm.

"What—" I started, looking down.

"I did a little glamour. Just a baby one," she assured me. "It'll wear off by tomorrow. Do you want me to cover the scar?"

Turning back to the mirror, I stared at my reflection. "No. Leave it."

I looked like a fey, wild creature of fierce beauty. Skinny braids tangled with the natural wavy curls of my hair, some loose pieces falling around the nape of my neck and framing my face. Flora had woven slim golden chains through my ears that dangled to my shoulders. And my eyes—she had done something to make them smoky with a metallic sheen.

For once, I didn't see a stranger.

I just saw...me. Like this was who I'd been all along, beneath the worry and exhaustion and wounds. Someone who held her pain close, but wasn't afraid of it. Someone who'd suffered, and lived. The fearlessness showed in my eyes, in the shape of my lips and the angle of my chin. In my scars and my ink, the signs of my story that I never wanted to erase no matter how much they'd hurt.

I liked this woman. I just hoped she'd stick around.

"Thank you, Flora," I said softly, watching my painted lips shape the words.

Her cheeks pinked. "You're welcome. I have to go—see you there, *Lihta*." She threw open the terrace doors, then flew into the waning afternoon light.

Smoothing the dress, I slid into the pair of matching slippers Flora left for me and went downstairs to wait for Simon. Nervous energy pulsed through me. It almost felt like the old fire that used to crackle over my skin. I wished I had Folly around to soothe me, but he'd headed off after I got back from the training field. Something to do with having his own solstice celebration.

Making my way to the kitchen, I poured a glass of Faerie wine and downed it in a few swallows.

Simon's door creaked open. "Seph, are you ready?" he called up the stairs. He hadn't noticed me standing across the way in the kitchen.

He wore a soft gray jacket, the collar turned up to reveal embroidery of fine silver threads. His pants were the same color, tapered and tucked into short black boots.

"I'm here," I said. He turned sharply.

Each of us stared at the other. His gaze roved over me, starting at my feet and moving upward. My throat tightened as he lingered over all of my exposed skin, finally landing on my face.

Lightning struck, showing yellow in his gray eyes. "You look...." He struggled for a moment. "Nice."

I jerked a shoulder, then instantly regretted it as his eyes widened. It had probably done something obscene to my chest. "Um—thanks."

His shirt was open at the throat, revealing the line of his neck and collarbone. He'd combed his hair back, giving him an air of sophistication. Who was this sleek version of Simon? "You do, too. Look nice," I said.

He cleared his throat. "Well, now we've established that."

"Mhm." I chewed on my lower lip and twisted the ring on my thumb, grateful for the buzz of Faerie wine that dulled my nerves.

Simon looked pointedly at the open bottle. "You started without me?"

"Just warming it up for you," I said with palpable relief. I thrust the wine at him, and he drank straight from the neck. When he finished, he handed it back to me. I took a long pull as well.

"Should we bring it for the road?" I asked.

"Definitely." He hesitated, studying me again. I had the urge to stare at his boots. "You are a vision, Seph." His voice was soft. "Like...some figment of my imagination. A fairytale princess in a tower."

I forced myself to meet his gaze. I may look like a princess with this dress, but I wasn't one. I was the hag in the woods, one foot in the world of the living, and the other with the dead. However, I was Simon's friend first. So I smiled at him. "You're the damsel in distress, remember?" I said lightly.

He grinned, then crooked an elbow. "Will you do me the honor?"

"Of course." I linked my arm with his, muscle shifting under the fabric of his jacket. I still held the open wine bottle in my free hand and clutched it tightly.

We fell into step, our shadows blending together as we headed toward the setting sun.

28

Hundreds of Fae gathered in the sprawling gardens behind the palace. The air smelled sweet but not cloying, perfumed by endless summer blooms that rioted wild from the ground and arched over trellises. Tree branches dripped with strings of enchanted lights that would illuminate the scene once darkness fell. Thunderheads built in the west, but the last rays of sunlight washed everything in gold and turned the Fae in their finery from otherworldly to god-like. Some sat at long trestle tables set with aureate runners and overflowing vases of white flowers while they chatted and drank. The river Mona rushed in the distance, cutting through the gathering, then flowed into the darkness of the Bearu-Glom.

Bri caught my eye and waved, striding toward me and Simon. Flowers were woven into her loose braid, and she wore a halter gown of swirling orange and yellow silk that reminded me of a new dawn. Her lips were painted soft pink, her skin rosy and dewy. She looked breathtaking, and even Simon bit down on whatever retort he had prepared.

"Finally," she said, reaching out to squeeze my arm and grinning at Simon. "I've been stuck with my parents all day." She looked over her shoulder at two Fae men, one of whom had the same heart-shaped face and amber eyes as Bri. "I'll introduce you later. Come on, the queen is about to open the celebration."

We headed to the outskirts of the party, toward an enormous pyramid-shaped pile of wood. Other groups of Fae drifted over as well, resembling a moving garden dressed in all the hues of a sunrise.

The bonfire kindling stood twenty feet high at least. Flowers garlands wove through the wood, and small offerings of bundled herbs and cups of wine had already been placed along the edges.

Calytrix stood before the pyre, the midsummer incarnate. Her gown was like a living flame, red and orange and white, layers of the full skirt cascading to the ground in licks of fire. Even the material shimmered, as if lit from within. Tiny crystals sewn into the bodice sparkled, setting her aglow.

The gathered Fae fell silent as they faced their queen.

"Thank you all for joining me this evening." Calytrix inclined her head, bowing to her people. "I hope you have had a joyous solstice." The crowd murmured their assent.

She spoke in a clear, ringing voice. "As the sun sets on the longest day, we express our gratitude for the bounties and fruitfulness of the season. For the good fortune we reap as the wheel of the year now turns toward darkness." She gestured behind her, the rubies in her crown glittering darkly. "This is why we light the ceremonial fire. To give thanks, and to ensure illumination and protection through the long nights ahead. To recharge the wards, and to recharge ourselves. To celebrate life in all its radiant beauty. To affirm the interconnectedness of all beings in our realm."

Virid came forward from the crowd, handing a golden chalice encrusted with garnets to Calytrix. She nodded her thanks, every inch the powerful Faerie Queen.

"To the solstice," she said, holding the chalice aloft. The very last of the day's light shone right on her, and her gown blazed in a halo of white and gold. "To the spark that ignites our inner fire, and the light that keeps us. The flames could not shine so brightly without the darkness." She drank deeply, and the rest of us followed suit. Murmurs of "to the light that keeps us" echoed through the watching Fae.

"And now," she smiled, "I command you to enjoy yourselves." The sun disappeared over the horizon just as she spoke, and Calytrix pushed both hands toward the kindling. Fire erupted, catching and racing to the top of the pyre in a whoosh of heat. Cheers erupted all around, and I couldn't help but add my voice to the cacophony.

As if on cue, the thunderheads in the west boomed, heat lightning jumping from cloud to cloud. The pyre cracked and popped, the fire continuing its bright burn while night fell.

The atmosphere of the gathering shifted. It was as if a fever had spread through the crowd, infecting everyone with dark delirium. Bodies flowed in sensuous dance, laughter rang loudly, and the Fae all glowed as if they'd taken the light from the bonfire inside themselves. Firelight flickered over us all, casting long, shifting shadows.

Energy hummed along my skin, sending a shiver down my spine. My heart began to thrum wildly. I felt pulled to everyone in the garden, like we were all bound together in a web.

"What's happening?" I asked Bri, massaging my chest. Simon appeared dazzled, blinking slowly.

Her amber eyes had turned into dark, endless pools of onyx. "It's the ancient magic of the solstice. The strength of renewal can make you a bit...dizzy." She grinned, flashing white teeth. "We're all getting drunk on power tonight."

She pulled me along, and I reached out for Simon. He caught my hand, and we formed a chain, weaving through the crowd. I had a hard time not tripping on my skirt, but managed to keep up until Bri joined hands with another blue-winged Fae.

The frenzied beat of drums and fiddles wrapped around my limbs, coaxing me into a dance. I let go, allowing the music to pluck the strings of my control so that I succumbed to the savage pulse of solstice magic.

Vesper was in the crowd, her pale skin shining in the firelight, her dark red gown the color of spilled blood. She caught my eye and gave me a knowing smile before joining hands with another pale, red-haired man. The man twirled her, then pulled her into an embrace, and kissed her passionately.

I wasn't even sure how much time had passed when suddenly I was face to face with Alder. He held out a hand, eyebrow quirked in invitation. It didn't matter that I'd won the bet—suddenly, I didn't mind him so much. After waiting a beat, I took it. He spun me, and I turned my face toward the luminous stars dotting the sky, a thousand diamonds against midnight silk.

When I came back in, he put a hand around my waist and swung us into a lively jig.

"I don't know how to dance!" I yelled over the music. At least, I hadn't before tonight.

"Seems like you're doing just fine to me," he replied, eyes sparkling wickedly.

We twirled and spun until I was breathless, the heat of his hand pressing through the thin fabric of my gown. The songs never seemed to end, only flowed into each other like waves overlapping the shore. If the musicians were getting tired, they didn't show it.

"I need to stop," I panted, releasing his shoulder and pushing away. He simply gave a slight bow, turning to take Bri from another partner and drawing her into a dance.

Hitching my skirts up, I stumbled out of the melee and crossed one of the footbridges spanning the Mona. The full moon reflected on the water, so clear it seemed I could reach in and scoop it up. I leaned over the bridge and trailed my fingers across the surface, and when I lifted them out again the tips glowed pale—like I really was touching moonlight.

Past the bridge was another walled garden, thick with climbing roses. I entered beneath an archway heavy with white blooms, glad for the space and solitude. The sounds of the party were muffled, making room for the song of night creatures. But the solstice magic still pulsed in my chest, calling me back to the gathering like a moth to flame.

There was someone seated on a bench inside the walled garden, a dark figure with chestnut hair made visible by moonlight.

I stepped on a twig, and Simon startled at the noise. "Who's that?" he asked, breaking the silence.

"Just me," I answered, stepping out from the cover of the stone walls.

Simon's shoulders dropped, and he leaned back. "Ah. Good."

I sat beside him, smoothing my skirts. "Hiding?"

He cleared his throat, then brushed lint from his trousers. "I could ask you the same thing."

"Well, the answer is yes."

He chuckled, a low, throaty sound. "I wondered when you'd turn up. I know parties aren't your idea of a good time."

No, they weren't, and I knew Simon couldn't stand them either. "Not really. But for once, I don't mind it. Aren't you having fun?"

He shrugged, looking up at the moon. "Aye, it's all right."

I waited for a beat. "What's wrong?"

He exhaled loudly. "What could possibly be wrong? We're drinking Faerie wine under the full moon." As if to punctuate his point, he picked up a bottle from where it sat between his feet and swigged. "D'you know that the Fae make their wine according to lunar cycles?"

"No, but I bet you're going to tell me about it." I plucked the wine from his hand and drank, letting the spicy sweetness wet my throat. Lowering the bottle, I turned back to Simon.

A fine mist surrounded him, shot through with color. Gray, green, and yellow all wove together, overlaid with a sheen of pinkish red. I looked down at the bottle I still held.

Oh, no. Was this Simon's aura?

He grumbled, not having noticed my revelation. "Such a sweet girl, you are. Anyway, yeah. Wine bottled at the new moon is for fresh starts. The waxing moon is for preparation, the waning for reflection."

The green mist surrounding him flared as he spoke. "And the full moon?" I asked.

Now the red dominated, casting him in a bright glow. "The full moon is for truth telling."

I kept my eyes trained on the carpet of stars spreading across the sky. I didn't have to look at Simon's aura in order to see the truth; it was all right there in his voice. Silence grew in the space between us. Silence, and the something I'd been avoiding for weeks now. Months.

"Seph," Simon said, my name coming out low and hoarse. I clutched the skirt of my gown hard enough to rend fabric. I didn't want this. I did want it. My chest was full to bursting, and I couldn't breathe.

"I...I've wanted to say something for a while now." Another pause. "Maybe it's the magic, or maybe it's that I can't keep it in anymore. This isn't how I thought my life would turn out. Everything that's happened...with my parents, and my sister, and Penn. I just wanted to say that spending this time with you...well, I know there've been hard parts. Being imprisoned and stabbed, I could've done without."

I made a low noise of distress in my throat, finally turning to him.

His eyes were like quicksilver in the moonlight, his skin bleached white. Soft pink strands from his aura reached out their tendrils for me.

"I'm mucking this up, aren't I?" He kneaded his forehead, then dropped his hand to the bench. It lay between us, a white flag or a grenade. "What I mean to say is this time with you has been the best of my life." The face I knew as well as my own folded into lines of heart-breaking tenderness.

"And not because we're always doing mad stuff, like making deals with demons or getting our arses kicked," he continued. "Er, sorry, didn't mean to bring that up again. It's because...." He rubbed his lips together, perhaps steeling himself for what came next. "Because I'm with you. You make everything better, Seph."

I wanted him to take back the words. I wanted to turn back time, to have walked past the garden and never had this conversation. We'd been dancing around this for ages, him and I, each straining toward each other then pulling back. Afraid to get burned, afraid to face the truth.

"Simon," I warned, clutching my chest. Something was stirring in the hollow place, a dormant creature coming to life. And it hurt. Pain began to throb down my center, threatening to split me in half.

"Please, just let me speak," he said. I picked at my nails, silently pleading for him to stop, but he continued on. "You're my best friend. Well, my only friend, maybe, but it still stands."

I couldn't help the choking laugh that escaped my lips.

His voice dropped to a whisper. "But you're more than that."

A yawning pit opened in my stomach even as my heart skipped a beat.

He grimaced, twisting his long, artist's fingers together. "I've tried not to. Not to think about you, I mean. Not to see your determination and grit and stubbornness and bravery, and all that. But I...I've failed, miserably. Even though I've watched everyone around me die and know that love can't last, with you...I feel like with you, maybe it could."

Simon reached tentatively for my hand. I didn't stop him, focused as I was on keeping the breath flowing in and out of my lungs.

Now he was babbling, the words spilling out unchecked. "And I know you're in love with Eames. I know, but I love you anyway. And I... I want you to choose me, Seph. We could be so good together. I wouldn't ask you to risk yourself for me—to do anything that would put you in danger. We could stay here, together. Have a life together."

I saw it, too. Living in our cottage in Faerie. Early mornings with Simon, limbs askew and rumpled sheets. Night spent drinking enchanted wine in the glow of candlelight. He could paint, and I would read, and we would take care of each other. It was a gorgeous fantasy.

But this wasn't a fantasy. This was real life.

I was frozen, but the pressure of his thumb stroking my hand brought me back to life. My voice cracked like a splinter of ice. "I can't give you what you want."

"You could." He didn't even look hopeful. In fact, he looked utterly miserable, all the colors in his aura turning dark.

Tears pricked the backs of my eyes, sharp and painful. "No, Simon. Even if I could—I won't." I stood, jerking my hand away. He rose as well, shadows playing in the hollows of his face. Why had he said anything? What was the goddamn point of it all?

"You deserve someone who can love you the way you should be loved. Whole, and not—not someone like me." I massaged my throbbing chest. "I am ruined, Simon. There's something in me that's broken, and it can't be fixed." *Betrayer*, a voice hissed in my head. *False.* My wounds couldn't be mended by a pretty dress and some makeup. And I was a fool for thinking otherwise.

"No," he said, stepping toward me. I moved back, out of his reach. "That's not true, and you know it. You're getting better—healing. This place is good for you. *I* am good for you."

He was right about one thing, at least. Simon *was* good for me. He had become my safe harbor over these long months, the only bit of comfort I'd allowed myself.

Self-disgust filled me. I'd been using him all along, maybe not on purpose, but I'd taken advantage of his love—had gobbled it up and drank it down like I was some starving woman. Because deep down I'd known how he felt—the long glances, the private smiles. And I had no intention of returning those feelings. I couldn't.

Yet, a kernel of some emotion echoed in my chest, something else that wasn't repulsion or guilt or sadness. "It's not going to work. I can't be who you want me to be."

"You already are who I want you to be," he said, voice hoarse. When he reached for me this time, I didn't move away. Simon's fingertips traced down my shoulder to my elbow. He held me and, eyes on mine, leaned in.

My unfaithful heart pulsed once, then his mouth pressed against mine in a kiss. It was so soft, but oh so sweet. He smelled of mint and the turpentine he used for oil painting, and he felt like salvation.

On a lurch, my traitorous lips parted, and I was kissing him back.

We pressed against each other, and his arms came around my waist, gripping tightly. My fingers threaded through his thick chestnut hair, and I finally knew how soft it was after months of wondering. Simon made a small groan of pleasure from deep in his throat, the hum of it dancing over my skin. His tongue swept mine, and heat pooled in my belly, urging me on. He was hot and solid and real. On a heavy exhale, his lips left mine to trail along my throat, and I arched to give him access. A thorn from the climbing roses on the wall pricked the sensitive skin on the back of my neck.

The stinging pain had the same effect as being doused with a bucket of ice water. I gasped, surfacing from the kiss, and shoved Simon away. He lifted his head and gave me that furrowed-brow look.

"I'm sorry," I choked out.

Then, like the coward I was, I pushed past Simon and ran.

I sprinted out of the garden, along the river that wound into the Bearu-Glom. The forest enfolded me in its darkness, the shadows cast by moonlight holding me in a loving embrace. The wildness of the solstice magic returned tenfold, as if making up for a lack. A song of unbridled chaos beat in time with my heart, pulsing through my veins, urging me onward.

A new purpose filled me, one full of darkness and disorder. Something in the forest called to me, a siren to unwitting sailors. I was more than happy to chase it, to distract myself from what I'd just done with Simon. From what I finally admitted in my heart of hearts.

I loved him. I loved him, and I desired him, and I wanted to tear the flesh from my bones because of it.

Branches lovingly caressed my cheeks as I bolted past them, muscles burning and footfalls absorbed by the springy moss underfoot. I burst out of the trees into a clearing.

It was the *relick*, where Sceadu had brought me weeks ago. The dolmen glowed, its stones turning the silver of precious metal. There was a pattern illuminated on the ground in the center that hadn't been visible before in daylight. A triangle, three spirals connecting in a center point.

I knew that sign. It was the triskele, the same one inked onto my forearm. The same one that marked the precious stone I'd sacrificed to the goddess Iznir.

The air resonated with power that sent tiny jolts over my skin. I walked toward the dolmen, almost as if my legs moved of their own accord. When I entered, my whole body vibrated, and I had to clench my jaw to keep my teeth from chattering. What strange magic was this?

Moonlight poured over me as I stood under the symbol so that I, too, was bathed in silver. It was cold on my skin, and...pure. Clean. Safe, and comforting, and everything I didn't deserve.

Maybe it was because I admitted my feelings for Simon, or the moonlight itself that did it. But my defenses crumbled, the parts of myself that had been shoving everything down just to hold on, just to get through each day. I dropped to my knees, the carefully constructed lies of broken-me falling to pieces.

Every bad thought I'd ever had about myself swirled, attacking. I didn't know what the fuck I was doing. I disappointed people, hurt them over and over again. I couldn't give Simon the love he deserved. I was a traitor to even harbor those feelings, to think about him in that way while the man I loved was in hell. I couldn't get my power back. I couldn't be the savior of the worlds that everyone wanted me to be.

I couldn't save Alex.

And it was *my fault*.

My breath hitched, and hot tears I'd been holding back for months poured down my face like rain. I let them water the seed of pain in my chest, and I tore wide open.

It was the most exquisite agony, like finding something precious then watching it die a thousand times. It was the fear that dogged my steps, the guilt that haunted my nightmares.

I should have been taken. It *should* have been me.

By all rights, I should be dead.

I'd failed, and I'd let the person I loved most in all of the worlds—

the person who had been my home, who I thought was my future—disappear.

I'd hurt the man who loved me despite all the nightmares I'd dragged him through. And I loved him back, but didn't respect him enough to tell the truth.

I sobbed, my harsh, broken cries splitting the air. My throat felt like I'd swallowed razor blades, but I didn't care. I welcomed the pain. I needed it, to feel something else amidst the torrent of emotion that would surely drown me.

Other memories rushed to the forefront—my father's face right before he'd transformed into a hellhound, the disappointment in Bri's voice when I'd lied to her, hurting Simon, Penn dying, Fern's betrayal, my mom's heartache. They battered me, and I was helpless against them, tossed around like a rowboat caught in a tempest.

I was pain, and devastation, and one giant, pulsing wound.

In that moment, I hated myself with a depth I hadn't known I was capable of.

But.

There was relief, too, to have it all laid out in front of me. Every mistake, every lie, every failure stared me in the face. And I found that I could look back at them. I could look, and it hurt like hell—but I wasn't afraid any longer.

I picked up each memory, each feeling, and held them up to the light. I poked and prodded them, and every fresh assault brought a new ache. But, it felt better to see them than to pretend they didn't exist at all. This was the collision of old-me and broken-me, twining together to create a new third entity—the sum of every moment, good and bad and everything in-between.

The place beneath my ribs that had been hollow for so long filled to the brim with sensation, pain and joy and love and grief, full of shadows and light existing together. Needing each other.

Bowing my head, I surrendered.

And felt a whisper from behind the obsidian door that was the gateway to my power.

Closing my eyes, I went inward, racing through my meadow. The shriveled grass shrank away, and tender green shoots shot up to replace it. Leaves budded on trees, and birds broke out in song. My door flew open at the barest touch.

And beyond the threshold, it rained. Water spilled from dark clouds, pouring over the hills. It created a deluge that filled the dry riverbeds and turned them black and gold.

Healing rain mingled with my salt tears, and I turned my face to the sky so that it could wash me clean. Magic bloomed beneath my skin, hot and vital and alive. *Finally.*

The touch of cold steel on my throat brought me back to my senses. My eyes flew open, and I tried to scramble to my feet but was met by another blade in the center of my back.

A familiar face stood before me, her teal braids swept into a knot and wings spread wide.

"Hello, Seph."

29

"Fern?" I whispered, my jaw gone slack with disbelief. For a second, I wondered if she was a magic-induced hallucination. But the half-sword pressed against my throat was all too real. I swallowed, and the sharp edge scraped me. Chills broke out across my skin, even as heat gathered behind my sternum.

"I have to hand it to you." Her mouth, which used to always be turned up in a grin, was flat and bracketed with lines. The ropy muscles of her arms shifted directly below the skin as she tightened her grip on the sword. "We've been trying to track you down for a long time."

Anger flared at her use of 'we.' Fern and the Diurne, cozy in their treachery. "How did you get past the wards?" I demanded.

"We've been searching for weaknesses for days now, ever since we found you. Just a few minutes ago, they dropped for a second."

Fuck. How the hell had that happened? "How'd you find me?" I asked, desperate to keep her talking.

Fern licked her cracked lips. "You should have kept running, Seph." I could've sworn regret flashed in her dark eyes, if only for a moment.

"You don't have to do this," I pleaded, all the while flexing the magic that ran hot and thick through my veins. "You know it's wrong. Let me go, and we'll call it even."

Whoever was behind me snorted, and she shook her head. "I can't.

The Diurne renegotiating the extermination program is contingent on bringing you back."

The extermination program. I thought of Vesper, who was celebrating with the rest of the Weald Fae, clueless to the fact that the people who destroyed her world had followed me here. "Why didn't they just leave me for the demons to hunt down?"

"After Magoth's double-cross, the Diurne aren't taking any chances. They don't want the demons to have you." The hard line of her mouth wavered. "If you come quietly, I can help you."

This time, I couldn't prevent the rage from seeping into my voice. "Oh yeah? What are they going to do with me, Fern? Keep me in a cage for the rest of my life?"

"It's better than whatever Magoth had planned for you," she countered.

I eyed the sword at my throat. It hadn't wavered at all. "The Weald Fae can protect you from the Diurne. Stay here, with us. You don't want to hurt anyone else."

Sharp pain flared in the middle of my back, and I flinched. Fern's eyes cut over my shoulder. She gave a slight shake of her head. My blood ran cold as I wondered exactly how many Guardians were in Faerie. I needed to get out of here, to warn the Fae.

"I'm in too deep," she said, voice cracking on the last word. "The only way the Diurne will work with me is if I bring you back to them."

Yes, I was sure of it now—there was regret there, and I would use it. "And what's it going to be after that? There'll always be some task they want you to complete, something to hold over your head. You have to get out, Fern."

She blinked hard.

"What else are they threatening you with?" I asked slowly.

Fern shook her head. "It's time to go, Seph."

She reached for my arm, and I could sense the magic she sent toward me, trying to bind me in place. That was new.

Grasping for my power, I shot fire at her. But she was ready for my attack, and the flames hit an invisible wall.

Ducking and throwing an elbow into the Guardian behind me, I grabbed the arm holding the sword and flipped them over my back, lifting the blade from them in the process. It was Yuto, shaggy hair covering his surprised face.

"Graduate early?" I asked, pointing the short sword at him. His eyes flicked to Fern, who stood there watching us. If I didn't know any better, she didn't want him to get back up. But then she clenched her fist and drew it in, and I began to slide toward her, my slippered feet catching on pebbles.

Shooting out a hand, I sent threads behind me where they hooked around one of the dolmen's supports. I tugged, rocketing backward and swinging onto the flat slab of its roof. From there, I caught the glint of nocturnal eyes in the forest, and antlers illuminated by the moonlight.

The *deor feya* were coming to defend their forest.

Fern alighted atop the dolmen and landed in a crouch. She leapt forward, attacking with her blade. I met her advance, parrying and thrusting her back.

"You'd better get out of here while you still can," I warned, spinning and slicing down in a blow that sent her stumbling toward the roof's edge. Yuto shouted from below, and Sceadu's voice pierced my mind.

The eudaemon and I will get this one, Lihta. More Golden Ones are in the forest.

My blood ran cold, and I risked a glance down. Sceadu and Folly circled Yuto. What if the other Guardians attacked Simon and Bri? What if people died?

Fern took advantage of my momentary distraction, sweeping her blade at my stomach. I jumped back, but the tip sliced the fabric of my dress. My legs were getting caught in the long skirts, so I gripped the fabric with my magic and tore. A large rip ran from hem to hip, freeing me.

Sceadu and Folly snarled below us, but I didn't look down.

Fern and I battled, the clang of steel on steel ringing through the night. Sparks jumped where the edges of our blades met, a shower of flickering lights.

"You're good with that sword," Fern acknowledged, panting.

"I have a good teacher." Advancing once more, I got below her guard and thrust my sword into her shoulder, using my threads to part her shield and drive it deep. She cried out, stumbling back. I jumped off the dolmen, slamming into the ground. Just then it began to rain hard, fat droplets, and a fork of lightning split the sky.

I bolted from the clearing as thunder boomed, skirt billowing behind me like a cloud. I picked up on Fern's footfalls coming fast as I darted into the trees. The dense forest swallowed me whole.

Pushing off the ground, I soared through the air and landed upon a low-hanging branch. I climbed until the thick foliage obscured me from view. Sticky sap coated my hands.

Fern appeared a few moments later, stalking cat-like through the trees. "I know you're here, Seph," she said quietly. "Come on out."

Barely daring to breathe, I waited until she was just past my tree. Then, I jumped.

She spun, but not quickly enough to dodge me. We hit the ground in a heap, and I threw her sword to the side, pinning her with strength and my power. I bound her wrists and ankles with my black threads. She struggled against the bonds, her power shoving against mine. With a start, I realized I was the stronger of the two of us.

"Are you going to kill me?" she asked, dark eyes boring into mine.

I hesitated for the space of a single heartbeat. "Not if I can help it."

I'd fantasized about this moment. Had imagined torturing her with aching slowness that would stretch her agony into an eternity. That would give her pain equal to mine.

Now that she was standing in front of me, flesh and bone where there had been only memory, I didn't feel the hatred I expected. Yes, there was fury, betrayal, hurt—but I didn't want her to die. "I want you to take the others and go," I said roughly.

"I can't do that. They know you're here now." She cocked her head, listening for something. "They have my family, Seph." Her voice wavered. "If I disappear, the Diurne will hurt them."

My chest clutched. "Are you going to attack me if I let you up?" She shook her head, and I stood, letting her rise but still cuffing her with my threads.

"Edward is having them watched by his personal death squad," she told me, forcing the words out with effort. "I regretted everything immediately, as soon as Magoth showed up in the prison world. We ended up in some sort of water world, and when we got back to head-quarters, I tried to run." Her voice broke. "I can't believe I betrayed you.

I was so wrong. So fucking stupid. I got carried away. I just...I'm a fool, Seph. I want out. You'll never know how sorry I am."

"Sorry," I repeated incredulously. As if that one tiny word could make up for everything she'd done. And yet, I couldn't entirely shove down the part of me that missed her friendship. I shook my head to banish it.

"Where are the others?" she croaked. "Davina, and the rest."

"Gone." I made my voice hard to mask the pain that brought. "Not that you would care."

Her forehead puckered as her brows dipped. "What do you mean, gone?"

"The rest of the unit are somewhere in the worlds, probably looking for us. And Alex...." The lump rose in my throat, and this time, I let it come. "Alex was taken. By Magoth. The demons are using him as bait to get to me." The space beneath my ribs erupted with pain.

Fern's face was a mask of horror. "No," she croaked. Tears slid down her face, and she dropped to her knees. "What have I done?"

"You fucked us all." I looked down at her squarely as the gears in my brain worked overtime, searching for a solution to this disaster. "If you want any chance of making this right, you can help me now. Maybe we can protect you, if you're willing to turn on the Diurne."

"I told you—"

"I have a plan." A risky one, but there was no time to think of something else. "Follow me." I let Fern's bonds fall away and turned my back on her.

We spilled out of the forest, me sprinting, and Fern on my heels. Without looking back, I shot an arc of blue flame at her, then raced over the footbridge. Rain drenched the boards, and I almost slipped.

The solstice gathering was utter chaos. Screams reverberated through the air, as dozens of Guardians bore down on the Fae. I couldn't see Simon or Bri anywhere. Leander squared off with one of the Guardians, sending a rock hurtling toward his opponent. Another Fae had their feet planted and hands spread, calling the river to breach its banks. Lightning struck a Guardian, and they were thrown back, smoking.

Folly appeared then, galloping out of the Bearu-Glom. A snarl rippled through his teeth, and he lunged for a Guardian's throat.

My power swelled inside me, like it was clamoring to be used after all these months. The rivers felt endless, as though they could never be drained.

"Get back!" I yelled. "Evacuate to the palace!"

Someone had the sense to listen. Fae took to the skies, some winging for the castle, others raining attacks on the Guardians.

Calytrix was in the fray, sword flashing as she stabbed and sliced. She had one Guardian at her front and one at her back. I rushed toward her, just as one of her attackers stabbed her in the leg. She fell, and they bore down on her.

I shoved both hands out, and my gold threads turned into lightning, shooting straight for the Guardians. They both glowed briefly before crumpling to the ground. I reached the queen, shielding her with my body.

"It's just a scratch," she said through gritted teeth. Her crown was gone, and blood trickled from a cut above her eye. "Where is Virid?"

"Respectfully, you need to get the fuck out of here." I snagged a passing Fae, then pulled Calytrix to her feet and shoved her into his shaking arms. "Get her up to the palace. Now."

I ran back into the battling pairs of Guardians and Fae. Alder had taken on Fern, sword arcing gracefully as he vaulted into the air. She slashed down with a hand, and blood bloomed across his cheek. He faltered, and she struck again, slicing across his sword arm.

Charging toward them, I shoved Alder aside and met Fern's attack. I superheated the metal of my sword, and flames jumped to hers as we clashed. They raced up the pommel and she dropped her blade, reaching for a dagger at her ankle. She threw it at me, but my magic caught the dagger and reversed its direction so it arced toward her.

Fern dodged, and I lunged, hitting her with an uppercut then kicking her exposed midriff. She caught my foot and twisted. Going with the motion, I spun and landed in a crouch.

I got up, then waited for her to strike again.

Her eyes glittered darkly, and a smile curved her lips. "You can't hold out forever," she said, circling. I moved with her, fists raised.

"Neither can you," I countered.

"You forget that I know all of your moves. I taught them to you."

I stared at her, concentration never wavering. Then I looked over her shoulder, and gasped.

Fern's eyes flicked away from mine, and she swiveled her head. I sprang, closing the ten-foot gap between us, and stabbed her.

Blood poured from the hole in her torso, and she collapsed, eyes fluttering closed.

It was time to end this.

Gathering my power, I waited until it frothed and roiled. The edges of my control frayed, and some trickled out, flattening a Guardian who charged at me.

I breathed deeply, then shut my eyes. Time seemed to slow as I expanded my senses, noting the differences between Guardian and Faerie. Fae pulsed blue in the darkness behind my lids, while Guardians were brilliant gold. Shouts tickled my ears, and steel sang through the air.

On my next breath, I unleashed my power, energy crackling as it surged through me.

Black and gold threads snaked out from my open palms, encircling the Guardians. They twined around their throats, squeezing. Choked cries split the air, and I felt hands pulling at my power in an attempt to throw off the binding. I squeezed harder, then one by one, their spluttering gasps cut off. Silence fell.

Spears of light shot over the horizon as dawn broke, illuminating the unconscious Guardians that littered the grounds like fallen statues. I removed my threads from their throats, instead sending them to bind wrists and ankles.

The Fae who had remained behind to fight stared at me with slack jaws. "We need to get them out of here. Someone open a portal," I commanded. "And separate the dead bodies from the live ones. The wards need to be checked and secured, too."

Leander began shouting orders, and the Fae jumped into action. The wounded were gathered and healers began to triage. Others dragged unconscious bodies through the mud, forming neat rows, while portals were opened on the river's edge. The rain began to let up, then stopped altogether. The sky was turning the pale gray of dawn.

Folly crested the rise behind the river, his muzzle coated in dark red. I dropped to my knees, hugging him. "Are you okay?"

"I am well." He did a full body shake, spraying me with water, and his ears flopped haphazardly.

"Will you check on the queen for me?" I said, eyeing Fern as she limped over, blood seeping from the flesh wound in her side. After one last sniff, Folly loped off toward the castle.

"Did you have to stab me so deep?" She grimaced, pressing her hand over the puncture.

"Consider it payback for my arm."

Her face fell, and she nodded. "I deserve that."

Leander approached us from the riverbank. "I assume there's a good reason she's still alive?" he growled.

"There is," I answered. "Put her in...I don't know, jail or something."

He grunted, and we both ignored Fern's wounded look. "Where should we send the Golden Ones?"

"I don't care. Anywhere that's far away from here." I turned back to Fern. "Do you think any of them saw you go down?"

She nodded. "I'm positive. But what are you going to do with Yuto?"

I jerked a shoulder. "That's for the *deor feya* to decide. Hopefully, the survivors will think he's dead, too."

Death was the only solution I'd come up with for releasing Fern from the Diurne. She was one less soldier for them to control, and her family's grief was a small cost for her freedom. There was also the fact that she was now indebted to me.

"Right. You, come with me." Leander cuffed Fern by the back of her neck. If looks could kill, he would've been bleeding out. But she bent her head and allowed him to lead her in the direction of the barracks.

I went to assist the healers, helping them bind wounds or heal shallow cuts. I promised myself I'd learn more about healing when this was all over with.

Simon stumbled up to the triage area, supporting a bleeding Bri. I dropped a roll of bandages and ran to them, jumping in to take her other side. They were both soaked and covered in dirt and streaks of blood.

"How bad?" I asked, fear clogging my throat.

"I'm fine," Bri assured me. "It's just a burn." Indeed, her dress was charred and the exposed skin of her left thigh was an angry, blistered red.

We settled her on the ground, and I flagged down a healer. "I think I can take the pain away," I said as I knelt next to her. Simon stood beside Bri, seeming disheveled but unhurt.

"Don't worry about me," she said, waving her hand in my direction. "Take care of yourself." Catkin arrived holding a glass bottle, and I shuffled aside to make room for him.

"It would be best if you give us space, *Lihta*," Catkin said, pouring a few drops from the bottle onto a cloth and holding it to Bri's leg. Her face went slack with relief. "Please, take your rest. I noticed that you have your own injuries."

"I'll come back to check on you," I informed Bri. "In an hour."

Giving a faint smile, she lay back and closed her eyes. "Looking forward to it."

I walked toward the edge of the forest, Simon falling into step beside me. My pulse skittered more than it had during the battle. "You're okay?"

He nodded, and something held tight in my chest softened. "None of this blood belongs to me. I was helping the healers."

"What happened to you? After I...left."

His eyes were bleak and tired, ringed with purple shadows. We'd all been up for over a day. "I heard the Aureum coming and ran to warn the Fae."

My shoulders dropped. At least they'd had some notice. "You saved a lot of lives, then."

"As did you. Your power came back, I see." Then, he wet his lips. "Look, Seph, about before—"

I stopped Simon by throwing my arms around his neck. After a brief pause, he clutched me tightly, burying his face in my hair. I breathed in his mint and turpentine scent, now mixed with sweat and hints of copper.

Holding Simon felt right on so many levels. He was my safe harbor, my best friend. The only person who'd been able to bring me peace when I was steeped in misery. The voice in my head that had told me to keep moving when I wanted to give up belonged to him.

But.

"I can't be with you, Simon," I finally whispered, still clutching him. "The only thing I can offer you is friendship."

I'd known after the kiss. No matter how much I loved Simon, it just wasn't right. My soul belonged with Alex's. They were already merged, so intertwined I couldn't possibly pick out where mine ended and his began. There was no room for anyone else.

Simon's chest moved under mine, heaving in a long sigh. His grip on me tightened. "You could, you know."

I shook my head. "I couldn't." Releasing him, we drew apart.

"But you love me, too," he insisted. There was no heat behind his words, more of a subdued acceptance.

I didn't bother to deny it. He was owed the truth. "I do."

He gave a wry smile, his eyes a soft, sad gray. "Not enough, then."

Another piece of my heart splintered, an ache radiating through my chest. I couldn't answer that. I'd never imagined myself falling in love with one person, let alone two. But Alex had staked his claim on me, and I him, before I'd even known of Simon's existence.

Maybe in another life, Simon and I belonged together. But in every world, I was Alex's. And he was mine.

I picked at my thumbnail, staring into the shadows of the forest. "I understand if you don't want to...if you can't be around me anymore."

Soft pressure appeared on my chin as Simon tilted my head toward him. "Beyond anything else, you're my best friend in all the worlds. My family. I don't want to lose that."

"I don't, either," I said, voice cracking on the last word. I screwed my eyes up against the tears, but they overflowed my lids and dripped to the ground.

Simon dropped his hand and cast his gaze downward, chewing on the inside of his cheek. He took a long breath, and when he released it, he met my eyes. "If that's how it has to be...I understand. Friends, then?"

I nodded, hating the pain riding just beneath his veneer of lightness. Hating that I put it there. But if I had to do it all over again, I'd make the same choice every time.

"What do you say we wash the blood off and sleep for eighteen hours?"

He snorted. "Sounds like a bloody good plan."

30

Cleaning up the aftermath of the battle took weeks. Once all the surviving Guardians had been sent through portals and the dead buried, the Fae turned toward tending their own wounds. Two Fae warriors had been killed, leaving the whole community in mourning. We laid them to rest under rainy skies, committing their bodies to the earth they cared for so deeply.

The return of my magic set the wheels of planning into motion, and every waking second was filled with preparation for the mission to Tristia. In addition to ramping up training with Leander to include practicing with my power, I spent my evenings with Vesper learning about Lightbringer magic. Sunset was in a few hours, and I'd need to head to her guest apartments in the city to meet her soon. But first, I went to see Calytrix.

The queen had refused to take any time off after the battle, despite Catkin's urging that she needed rest. I still wasn't her biggest fan, but I'd gained new respect for Calytrix after watching her in the fray. She wasn't content to wait on the sidelines while others fought her battles.

Her only nod to weakness was that she didn't rise to greet me when I entered her office. "Ah, Persephone," she said, nodding to the chair across from her. There was a grimness lurking around her mouth that hadn't been there before the Guardians invaded. "Please, sit."

I waited while she shifted stacks of papers around her desk, lifting one to the light and squinting at it. "Leander informs me the strategy meetings are proceeding well."

Proceeding was certainly a word for it. We'd spent hours studying the geography of the island of Tristia and this Vale of Shadows where the Book was supposed to be hidden. I saw topographical maps in my dreams now, which was a welcome reprieve from their usual nightmarish content.

But what Queen Calytrix had neglected to mention when we made our deal was that the Fae weren't the only ones seeking the Book of Shadows.

That came out during a strategy meeting, when talk had turned to defense tactics. Vesper, Leander, Indigo, Folly, and I were clustered over yet another map in the dimly-lit suite of rooms where I'd first met the vampyre. The outermost apartment had turned into a sort of central base for operations, a commandeered war room. Paintings of a dark forest had been removed from the walls, replaced by astrological diagrams and charts.

"Defense tactics?" I'd asked. "Shouldn't we be thinking about how best not to get our eyes burned out by the Book?"

Vesper turned her cool hazel stare on me. "You thought we would be the only ones after the first grimoire?" Her tongue slipped out to wet her fangs. "Rumor says that what is inside that book can unknot the very threads that bind the worlds together—that bind life together—disintegrating us all en masse. Now, tell me who would not want that sort of power."

Leander and Indigo, who had been pinning maps, stilled. It didn't seem to come as a surprise to them, but they still hung on Vesper's every word.

Once, the promise of facing off against hordes of unknown magical creatures would've scared me boneless. Now, it was nothing more than another obstacle standing between me and Alex. "Isn't it supposed to be hidden? A secret?" I asked.

Vesper huffed, flicking a long lock of hair over her shoulder. "Any secret can be unearthed. If my spies can discover the Book's location, surely others will have. Unlike you Guardians, vampyres do not think we are the supreme beings of the worlds. There are countless stronger and cleverer creatures." She tapped a finger on her fang. "Well, perhaps not countless."

"Fine," I acknowledged. "So how do we beat them?"

Indigo placed her palms on the table and leaned toward me, a wicked grin on her face. "We use you."

That discussion had been just over a week ago, and we only had days remaining until we left for Tristia. "They're going well," I told Calytrix. "We'll be ready."

"Of course you will. However, I would like you to consider an alteration to your team."

A wary feeling crept over me. "Who's that?" If she was about to suggest Alder...

"The prisoner."

My eyes, which had been wandering over the queen's desk, snapped back to her. "What?"

Everyone had taken to calling Fern "the prisoner," which she technically was. She'd been staying in a holding cell in the lower levels of the barracks, though she'd been allowed some privileges after her interrogation. Turned out the Faerie truth serum Vesper had threatened me with was a handy tool for learning whether your enemies harbored ill intentions.

However, it was a far cry from trust. Which left me wondering why exactly Calytrix wanted to send her to Tristia.

"This is her chance to prove her intentions to our cause. If she helps you retrieve the Book, she will earn her freedom here." The queen leaned back in her chair, stroking her hands over the gold fabric of her dress. "And, if you must know, she is expendable. I would rather lose her than one of my own."

Ah, there it was. The calculating queen I knew and—well, tolerated. "You aren't worried she'll betray us? She doesn't exactly have a great track record."

"If she tries, you have orders to eliminate her." She said it with such calm certainty that a chill ran down my spine. No, it would not be wise to cross this queen. I couldn't bring myself to kill Fern when she had a sword to my throat—but would I do it if she betrayed me again? I didn't like that no clear answer presented itself.

"And when you return with the Book," Calytrix continued, "I will make my soldiers available to you. You can leave to fetch your captain any time once it is in our hands."

My stomach fluttered as though a hundred butterflies had taken up residence there. I was so, so close. Every cell in my body longed to hear Alex's voice, to feel his skin on mine. It was as though our very atoms strained to be together, and I ached with it. "Thank you, Your Majesty," I answered, standing to dismiss myself.

She held up a finger. "A moment." I lowered back into the chair.

"As you know, I am due to give birth soon. Very soon," she said, rubbing her belly. It had grown so large that she had to sit quite far back from her desk. "We have decided—well, Virid has insisted, actually— that I go into hiding during and immediately after the birth."

My forehead crinkled. "Why?"

She huffed. "Because in marriage, you must compromise. Despite no threat to the wards—not since the return of your power disrupted them, at least—he doesn't feel it is safe here."

Oops. "Where could be safer than here?" I asked, picking at my thumbnail.

"If I told you, it wouldn't be very secure." The grim lines around her mouth softened as she looked down at her belly. "I will do anything for the wellbeing of my child. Even if it means leaving my home. Temporarily," she added. "Alder will be in command during my absence, and will know my location. Anything you need will go through him."

Oh, goddess. Alder, in charge? I tamped down on the urge to roll my eyes. "Understood."

"You know...Ezekial would be proud of all you are doing here, Persephone," the queen said. I stilled at the mention of him. "You are your father's daughter."

My father's daughter. Before I'd learned the truth, I would've laughed at the very idea. But my father was a good man. "Thank you," I said, the ghost of sorrow in my chest.

Calytrix nodded, then turned back to the papers covering her desk. I left, walking swiftly beside the small tributary of the Mona that ran through the castle. After being with the Weald Fae all these weeks, I still had moments of wonder at the seamless blend between architecture and landscape.

I found Fern on the training field, drilling with Leander. He was the only person apart from me who didn't treat her like a pariah. Well, not entirely.

They were sparring in hand-to-hand, evenly matched with his muscular bulk and her enhanced abilities. She certainly hadn't been slacking on training during our time apart.

After dodging Leander's kick, she flipped backward like there were springs attached to her feet. He took to the skies, flying at breakneck speed and landing behind her, swiping out again. They tangled, landing punches and kicks. Finally, he got under her guard and flipped her onto her back. He leaned over her, chest billowing as the cords in his neck strained. Fern's glazed expression didn't seem entirely to do with shock.

Watching them spar brought back memories of training with Fern at Aureum headquarters. She'd been the first of Alex's unit to accept and welcome me into my new world. I knew she was happy to spend time with someone else who looked like her, though our experiences growing up had been so different. And I was happy to have that, too. There'd been an unspoken bond between us from the very start, which made her treachery hurt all the more.

Yet, she thought she'd been doing something for the greater good, something that would save countless lives. And how many times had I put other people at risk in service of getting to Alex? True, I hadn't shot or promised anyone to a demon, but I'd summoned Gamori out of a moment of reckless hopelessness. I'd let my pain and my fear get the better of me, and ended up threatening Simon's life. Fern, like all of us, was the sum of every moment. Good and bad.

The fact was that I missed her. The past couldn't be changed, but the future could. I'd experienced so much loss, and beneath all the hurt, I wanted her friendship back. I wanted her back. Only time would tell if that was possible.

"Am I interrupting something?" I asked, strolling toward Fern and Leander.

Leander started and jumped up, brushing grass and dirt from his tunic. Fern did the same, studiously avoiding eye contact as she squirmed under my gaze.

"No," he said, a little too carefully. "I was just showing the prisoner some new defensive maneuvers."

"Sure." Fern snorted. "As if you could teach me anything."

Leander's eyes gleamed, and I cut in before they either started trading insults or jumped each other's bones. "Enough. I have something to tell you." I turned to Fern, and her face blanked apart from a muscle jumping in her jaw. "You're coming with us to Tristia."

Her brows shot up. "Really?"

"Queen's orders. If you have a problem, take it up with her."

"Um...no. No problem," she said, shifting back and forth on her feet. "But why?"

"Probably sees you as expendable," Leander offered. Fern shot him a glare. I didn't bother to tell him he'd guessed correctly.

"I want to help," she said quietly. "And, it's better than...well, you know." She jerked her head back toward the barracks, where her cell was.

Certain danger *was* probably better than being semi-imprisoned and universally hated.

"You'll join us at our next strategy meeting," I said, nodding toward Leander.

"You know...." Fern ventured. "You remind me of Alex right now." She flicked her gaze to the side, then back to me. "Being in charge looks good on you. He'd...he'd be proud to see you stepping into your power."

Hearing her say that was bittersweet, but she was right. Alex would be proud of me.

"Well," Leander said gruffly, "if you're here, then I'm off." He crouched, then launched into the sky and arrowed toward the palace.

"I guess that means I'm headed back to my cell. Unless you want to supervise me?" she asked, eyeing me hopefully.

"No," I said curtly. Then, I took a long breath. "I just have something I need to do. Alone."

I watched until a guard flanking the main entrance to the barracks intercepted Fern, and they disappeared inside.

I searched the training field until I found the two handprints of dead grass I'd left after my first meeting with Leander. Kneeling before them, I reached into my pocket and removed a pouch of bulbs. I'd chosen to replace the grass with narcissus—the flower of renewal.

Placing my hands on the earth, I closed my eyes and felt for my threads. They were just under my skin, flowing like smooth water. I sent both the gold and the black into the earth, scooping up death and pushing out life.

The soil changed from dust to rich, dark humus. It smelled of damp earth and the promise of new beginnings.

Parting the dirt, I lowered the bulbs into their new home and covered them. My magic sensed the potential lying just beneath the protective outer layer, and, unbidden, caressed it. Roots sprouted and wove through the earth, while green stems shot upward. White petals unfurled, revealing a center, cylindrical orange blossom.

Life and death. I smiled and headed toward the docks, glad I'd left my mark.

———

Vesper's apartment in the city was all whispered elegance and quiet sophistication. A simple candelabra cast a dim glow on the creme walls of the living area, where we were seated on a plush carpet. She, who was happiest in pure darkness, lit the candles only for my comfort.

"Your shield is your most important weapon," Vesper began, tucking her legs beneath her. Her black velvet trousers swished against the carpet. "And because you have two sources of power flowing within you, it will always be stronger than your opponent's."

"Unless they're another Lightbringer," I muttered, going inward to grasp the black and gold filaments of my magic.

"Those seem to be rather short on the ground." The corners of her red-painted mouth were drawn, like she was trying to swallow down a feeling.

Fuck. Her sister, Seraphyna. "That was stupid of me," I told her, all thoughts of shields forgotten.

Vesper waved her hand. "Never mind that. Now, concentrate. Your power is not two separate entities to be used individually, which is something you still seem unable to grasp."

I accepted her redirection, quietly chastising myself. Maybe 100 years was long for a human, but not for a vampyre. The wound of her sister's loss was probably still fresh.

Soon, I lost myself in the throes of magic, sweat beading on my hairline as I focused on knotting the threads with my mind. They resisted each other like oil and water.

After an hour with little success, Vesper sighed. "Why don't you bring your keeper to our meetings?"

"Hm?" The black thread kept slipping off of the gold.

"Your keeper. The boy, Simon."

I dropped the threads. "Simon isn't responsible for me. He's been busy volunteering at the refugee camp, anyway." Busy avoiding me. Things had been uneasy between us since I told Simon I couldn't be with him. Wouldn't, I corrected. I'd made my choice and had to live with the consequences. He'd said he still wanted my friendship—I would have to hope that he came around, eventually. Because I missed Simon terribly. It was harder to get through my days without his disapproving snorts and sarcastic overtures. He wasn't the only one who'd come out of the solstice with a wounded heart.

Vesper clucked her tongue. "That is not what I mean." Waggling her fingers as if trying to pluck the correct word out of the air, she said, "The keeper is the one who strengthens your power. They sense your magic and are tethered to you."

A strange, cold feeling erupted in my stomach. "Tethered?"

"Connected, by a thread of your own magic that hooks into them when your power develops," she replied. "Your magic will choose who it believes to be the strongest conduit." Then, she smirked. "It is difficult for a Lightbringer to be separated from the keeper. Many become lovers. For my sister, her keeper was the woman who would become her wife. Elysande."

"What—what happened to Elysande when Seraphyna was taken?" I cleared my throat, which had suddenly gone dry.

Vesper's expression clouded. "The keeper bond went dark. She took her life about fifty years ago."

I barely even heard her. "Simon isn't my keeper," I rasped.

Alex was.

The bond between us—our linked minds, the thread of connection tugging from the center of my chest—that explained all of it. I finally had an answer for why we were tethered in such a way. Why Alex could feel my magic before I'd been aware that it or he existed.

The link between Seraphyna and Elysande had gone dark, just like it had between me and Alex. The titanium threads of our connection still remained, but there was nothing on the other end. For the first time since he'd been taken, a horrible thought burrowed into my brain like a parasite sinking its hooks into me.

Was Alex still alive? Seraphyna's keeper surely wouldn't have gone to such drastic measures without good reason. But I refused to believe that. I couldn't.

"Perhaps we should end here for tonight," Vesper suggested. The shadows had lengthened as full night settled in, and her moon-white skin glowed in the candlelight. "Practice your shield before you return tomorrow evening."

I nodded, then rose mechanically and headed to the riverboat that would take me back to the cottage. I sat on the deck, studying the unfamiliar constellations dotting the sky. They glowed white, brilliant as any diamond. My mind churned like the water beneath the boat.

Why did the tether go dark when Seraphyna was taken, and what did it mean for me and Alex? And the thought that buzzed like an angry wasp: were our feelings for each other artificial, due to some magical influence? Some hand of fate tied us together, but what had our choice been in the matter?

Perhaps it was impossible to tell. In the end, I wasn't certain the reason why I loved Alex was as important as the simple fact that I did.

The boat bumped against its moorings at the dock, and I wound my way back to the cottage, still turning over questions. I almost didn't notice Simon and Folly in the kitchen sharing their evening meal together. Folly hopped off a chair and trotted over to me. I knelt to scratch beneath his chin.

"Hungry?" Simon grunted. He'd neglected to shave, and the shadow of a reddish beard covered his jaw. But otherwise, he looked the same—hale, handsome, irate, sleeves shoved past his elbows to display paint-splattered forearms covered in freckles.

"Starved," I answered.

He plated me up steaming scrambled eggs and toast and shoved a mug of tea in my direction. I sipped, wetting my dry throat. Folly let out a soft whine and placed his heavy head on my knee. He knew, as he always did, when something was on my mind.

"How was the refugee camp?"

He shook his head. "Poor buggers. They just want to go home, but there's no home to go back to."

"Maybe there will be soon, now that my power's back. After I get the Book and Alex."

"After *we* get them," he corrected, slathering his toast with a thick layer of blackberry preserves.

I was mid-chew when his words sank in, and I swallowed hurriedly. "You want to come?"

"I've seen it through this far, haven't I? Seems like a waste to stop now." His gray gaze bored into me. "You're not going to try and stop me?"

Would I rather he stay safe behind the wards, out of Gamori's reach? Absolutely. But I was done preventing Simon from making his own choices. He'd survived a dying world, demons, imprisonment, stabbings. Every time I'd underestimated him had been a wound, and he'd borne them all because he loved me.

I would worry about him, but it was his decision to make. I shrugged. "No. If you want to come, you're in."

Surprise skittered across his expression before he gave me a smug smile. "Good. I mean, as if you'd have been able to stop me. You need looking after. And if anyone's an expert on books, it's me."

I returned his smile. "Of course." Then, I sobered, thinking about me and Simon and Alex and tethers and all the space between us that was filled with grief and pain and love. "Are we okay?"

Simon leaned back in his chair and interlaced his fingers behind his neck. "We will be."

It would take time. But I trusted him. I sent a gust of air across the table to ruffle his hair.

"Ugh." He shoved stray strands out of his eyes. "Can't say I missed that."

"I'm better with my magic now. There are so many more ways for me to fuck with you."

He snorted. "Guess I'll have to start sleeping with one eye open."

I rose from the table, yawning. "Nah, you need your sleep. We leave in a week, so rest up." He gave me a bemused smile, saluting before rising to deal with the dishes.

As I headed up the spiral stairs with Folly's footsteps thumping behind me, I felt a sort of peace. Everything was falling into place. Alex would be home soon.

I hoped I'd dream of him that night.

PART IV

"How do you know I'm mad?" said Alice.

"You must be," said the Cat, "or you wouldn't have come here."

— LEWIS CARROLL, ALICE IN WONDERLAND

31

Time passed like someone bespelled the hours to disappear. I blinked, and our week was up. Tristia and the Book of Shadows waited.

Myself and the rest of the team, plus Bri, were gathered around a portal Indigo had opened on the roof of Calytrix's city palace. Lavender clouds had swept in as night fell, though Vesper cinched her hood tight around her face. We were in the strange hour now, the time where anything and everything could happen.

Leander, tawny eyes gleaming, was spoiling for a fight. Fern, her teal braids twisted back, bristled with weapons. Folly's nose twitched and his ears were alert. Vesper managed to look bored, but her fangs extended over her bottom lip. Indigo, a crossbow strapped across her back, was deadly focused. And then there was Simon, face taut with tension and paler than usual.

As for me, hope was no longer a flickering ember in my chest, but a steady, blazing fire. It warmed me from the inside out and fueled my determination. Nothing would stop me from getting the Book. Nothing would stop me from getting Alex. It was that simple.

I'd lost faith in myself after he'd disappeared. Instead, failure had become my god, and I'd worshipped at its knees. I'd been a supplicant to my own destruction, needing to prove how worthless I was.

Broken-me was still inside, nestled next to all the other versions of myself. Val had been trying to impress upon me for months that only through acceptance would I find my power.

I flexed my hands, and lines of blue flame shot from my fingertips to wrists. I felt stronger than I ever had, more ready to face what was coming.

"Everyone clear on the plan?" I asked, nerves jumping in my stomach. They all nodded in unison. We'd been over it so many times the past few days, I'd seen it written across the backs of my eyelids when I collapsed into bed every night.

"Wait," Bri said, biting her lip. "You have the *frithcloth*?"

I patted my midriff, where a special bag was tucked inside a pouch tied around my waist. The enchanted fabric, made from special plant fibers, would supposedly contain the magic from the Book—or at least soften its effects, whatever they may be.

"Okay, then." Bri pulled me into a tight hug. "Be careful," she whispered. "Get that book, and come back. I don't want to lose you again."

I clung to her for another moment, not willing to lie just to soothe her.

"All of you be careful," Bri instructed, amber eyes skimming the rest of the group. She lingered on Simon, who gave her a crooked grin.

I nodded to the others. "Let's go get us a book."

The portal swallowed me whole, enveloping me in blackness before spitting me out into a night-darkened jungle. The air was humid and sticky, and I felt like I was breathing through a heavy mask. As I stepped back to allow the others through the portal, dewy vegetation dampened my trousers.

"Bloody thick here, isn't it?" Simon said in a hushed whisper. "Where are you, Seph?" I took his hand, guiding him toward me. The others trailed out after him.

"It is oppressive," Vesper replied, wrinkling her nose with distaste. "Better to get moving, I think."

"I'll lead," Folly said from below. The thick undergrowth of the jungle was taller than him, but the tip of his tail poked out, waving like a flag.

"Let's sound off every so often to make sure we're all here. I don't want to lose anyone on the way," I said. Humidity wasn't the only presence pressing against my skin. Magic was a low thrum in the air, pulsing in time with my heartbeat.

We fell into a line, Folly at the head, Leander bringing up the rear.

Tristia was a mountainous island, with a rocky coastline and densely forested interior. The Vale of Sorrow was about two hours north of where we landed. No one could get closer, apparently—the island held its own magic to keep intruders out. So we would head north, arriving shortly before the Lacrima meteor shower exposed the bridge into the Vale. Beyond that, no one knew what we would find. Or who else might be waiting for us.

The moon was a vast orb overhead, outshining all the stars in the sky. I couldn't help imagining it as a glowing crystal ball that held our fates inside. Whining insects and croaking frogs formed a clamorous backdrop as we picked our way through the jungle. I swatted a mosquito trying to make a meal of my neck. Indigo cranked her head around and put a finger to her lips.

Treetops rustled, and pairs of large eyes blinked down at us, shining eerie green in the moonlight. Whatever creatures they belonged to only watched our progress. After an hour of walking, we hadn't run into anything threatening.

Sweat soaked through my clothing, running down my face and stinging my eyes. Even if we made it to the valley, we'd be on the verge of exhaustion.

As we pressed on through the crowded undergrowth, the terrain changed. Thick foliage gave way to small clearings, and the ground turned rocky underfoot. My legs burned with the climb, and unease gnawed at me as I sensed the creatures in the trees tracking our progress.

"It's too quiet," Leander muttered from behind me. "I don't like it."

"Quiet is good, right? Maybe no one else is here." Not a fat chance in hell, but I didn't want to invite trouble by thinking about it.

"There could be an ambush waiting for us at the Vale," he said.

"And if there is, we'll handle it," I reminded him. "Okay, sound off everyone."

Folly yipped.

"Unfortunately, I am still here," Vesper intoned.

"Here," Fern said.

"Yep," said Indigo.

Silence.

"Simon?" I said in a harsh whisper, my pulse rocketing in an instant. We stopped, and I turned a circle, scanning for him. "Simon!" I called as loud as I dared. I held my breath. There was no answer. The others searched the undergrowth, but didn't venture too far from our path.

"Fuck, fuck, fuck." The last time Simon disappeared into a forest had turned out very, very badly. Closing my eyes, I sent questing tendrils of power out into the jungle.

Creatures chattered, their furry animal bodies warm and busy. Water dripped from tangles of vines and vegetation. Beyond that was the thick, pulsing rhythm of a heartbeat. A human heartbeat.

Not one, but....

Six.

I crashed through the undergrowth, stealth be damned. The others followed, shouting for me to stop, to slow down, but I carried on, running west until I made out six figures and six voices babbling over each other in the gloom.

Sage, Sylvan, Davina, Hollis, and Casey stood with Simon, shocked looks mirrored on each of their faces. Joy flooded through my limbs, making me light as air.

Hollis let out a strangled cry, then rushed me, yanking me off my feet. How the hell were they here? I clutched him tightly, then the others piled on, making happy noises until I shushed them.

"Put me down!" I laughed, beating Hollis's shoulder. After one last squeeze, he did.

Sylvan had a bevy of new lines in his face, his jaw heavily shadowed. Casey's shirt was torn, and leaves were stuck in her hair. Sage's silvery locks were buzzed down to their scalp. Hollis's face was thin, his usually ready smile turned flat. Davina bore a white scar down the side of her neck. But they were alive, and that's what counted.

"Where's Alex?" Hollis said through cracked lips. "And who are they? Is that a dog?"

Folly growled. The rest of our companions stood behind me, examining the Guardians warily.

I turned back to them, still holding Hollis's hand. "They're friends.

And Alex...." I took a breath, bracing myself as I met Hollis's eyes. "Alex was taken by Magoth in the prison world."

"No," Davina said through a sharply in-drawn breath, her doll-like features turning stricken.

"Taken?" Sage echoed, their voice like a cracked bell. Hollis froze on whatever he'd been about to say next, horror ravaging his face. Sylvan was simply silent, but he paled to ghost-white. Casey stared into the jungle.

"We're going to get him, soon. I'll explain later. But what are you guys doing here? How did you find us?" I asked.

"We weren't looking for you," Sylvan answered. "Well, not at this particular moment. We came for the Book of Shadows. We were hoping it would help us find you."

"Ha, what a coincidence. That's what we're here for!" Simon said.

"How did you know they were here?" Leander asked suspiciously.

"I didn't," Simon answered. "Just stopped for a piss, and...well, next thing I knew they were pouncing on me."

"I don't pounce," Hollis drawled.

Indigo cut in, hand inching toward her crossbow. "This isn't a playdate."

"What's up with the wings?" Sage asked, looking at Indigo with interest.

I raised my hand to silence the chatter. "How do you know about the Book?"

"Well." Hollis scrubbed a hand over his jaw, eyes tight. "You're not gonna believe this."

"Try me."

"We got the information from a demon."

Silence descended upon us, only broken by singing insects. "A demon," I repeated. "Why would you listen to a demon?"

"Because we didn't have any other options," Davina cut in. Her eyes were red and glistening with unshed tears, her voice rough. "We thought it might be a trap, but...it was worth the risk."

"Which demon was it?" Simon asked.

"Gamori," she whispered.

A cold sensation erupted in my stomach, and I whipped around, like she'd appear over my shoulder at any second. Fuck, *was* it a trap? I grabbed Simon's elbow and jerked him toward me. Our eyes met, and his were wide.

Then, Casey charged Indigo. A dagger appeared in Indigo's hand, and she threw it at Casey. I lunged with my magic, sending out threads to snag the dagger and bring it to the ground.

"What the—" Indigo said, then Casey was past her, tackling Fern, who'd been hiding in the shadows.

"For the Mother's sake," Leander hissed, plucking Casey up by the scruff as if she weighed no more than a feather. "Stop that."

"You fucking traitorous *bitch*," Casey snarled. Leander flinched like he'd been scalded and released her. She went for Fern again. I ran over and pulled Casey away, standing between the two Guardians.

"Casey, no! It's not what you think. Fern is on our side."

Davina snapped her teeth. "Once you're done, Case, I'll take the leftovers."

"Hm. I like her," Vesper mused.

"*No*," I repeated, battling the urge to tear my hair out in frustration. "We don't have time for this. If we don't leave right this second, we're going to miss our window." Because even if Gamori was waiting for us, we didn't have any other choice but to move forward. I couldn't miss my chance at the Book.

Casey was still seething, her lip curled. "If we don't get this Book, we're not getting Alex back. If you want to help, you will put this aside and listen to me. If you keep fucking around, I will make sure you can't follow us. This is about him, not your revenge," I said sharply.

She stared at me, mutiny written all over her face, then nodded, backing away.

My shoulders dropped. "We're heading north. And keep your guard up." I turned to Simon. "I'm putting a leash on you."

I forced a thread down my arm, wrapping it around my wrist, then tied the other end to Simon's. I tugged experimentally and felt answering tension.

"Weird," Simon murmured, wrinkling his brow.

Turning to the others, I said, "If Gamori is already here, it doesn't matter if we're heard. From here on out, it's full speed, full power. Take out anyone or anything in your way. We are getting that book. If anyone gets separated, meet back at the entry point, five miles due south."

I took off toward the Vale of Sorrow.

We sped up the mountain, our group of twelve supernaturals laying a blazing trail. Folly kept pace in the front of the pack, ears flying behind him like streamers in the wind.

Moonlight beamed through gaps between trees, casting pools of silvery light that we split as we charged through them. At last, we stumbled out of the jungle and into the Vale of Sorrow.

It was more of a pit than a valley, or perhaps the inside of a dormant volcano. The mountain extended a hundred feet beyond the jungle's edge, then dropped off into a sheer cliff. The chasm spread wider than a football field, with an outcropping spearing up from the center of its depths, perched atop a slim column of stone. The outcropping had some foliage amongst the barren rock, and it was no longer than two buses lined up end to end.

"That's where the Book is?" Fern asked, drawing up next to me.

"Either the Book or some great magic," Folly said, nose twitching as he scented the air. "There are other creatures here already. Arm yourselves." His hackles rose, a growl rippling through his lips.

"Where?" I asked, drawing the short sword sheathed between my shoulders. Every muscle was wound tight as a spring. The meteor shower that would reveal the bridge to the outcropping was due to begin in seconds.

Folly sniffed again. "Demons on the western ridge. In the skies, on the ground. And from the north." He turned to the expanse stretched out before us. I caught sight of winged people taking to the skies. They flew toward the outcropping but halted in midair, just off the cliff's edge. As if they'd hit an invisible barrier.

"The Aureum," Davina said, face ashen.

"At least they're far away?" Simon suggested.

"They won't be for long," Indigo replied. "As soon as the bridge is revealed, they're going for the middle." She unshouldered her crossbow and loaded a bolt, then cocked it.

"But where will the bridge appear?" Sylvan asked, flexing his hands.

"Your guess is as good as ours," Leander replied. "I suggest the no-wings pair up with one of us so we can fly you in."

As if on cue, the Guardians in our party unfurled their powerful wings.

"Hm," Vesper said, swaying over to Sylvan. "I choose you."

"Guys, I think it's starting," Casey said, pointing above our heads.

Spits of blazing light began to rain from two points in the sky, like tears trailing down a face. The meteors dazzled, casting a bright glow over the Vale. As the first of the meteorites fell into the chasm, they illuminated two bridges of pure, glittering silver arcing from the east and west sides of the surrounding cliffs.

Two bridges. *Fuck.* "Split up!" I yelled, jumping into Leander's arms, even as Indigo spread hers wide for Simon. "Head off the others. We need to get there first!"

We flew at breakneck speed toward the western bridge, and from the corner of my eye, I caught Fern trailing us. Folly howled in her arms. The air pushed against us as we zoomed along the rim of the chasm, preventing us from flying directly to the outcropping.

The Guardians who'd come from the north had the same idea. They'd split their forces, sending half to each bridge. The ones heading toward us came on furious wingbeats, and I could see the battle-light in their eyes, the power pulsing in their hands. The Diurne would have sent their most experienced Guardians for this mission. The deadliest.

The eight demons at the western bridge were already a quarter of the way across. As soon as we got to the mouth entrance, Leander tried to fly us straight in toward the outcropping.

But that wall of air hit again, more solid than stone. We all dropped to the ground and sprinted after the demons. I didn't look back to see what was happening with the Guardians, if they'd caught up yet.

Some demons had human-shaped bodies and features, while others were amalgamations of animal parts—wolf heads and serpent tails, boar tusks and horse hooves, feathers and scales. A demon with hooves skidded on the bridge's diamond-slick surface. It backpedaled, but wasn't able to stop from plunging over the side of the bridge into darkness. Its companions didn't spare it a glance.

The demons were gaining too much of a lead. Shooting power, I tried to bind them with my threads. Most of the threads slipped off, but one demon, a serpent's body with a woman's face, got snared in a loop. I pulled hard, but it reared back with a hiss.

Still running, Indigo aimed her crossbow and fired. The bolt hit right between its eyes. The demon fell, unable to remove the arrow. With a push of power, Fern shoved it over the side of the bridge, its tail rattling as it disappeared.

They couldn't be killed, but we could sure as hell make it hard for them to come back.

We caught the attention of the remaining demons. Half of them kept on toward the outcropping, running and galloping and slithering, while the other half stopped on the bridge and faced us in a line.

Leander took the lead, legs blurring with speed as he ran at them. Drawing his sword, he pounced on a demon with skin like pond scum. The blow slashed across the demon's chest. It rippled, then became a puddle of green sludge, pooling across the bridge. Folly bayed, turning and galloping away from its spread.

I flung out a hand to stop Fern, but Simon barreled ahead and slipped on the ooze. My heart jumped into my throat, and I yanked on the thread binding us. It held. He flew back toward me, but not before the sludge reformed into the demon.

This was going to be a fucking problem.

"Shit," Fern grunted, before leaping into the fray to join Leander.

Indigo was already battling the scum-demon, slicing out with a wickedly curved knife. "Go!" she yelled, sliding away from a gooey tendril the demon shot from its midsection. "Get the Book!"

Right. That.

I turned to Simon. "We can't stop, no matter what."

He nodded, face wan but eyes blazing.

"I'll lead," Folly growled.

Gritting my teeth, I wove a quick shield to cover us as we ran. "Let's go!"

Folly led us through the minefield of demons, his luck keeping us out of harm's way. Once we cleared them, we ran full tilt toward the outcropping. The other demons were so close to it. Too close.

Folly's nails clicked on the bridge. Simon panted beside me, and screams pierced the air. Jets of light split the darkness, almost blinding as the meteorites fell into the gorge on either side of us. The demons cringed away from a particularly brilliant spear that flashed overhead.

It gave me an idea.

I stopped abruptly, Simon and Folly flying past.

"I thought you said don't stop!" Simon yelled, backpedaling. Folly tilted his head, studying me.

"Shh." I closed my eyes and went inward. If this gamble didn't pay off, the demons would get the Book first. They were already too far ahead for us to have a hope of catching up.

Thinking of Alex and his light, I gathered golden threads, drawing them from my river until every corner of my body was bursting with them. I didn't know if it would be enough. It *had* to be enough.

"Close your eyes," I warned. I hoped Vesper was still wearing her cloak.

On an exhale, I let go, shoving the mass of power out into the world.

When Simon gasped, I knew it had worked.

I opened my eyes. Dazzling golden threads joined the bevy of shooting stars, covering the whole chasm in a bright, shining dome that glowed like the sun.

The demons ahead of us disappeared, sent back to wherever they'd come from. Demons bound to the hours of darkness couldn't exist in the light.

But there was still another threat. Leander, Indigo, and Fern tangled with the Aureum who were behind us. Indigo shoved her hands forward, and hail pelted the Guardians. One of them shot a spear of flame back, singeing her hair.

"Folly, help them," I urged, taking Simon's hand. "We're going for the Book." He howled his agreement, charging for the Guardians.

The outcropping was mere seconds away. We were so, so close, but the effort of keeping the light dome erected was beginning to drain me. My muscles dragged, and a wave of fatigue swept me. I shoved it down. I didn't have time for weakness.

We sprinted the remaining stretch, then clambered onto the outcropping. Spindly trees, their roots clinging to gray rock, jutted out to create perfect handholds.

"You take the left side, I'll take the right. And watch yourself," I cautioned. We split up when we reached the top. Scrubby bushes and a thin layer of dirt covered the rock. There was no sign of a hidden chest, or an altar, or a handy sign staked into the ground.

I drew a thread of magic away from the dome of light and sent it spinning over the outcropping as I crawled, hands scrabbling over roots and weeds.

But there was no book, not even a singular, torn page left behind.

32

My heart plummeted to my stomach and a hollow feeling crept in. Where the fuck was the Book?

"Did you find it?" I asked Simon, spying him shaking the branches of a scrawny tree.

"No," he said, jaw tight. "Calytrix was wrong. We all were."

It was for nothing. This dangerous, stupid, wild goose chase. More time wasted when I could have been bringing Alex home.

Stinging pain tore across my upper arm, then a bullet buried itself with a thunk in the tree Simon had just shaken.

We ducked, diving behind a scraggly bush. The Aureum must have made it past the rest of the team. Icy tremors wanted to overtake me as I thought of them lying on the bridge, injured or dead.

Two winged Guardians were on the outcropping by the east bridge. I glanced at Simon, face grim. I couldn't defend us and keep the glowing dome up at the same time. Already, my power was strained so thin the merest touch might snap it.

I withdrew the threads, letting the dome drop. The light evaporated, and darkness descended once more. Shooting stars still fell, but there were less now. Much less. If they stopped entirely while we were still on the outcropping, would the bridges disappear, leaving us stranded?

338

"She's over there!" one of the Guardians yelled, pointing some ways to our left.

Touching Simon's shoulder, I gestured toward the bridge we'd just crossed. He nodded, and we dragged ourselves along the ground by our elbows, hidden by the scrub. Scraping the dregs of my power, I cloaked us in another protective net. My threads had become spindly, and I feared they wouldn't hold up to much strain.

"Come out, traitor," another voice crooned. "Such luck, finding you here. The Diurne will be pleased."

We crept along, reaching the point where the outcropping curved down toward the bridge. The voice spoke again. "You have ten seconds until I start shooting. Councilman Eames wants you and your accomplices alive, but I don't think he'll mind as long as we bring a body back. We've already killed two of you on the bridge."

My blood ran cold, my friends' faces flashing before my eyes. I had to believe the Guardian was lying. We had to get off this damn rock and help them.

Long moments passed between meteors. I hoped to god the others had already left the Vale of Sorrow.

Almost there—just a few more feet—

Something jerked me backward by the ankles. I slithered across the hard ground, scraping my stomach on the rock. Muscled arms wrapped around my chest, then a forearm thrust across my neck, choking me. "Simon," I wheezed, kicking, but the hold was too tight. My captor smelled of sweat and smoke, and blood.

Simon struggled against another winged silhouette, cursing and spitting. The Guardians had us trapped.

My mind went blank, any plan evaporating as a man with short, black hair trained a gun on the back of Simon's head. The one holding me wrestled my arms behind my back, slipping cuffs over my wrists and pulling tight. Cold, unyielding metal bit into my skin.

"If you struggle, I'll shoot him," the Guardian holding the gun said. "Tell me you understand."

My captor loosened his grip marginally. "Yes," I said quietly. Simon's face was bone-white in the darkness, his eyes flitting back and forth between me and the Guardian who held me.

"Good. Now turn around and walk toward the bridge."

I couldn't turn my back on Simon. "What are you going to do with him?" I fought to keep my voice steady.

The Guardian cocked his gun, the ominous click sending a quiver down my spine. "Get moving."

They had no reason to keep Simon alive. As soon as I walked away, they'd shoot him. If they'd already killed two of our group, why would they save a Watcher? The Aureum wanted to get rid of them all.

"Okay, I'll go. Just don't hurt him." Every nerve ending in my body prickling, I gathered the strings of my power that had faded to a whisper. It wouldn't be enough. My tongue was like sandpaper on the roof of my mouth, and my pulse thudded in my ears. I was desperate, muscles rigid and straining for anything that could save him.

The Guardian holding me shifted their grip to clamp down on my upper arms, preparing to steer me away. Touching the bare skin of my arm through a rip in my sleeve.

There was no thought involved with my next move, just pure instinct and love and fear.

I siphoned, pressing my exposed skin into the Guardian and latching on. The golden rush of their magic washed over me in a warm wave, swirling down to my bones. I pulled and pulled, greedy, not caring if I sucked the life right out of him. A soft groan sounded in my ear. The Guardian with the gun looked over my shoulder at his comrade.

My captor dropped with a thud, and in the same moment I sent the gun spinning out of the other Guardian's hand. Simon jumped off the outcropping and landed on the bridge. He staggered close to the edge before righting himself.

I shot a bolt of fire at the black-haired Guardian, who ducked and sent a flare of white-hot power back at me. Stinging pain flared down my neck where it struck.

"Run!" I yelled, breaking my bonds and throwing up a wall of fire between me and our would-be captor. The other Guardian who'd been holding me was unconscious, or maybe dead. "I'll hold him off."

Simon's feet pounded on the bridge's slick surface.

Metal clinked, and a long chain sailed through the wall of flame, wrapping tight around my neck. Choking, I snaked a hand between my throat and the chain, but it still hurt like hellfire when he pulled. I bumped along the ground like a tin can rattling after a car. My other hand clawed in the dirt, trying to find some purchase.

Clutching the chain, spots appearing at the edges of my vision, I sent fire racing down it and superheated the metal links. The Guardian bellowed, and I stopped moving.

I scrambled to my feet and ripped the chain free. I swung it like a flail, the links whistling through the air.

Where had the Guardian gone? There was only night-dark sky, the outcropping illuminated by a meteor every now and then.

I didn't have time to look. Still holding the chain, I turned and ran.

Straight into the ugly metal barrel of a gun. It floated in the air at chest height, digging between my ribs. Pointed directly at my heart.

The black-haired Guardian stood some ways behind it, his ruined hands held out before him. I took dark satisfaction in the ugly white blisters covering his palms, although perhaps now wasn't the time.

The hammer cocked, clicking loudly. "Die, bitch," he said with a sneer, lips twisting.

This gun wouldn't be the last thing I ever saw. I looked up at the sky, the millions of stars winking back at me. I hoped Simon had gotten away.

A crack rang through the air.

Being shot wasn't how I remembered it. My body didn't jerk away from the bullet, as if in protest. There was no sharp retort of pain, no heat. No slippery spray of blood.

I looked down at my intact chest. The gun had fallen to the ground, the hammer still cocked. Unfired.

What the fuck? I found the fallen body of the Guardian. A figure stood above it, clothed in bloodred robes. Raven hair swept to her waist, an obsidian crown atop her head.

Gamori gave a cruel smile. "Well met, daughter."

Heat flashed over my skin, followed by ice. My lungs wanted to seize up, but I forced a ragged breath through them. "You can't have Simon," I growled.

Gamori tilted her head, the planes of her face hardening, growing rougher. "That trifling matter? Consider the deal null." She flicked her fingers dismissively.

I clamped down on my next retort. What was she talking about?

We'd made a binding agreement, and I'd never known a demon to let that go. "You said—"

"My dear, I have said many things. And in the end, they have gotten you where you needed to go. Where *I* needed you to go." Her eyes glittered, as black as her crown.

"Where you...." I trailed off, comprehension dawning. If she didn't care about the bargain, then the quest to get the stone must have been bogus. She'd gone to Davina and the rest of the unit on purpose to send them here, to meet me. She had an ulterior motive all along, and I hadn't even stopped to wonder what other reasons she might have for making our deal.

She laughed, the sound unnervingly cold. "Yes, Lightbringer. Now you have Malistir's stone, and will soon have the Book of Shadows. With those, you will have the power to defeat Magoth and his ilk."

My head spun with shock. There was some greater scheme at play here, and I'd been utterly blind to it. "Malastir's stone? I thought it belonged to Vadyron." I hadn't heard the name Malastir since Alex had given me the book on the Aureum's origins, after he'd pulled me through a gateway in the Norton Cemetery. Back when I hadn't believed in supernaturals, or demons, or even known I'd had magic.

The dark god Malastir was alleged to be the whole reason why the gods-touched Guardians had been created by Malastir's twin sister, Iznir —to defeat his evil rise to power.

"The stone was Malastir's first—the star he plucked from the heavens to hold the souls of those whose lives he stole. After Malastir's fall, the stone was lost to time. Vadyron, the mad fool, simply found it. The Soulstone has powers beyond even my understanding." Her lips curled, as if she was disgusted that anything could have power she didn't comprehend.

"Aren't you—aren't you on Magoth's side?" Even as I posed the question, I knew the answer. Demons served their own interests first. Hadn't I learned that already, with Beelzebub's dream visit? *Child, I am not helping you. I am helping myself.*

She walked toward me, long sleeves swaying with every step. "I have been steadily rising through the ranks for a thousand years. And this—" Her eyes closed briefly, as if savoring the thought. "Magoth is in my way. He seeks power that would come to destroy our worlds—all of the worlds, not just demon, but human and Fae, and every other kind. He means to rule them." She licked her blood-red lips. "And there isn't room for two kings on a throne."

My pulse thudded hard at the base of my throat. "Why tell me this now?"

Her full mouth thinned. "Because you are out of time."

"What do you mean?" I looked up. Only four meteors had fallen in the time we'd been talking. The bridges were wavering, flickering in and out of sight.

"Not that. Although yes, the Lacrima shower is almost over." Her eyes met mine, gaze branding me. "I will tell you how to get the Book of Shadows. But he is waiting for you there."

"Who?" I asked, my throat tightening.

"Magoth. He has been in possession of the book for some fifty years now, and hid it in the Vale of Shadows. I have been seeding rumors of its whereabouts since the last time the Vale opened."

Clammy sweat coated my palms. "But that's not—" I bit my tongue. I needed to stop assuming that what I knew was true. This was all a game of smoke and mirrors, of mirages and trapdoors. And I was stumbling through it blindfolded. "Fine. Take me to it, then."

"Before I do that," she said, "we need to make a deal."

"I'm done making deals with you," I spat.

"Then you will not find the Book, or your lover."

I glared at the haughty lines of her face. "You need me more than I need you."

She bared her teeth. "Brava, my dear. You have some spine after all. Although, I believe we are at an impasse. We both want the same thing, and you *do* need my help."

I hated that she was right. "I can't trust you."

"Yes, and the sky is blue. I thought we were beyond stating the obvious."

My heart raced, adrenaline rushing through my veins. I had a decision to make, and it needed to be done quickly. Though, there was really only one choice. I had to find that book, no matter the cost.

"When I get the Book, you don't get to use it for whatever your agenda is. The Fae will keep possession of it for as long as they deem fit." I took a deep breath. "But I won't get in your way and stop whatever plans you already have—unless you're maiming, murdering, or destroying. Or trying for world domination," I added, trying to be specific enough to close any loopholes.

Gamori extended a long-fingered hand. "You have a deal."

We shook. My right forearm instantly began to prickle. I released her hand and pulled up my sleeve. A crown marked in black ink, a twin to the one Gamori wore on her head, had appeared on the skin beneath the crook of my elbow.

"This is not like our other false bargain," she warned. "I will expect payment if you fail to retrieve the Book." She cocked her head. "Your friends approach."

Footsteps sounded on the fading west bridge. Simon, Fern, Folly, Davina, and Vesper appeared over her shoulder, sprinting for the outcropping.

Fern had a hand outstretched, and shot a jet of orange light at Gamori. Gamori sighed, swatting it away. "Call off your dogs," she instructed.

"Don't," I called to the others. "She's here to help."

The rest pulled even with us, streaked in blood and gore, but appearing mostly unharmed. Folly growled at Gamori. She studied him, then spoke an unfamiliar word that sounded like lightning cracking through black clouds. His lips drew back to display sharp teeth.

"Where are the others?" I asked, fearing the worst.

"They went back to the entry point. Everyone's alive, but Sylvan and Casey are hurt badly," Fern said steadily. I had to remember that she was a trained soldier, used to battle. "Leander's taking care of them."

"You should've gone back with them," I said.

"No," Simon answered, stepping up, jaw set. "We're in this together. Until the end."

"Which will be very near, unless we all get off of this rock immediately," Gamori cut in. She turned to me. "The Book is being held in another world, only accessible through a seam in the Vale. You must enter from one of the bridges."

"And how will we do that? These bridges are dead ends," Vesper snapped. Pink smeared her hairline, and I realized she was sweating blood.

Gamori narrowed her eyes. "Quiet, vampyre. You will jump from the bridge, into the seam."

"You want us to jump off a bridge?" Indigo said slowly.

"Indeed, that is exactly what you *must* do if you want to get to the Book," Gamori replied.

"How do we know you're not trying to get rid of us?" Davina hissed.

"I lead you to your friends, did I not?" the demon said lazily. "Moving your pieces on the game board has taken a great deal of effort. Why would I do that just to kill you?"

"I believe you," I said. If demons could be counted on for anything, it was to serve their own needs and vanity first. Plus, we had a deal—a real one—the evidence of it still stinging. "All we have to do is jump?"

She arched a dark, finely tapered brow. "Believe it or don't, it's your choice. In the end, it matters not. There is always someone willing to bargain." She turned for the bridge, gliding across with a speed that turned her into a streak of crimson.

"And now she's just taking off?" Davina exclaimed. "What the hell?"

"We have to try," Indigo said, turning her face up to the sky. One meteor fell, its tail spindly and dull. "We're out of time."

"Follow me," Folly directed, running for the bridge. "Perhaps I can scent the seam."

The bridge swayed beneath us, like it was there but not quite there at the same time. We ran, slipping and sliding while trying not to lose our footing. Folly had his nose to the ground, tail waving in the air like a flag.

He stopped in the bridge's dead center, sniffing in a circle. I slid past him and had to backtrack. "The pull is strongest here." He looked at me. "Whatever is on the other side of the seam will put you in extreme peril."

I ran a hand down his soft ears. "Extreme peril is my specialty." I turned to the others. "You can follow me, or not. But I'm going for the Book."

Simon came forward and took my hand. "Together?"

Nodding, I squeezed his hand. Then I felt pressure on my other hand. It was Fern. "I'll do whatever it takes," she promised. "I owe you that."

"Why must everything be so maudlin?" Vesper grumbled, taking Fern's hand. Davina and Indigo linked up at the ends of the chain we'd formed. Folly stood between me and Simon, his head bumping against my leg.

"Be ready for anything," I warned. "We'll jump in three. Two—"

The bridge disappeared, flickering out entirely so that we were suspended for a moment in the pitch-black night.

We plummeted through darkness. Yells of surprise sounded in my ears, and I gripped Simon's hand harder as our damp palms threatened to slide apart. The tether between us was still somehow connected, and I added more threads to it. Folly had nipped my pant leg, hanging on with his teeth. I sent another thread out to him, then to all of the others, connecting us like insects caught in a spider's web.

We're going to the Book of Shadows. We're going to the Book of Shadows.

Slivers of doubt crept in. Where was the damn seam? We'd only been falling for seconds, but it seemed like hours. Windy fingers plucked at my hair, loosening it from my braid. My eyes streamed, and my heart jumped into my throat as if trying to escape, to get back onto solid ground.

Finally, we slowed, like flies that had become trapped in a pot of honey. The air was sticky, pressing against my skin, then the walls of a seam rubbed against me. Claustrophobia descended, my throat closing and panic clawing at my chest, dying for air, for escape, for light.

We crashed to the damp ground in a tangle of arms and legs. All except for Vesper, who was on her feet and arranging the folds of her cloak just so.

Indigo offered a hand and pulled me to my feet. We were at the edge of a forest. A grassy lawn spread beyond the trees, ringed by high iron gates with wicked, pointed spikes. I drew my short sword, prepared to meet an attack.

Nothing crawled out of the seeking mist that swirled around our ankles, nor from the wild, thorny rose bushes that guarded the entryway of the gothic castle looming ahead. The air was oppressive in its stillness, like a closed fist.

"What is this place?" Fern asked, her voice reflecting my unease.

"I don't know, but the Book better be here," I said. Was Magoth here, too? Waiting somewhere behind the castle's long, diamond-paned windows? Or perhaps he was in the topmost spire that was straight out of a fairytale, one with desperate princesses and evil queens.

"So what, we just walk in?" Davina said, staring around at the fog-shrouded grounds. More forest lay behind the castle, the tops of evergreens poking out of the mist.

"What else can we do?" Simon chimed in, looking determined but afraid.

"It smells of demons and—and humans," Folly said, front leg lifted into a point.

"Let's separate," I suggested. "Simon, Folly, and Vesper with me. Davina, Fern, and Indigo together."

"Have you ever seen a horror movie?" Davina said, narrowing her eyes. "We don't split up."

"Well, make a decision. We might as well dash through the castle nude for all the attention we're drawing to ourselves out here," Vesper said, clutching her cloak tighter around her shoulders.

"There is no way to hide from powerful demons," Folly agreed. "They will know we're here already."

"That's fine. We just won't get caught. Indigo—if things go wrong, open a portal and get everyone back to the Weald Fae," I instructed.

Indigo looked like she wanted to argue, but nodded instead.

I checked my weapons, noting I'd lost a couple of throwing knives somewhere on Tristia. My magic was still limping along, and the power I'd siphoned was running low as well.

Siphoning from that Guardian had been like drinking room temp water, whereas demon magic was aged whiskey—powerful, complex, layered. It didn't give me the same rush, either. That was a good thing, I reminded myself. I needed to keep a clear head.

"We stick together," I told Davina. Her face relaxed into relieved lines. "We'll have to search room by room, and look for the Book's signature. As soon as we find it, we get the hell out of here." I looked into each one of their faces, and thought of what Alex always told me before we threw ourselves into danger.

"Be strong, and smart, and take care of yourselves."

33

Entering the castle was easy—suspiciously so. After we flew over the spiked gates, Folly sniffed the perimeter to determine the best entry point. It was still eerily quiet, with no sign of life anywhere.

We scaled the castle wall, its rough stone providing easy handholds, and climbed onto a balcony. I tried the handle on a set of French doors. They swung open easily, as if inviting us in.

Whatever I was expecting the inside of a demon's lair to look like, it certainly wasn't a nineteenth century English country manor. The richly carpeted floors and canopied bed looked more appropriate for a Jane Austen heroine than a creature of evil.

"Where is everyone?" Simon said in a hushed whisper. "This emptiness is almost worse than a horde of demons."

"Be careful what you wish for," Folly advised. His hackles stood on end. "I can feel...echoes. Imprints of what has been."

"What imprints?" I asked, keeping my sword in one hand and a ball of flame cupped in the other.

Folly's nose twitched, then he blinked. "Creatures who have been here before—it is strange."

"Do you smell Magoth?" Fern asked.

"Not here," Folly answered after a moment. "Let us move on."

The hallway was lengthy, at least ten doors on each side. "This is going to take forever," Davina said in a low voice.

"Then we need to get started," Fern answered. Davina glared at her, but didn't respond.

"You three take the left," I said, gesturing to Indigo, Davina, and Fern. "The rest of us will take the right."

Vesper, a blur of movement, opened the first door on the right. She'd probably be able to search them quicker than any of us, but I followed her in.

It was another bedroom, with a glittering black chandelier and crimson rug—not the torture chamber I'd envisioned.

"The decor is a little obvious, no?" Vesper sniffed. "The Book is not here." She zoomed away, leaving the heavy brocade drapes fluttering in her wake.

There was no sign of the Book on this floor, no telltale hum of magic in the air or magnetic pull. We ascended a flight of stairs, searching the next floor, then the next after that, until we'd gone three stories and had nothing to show for it but mounting frustration.

I'd doused my flames, sure that if no creatures had shown up an hour into our search, we were probably safe for the next five minutes.

"I swear to the goddess, if it's not in this next room," Davina said, wrenching a door open, "I'll—" She stopped cold, pausing on the threshold.

"What?" Indigo said, coming behind her with a knife drawn.

"Does this look familiar to you?" Davina asked, stepping away from the door. Beyond her was a sort of parlor, with cream settees and gold leaf wainscotting.

Indigo scanned the room. "Fern?" she called, beckoning.

Fern joined them, poking her head in. "Shit," she growled. "That painting of the fruit—I swear it's the same as the first floor."

"What?" I said, going cold. I burst into another room on the right side of the hall, then another. They were copies of what we'd already searched—the same black chandelier, same crimson rug. "Fuck. We're going in a circle."

Vesper pushed Indigo aside, entering the room. "But how? We have only gone up, not down. Perhaps they simply ran out of ideas. I would not put it past a demon," she said.

"Folly?" I called, looking around for his silky black and tan head.

"I would have smelled if we backtracked. None of our scents were here," he confirmed.

Vesper was already a step ahead of us, racing down the hallway and up the next flight of stairs in a dark blur. The rest of us dashed after her, but her expression confirmed our fears when we reached the next floor.

"All of these rooms are the same. A repeating pattern every three floors, I think." She drew her lips back in a snarl, exposing her fangs.

Fern pushed at her braids, swearing. "We're stuck in a labyrinth. It's a fucking illusion."

"That's why you're only sensing imprints," I realized, looking down at Folly. "This must be some kind of...veneer. It's hiding what's beneath." My thoughts went to Gamori, to her deceptiveness and duplicity.

We were like rats in a maze, wearing ourselves down, while the real danger waited for us out of sight. Whichever demon was controlling the illusion could be watching us right now. Or, maybe the Book of Shadows was the one responsible. Hadn't the crone told us the Book liked to play games?

"We need to think for a minute," I said, kneading my forehead. Pain pulsed behind my right eye, sharp and unforgiving. I sat on the floor, drawing my knees up and resting my head on them.

Simon dropped down beside me. "Let's all take a break. We need water and food." The rest followed, although Vesper elected to remain standing. Folly circled and sprawled on the floor, exhausted. I rubbed one of his ears while we took out our packs and refueled. That water was the best thing I'd ever tasted—crisp and cool, cutting through my fatigue like a knife.

"How do we break an illusion?" Simon asked, wiping a crumb from his lip.

"There are a couple of ways," Davina answered, passing Indigo's waterskin back to her. The Guardian had a pallor to her olive skin that I didn't like the look of. "The first is to use a word to break the illusion's binding. Usually, whoever has set the illusion creates this word in advance, should they need to break it, or for others to bypass it."

"What word?" Vesper asked.

Davina's jaw tightened. "That's the problem. The word could be anything. Pineapple, or muffin, or—"

"Stop, I beg you," Simon groaned, putting a hand on his stomach.

"Sorry. But you get my meaning."

"Okay, so guessing the word is out," I said. "What's the other way?"

Fern cut in. "To see reality. Find what is beneath the illusion, and it ceases to have power over you."

Everyone fell silent, then all eyes turned toward Folly. His were closed, his twitching nose producing soft snores.

My heart ached for the innocence of a sleeping dog. But Folly wasn't just a dog—he was an ancient eudaemon, part guardian angel and part good luck charm. Nor were any of us how we appeared on the outside.

"Folly," I said softly, shaking him awake. He opened one eye, then yawned widely and sat up, giving a full body shake.

"Apologies. This body requires much rest," he said.

I scratched his chin. "We need you to describe what you've been feeling—those imprints."

A shudder began at his head and ran through the tip of his tail. "It is...unpleasant."

"You don't have to spare us," Davina said. "I guarantee I've seen worse."

Folly cast his warm, downturned eyes on her. Then he ambled through one of the doors, into a room decorated in varying shades of green. We followed him, watching as he went to the center of the floor.

"I hear screams," Folly began. "And I smell blood. Human, Faerie, witch. So much blood, soaking into stone." He blinked, the long whiskers on his eyebrows quivering. "Here, a young human woman was eviscerated. She was cast out of her home by her family for becoming pregnant out of wedlock, and made a bargain with a demon to rid her of the child. She did not know they would take her life, as well. And here—"

"Stop," I choked, hating everything that he was saying. Hating that he had seen this horrible suffering. I could imagine it exactly as he'd described: the young woman, her belly splayed wide, shrieking as she was torn apart. Her blood, a dark red river, coursing over stone floors, flowing into cracks and staining them in great rusty brown swathes.

Torchlight flickered, throwing shadows across the bloodstains.

Crumbled stone archways soared overhead, and a crescent moon glowed in a midnight sky. Tattered silk panels hanging from the arches fluttered lazily in a light breeze that cut through the warm night.

I stood swiftly and drew my sword, the edge of the blade whispering against the sheath. Stars winked at us from above, as if they were in on some cosmic joke. "Is everyone else seeing this?" We'd automatically drawn together and formed a circle, our backs to each other.

"If you mean creepy ruins, then yes," Indigo answered from my left. Simon was on my other side, his hand finding my sleeve.

"What is this place?" Vesper said, her voice echoing eerily off the stone.

I don't know hovered on the tip of my tongue. Until the breeze caressed my cheek and whispered in my ear, drawing my gaze toward a tower that jutted far off in the distance, over rocky crags. The white column was massive, with an exposed staircase wrapping around the outside toward a crenelated spire.

A familiar voice floated toward me on the wind. *You found me.*

My heart clenched, the click of recognition a sweet agony.

Come closer. Come to me.

"It's there," I croaked, pointing to the tower with my sword. "The Book of Shadows." And maybe someone else, too, but I barely dared believe it.

The others turned their gazes on the tower, a hush falling. "I can hear it," Simon said, rubbing his chest. "It...it sounds like Penn."

"I hear my mom," Fern said, faltering.

Disappointment curdled my hope. I looked at Davina, her eyes glazed with a sheen of unfallen tears. Who was she hearing?

"It is a trap," Folly growled. "Do not believe what you hear."

"If it's a trap, then we're in the right place," I replied. I flexed my fingers, the rivers of my threads moving with me. They were getting stronger, not quite like their usual supple steel, but close enough. "Last chance to turn back," I offered.

"Quit trying to get rid of us," Davina said, locking eyes with me. "We're doing this."

I nodded. "Then be ready."

With weapons drawn, we advanced on the tower. Its white, bumpy stone shone with an inner light, as though it was made of millions of strung pearls. All the while, I heard the deep, warm voice I loved whispering. *Come. Come to me.*

Was Alex actually there, or was it the Book playing another trick? His face floated in my mind's eye, joined by Magoth's cruel smile and an ancient, tattered leather-bound book. I pulled on the cord that tethered us, but it hung slackly, just as it had since he'd disappeared. Shelving the disappointment, I focused on putting one foot in front of the other.

We fell into pairs with Folly leading, Davina and I right behind him.

"So," Davina said, easily keeping up with me despite her shorter strides. "What happened after we left the prison world?" She'd carefully modulated her voice, but I heard the choked sorrow beneath it.

"He..." I swallowed, wishing I could drain my waterskin. "We were leaving. I opened a gateway at the bottom of the lake to trap Magoth—to send him through it. I didn't know where it led, I just wanted him away from us. I thought I'd done it."

For a moment, I was back in the prison world. Alex's hand was in mine, and the hopeful, unbelievable flush of our near escape filled me. In the seconds before he'd been taken, I'd had it all—more than I'd ever had in my life. Even amidst Fern's betrayal, I'd had friends I could count on, someone who loved me—everything I'd longed for, yearned for, had been mine for a brief, sweet moment.

And then it had all gone to hell.

"Alex was right behind me," I continued, not bothering to hide the thickness of tears clogging my throat. I was done pretending I couldn't feel. "And then...and then he wasn't. I was already halfway through the gateway, and I couldn't reach him in time. Magoth pulled Alex into the pit."

Davina simply nodded, although her throat worked as mine did. When she mastered herself, she said, "When you didn't come through after us....Well, we hoped you'd made it. And we've been looking for you ever since, on the run from the Aureum."

"How did you manage to avoid them?"

She grimaced, then stroked a finger down the nape of her neck. "We burned our marks off. And we never stayed in one place for more than a few days."

"We did the same." I glanced at her, then looked ahead again at the looming tower framed against the dark sky. It was much closer now, but we still had a few minutes until we reached it. "How are you, really? And the others?"

She gave a humorless laugh. "About the same as you, probably. We've been on the run for months now, being hunted by our former brothers- and sisters-in-arms. We've been shot, burned, beaten, stabbed, nearly drowned, and tricked. We've seen dying worlds and starving creatures. But," she said, a sardonic grin pulling at her lips, "it wasn't all bad. We ended up in a world called Aetheria. It was beautiful—crystal clear ocean, white sand, fruit so juicy and perfectly ripe it practically jumped off the branch and fell into your mouth." She threw me a narrow look. "But it's hard to enjoy paradise when your closest friend is missing, and the land is crumbling into a howling void."

"Right," I said, aiming for nonchalance and missing by a mile. Guilt seared through me. Did Davina blame me for losing Alex? For not diving into that hellish lake after him? The charring heat cooled as I realized that she would never blame me as much as I blamed myself. She could never punish me more than I already had.

The base of the tower was only fifty yards away now, and we hurried the rest of the way over the mountainous ground in silence.

The tower soared above our heads, much taller than I'd initially thought. The stairs were steep and treacherous, coiled around the facade like a snake. In addition to the steps, there was a door set flush with the pearly stone, made of the same material. I tried the pull ring, but it didn't budge.

"What the bloody hells is this thing?" Simon muttered, craning his head back to take in the tower's expanse.

"I can fly up, see what's what," Indigo offered.

"No," I said automatically. "What if something's waiting up there?"

Fern touched my elbow. "It's basic strategy, Seph. We send a scout first, then the rest of us follow. I'll go with Indigo. That way, there's two of us."

The tightness in my chest loosened marginally. "Okay."

Indigo hovered above the ground. Fern unfurled her wings then launched upward, the two of them flying to the top and disappearing from sight.

I paced, feeling the pressure of Folly's gaze tracking me. The pull toward the Book was stronger than ever. The unmistakable feel of magic curled over me, pricking my skin, like I'd been caught in a tangle of thorns.

Wingbeats sounded overhead, then Fern and Indigo landed. "What did you find?" Vesper asked, tapping her nails on her chin. She'd been unusually silent during the walk, no snide remarks to be had.

"Nothing," Indigo answered, disappointment clouding her features.

"Then the Book must be inside the tower," Vesper said. "Because I can feel it. I can hear her." She must have meant Seraphyna, her sister. The other Lightbringer.

"How do we get in?" Simon asked, approaching the door. He laid a hand there before quickly removing it. "Blimey, it's freezing."

"Do not touch things you don't understand, pup," Folly warned.

"Here, let me," Davina said, shouldering Simon aside. She spread her hands, palms outward, then shoved them forward.

I would have bet none of us were prepared for the great jungle cat that appeared out of thin air and launched at the doors. Its claws, thicker than the daggers on Fern's belt, raked down the pearly material. A horrible screech rang out, like nails on a chalkboard. The panther, with its jet-black fur and emerald eyes, swiveled to face us and released a scream.

Indigo drew her crossbow and aimed it at the beast. I called fire to my hands, while Vesper sank into a crouch. Folly appeared wholly unconcerned, releasing a wide yawn.

"Stop!" Davina commanded, throwing herself in front of the animal even as it faded from sight.

"What in Asael's name was that?" Simon croaked, staring at Davina.

"How—how did you see that?" she asked, searching our faces as if the answer lay there.

"*What was it?*" Indigo repeated.

I walked up to Davina, extinguishing my flames. "It was your magic, wasn't it?"

She eyed me, then nodded. Fern and I exchanged a glance. Sleek, powerful, a fierce hunter—that fit Davina perfectly.

Davina's eyes widened. "That's never happened before. A Guardian's power source is only visible to the individual who wields it," she said, sounding like she was trying to convince herself of the words.

"Let me try something," Fern said, extending a hand. She made a coaxing motion, and a vine sprang from the rocky earth, growing rapidly until it was wide and tall as a sapling. It wound around the door, seeking to infiltrate its margins, but failed. The vine retracted into the ground and disappeared.

"Well, that answers that," she mused.

I sent an experimental gold thread—my Guardian magic—to the pull ring, wrapping tight and yanking. It didn't budge, not even a millimeter.

"Use your other one," Simon said from behind me. "Go on."

Feeling penetrating stares on my back, I lifted a hand, sending black threads toward the door.

They snaked through the air, closing the gap swiftly. When the threads touched the ring, wrapping around it and pulling, I expected the same result as my previous attempt.

The tower door swung open in invitation.

34

The darkness beyond the door was like the vastness of the void, swallowing all light and sound. I squinted, but couldn't make out a hint of anything on the other side.

"So, who wants to go first?" Simon said, sounding far away to my ears.

"I will go," Folly volunteered. Before I could say a word, he trotted into the opening.

Or, he tried to. Upon reaching the threshold he bounced off, like a coin thrown at a wall. I ran to where he lay on the ground, but he was up before I got to him. Folly shook himself.

"Are you okay?" I asked, kneeling.

"I am well," he grunted. He looked more embarrassed than anything. "I did not see that coming."

Fern picked up a loose stone and threw it at the opening. It bounced off as well, clattering to the ground.

"So the door is open, but we are no closer to getting through it," Vesper said, squinting at the black expanse.

"Perhaps Seph should try?" Davina suggested. "It stands to reason that since her magic opened the door, she's the one who can enter. Like calls to like, after all."

Somehow the black behind the door deepened as I approached.

Without looking back at the others, I tentatively reached a hand toward the opening. It slid through with no resistance, disappearing completely. I jerked backward on a harsh breath, and my hand reappeared.

I reached back into the dark, this time up to my elbow. The temperature beyond the door was slightly cooler, but otherwise it didn't seem much different. I looked over my shoulder at the others, withdrawing my arm. "I'm okay."

Simon let out a long, silent exhale, his shoulders dropping. "Well, if you're able to go through, I might be able to as well. And Vesper, and Indigo. We all have Watcher blood."

"What about us?" Fern asked. "I'm not waiting here while you throw yourselves into danger."

"I do not think you have a choice," Vesper said, marching up to me. "Let's get on with it." She plunged a hand through the doorway, sinking up to the shoulder, then gave a satisfied smile.

A wet nose bumped me. Folly was there, his soft eyes drooping in sadness. I crouched beside him. "I'm sorry you can't come," I whispered. "Will you watch after Fern and Davina?"

He gave a solemn nod and leaned into me. I wrapped my arms around his warmth, digging my fingers into the soft folds of his fur. After a long moment I released him, dropping a kiss on top of his head before straightening. "Be careful, all of you," I cautioned. "And be ready to run like hell once we get out."

Fern, a dissatisfied look on her face, nodded. Davina stepped up to me.

"You be careful, too," she said. "And...if he's in there...." She trailed off, looking up the length of the tower. "Bring him back."

I waited until she met my eyes again. "That's a promise."

Indigo and Simon joined Vesper and me at the threshold. I looked back one last time at Fern, Davina, and Folly, standing in a huddle. Folly let out a soft whine that pierced my heart.

Giving myself a mental shake, I squared up to the door and stepped through into a thick darkness that blinded me. In fact, all of my senses had been wiped out, not just my sight, and I floundered for a few petrifying moments.

As if a light switch had been flicked, a room materialized around me. Well, it wasn't a room so much as a hallway, with speckled vinyl floors and ceiling tiles stained with yellowing water rings. Lockers lined the maroon and white cinderblock walls, and irate voices floated through doors that peppered the hall in regular intervals.

Cold sweat dotted my forehead.

Turning a circle, I called for the others. "Simon? Indigo? Vesper, are you there?" My voice was high and thin, echoing down the hallway. No one appeared.

What the hell was this? I groped for my sword, but instead of feeling its leather hilt my fingers closed over the nylon handle of a backpack. I looked down, horror filling me.

My pants were two sizes too big, but somehow still too short for me. I brushed a hand down my T-shirt that bore a technicolor image of Mickey Mouse wearing sunglasses, feeling the flatness of my chest.

A hot trickle of embarrassment spilled down my neck. I never liked Disney—I figured there was no point when there wasn't a chance in hell I'd ever get to go there. But the shirt didn't have holes and fit decently, so when Mrs. Bram had fetched it from the hand-me-down closet, I eagerly accepted.

The bell sounded, a tinny *beeeeep* that signaled the hall would be flooding with middle schoolers soon. One of the many clocks dotting the walls—meant to keep us on time, but in reality just posing a challenge for the chronically tardy kids—read two o'clock.

I should've been in sixth period English. What was I even doing in the hallway? Skipping class never crossed my mind, so eager was I to fill my head with something other than images of scattered bottles and my mom's darkened room, the musty smell of unwashed sheets hanging thick in the air.

I tried to wake her up before I got on the bus this morning, but she was still out cold. I fretted about her making it to the country club later on to clean, but I had more important things to worry about at the moment. Such as the hormone-ridden flock of preteens who spilled out of classroom doors, descending on the hallway like a tidal wave.

They caught me in a melee, and I was spun around and carried by the tide of students, flowing down the hall and into the cafeteria. My chest tightened as I was jerked along, unable to wriggle free. I finally caught my breath, just to have it flee again.

The cafeteria. Turning, I tried to leave through the wide double doors, but was stopped by the wall of kids. Their bodies were packed thick as sardines, and they just kept coming, filling the room. It was too full. My head buzzed. I had to get out.

I fought my way to a window, lunging past a group of giggling girls. They stared at me, pointing at my too-short pants. My hands scrabbled at the sill, trying to pry it open, but either time or a thousand layers of paint had it stuck fast.

Sweat slicked down my back and my armpits. I caught a whiff of body odor, and with a wash of embarrassment I realized it belonged to me.

"God, you stink," one of the laughing girls said loudly. She tossed her long, blonde hair over one shoulder.

Ashley Gladwell, the most popular girl in sixth grade—in no small part due to the breasts she'd already sprouted. One of her favorite pastimes was making fun of me at the top of her lungs.

Ignoring her even as shame prickled my cheeks, I kept trying the window, about to bang on the panes and knock the glass out. Bodies pushed against me from behind, and I cringed away from them. There were too many people. Too many. Shallow breathing caused the walls of my throat to close, or maybe it was the other way around. I didn't know, didn't care.

Pinching hands grasped my shoulders and spun me around. The milling students formed a half circle around me. Through my panic, I had the thought that at least now there was some breathing room.

Ashley sashayed up to me, pouting lips that were sticky with pink strawberry Lip Smacker gloss. I coveted that gloss, the way it made her look so perfect. Untouchable.

I quivered and crossed my arms over my flat chest, voice shaking. "Leave me alone."

Ashley's shiny lips parted to emit braying laughter that seemed far too adult for a twelve-year-old. "You do it to yourself, you know." Her eyes flitted around, egged on by the crowd's harsh giggles. "If you didn't smell like *shit*." Her voice faltered on the illicit word, as if she couldn't believe she was that daring. "We wouldn't have to tell you."

My head hung as I willed back tears.

Emboldened, she continued. "You're a freak, with your stupid name and your loser mom. That's probably why your dad left. He must have been smart, since he took one look at you and ran." Brash laughter and tight giggles rippled through the gathered kids.

I lost the battle, tears of humiliation coursing down my face. Ashley was right. I was a freak. A loser. Unwanted.

"Freak," she taunted again, then the crowd of students took up the chant. "Freak, freak, freak!"

It pounded in my ears, too much to bear. What was the point of it all? Why even try? I raised my head, ready to tell Ashley to do her worst—to end this and take me out of the misery so deep I didn't even have a name for it. But I caught a flash of a face in the throng that made me pause.

A girl stood about two rows back, with dark hair and quiet, amber eyes. She wasn't shouting, and maybe even wore a look of sympathy. She reminded me of someone.

Bri.

The unfamiliar name popped into my head, floating there like a leaf on a stream, whisked away almost as soon as I'd thought it. I didn't know anyone named Bri.

Didn't I? A voice entered my mind that somehow matched the name. *I don't want to lose you again.* I saw a pair of wings, and a familiar face. A small-framed woman, reaching out for me. Calling me her best friend. Sitting on the couch in my apartment, watching *Buffy*. Sparring with me, using a wooden sword. Eating, laughing, talking.

This was another illusion. I *did* have friends. A whole lot of them. I was wanted and loved. And I wasn't twelve anymore, at the mercy of the Ashleys of the world who were likely as damaged as I had been back then.

I was an adult. The goddamn Lightbringer. And I had better shit to do than relive old nightmares.

The kids seemed smaller now, the weight on my back heavier. I reached around, finding the hilt of my sword.

The chanting stopped. For the first time, I noticed how cloying the scent of fake strawberries was.

The cafeteria disappeared and suddenly I was in a circular room, cold stone biting into my knees. Torches flickered in wall brackets, casting small pools of warm light over colorless walls that appeared smooth as glass.

I stood, my knees aching. How long had I been kneeling there? "Hello?" I called, turning a circle. But I was alone in an empty room with only old misery for company.

Pacing the perimeter, I ran my hands along the walls, then lifted a torch out of its bracket to inspect the room. There were no doors or windows, not even a handy hollow panel hiding a secret exit.

On my fifth turn around the room, the air shimmered and Simon appeared. He was also kneeling, but immediately fell over, coughing.

"Simon!" I put the torch back and went to him. "Are you okay?"

He reached a hand out, and I pulled him to standing. His eyes were puffy and slightly red, but he otherwise appeared unharmed. "I'm all right," he said gruffly, waving a hand. "Where are the vampyre and Indigo?"

"I don't know. I was the first one here."

"What a bloody welcome. I could've done without reliving that, but here we are." He was trying too hard to be casual. "Why d'you think that happened?"

I sighed. "Maybe to weaken us emotionally?" The ache in my chest had faded, but still throbbed.

"I wonder if the others will be able to get out of theirs?" he said, scrubbing a hand over his stubbled jaw. We must have been awake for at least a day at this point, and I felt every hour of strain.

"We'll just have to wait and see," I replied, settling back against the curved wall. Even though I hadn't used any power, the illusion drained my energy. Still, I pushed out a singular black thread to curl around Simon's wrist, connecting him to me. I didn't want us to get separated again. He leaned his head back against the wall, not seeming to notice the intrusion.

We passed another half hour in silence before Vesper appeared in the middle of the room, pink stains smeared beneath her eyes.

"I am tempted to tear this book to shreds when we get our hands on it," she seethed, smoothing her fiery hair. Looking around the room, she asked, "Where is Indigo?"

"No sign of her," Simon answered. After he spoke, there was a mechanical sound like gears turning, and the ceiling retracted. A rope dropped through a hole big enough for two people to shimmy through.

We exchanged glances. "I don't think we should leave without her," I said.

"If the Book is allowing the three of us to proceed, she must have failed. We need to move on. I regret it, too, but it must be done," Vesper said resolutely, though her face was gaunt with worry.

I hated it, but I agreed. Fear for what had befallen Indigo settled over me like a layer of fallen snow, but we needed to keep moving. I didn't know how much longer this could last. How much longer we could last. Simon, the least powerful of the three of us, had purple half-moons under his eyes, and his skin had taken on a waxy cast.

"Who wants to go first?" he asked, echoing his earlier statement. It seemed like we'd entered the tower a year ago.

"I shall," Vesper said. "Wait here, and I will call for you." With that, she took hold of the rope, clambering up with a primate's agility.

"What do you think is up there?" I asked Simon.

"Dunno. Guess we'll have to—"

A whistling noise cut him off, similar to the sound a blade would make while swishing through empty air.

"*Shit*," I muttered, going for the rope.

"Stay where you are!" Vesper called, her voice floating down from the opening. Her freckled face appeared through the hole a second later. "It is an obstacle course. Grab the rope, and I will pull you up. But you must not step off the platform. Do you understand?"

I nodded, tightening my grip. Vesper hauled me up as though I weighed no more than a feather. When my head cleared the hole, I cursed.

The room was one giant trap. Vicious contraptions of metal and wood climbed the walls, centered around a series of steps and ropes. Another hole waited in the ceiling, perhaps three stories above our heads.

Just beneath the opening, a long rod balanced upon a fulcrum. Impossibly, it floated untethered in midair, like some magical seesaw. I supposed that's exactly what it was.

"Down!" Vesper commanded, shoving me to the floorboards of the platform we perched on. A breeze whispered as an ax blade arced above our heads in a pendulum swing.

"Oy, what's going on up there?" Simon called, peering upward. I caught a glimpse of concerned gray eyes.

"We're fine!" I returned, then sat up. "How are we going to get out of this?" I said to Vesper in a harsh whisper, tracking the ax's course.

"The ax will fall in another thirty seconds. After that, we will pull Simon up and climb the pegs." She pointed to a series of iron pegs hammered into the wall. "It seems to wind toward the top. You see?" She traced a pattern with her finger, from the pegs, to swinging ropes, to spinning logs. A host of deadly implements lay between each level.

Cold realization hit me. "Simon will never make it." I could use my magic to help him, but it wouldn't be enough. I wasn't strong enough yet, and if I expended all of my energy before we reached the Book....

"No, he will not make it on his own," she replied. "But with me, he will be fine. I shall take him to the top."

Relief flickered like a guttering candle. "Thank you, Vesper."

She nodded, then grabbed my collar and threw us down again as the ax whistled by.

"Grab the rope, boy," Vesper instructed, already on her feet again. She pulled Simon up. As soon as his feet touched the platform, she addressed him, the words coming so fast they blended together. "You will climb on my back and hold on tight. Understand?"

Wide-eyed, he nodded, making the wise decision not to question her.

"Get on." Vesper presented her back, and Simon awkwardly looped his arms and legs around her. If we hadn't been running on the verge of total exhaustion with the fate of the worlds hanging in the balance, I would have laughed.

Without warning, Vesper jumped for the pegs, Simon riding on her back like a baby monkey. They were already halfway up the dozen pegs when I jumped a second later, the ax falling swiftly behind me.

Momentum slammed me into the wall hard enough to knock the air out of my lungs. I hung there for a moment, gasping like a fish out of water. The metal pegs bit sharply into my palms. Rocking my legs from side to side, I drove upward, catching the next set of pegs.

They were so damn slippery, or maybe it was just the slickness of my damp palms. Fighting for every inch, I climbed. My world narrowed to the iron tang of wet metal, dripping sweat, and harsh panting. This was as bad as the Weald Fae's beast—worse, in fact, and I hadn't even cleared the first element.

But I'd beaten that course without magic. I could do this.

After another few seconds, I cleared the next platform. The other two waited for me, Simon no longer on Vesper's back. His eyes were tight as he studied me, a deep line furrowed between his brows.

I bent over, hands on my knees as I caught my breath. "What's next?"

"We have two choices." Vesper gestured to two sets of stairs that were roughly a six-foot jump from the platform. One went flush against the wall to our left, and the other jutted out into the center of the cavernous space. For the first time, I noticed water lapping far below us. There was a splash, then I caught a glimpse of a sinuous, scaly body breaching the surface. I quickly trained my gaze back on the staircases.

"These ones," she resumed, pointing to the stairs against the wall, "appear less dangerous—appear, being the key—but taking them will put us on the longer path. These," she pointed to the other stairs, "have blades coming at random intervals, swiping across the entire path. But it will give us a shortcut to the top, bypassing some of the other obstacles."

"Slow and steady is my vote," Simon said.

I turned to Vesper. "Can you do it? The more dangerous path?"

She nodded slowly, but with certainty. "Yes."

"Okay—"

The platform swayed, shuddering beneath our feet. I staggered, reaching out to steady Simon, my heart jumping into my throat. The wooden planks groaned, then broke apart, the gaps between them widening an inch, then two, three, four.

"Jump!" I yelled, lunging for the base of the right-hand stairs. As my feet left the platform, the tendril of black thread connecting me to Simon dragged him along after me. We landed on the base of the stairs just as an immense splash sounded, followed by a reptilian hiss as the remains of the platform sank into the water.

Vesper was a blur, pulling Simon onto her back midair and darting up the staircase. She leapt out of the way a millisecond before a long, honed blade appeared out of nowhere and speared across the staircase. It would have skewered Simon had she misstepped at all.

Fear was bright and hard in my throat, like a splinter of ice had lodged there. I didn't think, just moved, instinct taking over as I raced after them.

A slither of cold steel tore through my shirt. Hot pain bloomed across my back a millisecond later. If dropping to my knees was an option, I would have. I would have laid there, boneless, but I was so sick of pain. So sick of everything hurting all the damn time.

Magic responded, reading my desire like a book splayed open to the right page. Threads pulled me apart, and I dissolved, my atoms spreading out so that when the next blade came, I scattered. It was a curious sensation, like I was a champagne bubble rising to the top of a glass and bursting. Then I was at the top of the stairs, my nerve endings prickling as my cells aligned and I was made whole once again.

Simon's face was a mask of horrified anguish, his jaw working but no sound coming out. Vesper spat something in her native language, the shape of the words changing beneath their meaning. I was torn between relief and dismay—relief that I'd made it through alive, dismay that I'd drained my power to do so. My magic retracted again, depleted.

Vesper's words finally cut through my dissociation. "—why not do magic from beginning?" she demanded, losing a few words in her fervor.

"I didn't know that would happen," I replied, not exactly sure what question I was answering.

"Let's not argue about it here," Simon said, his gaze still locked on me. "It's enough that we've got this far."

But it wasn't enough. We still had one last deathtrap to clear. It was the seesaw, below the hole in the ceiling. The one I hoped marked the end of this nightmare.

"Fine," Vesper agreed, looking up to where the lever loomed over us. It seemed fairly straightforward, except...oh, shit. My stomach back-flipped.

"Someone needs to counterbalance it." At this, my power quivered into alertness, eager to meet my demands. Digging deep into the well that was already overdrawn, I pushed out to ensnare the far end of the lever. The threads stretched tentatively, shaking with effort. They snapped back like a rubber band. I pushed again, gritting my teeth. "It's not working."

We fell silent, and I wondered if Simon and Vesper had arrived at the same conclusion. One of us would have to stay behind to help get the others through. Although Vesper's skills were impressive, even she couldn't make the jump from the platform to the exit.

Flashing fire, needle sharp edges, and the heavy, iron teeth of the surrounding obstacles all flared in my vision. Vesper might have the best chance of getting the Book, and she had the strength to protect Simon. If I was very, very careful—I might make it back down to the next level, and from there...I'd find a way out.

I opened my mouth at the same time Vesper spoke. "I will stay," she decreed, giving us a look that brooked no argument. Her lovely face settled into hard, unforgiving lines.

"Vesper," I started, but she held up a hand to silence me.

"I will not hear another word. You will fetch the Book, and save your lover. I can get out of this." She smiled then, her fangs glinting even in the dark smokiness of the space. "How does your kind call it? Child's play?"

"Are you certain?" Simon asked, voice low but steady.

"Of course. I would not offer otherwise." She looked between me and Simon. "Watch after each other. I hope you survive. And..." Her eyes shone, tiny spots of blood welling in the corners. "If you find my sister—if you learn what has happened to her—"

I took Vesper's cold hand in mine and squeezed. "I will do my best."

She nodded, then shook out her mane of red hair. "You must jump, and not let go."

Simon and I clung onto the end of the lever that sloped downward.

"Good luck, Vesper."

Sinuous as water, she sank into a crouch, then sprung into the air. Her bright hair trailed behind her, turning her into a spark jumping from a fire.

"Hold on," I warned Simon, taking his hand as I tracked Vesper's arc. She reached the other side, grabbing onto the lever. It hung in space for a moment, then she dropped. Our side moved, shooting upward and flinging us into space.

35

We arrowed toward the hole in the ceiling, arms wrapped around each other like vines. We had to thread the eye of needle, and if I'd misjudged the angle, we were fucked. Or, one of us was.

I shouldn't have done it, but I shut my eyes, unable to watch any longer. Simon hyperventilated in my ear, his fear leaching into me as our sweat mingled.

I slammed onto cold stone, then we skidded and rolled across the floor. Simon and I broke apart and came to rest on opposite sides of the circular chamber.

My forehead throbbed from where it had struck the ground, but I sprang up, knife already drawn even though the room spun.

It was empty, apart from lit torches and Simon. Well, no—not empty. The hole in the floor we'd come through was gone, replaced by a round stone pedestal.

And upon the pedestal sat a book. A book that whispered in my ears, that called me like a moth to flame. Something magnetic pulsed inside me, urging me forward.

"Is that..." Simon trailed off, scrambling to his feet. Blood trailed down his face from a cut on his brow.

"I think so." My voice rang unnaturally loud as it echoed off the walls. I darted a look around the room again. Part of me expected

someone or something horrible to pop out and try to kill us. But everything was still, apart from the rasp of our harsh breathing.

Our eyes met across the room, and in silent agreement we
approached the pedestal.

The Book of Shadows was bound in dull black leather and roughly
the size of a dinner plate. It had no title on the cover or spine, and
wasn't even especially thick. I'd imagined something grand, or dangerous. But this could have been any old book.

"So, do we...take it?" Simon asked, still staring at the Book.

"That seems too easy."

"Easy? We've had to fight demons, jump off a bridge, find our way
out of an illusion, relive our worst moments, and climb through a death
trap. None of this has been easy."

He had a point.

I reached beneath my torn shirt for the *frithcloth* bag tied around my
waist. Miraculously, it was still there.

"Wait!"

I jumped, bobbling the bag. "What?"

Simon wiped blood from his face. The gash wasn't showing any
signs of stopping, and a new frisson of worry ran through me. "How are
we getting out of here?"

How *were* we getting out of here? The only exit had been sealed by
the pedestal. "Maybe another door will open after we get the Book, like
how we got into the obstacle room. I don't know, Simon. But we can't
turn back now." What I didn't have to add was that we couldn't even if
we wanted to.

He came around the pedestal to stand beside me. There was so
much yellow in his gray eyes that they resembled the golden gaze of a
fox. "Let's do it then, and get this damn thing over with."

I passed Simon the silvery *frithcloth* bag, and he held it open
for me.

My heart slammed against my ribs so hard that it reverberated up my
throat. If I was to speak, my voice would come out garbled and unintelligible. I fought to keep my hands steady as I reached for the Book of
Shadows.

I'd never been afraid of a book before. In fact, they'd been my refuge
for as long as I could remember. I tried to shove the fear aside, to put it

in a box and close it away. The Book of Shadows didn't have to be frightening. Maybe, just maybe, it could be an ally.

With one last look at Simon, my fingers closed around the edges of the Book.

Nothing happened. The room stayed where it was, and there were no flames, no demons who sprang from the shadows. A relieved smile broke out on my face, and Simon released a long breath.

"Thank Asael," he croaked. "I thought we might be goners."

A disbelieving laugh burbled up my throat, and my heart resumed its normal rhythm. If the Book didn't exactly feel friendly in my hands, it didn't feel hostile, either.

"Don't let down your guard yet," I cautioned. "We still need to find our way out."

I lifted the Book from its pedestal.

The room disappeared, Simon and the Book with it. It was like I'd been sucked into a vacuum and spread on a torture rack, compressing and stretching at the same time, burning and suffocating and disappearing. Through the agony, I held onto the hope that Simon hadn't been pulled into whatever *this* was.

Then a voice pushed into my head, arrowing through the pain. *At last, little witch.*

Cold, sickening dread pooled in my stomach and sent nausea flooding into my throat. When I spilled onto a tiled floor, I vomited, my hands sliding through the bile. Feverish chills ran up my spine as I pushed to my knees.

Magoth sat upon an obsidian throne, a nightmare wearing skin. A twisted crown of blackened metal that curled into two horns and seemed to swallow the light sat upon his head. His features were still cruelly handsome, his sharp smile malevolent.

And he wasn't alone. Beelzebub, his ice-blue eyes frozen on me, stood beside the throne. His great black wings were folded in at his sides. If extended, they would've thrown the whole room into shadow.

"Welcome to my realm, Proserpina. But I must say, it is considered rude to bring an uninvited guest to the party," Magoth drawled.

With dawning horror, I turned to see Simon's limp body behind me. I rushed to him, terror laying a blazing trail through my gut, and felt for his pulse. It was weak, but there. Pressure tugged on my wrist, and I looked down. It was the black thread, binding us together. I should have severed it before I touched the Book.

I was a fucking fool.

Turning back to Magoth, I rasped, "Where is he? Where's Alex?"

"All in due time," the demon said, wagging a finger at me. "We have a little catching up to do first. It's been so long, after all. If I'd known all it would take to bring you here was a little reading, I'd have thought of it sooner. It seems to run in the family."

"I'm not playing this game with you." Fury rioted wild through me, heating my skin. This bastard, this devil, had cursed my father, stolen my love, then set the world on fire—and laughed about it.

His dark eyes flashed serpentine for a moment, the pupils going to slits. "You'll play whatever game I want you to." Magoth rose, walking toward me on heeled boots that clicked with each step. For the first time I noticed the statues of horrible creatures, human and beast, that were scattered throughout the marble-walled room. "You are in my world now. And you will follow my rules."

"Fine. Then send Simon back if it's me you want." I glanced behind me. Simon stirred, his eyelids fluttering as he emitted a small groan.

"Hm." Magoth tapped a long-nailed finger to his chin. "No." He snapped his fingers, and the pool of vomit vanished. Two smoky, wraith-like creatures appeared, one latching onto me with frozen fingers and the other taking Simon. He struggled weakly, then fainted dead away.

My hands closed over thin air when I reached for a knife. Our weapons had vanished. "Please, don't hurt him," I begged, even though I had nothing to offer the demon for his safety. My eyes found Beelzebub's again, but he looked at me with cold disdain and not a flicker of recognition.

Magoth shrugged. "That depends on you. Comply, and don't give me a reason to. For now, you will go to your chambers and clean your-self up." He sniffed, wrinkling his nose. "I need you well rested."

Gray smoke covered my eyes and ears so that the world went foggy. The icy fingers clamped around my wrist dragged me, and I stumbled along blindly. I twisted and clawed, fighting the wraith's pull, but it only served to make me so dizzy I almost vomited again.

We eventually stopped and the smoke cleared, revealing a bedroom with richly colored tapestries hung on white marble walls and an immense canopied bed covered in creamy linen. I broke away from the wraith, shivering even as fevered heat flashed over me. Running for the door, I jerked the handle. Not only was it locked, but a jolt of something hot singed my palm and left a red burn.

The wraith floated a foot off the ground, wisps of smoke arranged into a vaguely human silhouette with no definable features. Cold radiated from it like a block of dry ice. It lifted an arm to point toward an immense copper tub. Steam rose from the surface, curling before it dissipated in the chilly air.

"I'm not g-getting in your b-bath." I bit down hard to stop my teeth from chattering. I didn't know if it was from shock, but the cold was bone deep.

Although...the water would warm me, I reasoned. Visions of sliding into the tub filled my head. How soothing would it be to sink into the hot water and do what I was told?

I walked toward it, grasping the hem of my shirt to pull it over my head.

Then, through the visions of obedience, I felt it. The grip of icy fingers around my mind, directing my thoughts.

I took a deliberate step backward. "Get the fuck out of my head." Scraping for power, my fingertips smoked, but no fire appeared.

The wraith shoved an image into my mind. Simon, pale as death. *We can stop his heart*, a frosty voice spoke into my mind. *All it takes is one thought, one word.*

With trembling fingers, I reached for my belt. "Get out."

In an instant, the chill in the air disappeared. I stripped, then stepped into the copper tub. The hot water felt like both a miracle and a curse, and I scrubbed away the blood and dirt as quickly as possible. Myriad cuts and bruises covered almost the entirety of my skin, but there was nothing I could do about that.

Clean clothes waited for me on the bed. A gown of red velvet with white slashes in the long sleeves and a square neckline lay against the pale coverlet like a bloodstain.

I picked up my begrimed and torn clothes that smelled of sweat and smoke and something even worse, and dressed. There was no way in hell I was playing dress-up for Magoth.

After it was done, I sat on the end of the bed and stared at a tapestry depicting a feast scene. The mattress gave as I sank into it. I was a statue, weighty and arrested in time.

If I was being optimistic, I could acknowledge that getting captured was not ideal. But I'd been in…if not worse situations, similar ones. I had my power back, though I was weak at the moment after the fight in the Vale of Sorrow. The Book was here somewhere, and so was Alex. Simon…I shut my eyes and took a shaky breath. No. I would not let thoughts of him unravel me. My hope would not extinguish. I was stronger than I knew, strong enough to save the people I loved and defeat the darkness that threatened us. I was scared, but I would not fold. I would not fail. Everything I wanted was within reach.

I just had to figure out a way to get it.

Turning inward, I found the cord that connected me to Alex. I picked it up and pulled.

And felt an answering tug on the other end.

Stilling for one shocked moment, I placed a shaky hand on my chest. My heart beat strong and steady into my palm, and my nerve endings fizzed, light and bubbly.

Alex, can you hear me? It's Seph. I'm here, in Magoth's world.

I waited for a minute, then five, ten, twenty, reminding myself to breathe. He didn't respond, but the tether's presence meant he was here somewhere. The weight on the end of the cord was directionless but exerted steady pressure.

Getting up, I tried the door again and was rewarded with another singed finger. I explored the rest of the room, stomping on marble tiles and ripping tapestries from the walls in an attempt to find some weakness through which I could escape. When I was finished, the room looked like a tornado had hit it. But there wasn't a single loose panel or hollow bit of wall to be found.

I slid to the floor, drawing my knees up to my chest. The adrenaline that had been surging through me for hours was fading, leaving me wrung out and drained. My eyelids began to droop, and in the end, I couldn't fight it.

Though sleep took me, I held tight to the tether. Held tight to hope.

———

The cold woke me. I shivered, my breath crystallizing into a cloud. There was hardly a place on me that didn't ache, but my mind at least felt sharper, the fear dulled and tucked away. I checked on my power source. The rivers flowed strong, but hadn't risen nearly enough.

The wraith was back, hovering in the doorway. *Come with me,* the frosty voice instructed.

I peeled myself off the ground, grimacing as my joints popped. "Are you going to blind me again?"

Do I need to?

I shook my head. If I was going to come up with an escape plan, I needed to get the lay of the land.

Follow me.

The wraith moved through black marbled corridors like smoke being carried by the wind. I jogged to keep up, my footsteps echoing loudly. Corinthian columns were interspersed along hallways that branched off every few feet. The place was a damn maze, every inch identical in its lifelessness

The wraith stopped on the threshold of a cavernous room set with a long dining table. Black-veined marble covered the walls and floor, all illuminated by a circular candelabra strung high above my head. The table was laden with food, the peppery aroma of spices making my stomach grumble. I only hoped Magoth, who stood at the head of the table, couldn't hear it.

Black pants covered his long legs, and a breezer-style jacket of red brocade skimmed to mid-thigh. He still wore that burnt, twisted crown. My skin crawled as he surveyed me, forked tongue flicking out to moisten his lips.

"You are not dressed for dinner." Magoth snapped his fingers, and my filthy clothes disappeared, replaced by the red dress I'd refused to wear. Revulsion flowed through me as I realized the color was an exact match for his jacket.

"That looks lovely with your complexion," he said with a smirk. "Do sit." A chair partway down the long side of the table slid out, scraping against the dark, patterned rug.

With the cold wraith still at my back, I sat in the proffered chair, spine stiff. Magoth snapped his fingers again, and the wraith vanished.

"Relax, dear Persephone," Magoth drawled, slouching artfully in an ornate chair with black upholstery, surely designed to resemble a throne. "We're all friends here."

"Are we?" My voice cracked across the room like lightning. "Then where are Simon and Alex?"

He waved a hand, picking up a golden goblet with the other and taking a deep draft. "No harm has come to them. Yet."

I almost sagged with relief, but infused iron into my spine. No weakness from here on out.

"You must be hungry. Eat."

I eyed the dishes crowding the table, roasted meats and vegetables and sugary confections. My stomach gave an uproarious growl, but I'd rather have eaten broken glass than anything from this demon's table. "No thanks."

"Suit yourself." His eyes flashed, sharp as bitter herbs. "But you will give in eventually."

I wouldn't be here long enough for that to be an option, I vowed. "What exactly are you going to do with me? I assume if you wanted to kill me, I'd already be dead."

"Indeed," he acknowledged, picking up a ruby pomegranate from a pile of fruit. Using his sharpened fingernail, he sliced it into wedges then broke it open. Wet arils that resembled tiny gems glistened in the candlelight. "I have plans for you."

"Don't keep me in suspense."

He chuckled. "You are a fun playmate. Not like the others. They were too frightened to give me much of a challenge."

My heart struck up a wild beat, but I willed my breathing to slow. "Like Cora Roth?" The previous generation's Lightbringer who'd also been part of the Auruem—before they sold her out.

"Like Cora Roth," he agreed. "And Mei Shuyan, Bronagh Cailleach, Arianwen, Calista Silverfang, and dear Seraphyna. All Lightbringers, like yourself."

I tried not to let the surprise show on my face. I'd known he was abducting Lightbringers, but so many? And he'd mentioned Seraphyna. "What happened to them? Where are they?"

Magoth stared at me with coal-dark eyes. "You will find out soon enough, my dear. Patience."

I waited in silence, staring down at my empty plate. Wondering how long he'd had them, and if they were all dead. No, I wouldn't think that way. Instead, I imagined the look on Vesper's face when she was reunited with her sister.

"Tell me, how do you like my home?" he asked.

I'd nearly forgotten how mercurial the demon could be. "It's a little grand for my taste."

"I modeled it after your world's Renaissance. Such a genius time, all that creativity and wealth. Such *life*. Artists were selling their souls for talent, for the favor of kings and queens, for luck and fame." He smiled fondly. "I don't even need a home, not really—only when I'm in this form. But it is an indulgence, and as you may have gathered, I do like to indulge. And, I needed a place to house my mates."

During his speech, I'd been searching the table for weapons. There was no cutlery, not even a spoon with which to dig his eyes out. But I stopped cold at the mention of mates, the rush of fear, of disgust, so strong and instinctive I couldn't tamp it down. My lips drew back in a grimace, my stomach curdling as an acid taste climbed the back of my throat.

"Don't look so sour, my dear. Am I that repulsive to you?" His smile said that he didn't care—no, he enjoyed my outrage.

I didn't answer, but forced myself to meet his gaze. A sensation like fingers stroking my bare flesh slid over the nape of my neck, then around my sternum. When it glided over my breasts, my nipples peaked. I shuddered, and Magoth's lazy grin widened. Anger and shame joined the flush of arousal he was forcing on me. Fucking bastard. Power stirred under my skin, waking from its nap.

"Given you are named after the queen of an underworld, I imagine you know Proserpina's story," Magoth said, changing tack again. He finally released me from his prurient grip.

I nodded, schooling my features back to blankness even as the desire to rip his throat out with my bare hands swelled. He was getting closer to making his point, which meant my sojourn outside of my prison might be coming to a close. The gears of my mind clicked, trying to find any weakness, any way out. Could I get him to let slip where he was holding Alex and Simon?

"Ah, but do you know what happened to her after the abduction?"

I barely heard him, distracted as I was by my own plotting. But he didn't wait for my answer this time.

"Six months out of every year, she resided in the underworld. One for each seed she ate while with Pluto." He picked up a wedge of pomegranate and plunged his fingertip into the pulp with a crunch. Juice sprayed, landing on the snow-white tablecloth like blood spatter. "Proserpina had a whole life there, you know. One she enjoyed."

My pulse skittered, heart dancing wildly in my rib cage. "What's with the history lesson?" I said through a clenched jaw.

His forked tongue skimmed over long canines. "Just trying to broaden your mind, my dear. To help you understand."

I couldn't help the frustration that leaked into my words. "Understand *what*?"

"Your purpose." He skimmed a juice-drenched fingertip along his lip, then leaned forward. "Tell me, did you know that Proserpina had a daughter?"

I was beginning to go numb. My body knew something I didn't. I bit down hard on my lower lip, welcoming the sharp pain. Then I asked the question he wanted me to ask, because I wanted to get it the fuck over with. "Who's her daughter?"

Magoth smiled, his blood-red mouth stretching wide. "Melinoë. The bringer of nightmares."

<h1 style="text-align:center">36</h1>

I held tight to the edges of my seat, tasting salt-tinged blood. *Bringer of nightmares?* This demon was already a nightmare himself—what did he need that for? Magoth had control over the Aureum, over demons like Beelzebub. But the quest for power was a never-ending game of chess. Everyone was a pawn on someone else's board.

Magoth continued. "A creature like Melinoë is a tool to be wielded, one that would help my master cement his dominion. Imagine, a race of creatures specially bred for destruction—an army."

My mind slowly stitched together the threads of information. Bred for destruction. Persephone's daughter. This horrible fucking mausoleum, built to house the women Magoth abducted.

Every part of me recoiled, denying it. No. No fucking way.

"You're...trying to have a *child*?" The words were acid on my tongue, and I fought nausea again.

Magoth preened. "Yes, clever girl. Melinoë was carried by a woman who walked between two worlds, between life and death, just as you do. Just as the other Lightbringers have." He selected a gold-handled knife from his belt, and began to pick his teeth. "It is your womb that makes your kind valuable to us."

I wanted to hyperventilate. I wanted to be sick. I wanted to go back five minutes, five months, five years, and never hear those words again. Never learn what I was.

"I will take my own life before you ever touch me," I snarled.

Magoth shook a finger at me. "I thought you'd say that. You know, you could make this easier on yourself if you just embraced your nature. Let your inner demon take over, and choose darkness."

I pressed my lips together, shaking my head in denial of it all. This was worse than anything I'd imagined.

He sighed heavily. "Well, then. That's why I have two helpful bargaining chips to ease the process. I only really needed one, but fate delivered."

As long as he held Alex and Simon in the balance, I was paralyzed. "But the other women, what happened to them? Why do you even need me?" I was babbling, the words overlapping and blending together.

"We are creating an army, my master and I." Some emotion shone behind his eyes, and they took on a red sheen. "Rome wasn't built in a day. The more breeders we have, the more offspring, and the stronger we become. Soon, we shall be ready to take our soldiers on the march and possess what is rightfully ours."

The wild urge to laugh seized me. A year ago, my biggest problem had been deciding which book to read next, and now a demon prince wanted to rape and impregnate me with a monster so he could take over the worlds.

And there was an even bigger problem. Magoth was acting on behalf of a higher-ranking demon, and I feared it was only a matter of time until they appeared, too.

My fingers twitched, and I imagined snatching Magoth's knife and turning it on him, or even myself. But before I did either of those things, I needed to get Simon and Alex out. Get them out, then I would do what I had to do.

"You are a sick fuck," I said, enunciating every word and summoning all my courage. "And your plan is never going to work."

"On the contrary, it is going to work splendidly. And you will mind your tongue." He shoved up from his chair with sudden violence, and it flew backward, crashing into the wall. "I have forgiven you for your antics in the prison world," he said, stalking toward me, "but I am disappointed by this childish refusal to accept reality."

"Reality? This is a delusion. Your delusion."

"You think this is fantasy?" He looked down at me, sliding a finger beneath my chin to tip my face up to his. My throat constricted, my lungs refusing to draw air. "Then I shall have to show you something real to convince you otherwise.

"You are too headstrong by half, Persephone. If you cannot learn to listen.... Well, let's not visit trouble yet. Come."

"I'm sorry," I rasped. Had my insolence just threatened Alex and Simon? "Please, I...I believe you. I promise I'll do what you want, if you let them go."

"All in due time. Now, shut up. I've heard enough whining."

I touched the black and gold threads shimmering inside me. Their strength was reassuring, although I didn't know if I should try and use them yet. Nothing had prepared me for this possibility. I knew that I would have one shot, and one shot only to escape. I released my hold on my power, following Magoth as he exited the room.

We entered a chamber with stone walls and floors, dank and damp in contrast to the airiness of the rest of the dwelling. Lit candles cast shallow pools of golden light across the bound form of a man strapped to a chair, shining on a bedraggled mop of chestnut hair.

"Simon!" I cried, rushing toward him. Magoth still held my elbow, his talon-like fingernails digging in painfully.

He threw me to the floor, and I skinned my palms on cold stone. "Stay. And don't move a muscle."

I didn't dare. A bandage wound around Simon's forehead, covering the gash above his eye. He looked clean, and was also wearing a new set of courtly clothes. His eyes widened when he saw me, and he struggled against his bindings.

"What have you done to her, you bloody monster?"

"Simon, don't," I urged, heart in my throat. "Don't say another word."

Magoth walked toward Simon, placing a hand to the back of his chair. "Yes, boy. You would do well to heed my bride."

A curiously blank expression crossed Simon's face. "Bride?"

I shook my head, wishing I could speak with him mind to mind. To give him false words of comfort, to tell him how sorry I was about all of it.

Magoth waved a hand and Simon's restraints fell away. He immediately lurched to his feet on a snarl, but froze midstep. The demon produced a heavy chain out of thin air, then looped it around Simon's wrists. He hooked the end of the chain over a bar running the width of the ceiling, then clipped it back on itself.

Simon was strung up like an animal ready for slaughter.

"There," Magoth said, giving the dangling Simon's stomach a hard slap. "Nice and tidy. Now—Simon, is it?—I need your assistance. Our other friend is a tad indisposed at the moment."

Simon only emitted a pained groan, but I almost went limp as weakness flooded my muscles. I covered my mouth with a shaking hand, biting back tears. Indisposed. What did that mean? Alive, surely, but in what state?

"Excellent. You see, our darling Persephone is a bit obstinate. Not an unattractive trait, but it is most decidedly inconvenient. Hence, where you come in. Now, I wonder...what would cause you the most pain? Or rather...what would cause her the most pain?" Magoth turned his black, glittering eyes on me.

I made my expression cool and hard. If the demon couldn't see, couldn't sense how much Simon being in danger hurt me—that I was responsible for causing him pain—perhaps he would release him. Magoth easily grew bored, and if he didn't get a rise out of me, I hoped to god he'd leave Simon alone.

Magoth tapped his fingers together rhythmically. *One-two-three-four-five, one-two-three-four-five.* "Ah-ha!" he crowed, snapping his fingers. "I have it!"

A whip appeared in his hand, black as night and coiled like a snake with a barbed tail. Magic sparked under my skin, begging to fulfill my desire to save Simon. I clenched my fists. The only way I could protect him, to make it up to him, would be not to show any reaction. It was the only thing keeping me from screaming.

Instead of unfurling the whip, Magoth snapped his fingers again. A shape materialized beside him—the shape of a man.

My father.

Our eyes met, and the agony I found in his stole my breath. I was torn between joy and horror at seeing him again. Seeing him here, like this. But at least he wasn't in the form of a beast with dripping jaws and a stare like live coals.

"Show your daughter what will happen if she does not follow my orders and keep that sharp tongue of hers sheathed," the demon commanded, handing him the whip.

When my father hesitated, Magoth struck out with the whip, flaying his cheek. Flesh tore, and scarlet dripped down his face. "Do it now, or I will have you beat her after."

My dad's shaking hand closed over the whip, and he finally tore his gaze away from me and focused on Simon. I wanted to close my eyes, but kept them open. It would be cowardly to look away, and Simon didn't need a coward. He needed strength.

The whip whistled through the air, the first blow landing with a crack that made me flinch. Simon's back arched, bowing away from the pain. A harsh cry tore through him, but he gritted his teeth. His smoke-gray eyes, almost black in the light, stayed on mine.

Using precious threads of magic, I covered his back to absorb the worst of the blows.

Another lash. Another. Another. They fell in time with my heart-beat, my own back searing.

"Stop," Magoth said after the tenth lash. Simon swayed on the chain, his eyelids fluttering, saliva bubbling at the corners of his mouth. Flecks of red covered my father's brown skin, his face, glistened wetly in his curls.

The demon crouched in front of me. I still didn't look away from Simon. "You're learning already," he murmured. "If we have to do this again, I will spare his back and take an eye. Then the other. Then his tongue. You understand?"

I nodded once.

"Say it." His voice curled around my ears, the threat a whisper.

"I understand." My voice belonged to a corpse, something empty and rotting.

"Good." Magoth rose, then beckoned to my father. "Take her back to her chamber. You're past due for a little daddy-daughter time. And you, my dear, need to have a long think about your behavior."

My father's eyes—the mirror image of my own—latched onto mine, then his hand was around my waist, steering me away from

Simon's limp, bloody body. Turning my back on him felt like betrayal.

We didn't speak until the door of my room was shut tight. The fire burned merrily in the hearth, but each snap and pop sent a shiver crawling over my skin. It sounded too much like a cracking whip.

My dad stared at me, the anguished lines carved around his mouth doing all the talking. Blood still leaked from the gash in his cheek. "I'm so sorry, love. I never thought I'd see you again, that I'd...."

Beat your best friend's son? Kill his twin? Watch your daughter birth a monster?

"It's okay," I said, because there was nothing else to say. Even though this was the worst sort of hell imaginable...my dad was here. My face must have shown everything, because he opened his arms, and I stepped into them.

His solid warmth locked around me, and I buried my head in his shoulder. "Shh, darling. It's all right," he whispered, stroking my snarled waves. "I'm going to get you out of here."

Even if they were false promises, he gave me comfort. My magic swelled like an ocean wave, glowing and glittering. After another long moment, I pulled away, gesturing for him to sit on the bed next to me. His hand covered mine, maintaining the connection between us.

"Why aren't you turning into a hellhound?" I asked. "Last time, when I touched you...."

"I'm not a true hellhound. It's the nature of Magoth's curse." He sighed, running a hand through dark curls graying at the temples. "I guess I should tell you the whole story."

He didn't have to add that it might be the last chance we had. The only chance we had. I tightened my grip on his hand.

"Before I left you and your mother, I went to the Weald Fae. They've been allies to Watchers for a thousand years or more. I asked their queen for a boon and got that ring for you." He ran his finger along the warm silver. "It's a sign you're a friend to them, should you ever need their help."

"I found them. Or, they found me." I thought about trying to explain everything that had happened since I'd gone on the run, but words failed me. "I'm here for a reason. Magoth didn't find me. I came to him."

"Because of the Aureum boy? Persephone." He shook his head, a disapproving dad busting me after coming home late for curfew. Maybe that would've been true, in another life. The loss of what we could've had was the dull ache of a worn stone weighing on my chest.

"Don't tell me he's not worth it," I said, emotion roughening the words. "You made the same choices to protect me and Mom."

"And I never thought you'd have to do the same."

"Yet here we are." In some form of a horrible cosmic joke. Or maybe it was just that fate had a way of ruining best laid plans. "But there's another reason, too." I dropped my voice, although it probably didn't make a bit of difference. A wraith could be on the other side of the door, listening to every word. "The Book of Shadows."

He stilled, and another beat of silence passed. "The Book of Shadows," he repeated, something like malice tingeing his tone.

"You know it?"

"Know it?" He rubbed his cheek, where Simon's dried blood mingled with his own. "That's how I became enslaved to Magoth."

My jaw went slack. History really was doomed to repeat itself. "*You* were after the Book?"

"That's where I went after I left you and your mum. For years I studied it, hunted it. I thought it would free you. That I would find answers in it to help understand your magic. When I went away, it wasn't supposed to be forever." His voice cracked on the last word, and the weight on my chest took up residence in my throat.

"You found the Book." I knew from the confidence with which he spoke of it.

My father dipped his chin in acknowledgement. "I stole it from a warlock in a world called Uren, and when I summoned to escape, Magoth came. I never even had a chance to open the damned thing, didn't want to risk it in case things went wrong." He took a deep breath and shut his eyes, as if mustering the strength to finish this horrible tale. "I may be one of the only living people who's able to decipher it. Apart from Magoth. He...he forced me to teach him."

This time, he didn't close his eyes. He stared straight at me, and I watched the specter of remembered pain turn them glassy.

His calloused palm was rough on my fingers as I gripped tighter. "Dad?"

He blinked, the corners of his mouth curving into a gentle smile. "I've dreamed of hearing you call me that. Ever since I fu—botched the, ah, visit back home to see you."

My brow knit in confusion, then I realized Gravesville wasn't home to my father—Canhaben was. "I'm glad," I whispered. "That you came despite the risk." But the guilt rushed in when I remembered that it had cost Penn his life.

His arm wrapped around my shoulders, and he pulled me in close to his side. He smelled of smoke and a faint whiff of sulfur, but beneath that, I detected ink. I breathed deeply, letting the scent buoy me.

We sat in silence for a few beats before the muscles in his arm tensed. "How's your mother?" he asked.

"She's..." Married to a human piece of cardboard. Broken-hearted, but finally surviving. "Good," I landed on. "She moved back to Virginia when I was around three. That's where I grew up."

"Back to her family?" He shook his head, chin brushing my brow. "She didn't get on with them one bit."

"Well, no. Things changed, after..."

After.

His brow, only lightly lined despite being into his fifties, creased. There was so much pain living in our shared past, but I held hope for a better future.

"Do you know where he's keeping Alex and Simon?"

My dad drew back. "I don't, darling. He wouldn't pass on such information to me."

"Well, do you have any idea at all? Is there a—a map you could draw, or something?"

He stiffened, his brown-green eyes going unfocused, then gripped my elbows. "My love, I must go now."

"No. Please, don't." My heartbeat accelerated as he stood, lifting me up with him. I wanted him to stay with me. For the first time in my life, I'd felt the true comfort of a parent's embrace, the safety of it. I just wanted my dad.

"Do not eat the food, do not drink the water," he cautioned. "Whatever you do, do not trust anyone or anything here."

I paused, memorizing the lines and angles of his face once again. "Even you?"

"Even me. I am going to do everything I can to get you and your friends out of here. But at the end of the day, I am his creature. And if he commands me to do something, I must do it."

I clutched the worn fabric of his shirtsleeve, desperation overtaking me. "But the Book can free you?"

"Don't worry about the Book. Your first priority is to leave this world. If you see an opportunity, you take it." He cupped my cheek. "There's a seam in the throne room that's anchored by the Book's power."

"But—"

"Persephone," he snapped through a rigid jaw. Then, he softened. "Promise me this."

"I—okay." I hugged him tight enough to squeeze the air from his lungs. "I promise," I lied.

37

Three booming knocks sounded on the door. I jolted upright where I'd been lying on the bed, studying the ceiling since my father left a few hours ago. I was trying to plan my next move while ignoring my growling stomach and dry throat, but hadn't come up with anything except for trying to blast my way out of the room. After that...I didn't know what. My foray into the mansion hadn't given any indication where Alex or Simon were being held, so I'd have to—

The door swung wide. A person holding a large tray of food in front of their face stood in the entryway. Or, not a person, I realized. A demon —one I knew.

Beelzebub came inside then immediately dropped the tray, a sneer marring his handsome face. Fragrant meat pies and roasted vegetables crashed to the floor, along with a decanter of wine. Burgundy liquid spread across the plush carpet like a bloodstain.

I retreated until the backs of my knees hit the bed. Candlelight threw deep shadows across the demon's face, but his angular, icy eyes shone blue through the darkness. His stare pinned me in place as he advanced on me. It was impossible not to feel fear when a creature like that bore down on you—his very essence inspired terror.

"What do you want?" I ground out, resisting the way my voice wanted to tremble.

Beelzebub flicked his wrist, and the door slammed and locked. The air in front of the door shimmered, then turned an opaque white, hiding it from sight. "To bring you your evening meal, of course."

His voice was just as I remembered, hypnotic but hard enough to grind my bones into dust. "I didn't take you for a servant, but I suppose looks can be deceiving." I snorted when anger flitted across his haughty features. "Why are you really here?"

He stroked the jeweled hilt of a dagger worn around his waist with pale fingers. "You don't seem as foolish as most mortals. But time will tell."

"And it's wasting," I told him. "So get to the point, or get out." My head pulsed, and my throat burned with thirst. Even though I wasn't planning to eat anything, smelling the food was torture.

Beelzebub didn't step closer so much as appear inches away. We would've been nose to nose, except that he towered over me. I forced myself not to shrink backward, though it was a hard sell. My base instincts recognized him as a predator and screamed at me to flee. And yet, his spicy scent was almost seductive, drawing me closer.

"Magoth told you of his plans."

I shook my head, not in a denial but because a shiver of revulsion ran through me. "He's—it's—"

"Bad for business," Beelzebub answered. His face was calm, implacable.

"You don't agree with his plan for worlds domination?" I said, injecting venom into my tone.

"I don't agree with the power it will grant him." His upper lip drew back, revealing a row of sharp white teeth. "That insolent pup thinks that by coming to heel for his master, he can dominate the Fallen. But he is nothing but a thorn in the side of greater beings."

"What's the Fallen? And who's his master?" I asked, while pleading with my racing heart to slow. If Beelzebub wasn't here to goad me, then he must want something else—perhaps to make me an offer? My skin prickled in warning.

"Not a what, but a who. We are demonkind, yes, but I am of the worthier Seraphim—those who left the dominion of the gods to take control of our own existence. *We* created the infernal hierarchy. *We* are the kings and queens of legions. Magoth has always been below me, and will always be until someone does me the favor of removing him. As for his master, you should hope that you never find out."

Beelzebub's chest heaved, his eyes gone even brighter during his speech. His presence was overpowering, too overwhelming. I ducked beneath his arm, skirting crystal salt and pepper shakers and finally breathing air clean of his scent.

"Pretty bold of you to be plotting his demise in his own home."

"One thing you will not accuse me of is stupidity. He is away, entrusting you to my care."

For once, I was thankful for the scheming nature of demons. "Why can't *you* deal with him?"

Beelzebub faced me, but didn't come closer. "It is called the demon's bind. We cannot strike against our own kind, though it is in our nature to do so. That is why we make bargains—to fulfill our needs, while you fulfill yours. It's a win-win situation."

I scoffed. Yeah, it was a win-win all right. "You would've made a deal to get rid of him already, then," I hazarded. "So you can't do that, either."

"But I can deal with someone who has the power to do so."

And there it was. Suddenly, the fresh ink in the crook of my elbow burned, reminding me of all the bargains I'd made to get here. If I didn't get the Book and fulfill our agreement, Gamori would exact some kind of payment. I'd made a sacrifice to the goddess Iznir to gain my Guardian powers. My freedom was bound to Calytrix's agenda by a blood promise. And now, a demon king—one of the Fallen—wanted me to contract with him.

"What are your terms?"

Beelzebub smiled. "I will free you. In exchange, you will bring me Magoth's crown."

I blinked. "His crown?" The ugly, twisted thing would haunt my dreams if I ever got out of here.

"Yes. And if you happen to destroy the head it sits upon, I wouldn't take issue with it."

"Demons can't be destroyed, only imprisoned or controlled." I knew that from studying with the Aureum. Alex himself had told me.

Beelzebub clucked his tongue. "Oh, we can be—by your kind. Lightbringers walk on both the side of life and of death. That is one reason why they have been hunted for so long. Feared. Controlled. Killed."

"And you don't want to kill me?" I demanded. "Don't you fear me, if I can destroy you?"

He shrugged, bat-like wings flaring with the motion. "I'm not going to tell you *how* to do it, just that you can."

If we hadn't been in a life or death situation, I would've rolled my eyes. It was just like a fucking demon to be so cryptic. But here was the chance I needed. I would be an idiot to turn him down.

Except that I felt like a butchered animal, my pieces being sold off one by one. What would be left in the end for me? If I didn't draw the line somewhere, I might never be free.

And if I didn't sacrifice myself, Alex might never walk out of here. Simon might die in chains. My father would be bound to an eternity in this hell.

All my previous bargains had been made out of desperation, because I didn't have a choice. Because I didn't think I was good enough on my own. Now, I knew differently. I could do it without Beelzebub—some way, somehow. I was still afraid, but my faith in myself was stronger than my fear.

I was Persephone Hart. Daughter, lover, friend. Lightbringer, Watcher, Guardian, and mortal girl from Gravesville. I was the one who could save the people I loved. I was strong enough for this.

"This is going to be on my terms. And once it's done, I'm free and clear. You're not coming after me, or I'll be the one hunting you down."

"No, you're not as foolish as most mortals," the demon mused. A grin spread across his face, and it wasn't terrifying, but satisfied. "Let the negotiations begin."

———

I banged on the door of my room, fist smarting with pain from the burns. Beelzebub had left mere moments ago, taking the opaque shield away from the door that had blocked sound from exiting the room. We'd gone back and forth for what seemed like forever, but had both finally walked away semi-satisfied.

The demon was clever, I'd give him that. We'd concocted a plan that would help me escape without implicating him—much. I thought of the salt cellar hanging heavy in the pocket of my gown, how he'd thrown it a sidelong glance before disappearing. Giving me what I needed without actually giving me what I needed, in order to get around the demon's bind.

I didn't stop until a wraith appeared in the room, washing me in an icy breeze.

Cease this racket.

"Oh, you're here." I stepped away from the door and turned to face the shadowy wraith. "I want to see Alex."

The wraith released a hissing noise that seemed like annoyance. Good.

If you continue with this disturbance, I shall be certain your friend pays for it.

I ignored the chill that wanted to roll over my skin. "I want to talk to Magoth, then."

The lord shall hear about this upon his return, make no mistake. The wraith's words were sharp, slicing my mind. But the pain was worth the confirmation.

I gave an exaggerated wince. "Fine. Oh, and you can take that away," I said, gesturing to the food still covering the floor. "I've lost my appetite."

If it was possible for an incorporeal mass to roll its eyes, that's what happened as the wraith turned toward the tray. My heart thudded in my ears, so loud I was afraid the demon would guess my intentions.

As soon as it floated over the tray, I threw out threads of power, pulling hard to jump behind it in an instant. I whipped the salt cellar from my pocket and flung the crystals.

The wraith's human silhouette disintegrated as it became a dark, agitated cloud, churning like a storm. I darted around it, shaking salt until it was enclosed in a circle. It snarled, deep and animalistic.

"Where are Alex and Simon?" I demanded. Something Beelzebub had claimed he couldn't tell me, but that I would get from the wraith.

I will never tell you, witch.

"I think you will." Shaking a single, precious salt crystal to the tip of my finger, I flicked it into the swirling mass. The wraith released an anguished howl.

Pain is nothing compared to my master's wrath.

"It is nothing compared to my wrath." Then, steeling myself, I breached the salt circle and plunged my hand inside the wraith.

It was ice, and fire, and the biting edge of a knife slicing into me. But I held on, siphoning until I was awash in sickness, but also in power. The wraith's magic tore at me, then seeped under my skin, seething like an angry river.

Stop!

"Do what I tell you," I said through a shuddering breath, taking more. "And I'll let go."

Images pushed into my mind of winding corridors that ended in two locked doors. One was marble, the other stone.

I drew my hand back, part of me surprised to find it wasn't black with frostbite. "See, that wasn't so hard," I panted, struggling to subdue the wraith's gelid magic. It roared in my ears, and my gold threads recoiled from it. Almost without asking, my black threads wove a net around the icy power. My nausea subsided.

"Unlock the door for me," I commanded. "Now."

He will melt the flesh from you, and use your bones to pick his teeth. Despite the threat, the wraith's voice was weak, less than a whisper. The lock clicked open.

I returned the salt cellar to the deep pocket in the folds of my dress. Sweat clung to the back of my neck, the heavy velvet of the gown weighing me down. I used a precious thread of magic to shear off the bottom to my knees. "Maybe, but not before I get what I want from him."

The wraith's magic still rushed within me. I took hold of it, and though it hissed in protest, it gave into my will. Smoke rolled over my skin, covering me until I appeared as an exact copy of the wraith to the naked eye.

Opening the door softly, I ran.

Navigating the labyrinthine halls was easy when I had the wraith's images in my head to guide me. That, and the fact that if anything crossed my path, they'd only see a swirling, dark shadow.

The corridor forked, one direction leading toward the stone door, the other leading toward the marble door. I didn't know who was in which room. As I fretted, torn with indecision, a chill stole through the air. *Shit.*

I turned to see the other wraith gliding toward me. Would it be able to tell I was an impostor?

The wraith paused beside me, floating several inches off the ground. The siphoned magic squirmed, trying to flee, but my black threads wrapped tighter around it.

Greetings, the wraith said, the silken fingers of its voice caressing my mind.

I let a tiny bit of the wraith's power imbue my words, trying to emulate its speech. *Greetings.*

Why are you not with the prisoners?

It was so disconcerting speaking to something that didn't have eyes. *I visited the witch. She was causing a disturbance.*

The wraith hissed. *Foolish girl. She will soon learn her place, like the others.*

Yes, the others, I repeated. Then, another idea took hold of me. One that I knew I had to pursue. *The lord commanded me to bring her to them tonight.*

There was a long pause. *Indeed?*

I do not question the lord's wishes. Do you? I forced a little venom into my voice.

I do not. I shall assist you.

No, I said too quickly. I took a silent breath, hoping I could cover my stumble. *I need your assistance elsewhere. To prepare the...* I cast around, taking another gamble, *chambers for her.*

Silence hung heavy for a long moment, and sweat beaded at my brow. Could the wraith sense it? I tensed my muscles, preparing to fight, when the words entered my mind.

Of course. I should have assumed. The wraith bobbed, as though sketching a bow.

No matter. We can do it now. I tamped down on my relief as the wraith turned and floated down the left fork. I kept pace with it as we descended several flights of stairs, trying to act as though I knew exactly where we were going, too. But when it stopped abruptly, I walked into it, getting drenched in frigid air. A tiny gasp escaped my lips, no more than a forceful breath.

The wraith paused, but the door it stopped in front of clicked open, displaying a dark, low-ceilinged room.

Three people were chained by iron collars around their necks, one in each corner. They didn't stir when we entered, remaining sprawled on the floor or sitting with their backs against the stone walls. All three of them were gaunt and wore white, sleeveless shifts. Horror clawed up my throat, along with deep resolve. This risk was worth it.

Fetch the chains, the wraith told me, hovering in the doorway.

I moved through the room, walking slowly. The woman in the back right corner had red hair that still shone despite the gloom. Just past her was another corridor, cloaked in shadow. I made my way toward it, hoping that's where the chains were kept.

Suddenly, I couldn't breathe. I tried to draw air, but it was as if my lungs were made of stone. I choked, clawing at my throat. An icy blow struck me between the shoulder blades, and I fell. My knees slammed into the stone floors, pain reverberating into my bones.

You think I didn't know, witch? The voice raked my mind with sharp claws. *Where is Pryn?*

Black danced at the corners of my vision. The clink of chains sounded, and I heard a thin voice say, "What's happening?"

I shoved to my feet, releasing the siphoned power. It exploded through me, slapping frozen darts at the wraith. My airway opened and I drew a ragged breath, putting up a wall of solid ice between us.

By now, the chained women were all on their feet, shock on their rawboned faces. The one with red hair strained at the end of her chain, clawing at the iron collar.

A crack appeared in the ice wall, and on a groan, it shattered, a million shards skittering over the ground. The wraith blew over me, dissipating then re-forming. I dropped to the ground, throwing a dome made of ice over me as a shield while I dug around in my pocket for the salt cellar. The dome cracked, then broke, a sliver slicing my cheek so that warm blood gushed down my neck.

Springing up, I flung salt into the wraith's center. It recoiled, the smoky tendrils that had been hovering over the room coalescing again. I sprinted around the wraith, shaking salt into a jagged ring. Just as I was about to close it, a tendril lashed out, striking the center of my chest. The force was hard and cold enough to stop my heart for a beat.

The salt cellar slipped from my hand, hitting the ground with a crash, and I fell. Frost burrowed into my chest, joining with the last of my siphoned magic to freeze the blood in my veins. It was all happening too fast for me to stop it.

More of the wraith squeezed from the opening, heading for me. Until white crystals flew through the air like snow, sending the demon back inside the circle. One of the women, her black hair a cloud around her head, strained at the end of her chain. Her fingertips just reached the edge of the circle, and she spilled more salt, closing it.

Warmth chased away the cold in my chest as my magic flared, burning up any vestiges of the wraith's power. I looked at the women, and they looked back at me with wide eyes for a long second.

"I'm a Lightbringer," I said, getting to my feet. "And we're getting out of here."

The black-haired woman—actually, she looked more like a teenage girl—broke into keening sobs, tears streaming from her eyes. Pointed ears protruded through her curls. The two others approached me until they came to the end of their chains.

The red-haired woman had Vesper's exact bright, hazel eyes. She spoke first, her English heavily accented. "Who are you?"

"A friend of your sister's," I answered in the language of vampyres.

Seraphyna's mouth opened, and she covered it with a pale hand. "Vesper? How?"

"No time," I said, coming to her side. "I'm going to have to melt this collar off you. Keep it away from your skin."

Seraphyna complied, not saying a word as I ran a finger down the iron, burning a line through it. It fell away, clanging to the ground. The vampyre rubbed the livid scar that encircled her neck.

"You next," I said to the woman with bark-brown hair who was chained on the left wall. She flinched when I approached her, but stilled at Seraphyna's reassuring murmurs. "What's your name?" I asked as I worked.

Her voice quavered through scabbed lips. "C-Calista. I not know much how you speak."

"No problem, Calista. Almost finished." When the metal was pliant enough, I yanked the collar apart and dropped it before moving to the wailing girl.

"Be quiet, Bronagh," Seraphyna said, sharply. "Now is not the time."

Bronagh sniffled, but quieted as I worked on her. Once she was free, I turned to the other women. "Are there any others who need to be freed?"

"Mei died a week ago," Serphyna said, shaking her head. "We are the only ones left."

I told myself there would be time for grief later. "Do you know how to get out of here?"

"Passage," Calista whispered, her large, dark eyes flicking around the room, never hovering in one place too long. "Outside. From there, I know not."

"Are any of you familiar with inter-world travel?" I asked. Seraphyna raised her hand. "Okay. There should be a way out through the throne room—a seam. If you can get through, there's a tower. People are waiting there for me. You all go ahead. There are two others I need to find and free. Magoth is gone, but I don't know for how long."

I glanced at the growling wraith contained in the circle. "I don't know how long that'll hold, either." It was almost as if I could see the seconds tick by, dread gathering in my stomach and making my pulse race.

Seraphyna shook her head. "You will not make it alone. I shall help you."

"I come with," Calista said. "Come, Bronagh." She held out her hand, the palm lined with purple tattoos, and the younger woman clasped it. "We have power, us. But weak."

I nodded. "Don't be afraid to use it. Let's go."

Skirting the wraith, we fled the room and took off down the hallway. One of the doors the wraith had shown me earlier matched the ones in this corridor. I stopped at the one that had a chip in the facade.

My threads raced out, working on the lock. The door swung open to reveal Simon sitting on the edge of a cot with his back to us, hunched over. Rusty brown stripes of dried blood clung to his shirt.

He spun around, eyes tight. His mouth simply dropped open when he beheld me and the three malnourished women. They were panting in my ear, far too hard for the short run.

"What in Asael's pants?" Simon said, then he rushed over, throwing his arms around me.

I breathed him in. Somehow, the scent of turpentine still lingered beneath the blood and sweat. "You're okay," I whispered, taking care not to disturb the wounds on his back.

"Who are they?" he asked into my hair.

"Friends," I answered, drawing away. "Come on. We're getting Alex, and getting the fuck out of here." Not waiting for another word, I dragged him out of the room, and we ran full tilt for the stairs.

"How'd you find him?" Simon asked.

"Long story."

We went as quickly as we dared down corridors, although there wasn't any good way to hide a troop of escaped prisoners. If something came upon us, I'd have to trust the women would help handle it.

Finally, we reached the correct door. It looked exactly like all the others, but I was positive the wraith had shown me this one. I counted again, just to be sure—yes, it was the fourth down from the corner on the third floor.

Adrenaline surged through my blood, making me far more alert than I should've been. Once it wore off, I'd be in bad shape.

"Be ready for anything," I cautioned. I might have been warning myself more than the others.

"Seph, wait," Simon interjected, putting a hand on my arm. I met his stormy eyes. "Are you going to be all right?"

"I don't know," I answered truthfully. With my threads already racing to undo the magic on the lock, I shoved open the door.

38

He was there.

After all these months of waiting, searching, hoping—I'd finally found Alex. It almost didn't seem real, the way he lay on top of the sumptuous bed, eyes closed and arms at his sides. He was so still and perfect, like an angel fallen to earth.

My throat tightened with unshed tears, and for a heartbeat everything else faded away—the coppery smell of blood and the fear that pulsed inside me, the people who stood at my back, ringed around the door. Then the moment passed and I unfroze, dashing toward Alex.

His skin was pale, like he hadn't seen the sun for a long time. But otherwise he was clean, not a mark on him apart from the old scar crossing his eyebrow. His hair was longer than when I'd left him and neatly combed back, without the rogue lock flopping over his forehead. Despite that, he was the same as I remembered.

"Alex." I shook his shoulder, thrilling at the solidness of his body— that he was real, not some illusion my panicked brain conjured. "Alex, it's me."

He didn't move. "Alex," I repeated, shaking him harder. "It's Seph. Wake up." When he didn't respond, fear sliced through my relief. His pulse fluttered in his throat, but when I laid a finger on it to check, his skin was like ice.

"Is he...?" Simon trailed off, walking to the bed.

I swallowed. "His pulse is weak, but steady. He won't wake up."

"Drugged, maybe?" Simon offered. He leaned over and patted Alex's cheek. "Oy, mate. Rise and shine."

I prayed for his eyelids to flutter open, for him to peer at me out of forest shadow eyes and grin his breathtaking smile. But he didn't stir at all.

"Damn it," I breathed, stroking his cold cheek, the stubble prickling my palm. "Alex, come on."

A shadow moved over me, and I caught a glimpse of red hair. Seraphyna gave me a knowing look. "Is this your keeper?"

Simon threw me a sharp look. "What's a keeper?"

"Yes," I answered, ignoring him.

She laid a hand on my shoulder. "Go into his mind. Then you will know why he does not wake."

I glanced over my shoulder toward the door.

"We'll keep watch," Seraphyna assured me, joining Calista and Bronagh in the doorway.

The last thing I saw before closing my eyes was Simon's wary stare.

I turned inward, reaching for the tether that bound me to Alex. It was strong as steel again, and, encouraged, I grabbed hold of it with my magic.

The floor gave way. I free-fell into darkness, like someone had given me a hard shove off a cliff. My stomach flipped, and I shouted in surprise, but a moment later my feet were on solid ground again.

I was in a cemetery. Rain came down in sheets, the wind howling and whipping tree branches into a frenzied dance. Crosses and tombs speared from the ground in regimented rows, side by side with melancholic angels and grand mausoleums.

But I ignored all of that, even the rain lashing my face, after I spotted the man on the steps of a grave. His head was bent, elbows on his knees. A forlorn looking woman sat beside him.

Feet squelching in my boots, I approached Alex slowly. Upon reaching him, I realized that the woman next to him was only a statue, her grief immortalized in stone. The rain dripped down her face like tears.

"Alex," I shouted over the wind. "What are we doing here?"

He looked up, dark hair plastered to a face younger than the one I remembered. He was clean shaven, and missing the beginning of crow's feet around his eyes. "Who are you?" he asked. "And how do you know my name?"

I wanted to throw myself at him, to feel his lips under mine and the safe solidity of his body, and know everything was going to be okay. Instead, I knelt, mud seeping through the jeans I now wore. "I'm Seph. You don't remember me?"

His brows knit as he swiped soaked hair out of his face. "Should I? Did Councilman Eames send you?"

"No, your dad didn't send me. What are you doing out here, in this?" I looked pointedly at the puddle forming around my knees in the soggy ground.

Alex shook his head and kneaded his temple. "I fucked up."

God, I wanted to take his hand, to smooth away the sad lines furrowing his brow. "What do you mean?"

"Boone," he said. "I didn't have his back, and he's hurt. It's my fault." He squinted at me through dripping eyelashes. "Isn't that what you're here about?"

"No," I said softly. Whoever this Boone was, letting him down would've been the height of irresponsibility to Alex. An utter failure. "But I am here for you."

He stood abruptly, and I drew a surprised breath, rising with him. We were inches apart, and the smell of cedar mingled with warm rain.

"You look familiar." He raised a hand as if to touch me, then lowered it. "I'm sure we haven't met."

My heart gave a painful lurch. "We have. Many times." I took in the youthfulness of his face again. "What year is it?"

He drew back, peering down at me with confusion. "It's 2015."

Our paths wouldn't cross for six more years. "You're going to think I'm crazy." I mopped my face with an equally wet sleeve. "But I'm from your future."

His green eyes pierced me. "It does sound crazy. But stranger things have happened."

The scene shifted as I reached for him. I lost my balance and staggered, bumping into a suited man. It was dark, but the scent of freshly turned soil told me I was outdoors.

"Watch it." The man threw me an annoyed glance before walking into the sea of people surrounding us, all moving together like a school of fish.

Caught in the crowd, I let them carry me along, reminding myself to breathe through the pressure banding my chest. At least I had fresh air, the night sky studded with brilliant stars. But where was Alex? I couldn't find his tall frame amidst the black suits and dresses.

It was chilly, and the last of the dried leaves rustling on barren branches signaled late fall or early winter. I caught the rise of a hill covered in gravestones over the heads of the throng. We finally stopped at a gravesite, a rectangular hole filled with shadow. A plain casket sat beside it, ready to be lowered into the grave. Flickering spheres of light hung overhead.

I glimpsed Alex beside the casket, next to...Davina? She and her mother, Mindara, were to his left. His father was on his other side. The rest of the Aureum's governing body were there as well, and I glimpsed Yuto's face behind Councilwoman Kimura's. My stomach soured at seeing the Diurne Council assembled again.

This version of Alex was harder, the planes of his face sharper, his cheeks hollower. This was the man I'd left behind in the not so distant past.

I surged forward, hoping that this time, he might remember me. But a woman caught my arm. "What are you doing?" She pursed her painted lips. "Get into formation."

"Sorry," I mumbled, smoothing the skirt of my black mourner's dress. I followed the people ahead of me as they formed a semi-circle around the gravesite.

When everyone was in place, Mindara stood, the soft light illuminating a face devoid of feeling. "Thank you all for joining us today as we say our final goodbyes to Ernesto De Silva. He was a loyal Guardian, a good man, a cherished husband to me, and an exemplary father to our daughter."

Davina's mouth twitched and her eyes were red, but she didn't look away from the coffin.

Oh, no. Davina had never mentioned her father was dead. The grief must have been fresh, still.

Mindara cleared her throat. "Ernesto died doing what he loved.

Protecting the innocent, and helping to keep this world safe. Now that he has given his final sacrifice, we commend him to the gods. Let them watch over him in his well-deserved eternity." Her voice hitched on the last word, and she took a deep breath. "May his soul be with us. May his hand guide us. May his sacrifice strengthen us."

The other Guardians murmured those last words, their combined voices a musical hum. Mindara swept her hand, and the casket lowered into the ground. The circle of Guardians began to move, each person stopping by the grave and throwing something inside—a flower, a coin, fragrant herbs.

When it was my turn, I ducked my head, letting hair curtain my face. I plucked the tiger's eye pendant from where it nestled in the hollow of my throat, dropping it from my outstretched hand before moving on. Maybe it would be good luck for Davina's father, wherever he was. It had served me well, and I felt in my bones that it was time to pass it on.

The Diurne went next, Mindara and Davina last. The mother and daughter held hands in a rare show of affection. Davina's tears dripped into the grave, then she pulled back, wiping her face with her sleeve.

Flames shot high out of the grave. I flinched, treading on the toes of the person behind me. The fire burned orange, then white, then brightest blue. And almost as suddenly as it began, it was gone. The sudden darkness revealed a filled grave smoothed over with grass, set with a headstone displaying Ernesto's name. It was embossed with a golden lily.

The crowd dispersed, people forming smaller groups as quiet conversation spilled over the graveyard. I waited for Alex in the shadows. He took Davina's hand, squeezing and giving her a solemn nod, before heading off into the cemetery. I followed him at a distance. When we were far enough away from the others, I called out.

"Alex."

He turned, his gaze settling on my shadowy form as I closed in on him.

"Can I help you?" His tone held polite disinterest for the stranger disrupting his grief.

My heart gave another painful bump. "Yes, actually."

The corner of his mouth pulled down, dimple flashing. "If you want to pass on a message to the councilman, you can leave it with his administrator. This isn't exactly a good time."

"The message isn't for your father. It's for you."

He waited for a beat, then folded his arms. "Well?"

"I'm Seph. Persephone Hart. And I'm in love with you."

"I'm sorry?" Alex shook his head. "I don't even know you. You're confusing me with someone else. Look, this isn't appropriate—"

I put a hand on his arm, and he stilled under my touch. I waited to speak until the corona of gold in his eyes flashed. "I'm not confused. I've traveled the worlds to find you. To save you. And now it's finally time, and we need to go."

His eyes narrowed, and his dimple deepened. But he didn't leave. "Traveled the worlds? Impossible."

My breath came faster. If I didn't slow down, I would hyperventilate. Why wasn't this working? How the hell did I get us out of here? He turned to walk away.

"Wait! I need you!" My words rang out too harshly, too loud in the silence.

Alex, who would never turn down someone in need, paused. When his eyes met mine, I rushed toward him, throwing my arms around strong shoulders and pulling him to me until our lips crashed together.

His mouth was hard, unyielding. But after a second he softened, kissing me back, tentatively at first, then stronger. I lost myself in him, sighing with relief. In a few seconds we'd be back in Magoth's world, he'd be awake, and I'd rescue him at long last. True love's kiss to break the spell.

But when I opened my eyes, freezing air and a rust-red sky greeted me. Alex was gone.

I whipped around in a circle, looking for him. No. No. This couldn't be happening.

Lightning cracked across the sky, and sulfur fouled the air. A yell sounded over my shoulder, and I turned to see three people standing on a sheer cliff at the edge of a boiling lake.

It was my nightmare. My reality. The moment I'd relived a thousand times, the heart-rending pain of it all slicing straight through me. But I didn't have time for pain, because this was the moment. Alex and I were about to enter the gateway that Simon anchored. In a second,

Magoth's serpent's tale would coil around Alex and drag him into the pit.

I sprinted toward us, watching my arm disappear as I leaned into the gateway. Fuck, fuck, I wouldn't make it in time. I would have to see the look on Alex's face again as he fell. And this time, maybe it would be for good.

My back spasmed, and I lurched forward, almost taking a nosedive before righting myself.

The black, leathery wings that appeared over my shoulders were about to topple me.

Instinctively, I flapped, muscles burning from spine to wingtip. I was awkward and ungainly, but I landed in front of myself, Alex, and Simon just as the spiny tail snaked around Alex's ankle and yanked him backward.

Time slowed for a moment as I observed the three of us in our horrific tableau. My face was a mask of dread, mouth open and ready to shout. Simon was pale and otherworldly, the center of a dark, swirling mass.

And Alex's eyes were full of an acceptance that made me want to tear everything to shreds, to burn the world down until it was a ruined husk, a colossus of ashes in its wake.

"No!" I screamed it, the word carving the moment into a before and after. Sprinting toward the edge of the pit, I grabbed Alex.

His expression turned to confusion as his eyes floated over my shoulder, to the other me who stood frozen. "Seph? How—"

I pulled, throwing all my strength into it, as I laid a blazing trail of fire across the cliff's edge, right over the reptilian tail. It recoiled, releasing Alex, and we stumbled away from the pit.

Alex looked down at his freed ankle, then back at me. "What's happening? How are you here, and there?"

"Alex," I said, urgency lacing my tone. "I'm going to save you this time. It always should've been me."

His eyes widened as understanding dawned. "Seph, no!"

I turned away from him and ran for the edge of the cliff, diving into darkness.

39

"Seph! Come on, you, wake up."

I blinked my eyes open to Simon hovering over me, mouth drawn in a grimace. "That's a girl. Oh, thank Asael," he said, sighing and slumping back.

"I'm okay," I croaked. "How long was I out for?"

"'Bout thirty seconds," Simon said. "You just dropped like a stone. What happened?"

I used the bed frame to help me stand. But my knees went weak again as Alex sat up. He looked around the room with drawn brows, gaze landing on the three women huddled in a protective circle.

Then, our eyes met.

A shock ran through me like I'd grabbed a live wire. It was a jolt of recognition, of bone-deep connection that stole my breath. *There you are, and here I am. Just like it was always meant to be. And always will be.*

For I was certain that if Alex had died, my soul would've followed his to the ends of eternity.

I bounded on top of the bed, and he opened for me, crushing me to the miracle of his chest as I wrapped around him. This was real. It was everything I'd been missing for so long. He was warm, and solid, and safe. He was mine.

"Hate to break up the lovefest, but we should go," Simon inter-jected, a strained note in his voice.

I pulled back, searching every inch of Alex's beautiful face—his cupid's bow and stubbled jaw and fine-boned nose. "Are you okay? Can you walk?"

He nodded, staring at me like I was a cool glass of water and he was dying of thirst. "How—" His voice cracked, and he cleared his throat. "Why did you come for me?"

A heavy beat of silence passed. I cupped his cheek, and his jaw flexed beneath my palm. "Because nothing in this world or any other could stop me."

His expression tightened, and then his pupils blew wide, turning his eyes almost black. Something inscrutable flashed behind them before he lowered his gaze.

"Enough chit chat," Seraphyna barked. "Let's get on with it."

I wanted to smile at how like her sister she was. But Alex had me worried, the way he would no longer look at me. He swung his legs over the edge of the bed and staggered. Simon caught him, and they traded an indecipherable glance.

"I'm fine," Alex said, pulling away from Simon and scrubbing his face hard. "Do you have a plan?"

"Get to the throne room, go through the seam, and run like hell," I told him.

He nodded, his expression wiped clean and blank. He was trans-forming into a soldier again. "Lead the way."

Our merry band took off down the halls and descended flights of stairs, prioritizing speed over stealth. The ring of our footsteps slapping against slick marble floors announced our arrival to whatever might be lurking around the corners. Simon began to lag behind, so I took his hand and yanked him along beside me.

Alex was the first to arrive at a fork with three blank, identical hall-ways branching off to the left, right, and center.

"Which way?" he said.

We all looked at each other.

"Go s-separate?" Calista asked, her lip quivering despite the forceful-ness of her words.

"No," Seraphyna answered sharply. "We stick together." Then, she turned to Bronagh. "Darling, can you try?"

Bronagh tugged on a scraggly curl, her dark eyes full of fear. But she nodded and closed them, holding her temples as she bowed her head.

"What's she doing?" Simon muttered.

No one had a chance to answer, because we all doubled over at the same time. Something was wrong, terribly wrong. Dread rose, cold and slimy in my belly, and along with it came a cramping pain. Then a sulfurous wind swept over us, and a demon appeared in the crossroads. It materialized from ashen smoke into the form of a massive tiger, its fur shining in silver stripes and glinting like the strands were made of metal. The demon growled and sank into a crouch, exposing long fangs and claws like razors.

I gathered my magic close. Spheres of blue light appeared in each of Alex's hands, and he spread them wide. Seraphyna hissed, her own fangs elongating. Bronagh's eyes flew open, and she whimpered.

But Calista...Calista's skin rippled, and on a roar, the meek woman transformed into a great, brown bear.

Simon shouted a surprised curse as Calista charged the demon tiger, swiping a paw the size of my head. It connected with the demon's chest, and the creature careened back into the wall. Its jaws opened and, on a snarl, ejected a geyser of silver flames.

Even as he was throwing himself to the floor, Alex shot a hand out toward Bronagh and Seraphyna. Both dropped, missing the flames by inches. I'd done the same to Simon, feeling the heat race just overhead.

"Calista!" Seraphyna cried, but she needn't have worried. Calista's grizzly form seemed to absorb the flames, leaving her completely unharmed.

The demon leapt on her, locking its jaws around her throat. She shoved it back with a blast, but it bowled over into Alex. He crouched, then lifted his arms at the last second, using the demon's momentum so that it flipped over him. It sailed through the air, then landed on all fours behind our group. Directly in front of Simon.

And when it loosed an arc of shining flame, he was powerless to stop it.

"No!" I screamed, my magic racing out and dragging Simon away, but not soon enough. Fire engulfed his right arm from elbow to wrist, and the nauseating scent of searing flesh filled the hall. I shot a jet of blue flames at the demon to hold it off while Simon collapsed in my arms. I doused the blaze that ate up his shirtsleeve with my magic. Touching the silver fire felt like battering at impenetrable rock.

The demon tiger crouched, ready to spring on us. I caught Alex's blurred shape from the corner of my eye, but Bronagh stepped in the silver demon's path, as small as a mouse before a lion.

"Cover your ears!" Seraphyna yelled, and I did, shoving threads of power into mine and Simon's as Bronagh opened her mouth and released a scream.

The wail would have burst my eardrums had they been exposed. It reverberated off the walls, and a split appeared in the marble, the crack zigzagging like a fork of lightning. Dust rose from breaking plaster, and the whole world seemed to reverberate. A crystal chandelier shattered, glass raining down on our heads.

The demon tiger collapsed into a gargantuan heap, then went translucent and disappeared. Bronagh stopped shrieking, and we all tentatively removed our hands. I retracted the threads that I'd stuffed inside Simon's ears like cotton balls. He lay in my lap, staring at the ceiling, breath coming in harsh pants. I chanced a look at his burned arm, and couldn't restrain my gasp

Instead of the blistered, raw wounds I expected, his skin was smooth and gray from elbow to fingertip. His right arm rested on my leg, and I only now noticed how heavy it was. I ran a hand along the skin, but it wasn't skin.

Simon's arm had turned to stone.

"Oh, *fuck*," I whispered, rubbing the hard, cool surface with my thumb.

"Is it bad? It's bad, innit?" Simon wheezed, keeping his eyes trained on a spot above our heads. I had to focus on my breath, to not let the moment from the past when I had held his twin in the same way overlay the present.

Alex, Seraphyna, and Bronagh crowded around us. There was a popping noise, then a nude Calista joined them, her eyes widening.

"It's..." I couldn't answer. Simon's clever artist's fingers were curled, arrested mid-fist. Would they ever hold a paintbrush again?

"You'll be all right," Alex said, bending and hauling both of us up.

"We'll find a way to fix it as soon as we get out of here." Our eyes met, and I marked the unease in his.

But there was no time for worry, or questions. Simon was alive, and at least he could still run. Seraphyna and Alex each took a side and slung Simon's arms around their shoulders.

"Come on," Alex grunted, taking hold of the stone forearm. "It's now or never."

My hands shook, but I managed to keep the tremor out of my voice. "I'll lead. Bronagh, stay up here with me, and if we see any other demons, scream. Calista, bring up the rear. And maybe you should become the bear again."

Both women nodded, and Bronagh came to stand beside me, chin set. There was another popping noise, and Calista the grizzly circled to the back, padding on all fours.

I turned to Bronagh. "What were you trying to do before the demon showed up?"

Her soft voice had a musical quality. "Using the Sight to find our way to the throne room. I am Banshee."

"Do it again," I commanded, throwing a glance at Simon's pale face. His eyes were glassy with shock.

Bronagh bowed her head. She hummed a melody, quietly at first, then loud enough that it vibrated my chest. She pointed to the right. "This way."

I sprinted down the right fork, taking care not to stumble over cracks and gaps in the marble floors. Bronagh's wail had really wreaked havoc.

I wanted to scream, too, to do anything that would release the pressure building in my chest. It was joined by the drumbeat of fear, by the racing pulse of my thoughts. We would never get out of here, Magoth would catch us, we would all die—or worse. But at least it would be with Alex beside me.

The glimpse of an obsidian throne glittering darkly at the end of the hallway shoved down my terror. "It's just ahead," I called, maintaining speed. Alex and Seraphyna were hot on our heels, with Calista's heavy paws thudding just behind them.

My mind was already in the throne room, thinking about the seam, if we could even try to get the Book, if our friends would be waiting for us on the other side. My magic was about half depleted, but that needed to be enough for what I had to do next.

What I didn't account for was my father.

The hulking throne blocked him from view until I came skidding around the corner. I slapped a hand out to halt Bronagh, and the others bumped into us from behind. Calista let out an agitated snuffle.

"Dad, what are you doing here? What's going on?"

He walked around the throne to stand in front of me. His face was a ravaged mask of misery. I almost couldn't make out the slivers of green in his brown eyes because they were screwed up, tears leaking down his face. He threw a rapier at my feet, and the sharp edge sang when it hit the ground.

"What is this?" I said slowly, tracing the sword's bejeweled knuckle guard with my gaze as a sinking sensation filled my gut.

"Your weapon, my love."

It took a moment for realization to strike, but his irises were already taking on a red cast. "No," I pleaded. "Dad."

"Magoth has me under orders to summon him if you try to escape. And that I must stop you." He drew a harsh breath under lengthening canines. "If I cannot help you.... You must kill me. Please."

"No!" I cried again, like that word had the power to save him. But it wasn't magic, only the broken-hearted bid of a daughter who never got to know her father.

"You'll be all right, darling. I—I'm so proud of you. I love you." My father's back arched, and his spine popped. "Hurry," he said on a pained breath.

Calista snarled, rearing to stand on her hind legs. No. No, no, no, this couldn't be happening. I backed away, herding Bronagh with me. But I picked up the sword, gripping the pommel hard.

"Seph," Simon croaked. I hardened my heart against the entreaty in his voice.

Shoving Bronagh back, I felt for Alex's hand. When I found it, I squeezed. "Get the others through the seam. I'll hold him off."

With a final crack of a canine jaw, the transformation was complete. My father was again the black-furred beast that reeked of sulfur. A hell-hound, prepared to do his master's bidding, no matter how much the man trapped inside wanted to save his daughter.

Lips drew away from a slavering mouth, and the hellhound threw its head back and released a heart-wrenching howl. I knew it was a final call of grief. A plea I couldn't ignore.

Hefting the rapier's weight, I charged.

The hellhound roared, meeting my attack. Its fangs, as long as my forefinger, snapped over thin air where my shoulder had been a second before I dodged. I rolled, dancing out of range as it clawed at me. God, but it was huge, and fast, its lumbering form moving from here to there in the blink of an eye. I threw magic behind my movements, my threads adding springs to my feet.

I advanced, slashing out with the double-edged blade and catching the beast on its side. The hand guard was awkward, impeding my wrist movement, so my follow-through was too slow. The hellhound's tail whipped around and slapped the blade tip into the ground. It slipped from my grasp. I caught a glimpse of Alex pounding on the wall across from the throne where the seam should have been. They needed more time.

Leaving the sword, I let fire arc across my skin. Maybe the hellhound would be more hesitant to attack if its meal was being flambéed. But the beast didn't seem deterred, because it bunched back on its haunches and jumped. I ducked behind the vast throne at the last second, and it lost traction, sliding across the marble floors and hitting the wall with a resounding crash.

"What's going on?" I yelled, chancing a look at the others. They were still huddled around the seam.

Simon used his good arm to feverishly press against the wall. "I think the Book is holding it shut!"

The beast loosed a guttural snarl. I lurched around the throne, and dove for the sword. If I could only injure it, then maybe we could all get out relatively unscathed. My fingers closed around the hilt and I sprang, flipping over the hellhound.

But either I misjudged the landing, or the beast predicted where I was aiming, because I crashed straight into it. Wiry fur bit into my cheek, and I rolled off the hound's back, hitting the ground with a hard thud that knocked the air from me. In an instant, claws raked over my chest, and I shouted at the blaze of pain. The creature opened its jaws, and the scent of sulfur grew overpowering.

No. I wouldn't die like this. The others weren't out yet.

Hefting the sword with burning muscles, I struck the beast's ribs. I only managed a shallow swipe, but it yowled and flinched. I rolled, taking the blade in a two-handed grip and stabbing its shoulder.

"Got it!" Alex yelled. "Get ready, Seph!"

As if the hellhound understood that we were all about to escape, it galloped across the throne room toward the others.

Simon was half-in, half-out of the wall, good arm outstretched as if he held a curtain open. A wide, bloody streak marred the marble, a matching stain on Seraphyna's sleeve. Alex thrust his hands out. The hellhound flew backward, slamming into a statue. Then it slid to the ground, body limp and motionless.

I sagged, but didn't drop the blade. My head swam, and my lungs felt like they'd been shredded with razor blades. Yet, a strange sort of elation floated through my chest. Breath heaving, I crossed the room to join Simon and Alex. They must have sent the women through already.

When I passed the hellhound laying heaped at the foot of the statue, I glanced down at its unmoving form. I was beyond relieved that it— that my father—had survived.

Then, it snorted. A singular, red eye blinked open.

It was as if the beast's form turned to smoke. It gained its feet and lunged, going for my throat. Shock glued me to the spot as time slowed. But I was no statue frozen in marble.

Gripping the hilt with both hands, I stabbed—and watched the tip of the sword disappear into the hellhound's shaggy throat. I shoved, my warrior's training taking over, until it was buried to the hilt.

The beast dropped to the ground. And lay still.

40

I couldn't hear anything clearly through the blood beating in my ears—not the hellhound's death cry, or Simon's shout, or Alex calling my name. But I felt everything. Horror. Pain. Guilt. Rage. Somehow I ended up on the ground, hot tears slipping down my face as the beast's fur shrunk back into its body and the fangs retracted. After another moment, my father's body lay before me, my sword piercing his throat.

Sound flooded in all at once, and the keening wail I released rivaled Bronagh's. I choked on sobs, gulping and hiccuping and screaming, throwing myself on my father's body. He was warm, and it almost seemed like he could have been in a deep sleep. But no matter how I shook him, or how many times I shouted his name, he wouldn't wake up.

I killed my father.

Strong arms came around me and pulled me to my feet.

"No!" I sobbed, trying to break free. I didn't want this. I didn't want *any* of it, if this was the cost. "What did I do? WHAT DID I DO?"

"Seph, I'm sorry," Alex said in my ear, dragging me toward the seam where Simon still stood, shock on his face. "We have to go. I'm sorry, I'm sorry," he repeated, his restraining arms tight around my waist.

He was right. People were waiting for us. Depending on us. I stopped fighting him, though there was no fighting the agony flowing through me as surely as my own blood. But there would be time enough later, where I could fall apart so thoroughly I knew I'd never be the same again.

The ground quaked, and I stumbled, catching Alex for balance. Simon was ejected from the seam like he'd been shot from a cannon, his groan of pain ricocheting through the room while he slid along the ground. Alex spun, shoving me behind him.

Magoth reclined on his throne, resting his head back against the twisted metal. His horned crown sat at an angle, and he reached up to straighten it before dusting his hands off and rising. "When the cat is away, the mice will play. That is the saying, isn't it?"

Heart plummeting, I felt for Alex's hand and began backing toward the seam. He gripped me tightly, his bones like iron beneath the skin. My nightmare couldn't be happening all over again. I wouldn't let it.

"Oh, it's too late to retreat now. Playtime's over."

Magoth snapped his fingers, and ropes appeared from thin air and bound my wrists behind my back. My feet began to move toward the center of the throne room of their own accord. I fought the ropes, stabbing pain shooting through my arms. Alex and Simon were similarly restrained and marching beside me, both struggling against their bonds.

The three of us halted in a line before the demon prince—errant children brought to the principal's office. Alex's jaw was set, the corona of gold in his eyes flashing like they were on fire. Simon had a similarly resolute look. They were both much stronger than me.

Magoth tutted, pacing the length of us. "I'm not angry, but I am disappointed. I give you a little trust, and you try to escape as soon as I turn my back? And freeing the other Lightbringers...I thought you cared for these mortals, dear Persephone. It seems I was mistaken."

I shut my eyes and reached for the magic inside me. It was there, frothing beneath my skin. Burning slightly, just like the new tattoo of a coiled serpent that had been inked onto the base of my neck a couple hours ago. The artifact of my most recent bargain.

"Do you think you can just close your eyes and this will all disappear?" Magoth mocked. "It won't. In fact, we're back where we started. Just the three of us. But you know what they say." His lips stretched wide, revealing pointed teeth. "Three's a crowd. Why don't we eliminate one of you gentlemen? I think we'll all be much more comfortable that way. Persephone, darling, you do the honors."

Hearing my father's endearment for me on this demon's lips sent a flash of fury through me. I released a harsh breath, and stopped pinching the fabric of my skirt. "What?"

"It's simple enough for even you to understand. One of them dies, and one of them lives."

Simon spat at Magoth's feet. "Go fuck yourself with a sharp stick."

The demon stroked his chin. "You know, I don't think I will. But that may be a diverting exercise for you."

Alex bucked against his restraints, and a flare of white light blasted from him, ricocheting around the room before dissipating. He gritted his teeth, straining against some force.

"I was wondering when you'd try that," Magoth drawled. "Mister White Knight." The demon gave Alex a private smile that held a look of amusement. Like they had an inside joke, a secret only they shared. My stomach turned.

"Your bonds prevent you from directing your power, so you can take a shot, but you'll likely miss." Magoth stopped his pacing and dragged his gaze up my bared legs, over my torn, gaping bodice, and landed on my face. "So, which will you choose to spare? Your friend, or your lover?"

My fingers finally found the salt cellar that was still stashed in my pocket. I parted my lips, wetting them before I spoke. "I choose...." I looked back and forth between Alex and Simon, standing on either side of me. Simon's lip curled in defiance. Alex seemed...vacant. Almost lifeless, if I hadn't seen the rise and fall of his chest. I didn't know where he'd gone all of a sudden, what horrors he might be reliving.

"What was that?" Magoth prompted, cupping his ear. "Speak up, little witch."

Using my thumb, I unscrewed the top of the salt cellar. The crystal cut into my palm, and my shoulders ached from the awkward angle at which I was bound. "I choose both."

The minute the demon bared his teeth, jutting his face into mine, I spun around and hurled the salt at him. He cried out in rage, clawing at his eyes as he staggered backward. I shoved my shoulder into Alex and Simon, forcing them toward the seam.

"Get out of here!" I yelled, then sent fire racing down the ropes that bound me. Magoth was right—wielding the magic was like trying to drive while blindfolded. My skin burned and blistered, but the ropes fell away.

Magoth charged toward us, hands raised. His eyes were clear, but angry red spots dotted his face where the salt burned him. A pair of ragged wings sprouted from his back. When he flapped them, a jet of flame shot forward and threatened to engulf us.

I doused the fire with my threads, but they burned, too, the pain resonating through my chest. Then, faster than I'd ever done in practice, I wove a protective shield between us. It was weak, but better than nothing.

Alex rammed into me, back first. He shoved the sword that had been embedded in my father's throat into my hands. "Cut me loose," he commanded.

I did, ignoring the congealed blood on the keen-edged blade, and thrust the sword back into his freed hands. "Take care of Simon's."

My sloppy shield was already growing thin in places. On the other side of it, the whites of Magoth's eyes had turned wholly black as he snarled and roared. His magic punched a fist-sized hole in the shield. As if he'd shoved a massive vacuum hose through the breach, we were all suctioned toward it.

Alex cupped his hands, and darkness fled from the corners of the room to plug the hole. We stopped moving, teetering as the force we fought against vanished. He turned his head to me, keeping the rest of his body immobile. Cords of muscle bulged around his neck, and his eyes...why did they look so dark?

"Run!" Alex's voice was desperate, pleading. I shuddered as Magoth renewed his attack, agony slicing through my gut. Everywhere he touched the shield lit up a corresponding network of pain in my body. Clutching my middle, I shook my head.

"No. You take Simon and go," I wheezed.

"I'm not a bloody invalid!" Simon yelled, although his stone arm dangled limply at his side. "We all go together!"

Something slammed into the shield, too much for me to hold, and I spilled to the ground. My black and gold threads unraveled, then vanished. My magic was so low, the rivers depleting rapidly. It was almost time to act, but I needed Alex and Simon to get out first.

A great crack rang through the air as the marble statues lining the throne room leapt from their pedestals as one. Winged beasts and monsters with hunched backs and long claws circled, trapping us.

"You are almost not worth the trouble," Magoth boomed, pointing an accusatory finger at me. Then he swung it toward Simon. I couldn't see what the demon unleashed on him, but Simon ducked, shielding his face. He recoiled, then there was a deep, gong-like boom as a dark, filmy shadow rebounded off Simon's stone arm and hurtled toward Magoth. The shadow almost slammed into the demon, but he swept it aside at the last second. It hit one of the animated statues, and chips of pale marble exploded into the air. Shrapnel flew through the room, pock-marking the other statues and slicing at us. One of the statues behind us cracked and crumbled, creating a gap in the line.

With a heavy groan, I lifted a chunk of marble and launched it at Magoth. He laughed before batting it away. Alex, catching on, gathered more shrapnel and sent it flying in a rapid assault. Simon darted around, kicking larger chunks toward us to use as ammunition.

"This won't keep him busy for long," Alex grunted, hurling a slab. Then he glanced sideways, and his mouth tightened. "Behind you."

I turned to see the line of statues marching toward us in jerky, rigid movements. "Oh, fuck."

We were outnumbered and outgunned. Magoth was just playing with us now, not even trying because he knew he was going to win. As soon as we tired, he'd finish us off.

I lowered my voice to barely a whisper. "Alex, I need you to promise me something." I turned so we were back-to-back, and I prepared to take on the marble monsters while he attacked Magoth. Simon lingered next to us, eyes flicking across the line of statues, arm raised in a defensive position.

"Seph—" Alex's voice was tight, and held a note of something foreign. Defeat.

My chest tightened, but I breathed through it. One of the statues got too close, and I sent a lightning bolt to its chest. It shattered, pieces skidding across the floor and clanging off the walls, adding to the din.

"Do this one thing for me. Please."

His back flexed against mine, and I wanted nothing more than to sag against him. But I straightened my spine and shot another bolt of electricity, breaking the wing off a gargoyle with goat's horns.

"Fine," he gritted out. He probably thought it wouldn't matter anyway—because we'd all be dead or imprisoned forever.

"Protect Simon. Get out of here, and don't look back."

"I'm not leaving you." His voice cracked. "Not again."

"You have to. Because I can end this, but it has to just be me and Magoth. Only us."

Lightning cracked and marble crashed, all overlaid by the demon's crazed laughter. "Promise me, Alex," I urged.

His hand closed around mine, holding on. I wished I could freeze time. I'd just gotten Alex back, and now I didn't know when I'd see him again. If I ever would.

Love burned brighter than the immense sadness welling in my chest. I would do this for both of them. There was no world I'd want to live in if Alex and Simon ceased to exist.

Then, Alex spoke in a grating whisper. "I promise."

Time slowed. I breathed in. And on a breath out, I became darkness.

Black wings jutted from between my shoulder blades, the leathery skin growing and stretching painfully until they unfurled to their full breadth. My skin turned silvery and glowed with the rush of power that flooded me in an unchecked torrent. Black markings that forked like lightning raced across my arms as if spilled from an ink vial, and my fingernails lengthened into points. Fangs jutted over my bottom lip, the sharp points pricking the skin and drawing a bead of blood. My tongue flicked out, tasting iron and salt.

Stabbing pain in my skull signaled the transformation was complete. I reached a hand up to feel the slick bone of horns that protruded from my scalp.

Alex's eyes were wide with shock, his mouth drawn back in a horrified grimace at the monster I'd become. It made it easier, seeing him repulsed by me.

Already I felt wrongness encroaching my mind, twisting my thoughts. Urging me to kill, to burn, to destroy until the floor was slicked with blood and I stood amidst a pile of smoking rubble.

But not yet.

Simon's alarmed yelp drew my gaze. He struggled against Alex's grip, trying to reach me, shaking his head like he couldn't believe what he was seeing. I met each of their eyes, Simon's, then Alex's, and smiled gently.

"I love you."

Then I cast my stolen power out, shadows shooting from me in a diaphanous wave, and shoved both men through the seam. They sank into the wall and disappeared from sight.

Whirling back around to face Magoth, I struck out with a lightning storm. The air flashed scarlet, and every single statue shattered as a dozen loud cracks rent the air gone rife with ozone. Thunder followed, shaking the throne room.

Magoth was speechless, his black, red-ringed eyes narrowing. "How—"

The smile that spread across my face was in no hurry. "I made a deal."

Because the demon's bind prevented Beelzebub from telling me how to destroy Magoth, I'd had to guess how best to fight him. I didn't know the extent of my Lightbringer magic, let alone how to use the power to kill an immortal.

When I realized I'd never be able to outsmart Magoth—to best him at his own game—the answer had come to me.

If I couldn't beat him, I had to join him.

Beelzebub had granted me a single hour as part of our bargain. A single hour in which I didn't just have the power of demons—I became one.

"Are you certain?" he'd asked, midnight brows arched. "That kind of power can drive a mortal mad."

"I can handle it," I'd replied. And I would. I was betting on myself this time. I was strong enough.

The best part of it was that the demon's bind didn't apply to me because I was a Siphon. Or rather, all Lightbringers had the ability to Siphon. Calista had confirmed that when she absorbed the demon tiger's silver flames.

I'd been using demon magic against them all this time, ever since I'd first siphoned from the bone demons in the world with two moons.

Constance had given me the answer months ago. *Magic isn't an exact science, dear. It's ancient and persnickety, and just when you think you've figured it out, it goes and changes all the rules on you, because it doesn't have rules.*

Magic didn't have rules, because people—creatures—were the ones who imposed them. Magic didn't have will, or logic, or intent. It was a force unto itself, beyond law and order until it was bent to the user's purpose.

I'd been bending magic to my purpose all along and hadn't even known it.

"With whom did you bargain?" Magoth spat, frothing with rage.

I tapped a spiked fingernail to my lips, pretending to think. "I don't kiss and tell."

Magoth drew his lips back in a snarl, and his skin took on a raw, reddish hue. His eyes became the yellowed slits of a snake's. "We will find another Lightbringer. You are dead," he roared, his voice taking on a double timbre.

Ice crept into my heart, and malevolence stirred beneath my ribs, its sharp claws raking me in sweetest agony. Baring my teeth, I gave Magoth a wicked smile. It was finally time to heed his words.

I embraced my nature. I chose darkness.

EPILOGUE
ALEX

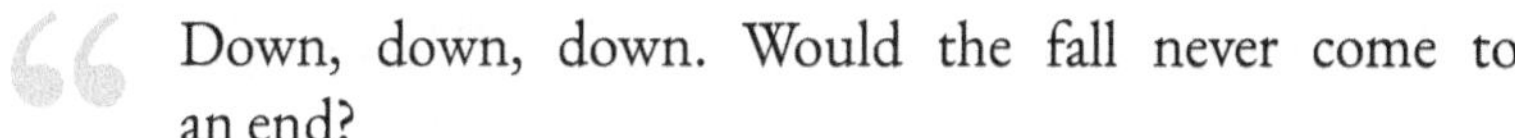

> Down, down, down. Would the fall never come to an end?
>
> — LEWIS CARROLL, *ALICE IN WONDERLAND*

She was gone.

Or we were, falling through the seam as Simon's stone elbow battered my ribs. I locked my arms tighter around him, stopping the worst of the blows.

Thoughts of Seph buffeted me just as Simon did. The way she'd transformed, beautiful and terrible all at once, with those great, sweeping black wings. Her eyes, that staggering brown streaked with forest green, were now blood-red and full of venom. And yet, it had been a look of love she'd given before her power shoved us through the darkness of the seam.

Wind whistled in my ears, then we landed, rolling on hard ground. The room was stone, walls and floors, with mounted torches throwing shadows. I groaned as I came to a stop. My body clearly wasn't used to being active, and protested at every turn. But still, I jumped into a ready position, sweeping the empty room for threats.

Simon was up and yelling at me. His eyes were hot with anger, but also fear. I recognized the look, because I felt it, too. We were both terrified for Seph, but I had to honor her wishes. I wouldn't allow Simon to return to that hellscape.

"What the fuck?" he spluttered, fist clenched. "Why did you do that? Why did you hold me back?"

I wanted to shut my eyes against his accusatory look, but I smoothed my face. He wouldn't see my anger, or my fear, or my shame. No one could. "She asked me to, Simon. I trust her."

"She's alone with a bloody evil demon!" he shouted, spittle flying from his mouth.

One of the torches flickered out, and it reminded me of Seph. Of that night at my house in Gravesville, when I goaded her into snapping and she shattered the lights with her power. She was so mad, so out of control—she was everything I fought to hide from the world. That was the first moment she'd made me want to throw away my restraint. To break the rules with her, and to hell with the consequences.

"If Seph said she had a plan, then she does." I owed it to her to listen, despite my instincts screaming at me to go back and protect her. My jaw tightened as I fought the urge.

"Fuck you," Simon spat, then lunged for a book that was laying atop a stone pedestal in the middle of the room.

Ice erupted from the center of my chest, stopping my heart. I couldn't breathe, couldn't do anything but stare at the unassuming, leather-bound tome. It was the same. I'd never be able to forget it as long as I lived.

Simon grasped it, his eyes shut tight as he mouthed silent words.

A surge of fury thawed the ice, loosening my tongue. "What are you doing with that?" I snarled. I almost didn't recognize my own voice.

Simon's eyes flew open, their gray like a lashing, angry storm. "Trying to get back there! But of course, this gods-damned thing won't work when I need it to. You like to play games, eh? Fine." Simon removed the book from its pedestal, tucking it under his uninjured arm. I took an involuntary step back.

A hatch opened in the ceiling. We traded a glance, then I walked beneath it and peered upward. A starlit sky shone down on me. "Wait here," I ordered, then crouched and jumped, catching the lip of the opening before hauling myself over. Fatigue clamped down on my muscles. They'd atrophied—not as much as I would've expected, being in a magically-induced trance for Iznir knew how long, but enough so that I felt my weakest since adolescence.

I was on top of a circular roof made of a white, ridged stone that glowed from within. After giving the space a cursory glance and finding no immediate threats, I walked to the edge and looked out on the landscape of barren, rocky crags. Ruins lay some way off in the distance. Then I heard voices, everything inside me going taut as I peered downward.

A group of women and a dog stood at the base of the tower. They were arguing. I recognized two heads with long, dark hair, and quiet elation flooded me. Davina and Fern. My unit, even though one of them had betrayed us. But where were Hollis, and Casey, and the twins?

Ducking down into the hole, I lowered a hand to Simon. "Come on. It's the way out."

Glaring daggers, Simon tossed me the book. I reflexively caught it one-handed, then dropped it instantly to the pearly stone as if I'd been burned. For a moment it had felt like that, as the power emanating from the Book of Shadows pulsed angrily.

I reached back down for Simon. He shoved out of my grip as soon as I'd dragged him over the lip of the hatch. I didn't mind his hatred. It barely registered among the fucked-up place that was my head, and anyway—I deserved it.

"Oy! We're back!" he called down to the others, the Book clutched in his good hand.

Fern, Davina, the dog, the three we'd rescued, and two strangers, one with red hair, and one with blue, stared up at us, wide-mouthed in shock. Simon was already descending the staircase that wrapped around the outside of the tower in a spiral. I followed him, my chest heavy and aching with the connection that bound me to Seph.

Even though she was in another world, it felt like I was walking away from her all over again. *She has to be okay*, I thought. *She will be okay.* But my gut didn't entirely agree with that statement.

Simon reached the bottom of the stairs and darted toward the group, words tumbling from his mouth. Davina had peeled off and rushed up to meet me, tears streaming down her face.

"You're alive, oh, my god," she babbled, flinging her arms around me in a crushing embrace. "Oh, thank the goddess. Alex, I thought...."

I shushed her, rubbing her back. "I'm fine," I murmured. "It's okay." Empty words, of course. Nothing was remotely close to okay, but that was my job. To put on a brave face and pretend everything would be all right, no matter how fucked it all was.

"What happened?" she asked, wiping her eyes. "Where's Seph?"

My throat closed. I shook my head, then cleared it. "She's still in Magoth's world."

"What?" Davina exclaimed. "Is she...."

"She's alive," I answered. *For now,* a dark voice in my head reminded me. *You should go back and rip Magoth's throat out.*

Davina's shoulders dropped. Her mouth opened again, but Simon's angry shout cut across her.

"We need to get back to the Weald Fae, *now.* Seph doesn't have time for us to sit around, blathering on while she's fighting that thing."

"What happened to your arm?" a deep, growly voice said. I looked around for the speaker. The dog, a black and tan hound with long, floppy ears, stared back at me.

"Never mind that," Simon said, waving in the hound's direction as he paced with the Book.

I finished descending the stairs, Davina still clinging to me. I extricated myself from her and approached the others. Someone had thought to give the bear shifter a coat to cover her nakedness. And why Fern was among them, I had no clue, but that was a problem for later.

"You got the Book," the blue-haired woman said, observing Simon marching around with it. "But aren't we going back for Seph?" She had black wings peeking above her shoulders.

I shook my head, compartmentalizing that for later, too. "She sent us on so that she could deal with Magoth, alone. She has a plan."

"I'm not leaving that to chance, then, am I?" Simon interjected. "I need my things—herbs, and such."

Fern finally spoke. "Why?" She looked at everyone but me.

Simon set his jaw. "Because there's one sure way to get Seph out of there. I'm going to summon her."

"Summon her?" Davina echoed, looking between me and Simon. "But that would mean...."

"That Seph is a demon, yes," Simon replied, already looking past her toward the ruins in the distance. Images of the black veins that had spread across Seph's burnished skin, so like the black threads of her magic, flashed across my mind. I released an involuntary breath.

Shocked silence settled over the group, and the dog whined low in his throat.

"Is that—do we think that's permanent?" Fern asked haltingly.

"Dunno," Simon said. Then, he turned to the blue-haired woman. "Indigo, can you open a portal here?"

Indigo swallowed, then nodded, gesturing to the roof. Simon turned and darted back up the stairs, not waiting for the rest of us to follow.

"Perhaps someone should stay here," one of the red-haired women said in deeply accented English. "In case we need to go after Seph." She'd been watching me curiously during this whole exchange. Her fiery hair, along with her sharp cheekbones, matched the other redhead. That, and skin so pale it seemed bloodless. Seeing them side by side, they had to be sisters.

"I'll do it," I volunteered. It would be nothing short of a miracle to be alone right now. After so long with being stuck in my head, absorbed by my own thoughts—by the worst moments of my life—the commotion was too much for me. Adrenaline still raced through my bloodstream, staving off the worst of the memories. But I knew they'd come flooding back in soon, and when they did, I didn't want any witnesses.

The redhead nodded slowly, her unnerving hazel gaze still locked on me. Then she and her sister raced for the stairs as well, blurring with speed. How had this motley crew of supernaturals come together? Almost as soon as I had the thought, I knew. Seph, of course. She couldn't see it, but she was a born leader. People would follow her anywhere.

"But how will you get back?" Davina asked. "We don't even know if there's a graveyard here. And you don't—"

I silenced her with a look. "I'll be fine, Davina. I can figure something out."

Simon's voice, heightened in irritation, cut through the night. "Hurry up, you lot. I don't give a damn if he wants to laze about here."

"I'll come back for you after Simon tries to summon her," Indigo assured me.

I nodded in her direction. My ears were starting to buzz, muffling their voices. "That works."

"I'll stay, too," Davina offered. Her generous mouth was set in a resolute line. She was loyal to a fault. But I didn't want her allegiance right now. I didn't deserve it.

"Go. You're wasting time," I said. When she didn't budge, I put immovable stone into my next words. "That's an order."

"You don't know what you're saying. You shouldn't be alone," she said, hands fisted on her hips.

"I'm fine." I sounded cold, the words' hard edges unfamiliar to my own ears.

She placed a hand on my bicep. I stilled, staring at the spot. Hot, bitter rage flooded the back of my throat, and my muscles seized. "Don't touch me."

"Alex—"

I met her eyes. The whites showed around her brown irises. She was afraid. Good.

"I—okay," she acquiesced, withdrawing her hand. My shoulders dropped, and I released a long, silent exhale even as guilt settled over me.

When they had all assembled atop the tower, Indigo raised her hand, palm out. A dark spiral appeared out of thin air. One by one, they entered the swirling mass. Davina threw one last look at me over her shoulder, then disappeared.

Finally.

The tremor I'd been working so hard to suppress took over my hands, then a shudder ran through my whole body. It was uncontrollable, an earthquake that wanted to tear me apart and send the pieces shattering to the ground. I let it, dropping to my knees. Harsh gasps tore from my throat as the tower spun in my unsteady vision.

A memory wanted to take over. Not a nightmare from my distant past I'd been forced to relive over and over again, but one from the near present.

Magoth's imperious, mocking voice sounded in my head. He was reading from a book. The book that had been tucked beneath Simon's arm, that he'd touched so casually despite it containing such devastation.

I shut my eyes, and let the images take me under.

After Magoth dragged me into his realm, his two wraith service strung me up in chains like a pig for butchering. I was so cold, and empty. Cold because it seemed like everything had frozen in the moment I'd been taken—the look of horror on Seph's face, her hands outstretched for me, fingers closing around nothing. Empty because I knew at that moment—hoped—I'd never see Seph again. She'd escaped with her life, and would move on without me. But I was happy for the same reasons. I knew wherever she ended up, Simon wouldn't abandon her. And I was grateful for that. I'd have taken her place again, and again, and again, if it meant she was safe.

She wasn't just the person I'd fallen in love with. She was everything. The one it felt like I'd been waiting for my whole life, who saw me, accepted me. Loved me, without conditions or limitations. Once a person earned Seph's heart, she gave it all. I'd had it for one brief, shining moment, and it had been the best of my existence.

As I swung on the chains, Magoth approached, his face twisted in a snarl. He was back in human form, but his black hair was mussed and ash stained his collar

"You think you've won this round, graveborn scum?" His voice had gone dangerously soft, and held such a terrible rage it quivered. "When the little witch comes for you—and she will come—she won't be able to stand the sight of you. Her favorite toy will be broken. Defiled. Corrupted." He closed in until our faces were mere inches apart, his sulfurous breath washing over me. "You just wait until I'm finished with you."

"Go ahead," I taunted, voice taut. "Do your worst."

Suddenly, a book appeared in the demon's hands. There was writhing, restless energy coming from its bound covers, like whatever was between those pages wanted to escape. Like it wanted to be anywhere but here. I could sympathize.

"Do you know what this is, Mister White Knight?" Magoth asked, the corners of his lips pulling into a chilly smile.

I didn't answer, just stared him down and refused to give an inch.

That's what my father had taught me—never let them see you sweat. Control was strength. Chaos was weakness.

"Well, since you asked me to explain so nicely. This, graveborn whelp, is the Book of Shadows. And it will be your undoing." He opened the Book, then ran his long fingernail down page after page as he flipped through them. A cold feeling spread through me until my breath came fast and shallow.

"Hmm, let's see. No, no, no, and no." The demon paused, and the grin that lit his face sent a shiver down my spine. I hardened my jaw, refusing to let him see my fear. This wasn't the most terrified I'd ever been. That had been when the demon Ventusiel took Seph and tortured her. If I'd gotten through believing she was dead, this would be a walk in the park.

"Yes, indeed. This will do nicely."

He began to read in a language I couldn't understand. It sounded… it sounded like death, or maybe the noises someone would make if they were dying.

A powerful chill stole over me, and I realized it didn't have anything to do with my fear. It was coming from the words Magoth spoke, some kind of spell or enchantment. *A curse*, a voice in my head whispered. *He's cursing you.*

I struggled against my bonds, jerking the chains like I could tear them from the ceiling. The metal squeaked, but didn't break. My body bowed backward, away from the demon. He only laughed harder as he read on.

An icy sensation radiated from the center of my chest, spreading through my torso and into my limbs. Then the shadows lurking in the dank stone room crept from their corners and advanced upon me, flowing over the floor and ceiling like dark water.

"No," I choked through gritted teeth, straining against the chains, but there was nowhere I could go that the shadows wouldn't find me.

They pooled around my feet, then slid up my legs. I groaned, the pain like being burned in a sacrificial fire. Soon the darkness eclipsed me entirely, and I was deaf and blind to everything except the agony.

On another harsh word from Magoth, the shadows sank inside me, threading their darkness beneath my skin like iron strings. They coalesced into the center of me, and suddenly I got an image of my power source. The landscape of light behind my door was surrounded by heavy blackness. The lights, brighter than the sun and more varied than a thousand rainbows, flickered and danced away from the dark. But they didn't go out. Not yet, at least. The shadows swirled around my arcana, lurking like hungry sharks.

The chains cut into my wrists where I hung limply, chin on my chest as my ragged panting filled the silence of the damp dungeon.

Magoth snapped the book shut, and it disappeared. His eyes turned wholly black as they lit with satisfaction. "The full transformation won't take effect for some time, but that's the beauty of it. The more you use your own magic, the closer the shadows will advance. Over time," he continued, explaining with the air of a bored teacher, "the darkness will claim you. The fear, the rage, the loathing, the agony of your basest instincts and deepest nightmares will manifest inside of you. Eventually, you will succumb to the power, going insane—perhaps even killing everyone you love, but that would be an added bonus. My my, that will be entertaining."

He leaned close to me again, lowering his voice to a stage whisper. "Let's see how the Lightbringer likes her golden boy being turned into a necromancer."

I went rigid. The chains rattled. Then the wraiths reappeared, blinding me until they deposited me into a room and put me into enchanted sleep. I spent the next—well, I didn't know how long, exactly —reliving the worst moments of my life in an endless loop. Until Seph had shown up.

I'd tried to hide the changes from her. But she was so observant—I was certain she'd seen the shadows lurking behind my eyes in the moments after I woke.

The trembling finally quieted, and I crawled to the base of the tower and leaned back against it, spent. The truth was that as much as I wanted to see Seph again, as much as I craved her touch and her laugh and the euphoria of just being around her—I was afraid. Because I was a creature of darkness now, bound by death magic.

A beat of anger replaced the fear. Why shouldn't I go back to Magoth's world right now, and rip that motherfucker to pieces for what he'd done to me? For what he'd done to Seph? Why shouldn't I feel his blood run between my fingers, hot and wet, as I tore whatever passed for a heart from his chest? He needed to die, and I was made of death.

The beat turned into a flow, then a flood, and I was up and striding to the tower's door, reaching out to open it.

I paused when I got there, fingers outstretched. My hand shook violently, and I clenched it into a fist, drawing a harsh breath through lungs that had gone tighter than tripwire.

This. This was what terrified me down to my bones. Even in the short amount of time I'd been awake, my thoughts had been disordered, jumping all over the place. My emotions were too close to the surface, and I hadn't been able to leash them like I'd spent almost thirty years practicing. This magic was wild, chaotic and dangerous, and resisted my control like oil did water.

That darkness had taken over during the fight with Magoth, despite how I tried to hold it back. When I'd reached for my arcana, the shadows gathered in the corners of the throne room responded instead. I sensed them even now, sitting heavily inside me like thick, oily sludge. Circling my light, waiting for the right moment to extinguish it.

I exhaled a harsh breath, digging my fingertips into my scalp. The pricks of pain grounded me, reminding me that I'd made Seph a promise. A promise I had to keep, if I was to retain any semblance of my former self. If I couldn't keep my word to the woman I'd give everything for...then who was I?

Bracing against the tower, I rested my forehead on the cool stone.

I wished she had left me behind. I wished Magoth had killed me.

Because Seph thought she'd saved me, but she hadn't.

She'd saved a monster.

ACKNOWLEDGMENTS

We did it—again!

I thought writing my second book would be easier than writing the first. Turns out, I was deadass wrong. It's the same amount of stress and delight, passion and frustration—all with an added layer of having to follow up on what you've already created. The joys of being a writer, I guess.

All that being said, this book took a village, and I need to first and foremost thank the folks who had their hands on this manuscript at one point or another.

To my husband: thank you for loving and supporting me through this crazy hobby-turned-life passion. Your encouragement to chase my dreams means everything to me. Thanks for believing in me when I don't believe in myself.

Next up is my writing group, who are much more than critique partners and beta readers.

Han, you were my first book bestie. Thank you for plotting and brainstorming with me at all hours. Jordo, thank you for the vocab choices that were truly so much better than what I'd written, and for your expert beta reading. Meels, thank you for your honest feedback about the vibes, and for the romance tips. Please feel free to write some devil's threesome fanfic. Laur, thanks for showing me how to condense my writing, though I fear I've failed you there.

Thanks to Margaux for being the best alpha reader around, and for Josie and David's work on CC.

Thank you to my editor, Melissa Durston. You helped this book grow in ways I can't even name, and I'm a better writer because of it! I will certainly never forget about interiority again. And thank you so much to my excellent proofreader, Ramona Mihai.

Ebook Launch smashed the cover out of the park, yet again! Thank you all so much for the gorgeous artwork.

Thanks to Andi for the invaluable beta read, and to my sister for brainstorming and hyping me up. I still think about your reaction after you finished TSH.

Writing has been my secret garden for a long time. So while they might not know it now, all of my friends and family have contributed to my books in some way, shape, or form. So thanks to them, too.

And last but certainly not least, thank you, dear reader. The fact that people resonate with Seph's story still blows me away, and I'm so happy for every person who's connected with these weird little books about graveyards and what it means to belong.

This book tackles some serious mental health issues. I hope that anyone who struggles that way finds comfort or hope in these pages. If you need support, please seek it out. There's someone out there waiting to help you. 988 is a great national resource.

ALSO BY R.G. WESLEY

The Graveborn Series

The Strange Hour
The Book of Shadows